Laura Kinsale

MIDSUMMER MOON
SEIZE THE FIRE
UNCERTAIN MAGIC

Praise for

The Prince of Midnight

"No one—repeat, no one—writes historical romance better
than Laura Kinsale. THE PRINCE OF MIDNIGHT is a
riveting read of bright words, dark deeds, and the most
irresistible hero ever to ride down the turnpike."

Mary Jo Putney, author of *Dearly Beloved*

"As always Laura Kinsale delivers a powerful, unique
romance laced with passion, danger, and compelling
characters. THE PRINCE OF MIDNIGHT is a wonderful
tale of a most unusual highwayman and his lady. Readers
will fall in love with the hero and that's the hallmark of a
first-rate romance."

Amanda Quick, author of *Surrender*

"Laura Kinsale is one of the most powerful and unique voices
in romance today, and THE PRINCE OF MIDNIGHT is
classic Laura Kinsale—beautifully written, totally compelling,
and utterly uforgettable."

Elizabeth Kary, author of *Midnight Lace*

"A love story you'll remember long after you close the book.
With eloquent and lyrical prose, Laura Kinsale breathes life
into memorable characters and their powerful story. Ms.
Kinsale stretches the limits of the genre, challenging the
reader's imagination."

Kathe Robin, *Romantic Times*

Laura Kinsale's previous bestseller
SEIZE THE FIRE
is a finalist in the
Romance Writers of America's
Golden Medallion Award competition

The Prince of Midnight

Laura Kinsale

This title first published in Great Britain 1991 by
SEVERN HOUSE PUBLISHERS LTD of
35 Manor Road, Wallington, Surrey SM6 0BW.
This first hardcover edition published in the U.S.A. 1991 by
SEVERN HOUSE PUBLISHERS INC of
271 Madison Avenue, New York, NY 10016
by arrangement with Avon Books,
a division of The Hearst Corporation.

Copyright © 1990 by Amanda Moor Jay

British Library Cataloguing in Publication Data
Kinsale, Laura
  Prince of midnight.
  I.Title
  813.54 [F]

  ISBN 0 – 7278 – 4214 – 5

Printed and bound in Great Britain by
Billing and Sons Ltd, Worcester

ONE

La Paire, foothills of the French Alps—1772

THE lad had the deep, burning eyes of a zealot. S.T.
Maitland shifted uncomfortably on his wooden
bench and glanced again over his wine across the
murky depths of the tavern. It was damnably disconcerting
to find that measuring stare still fixed on him, as if he
were up for admission to heaven and not particularly likely
to get in.

S.T. lifted his tankard in a lazy salute. He wasn't proud.
He reckoned he was a long enough shot for paradise that
a nod was worth the trouble. If this comely youth with the
absurdly black lashes and vivid blue eyes should turn out
to be St. Peter, Jr., best to be decently civil.

Rather to S.T.'s dismay, the youngster's gaze intensified. The straight, dark brows drew into a frown and the
boy stood, slim and silent, a figure of blue velvet and
shabby gentility amid the usual lot of peasants chattering
in Piedmontese and Provençal. S.T. rubbed his ear and
brushed his tie wig nervously. A vision of eating his *dé-
jeuner* in the clutches of an earnestly holy adolescent made
him swig the last half of his wine and stand up in haste.

He reached down for the packet of sable paintbrushes
he'd come into the village to procure. The string loosened.
He swore under his breath, trying to capture the precious

1

sticks before they scattered into the rushes that covered the dirt floor.

"Seigneur."

The soft voice seemed to be behind him. S.T. came upright, turning quickly to the left in the hope of escaping, but his bad ear tricked him amid the babble of laughter and conversation. His balance fluctuated for an instant; he grabbed instinctively for the table and found himself face-to-face with the youth.

"Monseigneur du Minuit?"

A bolt of alarm shot through him. The words were French, but it was very stilted French, and a name he hadn't been called in three years.

He'd been half expecting to hear it—for so long that it didn't even sound remarkable. 'Twas the voice itself that seemed improbable, gruff and toneless, coming from this infant with the fresh, high-colored face. When S.T. had envisioned the hunters who might track him for the price on his head, he'd hardly imagined a greenling who hadn't even started a beard.

He relaxed against the table and gazed glumly down at the youth. Was this youngster all he was worth? He could kill the poor cub with one hand, for God's sake.

"You are *le Seigneur du Minuit,*" the boy stated, nodding stiffly, managing the pronunciation of "seyn-yuhr" and "minwhee" with careful dignity. In English, he added, "I am correct?"

S.T. thought of answering in a torrent of annoyed French which would undoubtedly go right over the fellow's head. His schoolroom accent sounded none too steady. But those eyes of burning deep blue had a force of their own, enough to keep S.T. wary. Fresh faced or not, the child had managed to locate him—a disturbing fact on all counts.

The boy was tall for an adolescent, but S.T. still topped him by a head and certainly outweighed him by a good six stone. With that slender elegance and full, solemn mouth, the young whelp looked more like to grow into a dandy than a thieftaker. He dressed the beau, to be sure, even if the lace at his cuffs and linen jabot was frayed and grimy.

"*Qu'est-ce que c'est?*" S.T. demanded brusquely.

The dark, winged brows drew into a deeper line. "*S'il vous plaît,*" the boy said with a little bobbing bow, "will you speak English, monsieur?"

S.T. gave him a suspicious look. The lad was really outrageously beautiful, his black hair drawn back off high cheekbones into a short queue; a classical, perfect nose . . . and those eyes, *alors*, like the light through deep water: nightshade and violet and bluebells. S.T. had seen that effect once, in a rocky cave at the edge of the Mediterranean, with the sun shafts piercing aquamarine shadows and playing off jet-black stone—and this against skin soft and fine as a girl's. The superbly modeled face held high color, a pink that looked almost feverish. Against his better judgment, S.T. found himself growing curious about the brat.

"Little speak Eng-lish." He made up the worst accent he could humanly execute, speaking loudly above the tavern noise. "Little! Good day! Yes?"

The youth hesitated, staring intensely from beneath those slanted brows. S.T. found himself vaguely embarrassed by the farce. What a silly language, French—it made a man sound like some backstage cardsharp to imitate the proper Gallic inflections.

"You are not the Seigneur," the boy said in his husky, toneless voice.

"Seigneur!" Did the young dullard suppose that S.T. was going to announce it to any English stranger who happened along? "*Mon petit bouffon!* I look a seigneur, no? A lord! But yes!" He gestured down at his jackboots and paint-stained breeches. "*Bien sûr!* A prince, of course!"

"*Je m'excuse.*" The youth gave a second awkward bow. "I seek another." He hesitated, looked hard at S.T., and then began to turn away.

S.T. clamped his hand on the slender shoulder. He couldn't afford to let the cub go quite so easily as that. "Seek an-oth-er? An-o-ther? *Pardon;* but this I comprehend not."

The boy's frown deepened. "A man." He moved his hand in a slight gesture of frustration. *"Un homme."*

"Le Seigneur du Minuit?" S.T. put just a trace of patient patronage in his tone. "The Lord—of the Midnight, eh? Zut! Is a name absurd. I know not he. You seek? *Pardon, pardon,* monsieur, for why you seek?"

"I must find him." The youth watched S.T.'s face with the intensity of a cat at a mouse hole. "It doesn't matter why." He paused and then said slowly, "Perhaps he goes by a different name here."

"Of course. I give to you help, hm? Ah—the hair." S.T. tugged at the queue on his tie wig. "Color? The color, you know it?"

"Yes. Brown hair, monsieur. I'm told he doesn't like a wig or powder. Brown hair, dark, but with gold in it. Streaked with gold, all over. Similar to a lion, monsieur."

S.T. rolled his eyes, playing Frenchman. *"Alors. Le beau!"*

The boy nodded seriously. "Yes, they say he is handsome. Quite good-looking. Tall. With eyes of green. *Comprenez* 'green,' monsieur? Emerald? With gold in them. And gold on his eyelashes and brows." The boy stared at S.T. significantly. "Very unusual, I'm told. As if someone had sprinkled gold dust over him. And his eyebrows are quite distinctive, too, so they say—" He touched his own. "With a curl at the arch of them like the horns on a devil."

S.T. hesitated. The blue eyes held constant, no change in expression, just a shade too level, the tone of voice a trace too mild—he looked down at the youth and saw someone a thousand years old gazing out of that unfledged face.

It chilled him. There was a devil inside this one, and it knew full well who he was but chose to play the game S.T. had started.

He carried on with the performance anyway. The only other recourse was to lure the poor pup out back and hold a stiletto to his throat. S.T. needed to know how he'd been found . . . and why.

Tapping his forehead, he said wisely, "Ah. Eye-brow.

Je comprends. See this eye-brow you, and think . . . I is he. This seigneur. Yes?"

"Yes." The boy smiled faintly. "But I was wrong. I'm sorry."

The smile erased all trace of subterfuge. It was sweet and wistful and feminine, and S.T. had to sit down to keep from sinking under the sudden shock of revelation.

For the love of—

She was a girl.

He was certain of it. Abruptly and utterly certain. That soft, husky voice that didn't rise and fall in ordinary tones, but stayed stubbornly gruff; that skin, those lips, the slender build—oh, she was a female, the sly little cat. She had the face to carry it off, too, clean and striking, marvelous, with a full jaw and dramatic brows, and enough height and carriage to pass for a youth of sixteen. He'd wager a gold guinea that she'd cut her eyelashes to blunt them—that was why they looked so black and stubby.

And he'd wager a hundred on why she'd come. No threat of capture here. No cunning pursuit to drag him back to England for the king's reward. Just another damsel in distress, looking for help like a thousand others.

She'd traveled a devil of a long way to plague him.

But so beautiful. So beautiful.

"Sit," he said suddenly, waving his hand at the rough-hewn table. "Sit, sit, *mon petit* monsieur. I help. I think. Marc!" He shouted for the innkeeper above the mundane racket of lunchtime. *"Vin . . . Hé! Vin pour deux."* He slapped his sheaf of brushes on the table, straddling the bench. "Monsieur. How you are call?"

"Leigh Strachan." She gave her little bow. "At your service."

"Sra-hon. Srah-*hen.*" He grinned. *"Difficile.* Lee, eh?" He whacked his chest. "I name . . . Este." There was no use trying to hide that; everyone in the village knew him by it, and thought it was vastly Italian of him to call himself by a cardinal point on the map. "Sit. Sit. *Très bien.* You eat, no? Cheese—" He reached up and helped himself to a slab of sausage that swung with the cheese from a rafter over the table. Slicing off a generous portion of each, he pushed the food toward her, along with a pot of mustard. Marc brought hot bread, and gave S.T. a significant glance as he thumped another wine bottle down on the table. With a defeated grimace, S.T. promised in French to paint his ugly daughter before the winter was out, which was a considerable capitulation, and enough to send the *aubergiste* off with a smug look and no demand for payment, which would have been futile in any case.

Monsieur Leigh Strachan eyed the sweet-smelling bread as S.T. broke it into steaming chunks. She looked hungry, but shook her head. "I've—already eaten. *Merci.*"

S.T. glanced at her. He shrugged and poured her wine. If she wasn't starving he was a pig's knuckle, but these greenlings had their pride. He leaned back against the wall and smeared mustard on a large hunk of cheese. 'Twas a long walk uphill back to his castle.

He met her eyes in mid bite and grinned around the bread. She looked positively pale, but returned the smile bravely. How he ever could have thought she was a male, he couldn't fathom.

Those eyes. Magnificent. Now how the devil was a man to get up a flirt, with her dressed in that rig? "This seigneur," he said, finishing off his bread. "Hair bronze. Eyes of emerald. Tall man."

"Handsome," she offered, in that husky flat voice.

The little minx. S.T. poured himself wine. "What is this word? Hond-soom."

She took a swig of wine, quite a decent imitation of his. He considered belching, just to see if she'd copy him.

"*Un bel homme,*" she said. "Handsome."

"Ha. He is French?"

"He is of English parents." She drank again. "But he speaks French very fluently. That is why they called him the Seigneur in England."

"*Quelle stupidité.*" S.T. swept his arm around the crowded tavern. "All speak French. All lords here, eh?"

She didn't blink. "In England it is not so common. They say he has—a certain air about him. A newspaper dubbed him by that name, and now it sticks."

"Le Seigneur du Minuit," he mused, and shook his head. He'd really hoped that sobriquet had died along with his reputation. "Absurd. Midnight, *pourquoi?*"

She lifted her wine and took a long swallow. The chipped porcelain mug made a solid sound when she set it down. She gave him a straight look. "I think you know why 'midnight,' Monsieur Este."

He smiled a little. "Do I?"

She watched him silently as he poured her another portion. He leaned back against the wall again. He didn't want to hear her sad story. He didn't want to listen to her pleas. He just wanted to gaze at her and fantasize about the one great lack in his life these days.

She took a breath, and another swallow of wine. He could see her thinking, trying to reckon him. A faint touch of desperation had begun to seep into her brooding expression. After another generous gulp of wine, she came at him directly.

"Monsieur Este," she said, "I can understand that the Seigneur does not wish to show himself to strangers. I know the danger."

He made his eyes grow wide. "Dan-ger? What is this? I like not dan-ger."

"There is none. For him."

S.T. snorted. "For him I care not," he said indignantly. "Is for me I care! I think maybe well I do not know this bad Seigneur, yes? I think I do not help seek for he."

She looked a bit disconcerted. The wine was having its effect: the fire in those lovely eyes had grown a little smokier.

"*Mon cher ami,*" he said gently. "You go to the home. You no seek dan-ger . . . this Seigneur so absurd."

The cold blaze sprang up again. "I have no home."

"And so—" He examined his thumbnail. "You go seek. I think I know this 'prince.' I con-jec-ture. I hear 'midnight' and 'Seigneur,' and I know what kind of man this. Bad man. Bad dan-ger. He is a highwayman, no? He is chase from England like a *chien,* tail under legs, no? Here

we do not want him. Good men here only. Good king's
men. No dan-ger. No trouble. Go to the home, *mon petit.*"
"I cannot."
Of course not. Naturally he wouldn't get rid of her that
easily. He wasn't at all sure he wanted to. He watched her
gulp down the rest of her wine. When he did not offer to
pour, she served herself from the fresh bottle Marc had
brought.
"*Mon dieu.* What you want, boy?" he demanded suddenly. "Be criminal? Thief? Why seek you this bastard?"
"He is not a bastard." Her head came up. She frowned,
and when she spoke, the wine was already slurring her
voice. "You're *not* him, are you? You don't . . . understand."
S.T. rubbed his forehead. He drank deeply and leaned
on his elbow.
"He is a good man," she said, her voice breaking upward carelessly. She polished off her mug and poured herself another. Beneath the tattered lace cuff, her wrist
seemed touchingly pale and slender. "Not a thief."
He smiled in derision. "People give to him jewels, *oui?*
Rain on him gold."
She bridled, flashing him a glance of blue fire. "You
don't understand." She'd forgotten her male role completely, but her natural voice had a luscious soft huskiness.
"He would help me."
"How?"
"I want him to teach me." She tilted the mug up and
drank. She had to hold it with both hands, well on her
way to being half crocked. When she set it down, she
twisted a lock of loose hair around her forefinger with a
delicate gesture that was so feminine it made him smile.
Softly, he asked, "Teach you what, *ma belle?*"
She didn't notice the adjective. "Swordplay," she said
with passion.
S.T.'s mug hit the table.
"How to use a pistol," she added. "And to ride. He's
the best alive. In the world. He can make a horse do anything."
She looked feverishly at S.T., who was shaking his head

and swearing beneath his breath. He met that concentrated stare and looked away, pushing his hand into his hair in discomfort.

That was a mistake. He'd forgotten he was wearing the tie wig for his foray into the village of La Paire; it slid askew beneath his fingers and he had to pull it off. He cursed in French and tossed the scratchy nuisance on the table. Swordplay! Of all the damned crazy notions. He leaned on his elbows, chafing his hands in his hair.

When he looked up, he realized it was far more of a mistake than he'd understood. She was staring at him, intense and half-drunk.

"You *are* the Seigneur." Her lips worked. "I knew it. I knew it."

"*Allons-y!*" He stood up, hauling her to her feet. She was clearly one of those females who couldn't hold her claret. She'd passed the point of discretion—in a moment she'd be bursting into tears or performing some other purely female exploit—and whoever she was, or whyever she'd come, 'twas hardly chivalrous to leave her to reveal herself in a public ordinary. He grabbed the bottle of wine, slapped his tricorne on his head, and took her around the waist. She wilted against him. "Adolescent cabbage," he said disgustedly to Marc on his way past.

The tavern keeper beamed, all benevolence and grimy apron. "Don't forget my Chantal's portrait," he called after them.

S.T. lifted the half-empty bottle in salute, not even bothering to turn around as he carted Monsieur Leigh Strachan away.

He left her to sleep it off in a granary above La Paire and started home. He'd see her again soon enough—that was one thing as certain as death and the king's taxes.

It was sunset and he was breathing hard from the climb before the ruined towers of Col du Noir appeared, clinging to the cliff at the head of the canyon, silhouetted against a clear, cool sky. The ducks came out to greet him, nipping at his feet until he bought them off with a chunk of bread. He stopped at the garden and dug among the dry weeds for a garlic to flavor his dinner. Dusting dirt off his hands onto his breeches, he ambled beneath the turreted gate of his castle and through the lavender that grew wild in the courtyard.

He whistled, and Nemo came bounding out of some shadowed crevice where he'd been hiding. The great wolf leaped up and licked enthusiastically at S.T.'s face, then dropped down to fawn and whine in pleasure, getting a tussle and a bite of cheese for his trouble. He jogged circles around S.T. as he trudged up the uneven stone stairs.

S.T. paused in the armory, looking up at the huge painting just visible in the last of the daylight. With Nemo snuffling at his boots, he gave the portrait a fleeting stroke in the place where his hand had worn the painted luster from the flank of a shining black horse.

"Home again, old fellow," he said softly. "I'm back."

He gazed at the picture a moment. Nemo whined, and S.T. turned abruptly away, leaning down to give the wolf a hard shake. Nemo pressed against his leg, shameless, basking and groveling and groaning with ecstasy at the attention.

Dinner was short and simple, a pot of rabbit stew shared with Nemo, who'd brought the rabbit, and the last of Marc's good red wine. S.T. sat before the kitchen fire, tilted back against the table on two legs of a three-legged stool, wondering vaguely if he ought to try to plant some grapevines and asking himself if he wanted to paint badly enough to light the torches in the hall.

He decided that he didn't, and went back to pondering the mysterious process of making wine, which according to Marc was complex beyond reason. God only knew what kind of pampering the vines would require. Weeding garlic was bad enough. And something always ate his peppers in their helpless infancy if he didn't bleeding get down on the ground and sleep with them all night.

He sighed. The firelight flickered off plaster busts and pots of pigment, casting shadows that made it seem as if the room were filled with a silent crowd of people instead of books and canvas and smudgy charcoal sketches.

He clasped his hands behind his head and gazed at the

disordered sum of his life for the past three years. Half-finished paintings, roughed-out sculpture: he threw himself into each new effort with fierce energy, but the only thing he'd completed since he'd come here was the painting in the armory.

In one dark corner an unsheathed sword lay askew against the wall. He'd let it go to rust, along with the brace of pistols wrapped in their dusty rags. But the saddle and bridle he kept clean and oiled, hanging neatly from their pegs, just as if he were going to use them.

He rubbed Nemo's head with his boot. The wolf sighed in heavy pleasure, but didn't bother to bestir himself from his long-limbed sprawl against S.T.'s feet.

Two

It took Monsieur Leigh Strachan until late afternoon the next day to produce herself at Col du Noir. S.T. was a little surprised; he'd expected her by mid morning at the latest. He'd moved his work out into the courtyard as he usually did to catch the north light on these clear October afternoons, breathing the scents of linseed oil and tarragon and lavender and dust that clung to his paint rags and his hands. Nemo panted softly in a shady spot, his solemn yellow eyes following S.T.'s short perambulations back and forth to get a perspective on the canvas. But when the wolf lifted his head and looked toward the gate, S.T. put his brush in a terra-cotta pot full of oil, wiped his hands, and sat down on a sun-baked stone to wait.

Nemo heaved himself to his feet. A soft word from S.T. kept the wolf still. He heard the ducks break into disturbing muttering—a noise which seemed to him to come from somewhere off to the left where there was nothing beyond the wall but a sheer cliff. He turned his head to catch more of the sound with his good ear, then realized what he'd done and faced the gate directly with a little frisson of self-annoyance. He'd yet to become accustomed to the disorienting effects of his one-sided deafness. Even with Nemo's alert gaze trained on the obvious direction of approach, S.T. had a difficult time convincing his brain that their visitor wasn't somehow advancing on thin air across the canyon from the left. And worse, if he closed his eyes

12

or turned his head too quickly, the whole world seemed to
go into a tumbling spin around him.

Wisely, she created plenty of deliberate noise as she
came. A clever greenling, this. She knew better than to
try to sneak up on a desperate and dangerous highwayman
with a king's ransom on his head.

The thought made S.T. smile. Once upon a time, he'd
considered himself quite a perilous character.

He leaned over, tugged at some weedy bushes within
reach, and sat back armed to the teeth with a fragrant little
bouquet of lavender and chamomile. After a moment, he
added a few trailing stems of rockrose for color and com-
position. While he turned the nosegay in his hand, idly
inspecting the arrangement, she appeared beneath the
crumbling gateway.

She paused just inside the shadow. He waited. Nemo
stood still, growling.

S.T. could see her eyeing the wolf warily. Nemo was
something to see: huge, with his coat of black and cream
and silver, his teeth bared and a light afternoon breeze
ruffling his handsome markings. He was very clearly what
he was—no chance of mistaking him for a mere oversized
watchdog.

Ignoring S.T., she took a step toward the animal.
Nemo's hackles rose. She took another, and then began to
walk steadily straight at the wolf. Nemo's growl became
an open snarl. He crouched, his splendid tail waving
slowly, his yellow eyes fixed on the slender figure. She
kept walking. Nemo took a step forward, his whole body
rigid with the savagery of his warning. The courtyard echoed to the sound.

But she kept walking.

She was three feet away when Nemo's courage evaporated. The snarl gave out, his tail flagged, and he turned
in a little circle. His great head lowered and his ears flattened in dismay as he slunk across the open space and
crept into a safe place behind S.T.'s back.

"I know," S.T. said soothingly. "Terrifying creatures,
these females."

She stood silent, frowning at them.

"Watch this," S.T. said to Nemo. "I'm going to walk right up to her. No . . . don't whine, old chap—you can't stop me. It's a bloody awful risk, I know. I don't fancy my chances above half." He stood up, looking down at the wolf. "But mind you, pal, if I don't come back—" he gave Nemo a shake "—I want you to have my share of the cheese."

Nemo prostrated himself in abject humility, yelping faintly and trying to lick S.T.'s hand. S.T. pushed him over onto his side, scratched his belly, and left him lolling on his back in exuberant disgrace.

She watched S.T. as he approached, her dark, slanted brows drawn down with far more doubt than when she'd eyed the wolf. He offered the flowers silently.

For a long moment, she stared down at the little bouquet in his hand, and then looked up into his eyes. He smiled. *"Bienvenue, mon enfant,"* he said softly.

Her lower lip twitched. Suddenly those superb blue eyes were glazed with tears. She whacked his hand away with a hard fist. Flowers went flying, and the scent of crushed lavender drifted on the air. "Don't do that," she snarled, fierce as Nemo. "Don't look at me that way."

S.T. took a startled step back, nursing his hand. She possessed a dashed convincing right punch. "As you please," he said wryly, and then added with deliberation, *"monsieur."*

The glisten in her eyes was gone as quickly as it had come. Her jaw grew stiff and belligerent. She shook back her head and gave him a cold stare. "When did you realize?"

"That you're a girl?" He shrugged. "Yesterday." He held up one broken stem of rockrose and examined it ruefully. "When you smiled."

She scowled. "I'll take care to frown."

He flicked the rose into the dirt. "That ought to answer. You certainly unnerve Nemo and me."

She glanced past him at the wolf. S.T. imagined running his finger along the smooth plane of her cheek, warming to the color that burned there.

"That's Nemo?" She gave a little decisive jerk of her

head. "You've trained him well. I never saw you call him off."

S.T. turned toward the wolf. "Did you hear that? Well-trained. Come here and prove it, then." He whistled a command.

Nemo bounded forward. He stopped a yard away.

"Come along." S.T. whistled again, pointing at his feet.

The wolf trotted to one side, then turned and loped to the other, making an arc around them. When S.T. called him a third time, he crouched down and began to whine.

"I shouldn't wonder if you were quivering in terror at this spectacle," S.T. said.

She seemed slow to understand, watching Nemo with her back stiff and her lower lip set in a vaguely scandalized fullness. "He's really afraid?"

"It's women. Females petrify him." He nudged his boot at one of the flowers in the dirt. "No doubt he has his reasons."

A faint curve appeared at the corner of her mouth. She stared at Nemo with that little half smile but said nothing. On his side, S.T. stared at her. Her lips, her skin, the curve of her throat. He felt somewhat scarce of breath.

"I thought it was a test," she said.

He lifted his eyes to hers with a wrench of focus. "What?"

"I thought—you meant to test me. To see how I would face him."

"Oh, quite. And you passed. You're heroically stupid, I can see that. God knows I wouldn't have had the pluck to walk up to the snarling brute." He tilted his head, lost in the amazing depth of her eyes. "Of course, he'd tear the throat out of a man who made that mistake."

Nemo gave a long moan and rolled over in the dirt, wriggling and snorting as he tried to scratch his back. Then he relaxed belly-up, paws limp, looking toward S.T. with his tongue lolling in a canine grin.

"Well, you would, y'know." S.T. flicked his hand, signaling abruptly. "Get up, you great boor; there's a lady present. Go on with you. Hunt us up a pheasant."

Instantly, Nemo flipped over and scrambled to his feet. He sprang into his long lope and headed for the gate, already lowering his nose to cast for scent. As he disappeared, the ducks outside broke into a raucous quacking and then subsided. Nemo knew better than to raid them without permission.

"That's truly wonderful," she said, looking after the wolf. "The way you've schooled him."

S.T. rubbed behind his ear. "Well, most probably he won't get a pheasant," he admitted. "Perhaps a hare." He glanced at her sideways. "Will you . . . could I ask you—to stay? For dinner?"

Her brows drew together, and he felt something inside him sink. But she said stiffly, "Yes."

He let out a breath, trying to keep his smile from growing too inanely pleased. He felt as tentative as Nemo with her. It had been a long time . . . a very long time. It wouldn't be so remarkable to find he'd lost his touch entirely.

If only she weren't so damnably gorgeous. It made the base of his throat feel hot and funny just to look at her.

"You're not at all what I expected," she said suddenly. The scowl became a suspicious arch. "You *are* really the Seigneur?"

S.T.'s smile flattened. He didn't answer, but simply turned away and went back to his easel, setting the canvas carefully against a rock while he took down the framework and gathered his jars of pigment. He carried them inside and came back for the canvas, not looking at her. As he passed inside the door, he saw her long afternoon shadow trail slowly behind him.

She stopped in the armory. S.T. went on to the kitchen alone. He kicked an empty barley sack under the table, set the painting down, and stoked the fire to warm the chill stone walls. When he went back to the armory, she was standing in front of the portrait of Charon.

S.T. crossed his arms, leaning back against the doorjamb. He looked at her and then at the toe of his boot.

"I'm sorry," she said, with a trace of defiance.

"What for? I don't blame you for wondering. I don't much resemble Robin Hood these days, do I?"

Those blue eyes raked him coolly. She turned back to the painting of Charon. "Is he stabled here?"

"He's dead." S.T. hiked himself away from the door and left her. He went back to the kitchen, shoved aside some paint rags and books on the table, grabbed an onion, and started to hack at it with a dull cleaver.

He heard her come in; his good ear was to the door. He glanced up at her and wanted bitterly to see something less alluring. But she was beautiful, slim and straight, black lashes and fine, high cheekbones, running her fingers over a plaster cast and slanting a look toward him that held all the old fatal power of destruction.

And she didn't even mean it, that was obvious enough. She was dissatisfied; she thought he was a disappointment, not living up to his own legend. The other, the ache in his chest and his loins and his heart . . . that was his own affliction. His weakness.

Women. He whacked at the onion. No wonder they terrified Nemo.

Three bloody years alone. He wanted to go down on his knees and press his face against her body and beg her to let him make love to her.

He thought of Charon, of dumb animal devotion: a warm blow in his ear, when he could still hear with both of them; the reassuring thud of a hoof while S.T. slept on the damp English ground, all safe, all quiet, the watch kept by senses sharper than his own had ever been—by an honest, simple mind that knew no better than to trust in human wisdom.

The onion made his eyes blur. He set his jaw and tossed the ragged pieces into a pot. He could feel her, though he didn't look; she was like a bright flame in the cold clutter of his life. He wondered what blind folly this particular temptress might beguile him to commit, what he had left that she could take away.

His painting. Nemo. His life.

The list was longer than he would have thought.

"What do you want with me?" he demanded abruptly.

She looked up from a half-finished painting tilted against the bread chest. "I told you."

"You want lessons in swordsmanship?"

She nodded.

He gestured toward a corner with the cleaver. "There's a sword. A pair of pistols. You're welcome to 'em." He drove the cleaver into the table. "That's all I've got to teach you."

She regarded him steadily. S.T. decided to ignore her. He took the leather bucket outside, filled it at the stone well, came back and hefted it over the pot. Water rang inside the iron kettle with a crystalline splatter.

"Is it because I'm not a man?"

He didn't answer. He was busy peeling garlic. The papery skin crackled in his fingers; the familiar smell filled his nose. He concentrated on that. On simple things. He could see her feet from the corner of his eye, the buckled shoes worn down at the heels, the stockings darned meticulously with mismatched thread. Her legs were slender and strong, her calves delicately shaped. Female. He bit down on his tongue.

"That's going to taste terrible," she said.

He laid his hand over his heart. "And to think I was so confident that I gave my chef the afternoon free."

"I could prepare it better."

He set the garlic down. "How?"

She shrugged. "I know how."

"Do tell me."

She looked at him beneath her lashes. Her hands worked, open and closed, very slowly. "Will you teach me?"

He snorted. "I'm always interested in a new recipe for boiled onion, but frankly, no."

"I've a talent for cooking. And extensive training. I'm an accomplished housekeeper." She flicked an aloof glance around the chaotic cavern of his kitchen. "I can organize all your business affairs—keep your accounts. By next spring, I could have your garden producing enough to set an excellent table, with plenty left over to sell. I could outfit you properly . . . I have a gift for design and sewing.''

"And so modest.''

"I could make this place into a decent home for you.''

He tilted his head, glancing sideways at her. She stood very straight, clearly prepared to launch into a list of further accomplishments should he prove stubborn. With a little ironic smile, he said, ''Don't suppose you know how to make wine?''

"Certainly. I've been used to put up berry wine every year. And mint cordials. And beer.''

Her voice was cultured, her manner high-bred, but it sounded as if she'd been a household servant. The borrowed male clothes she wore had belonged to an aristocrat, that was certain. He allowed himself the indulgence of imagining her young body, slim and lithe and naked, and blew out a soft, private breath of desire.

His glance traveled upward. He met her eyes. She didn't blink.

"I'll do anything,'' she said. "I'll sleep with you.''

S.T. brought the cleaver down with a savage chop, sending garlic flying in two directions.

Curse her.

Curse her, curse her, curse her, the perceptive little bitch.

He wanted to say something vicious, something that would hurt her as much as that flat business offer injured him. But when he looked up at her, the high flush on her cheeks and rigid set of her mouth made her seem so young and mock-tough and defenseless that his words stuck in his throat.

All he said was: "No thanks.''

Just perceptibly, her shoulders relaxed. S.T. busied himself with another garlic clove. He could feel blood mounting in his own neck at that tiny indication of her vast relief. He tossed the garlic in the pot, parchment and all, spread his hands on the table, and looked down at them. Ten fingers, slightly paint stained. Two arms, one face . . . had he changed so much? No female had ever complained of him, looks or performance either. He'd never, never had to buy one.

He asked himself if he'd sunk that low, that he would do it now. He stood there, insulted and aroused, painfully aware of her presence in his kitchen, though he didn't dare look at her. For three years he'd put this into his art: when the urge for a woman came on him, he worked, painting thunderstorms and sleek greyhounds, nudes and horses, shaping curves in lumps of clay until he could stand on his feet no longer and fell asleep in a chair with the modeling knife still in his hand.

He never finished them. He could never decide if they were his best work or his worst.

"May I sit down?" she asked in a queer voice.

"For God's sake, of course you can—" S.T. turned . . . and she was falling, before he could gather his wits enough to lift his hand or take a step—she'd collapsed, sinking from the knees into a boneless sprawl on the dirt floor.

For an instant he just stood there, astonished. Then he moved, his body making the decision before his mind. She opened her eyes as he threw himself onto his knees beside her. The deep blue was hazy with stress, the burning flush on her cheeks gone to paleness. She tried to push herself up.

"I'm all right," she said huskily, trying to evade his support.

His heart was pounding. "The devil you are." He disregarded her feeble attempt to get away. She burned with fever; he could feel the heat without even touching her forehead.

"I am." She took a breath. "I am. I'm not sick."

S.T. didn't bother to argue further. He slid his arm underneath her shoulders, ready to carry her, but she fought free. With a grip that surprised him, she clung to his arm, trying to pull herself up.

"I'm all right," she insisted, holding herself in a sitting position against him. "I haven't . . . eaten. That's all."

He hesitated, allowing her to lean on him, her forehead against his shoulder, her blazing temperature refuting her own words. He smoothed his hand over her temple and felt her head droop as she passed out again in the circle of his arms.

S.T. panicked. Her skin looked pale as death, faintly tinged with an unhealthy sallowness. He couldn't feel her breathing. He grabbed her hand and chafed it, realized that was useless, and gathered her limp body into his arms. He staggered to his feet under the burden, his uneasy balance reeling.

She came to just as he passed through the armory on his way to the bedroom. "I have to get up," she mumbled. "I can't be sick." Her head tilted back and her white, slender throat vibrated with a low moan. "I can't . . . be."

He mounted the spiral stairs and gripped her tighter as she struggled weakly. By the time he reached the first floor, he was cursing the castle's builders to Gehenna, what with their uneven stairs and tight curves and narrow passage, devised to make the ascent as difficult as possible for any enemy. The nervous bastards must have been anticipating an army of midgets capable of twisting themselves into Gordian knots. When at last he put his shoulder to the bedroom door and swung her through, the rotation completely overcame his precarious stability. His back hit the door; he had to pause to find his equilibrium before he took a breath and crossed the room in a straight and unconfusing line to the bed.

Her body sank into the feather mattress. His nose filled with dust—it had never occurred to him until this moment to air the sheets, but at least the bedclothes were cool and dry, and smelled mostly of lavender and linseed and himself. She looked up at him, tried once more to rise, and then lapsed back under his hands on her shoulders.

She wet her lips. "Don't put me here," she muttered. "Is this your room?"

He pushed the damp black hair back from her forehead. "I'm not going to hurt you."

"I'll have to go away," she said desperately. "Leave me alone. Don't touch me."

"I won't do anything to you, *ma chérie.*"

She pushed at his hand. "Go away. Don't come near."

"You're ill," he exclaimed. "I'm not going to rape you, you little dimwit. You're sick."

"No! I'm not; I can't be. I can't be." She closed her eyes and tossed her head. Then with a defeated whimper she suddenly lay still. The strange, blunted lashes seemed outlandishly black against her chalky skin. She opened her eyes, fixing him with a fierce stare. "Yes," she said hoarsely. "Please go away. Please. I thought . . . I hoped . . . 'twas nothing. Poisonous food." She rolled away, shivering. "I was wrong."

He watched a shudder rack her body. His fingers curled in futile empathy.

"My head," she mumbled, and twisted over. "Oh, my head aches."

She turned onto her elbow. He pushed her back and held her down, cursing softly. His mother had died of a fever like this—sudden and devastating. Years ago; decades, it seemed, and all he could recall was her body lying in state in a cold marble hall in Florence, white and still as the stone. What had the damned doctors done for her? The wrong thing, obviously, but S.T. couldn't even remember that. They hadn't asked him into the sickroom, and he hadn't been breathless to go: seventeen and rebellious and stupid, not believing in death, never thinking that his impetuous, laughing, exasperating *maman* would not be asking him to carry another *billet doux* to her latest lover again.

The girl fought his hands. "Let go of me." She wrenched free. "Don't you understand? It's a mortal fever!"

"Mortal?" He grabbed her wrists and held them. "Are you sure?"

She tried to pull away, and then lay panting, nodding weakly.

"How?"

"I . . . know."

His voice rose. "How do you know, damnit?"

She wet her lips. "Headache. Fever. Can't . . . eat. In Lyon—" Her fingers trembled. "A fortnight ago. I hadn't

enough to pay. 'Twas a very . . . bad inn. I nursed the
little girl—''

He stared at her. "Oh God," he whispered.

"Don't you see? I couldn't just watch them send her off
on a hurdle!" She shivered, a tremor that went from her
hands through her whole body. "I had no money. I
couldn't pay them for the bed."

"And she had a pestilent fever?" he cried. *"Imbécile."*

"Yes. *Imbécile.* I'm sorry. I dosed myself; I thought
enough time had passed to be safe. I have to leave. I
shouldn't have come. But I didn't realize; until now—I was
sure 'twas only . . . some bad food. Please go away . . .
quickly . . . and I'll leave."

There was no doctor in the village. A midwife, at best—
and how could he send word? He thought frantically. It
was nearly dark—the walk down the canyon took him two
hours in the middle of the day . . . and no certainty he'd
find anyone who'd come, with fever to risk and no money
to pay, a fact the villagers were well aware of. He obtained
his brushes and canvas and wine with barter and promises,
and lived off his garden and the land otherwise.

"Go away," she mumbled. "Don't touch me. Go away,
go away."

He strode to the narrow window, pushed open the leaded
glass, and peered out into the twilight. He put his fingers
in his mouth and blew a piercing whistle.

Nemo might hear it. He might track Marc by the scent
clinging to an empty bottle of wine. Marc might allow a
savage wolf with a message tied to its neck within a hundred yards without shooting it dead.

S.T. leaned his cheek against the stone. From the edge
of his vision, he caught the dark shadow that slipped over
a break in the ruined castle wall.

His heart rose and tightened, caught between fears. Why
had he never told Marc about Nemo? He'd not spoken,
not even when the rumors of a lone wolf in the vicinity
had been ruffling the waters of village gossip. Instinct held
his tongue. S.T. was accustomed to murmur and subterfuge; he'd lived by it for years. He knew rumor. He'd used
it, let it grow and turn from hearsay into legend by the

casual drop of a word or a knowing smile. Let them worry about a wolf, he'd reckoned. Let them leave him alone in his castle to paint, the only one brave enough to walk up the canyon and sleep sound at Col du Noir.

He looked back at the bed. She was sitting up, leaning on her elbow, facing away from him. In a moment she'd have her feet on the floor, and a moment after that she'd be laid out on it—a sequence he could predict with perfect clarity.

Nemo came padding into the room. He slunk along the wall, skirting the bed as far as possible. After a perfunctory sniff of S.T.'s knees, he stood leaning against his legs, looking dubiously toward their guest.

There was a sketch pad and charcoal on the table by the bed. S.T. left Nemo cowering by the window and went to her.

"Lie down, you idiot," he said, pushing her back into the pillow. She barely resisted him, drawing her body up into a curl with a soft sound of distress. He tore a strip of paper and scribbled a note, folding it carefully in order to keep from smearing the charcoal.

He looked around the room for something to tie it with. Something obvious. Human. Unmistakably civilized.

The discarded wig hung where he'd left it on the bedpost. S.T. swept it up, rummaged in his chest for the satin ribbons he'd used to tie his queue in his damsel days, and advanced on Nemo. The wolf looked up at him, his head cocked, his pale eyes calm and utterly trusting.

S.T. tied the wig onto Nemo's head, smoothing down the fur and tucking the note beneath. He tugged it, to make sure it wouldn't slide into the wolf's eyes or interfere with his throat. Nemo accepted the decoration solemnly. S.T. stepped back, and the ridiculousness of the earnest picture the wolf made gave him a sick and guilty ache in his gut.

Why do this?

Send Nemo to the village, and someone would shoot him. 'Twas as simple as that. A wolf would come out of the dark, and no one would stop to ask why it wore a tie wig.

Hell.

She wasn't worth it. What did he know about her? A capricious, helpless, romantic female. He'd lost enough to her kind. He'd lost Charon, and half his hearing, and all of his self-respect.

He looked at her, a huddled curl of misery on the bed. He wanted her to live. He wanted to sleep with her because she was beautiful and he hadn't had a woman in three years, damn it all, and that was the sum total of it. Weighted against Nemo's life, it was nothing.

She was whispering something under her breath. He closed his eyes and turned his head away, but the move only brought her voice more clearly to his good ear.

". . . don't think I . . . can get up," she was saying. "You must go away, Monseigneur. A fortnight. Twelve days. Bathe in a cold stream to strengthen yourself. Don't come back before twelve days. Don't let . . . anyone come before. I'm sorry . . . I shouldn't have come . . . but please, Monseigneur—go away. Don't take this risk."

He put his hand on Nemo's head, on the silly wig, and moved it down to smooth the soft ruff of fur.

She wasn't asking.

Damn her pluck, that she wasn't asking for his help.

He knelt suddenly and pulled Nemo into a fierce hug, burying his face in the sharp scent of wolf and wildness. A hot tongue licked his ear; a cold nose sniffed curiously at his neck. He tried to memorize those sensations, tried to put them away in a safe place in his heart. Then he stood up and grabbed the empty wine bottle from the bedside.

He held the bottle for Nemo to sniff, and gave two simple orders before he had time to change his mind.

Find men. Find this man.

Go.

THREE

S.T. started awake to the sound of bird calls and a whispered muttering from the bed. He rubbed his neck, feeling on every bone the imprint of the wooden chair where he'd slept for the last ten nights. A bare, chilly glow of dawn sky showed through the open window. He squinted toward the shadows that lingered in the room.

She'd pushed the sheets off again. S.T. rose stiffly. He wiped his eyes, ran a hand through his hair, and took a deep breath. The place at his feet where Nemo should have been was empty, as it had been every morning. For a moment S.T. rested his palms and his forehead against the cold stone wall. He was past praying.

The whispered mumble became a low moan. He exhaled heavily and pushed himself away from the wall.

She opened her eyes as he ladled water from the bucket into a cracked clay cup. He saw her blink and moisten her lips. Her fingers moved fretfully, plucking at the white folds of her shirt amid the tangled sheets. Her wandering glance found him, and those dark brows drew downward in fierce disapproval. "Damn you," she breathed.

"*Bonjour,* Sunshine," he responded tartly. "*Ça va?*"

She closed her eyes. Her face was white and stark, set in hostility. "I don't want your help. I don't need it."

He sat down on the bed, catching both her wrists in one hand before she could start to fight. She tried to avoid him, but she was too weak to put up any struggle. She turned

her face away instead, her breath rapid and shallow ever.
with that small effort. He stuffed a pillow behind her head
and held the cup to her lips.

She refused to drink. "Leave," she whispered. "Leave
me alone."

He tilted the cup. She stared dully ahead, her eyelids
barely open. Her skin felt like paper, dry and ashen except
for that bright deadly color on her cheekbones. He pressed
the cup against her mouth. Water slid uselessly down her
chin and throat.

He stood up and added two fingers of brandy to the cup,
downing it himself. The welcome heat of alcohol swamped
the back of his throat and blossomed in his weary brain.

"Let me die," she muttered. "It doesn't matter. I want
it." Her head rolled. "Oh, Papa, let me die, let me die."

S.T. sat down in the chair and put his face in his hands.
She was going to die, yes; she'd made that choice somewhere in her delirium, and what the fever didn't burn up
simply faded with each passing day. She called for her
father with increasing frequency, drifting in and out of
sense, falling deeper into the hours of silent stupor.

S.T. hated her. He hated himself. Nemo was gone.
When he thought of it, he felt as if he'd been hit in the
stomach; his chest and his throat ached for breath that
wouldn't come.

"Papa," she whispered. "Please, Papa, take me with
you. Don't leave me alone . . . don't leave . . . don't
leave . . ." She turned her head restlessly, lifting one weak
hand. "Papa . . ."

"I'm here," S.T. said.

"Papa . . ."

"I'm here, curse it!" He strode to the bed and grabbed
her hand. Her bones felt like porcelain in his fist. He
reached for the ladle and filled the cup again. "Drink
this."

At the touch of the cup rim against her lips, she lifted
her lashes. "Papa." She wet her lips and opened them.
When S.T. tilted the cup this time, she swallowed.

"That's good," he said. "That's my girl."

"Oh, Papa," she mumbled. She drank again, her eyes closed, each breath and swallow an effort.

"That's my Sunshine," he murmured. "Keep trying."

Her fingers curled in his hand, seeking reassurance like a child. He held her tight, listening to her mindless whimper fade away into silence.

Don't die, damn you, he thought. *Don't leave me with nothing.*

She took a deep, shuddering breath and swallowed the last teaspoon of liquid in the cup. He smoothed her burning forehead, brushing the short, dark curls back from her face. 'Twas a true tribute to her beauty, he reckoned, that after ten days of nursing he could still see it.

He'd seen every inch of her by now. He wondered what her precious papa would think of that. Personally, S.T. was too damned tired and sick at heart to care.

He coaxed and bullied her into drinking a second cup of water. She managed half of it before he lost her to exhaustion and grogginess. After a halfhearted attempt to straighten the bedclothes, which he had a vague idea was proper sickroom procedure, he went downstairs to face the problem of food.

At the door to the courtyard he stopped and whistled. Twice. He had to restrain himself from a third time, or a fourth or fifth or a thousand. He stood in the dawn and listened to the sound of his own breathing.

He walked across the yard and whistled again. The ducks came waddling after him, irritable and hungry, but he left them to fend for themselves as he headed for the garden. He ought to butcher one, he knew—that was why he'd started the flock—but when it came to the decision he never could quite choose the victim. He'd reckoned he'd leave that to Nemo, who had no such scruples.

Nemo.

S.T. whistled again. He didn't allow himself to stop walking. The crunch of his boots on limestone and dirt seemed very loud, echoing faintly off the hillside. Every branch and bare rock stood intensely clear in the brilliant dawn light.

In the garden, he had to look hard for what was left

among the weeds. Five red peppers, a cylindrical green courgette—profoundly rabbit-nibbled on one end; some broad white beans, two fistfuls of wild rosemary and another of thyme, and of course the garlic, which was his sole agricultural success. He could throw it all in the pot with barley for soup. If she wouldn't eat it, he certainly would. And he'd mash olives and capers into a *tapenade* to spread on his bread. On his way back he collected pine kernels, eating them and tossing the cone husks over the cliff as he went.

After he started the soup, he looked in on her again. She was restless and petulant, drifting from sense to nonsense, taking one sip of water and then refusing the next. Her forehead and hands felt fiery. He might have thought she was reaching a crisis, except the past days had seemed nothing but one endless climax of fever and weakness.

He did what he could for her, bathed her in a decoction of rue and rosemary he'd been boiling daily, ever since she'd had a moment of lucidity and told him to rub himself with it to prevent infection. She seemed to be something of an expert in the matter of physicking, and when he could coax an instruction out of her, he followed it with alacrity. Afterward, he took a half hour, as he had daily, to climb carefully down into the canyon and steel himself to bathe in the icy river that rushed down from mountains.

To strengthen himself, she'd said—and God knew it took backbone to wade in naked and pour a bucketful of frigid water over his head. He'd never been known as a coward, but that little task bordered on being more than he could brave.

He did it, though. Mainly because he had no desire to die the way she was dying.

The sun had cleared the canyon wall by the time he retied his queue and shivered into his shirt and waistcoat. He walked a little way downstream, whistling for Nemo, looking for any signs, still clinging to the faint hope that a female's presence might be keeping the wolf in hiding.

He found nothing to reassure him. At last he took a different path up the canyon, emerging onto the track from the village. He kept his eyes on the ground, still looking for fresh signs.

The sign he found wasn't a wolf's. On a limestone ledge above the path, the scrambling marks of human footprints led him to a little crevice beneath a juniper bush. In the shadow, a battered cloak bag lay indifferently concealed. He pulled it out, turned it over, and flipped open the buckles, rifling the contents with seasoned efficiency and no compunction.

The elegantly lined interior held a crushed silk gown and matching slippers embroidered in an intricate pattern of Prussian blue birds. Beneath that lay a set of bone stays in brown twill and a few pieces of muslin worked in elaborate needlepoint.

He pulled out the clothing, spreading the carelessly wrinkled gown over a bush to keep it clean of dust while he ransacked the rest of the satchel. Underneath the layer of twill, there was a leather case that held a collection of small vials and medicines in tiny glass jars, all neatly lettered with labels such as, "Carminative Powder" and "Blistering Plaister," and "Lozenges of Marshmallows."

Stuffed inside a silver cup, wrapped in a handkerchief, he found a fine pearl choker. A painted fan and a pair of gold shoe buckles in a satin-lined case marked "Remember the Giver" lay at the bottom. He stuck his hand in an interior pocket and jerked back, swearing, sucking the cut on his finger. Investigating more carefully, he found a sterling letter opener engraved "LGS" and sharpened to a lethal point, along with the stable file that had done it.

There was nothing else but a purse full of small coins and a worn sketchbook labelled, "Silvering, Northumberland, 1764 to 17—, by Leigh Gail Strachan." S.T. flipped it open.

As he paged through it, he began to smile wryly. The bright watercolors inside were enchanting, the humorous and naive figures of a young country lady painting her family and daily life. Each sketch was carefully titled and commented upon in ink. "Emily falls off her donkey! (Must work on perspective)"; "Edward N. displays his ingenious electrifying machine to Emily, Anna, and Mum.

Anna swooning. (Staircase shown too wide but expressions good.)''; ''Assembly at Hexham. Captain Perry teaching Anna a graceful step.''; ''Stuck in deep mud. Castro barks most rudely at John Coachman. (Study proportions of equine hind leg)''; ''Papa asleep in the library after a difficult day cutting roses with Mum.''; ''Wassail, Wassail! Emily, Leigh, and Castro meet Papa and Edward N. returning with the Yule log.''; ''The Lord of the Manor curing a sick piglet by chasing it round the yard. Anna and Leigh looking on.'' ''Emily falls off a stile.''; ''Papa preparing Sunday's sermon.''; ''Emily, Anna, and Leigh save the kittens! (Dog very poorly done.)''

The sketch of the valiant rescue showed the three girls in their aprons and bonnets brandishing sticks and brooms at something that resembled a spotted pig with fangs. S.T. grinned. In the background of a hayrack, five splotches with feet seemed to represent the threatened kittens.

A folded clipping from the *London Gazette* lay between the last page and the backing. He smoothed it open.

By Proclamation of His Majesty the King, it read in grandiose lettering, above a long list of declared outlaws. S.T. found himself two-thirds down the page. *"Styled the Prince of Midnight, betimes in French, le Seigneur du Minuit. Passing Six Feet in height, Green Eye'd his Brown Hair Gold Favour'd, a Gentlemanly Air, Excellent Address and Brows of Uncommon upward Curl. Mounted upon a Fine Black Stud, Sixteen hands, no Markings. Whoever can discover the Person aforesaid to His Majesty's magistrates shall have three pounds reward.*

''Three pounds?'' S.T. said in shock. ''Only three bloody pounds?''

It had been two hundred in his glory days, and he'd been at the top of the list when last he'd seen one of these thieftakers' handbills. No wonder he'd never been disturbed in his lair at Col du Noir.

Three pounds. What a melancholy thought.

He slid the sketchbook back inside and stood up. Still nursing his cut finger, he folded the dress, stuffed it in, and shouldered the valise, shaking his head at the wonder of this gently bred young girl making it across most of England and all of France.

Alive. Alone. In search of him.

By nightfall, he'd spooned two bowls of soup into her. After a little rally, in which she'd cursed him feebly and called for both her parents, she seemed to grow worse, weaker and more lethargic. Sometimes he had to stare at the bed for long moments to make sure she was breathing.

He wished she'd just die and get it done with. In the dim firelight, he sat in his chair with his head resting against the stone wall, waiting. It came to him that he would have to bury her. He tried to think of where he ought to do it—God, some place that he'd not have to pass every day—he wouldn't be able to bear that. He thought of what it would be like, alone in the castle, without Nemo, and felt a deep black well of despair open inside him.

He got up and bathed her forehead. She didn't wake, didn't even move, and he stared down at her in silent panic until he saw at last the faint rise and fall of her breasts.

Asleep, warmed by the faint firelight, her face seemed softer. More human. He could imagine her smiling. He thought of the silk dress and slippers; envisioned a fine withdrawing room and a silver tea set, tried to put her in the setting . . .

S.T. knew those drawing rooms. He knew those ladies. Intimately. Their courage might extend to a rendezvous in the garden at midnight, an affair in the dressing room or the shadows of the back stairs: he'd conducted an intensely dangerous and passionate congress beneath a scaffold once in some state room under renovation in the Percy's great house at Syon, and the smell of sawdust and plaster was mingled ever after with sweetly scented powder and soft skin in his mind. The lady would have left her noble husband for him, she'd claimed that much valor for herself, but S.T. could not imagine she'd have walked alone from the north of England to Provence. In the end, she hadn't even left a message for him when that selfsame husband had arrived to put an end to her daring and take her home.

Women.

S.T. sat brooding on the past. There was something about Leigh Strachan that brought it back in all the glory and agony: what a splendid fool he'd been—but so alive, so electric, every step a gamble, every stake a fortune; even the memory seemed more real than the present. . . . *Charon in the moonless dark, a shadow with silver hooves, shouts and the yellow gold flash of pistol fire . . .* He closed his eyes. He could feel his heart beat faster, taste the sweat and excitement; he knew what the mask felt like on his face, how the black cloak weighted his shoulders and the gloves smelled of saddle soap and steel. His throat burned with cold air, with the effort of using his sword, of keeping Charon between bit and heel: a dance to the left or right, a *pirouette* or a *capriole* with those silvered hooves to distract and confuse in the night: a ghost horse that could ride the air.

It had consumed him, the cool art and hot thrill of it, moving in a twilight between wealth and dirt poverty, where the morality of what he did seemed fitting in the face of such consummate injustice. He was deliberate in whom he chose to champion and whom to torment. He'd studied his marks, gliding with them through the polite salons, the green parks and shimmering masquerades; a gentleman like the rest, unsuspected, shielded by the august and ancient name of Maitland—singling out the blindest, the most smug and self-concerned for his prey.

But he'd never been a true crusader. He'd never had an honest mission. 'Twas the sheer joy of the game, the risk and rebellion. He'd simply grown up an anarchist at heart: an agent on the side of chaos. Until chaos had turned on him.

He sighed deeply and rubbed his palms over his face. Then he glanced at the bed and sat up straight.

Her eyes were open. When he stood, she looked toward him. For a moment there was a trace of a smile on her lips, and then a look of slow realization changed her face, as if she'd woken from a good dream into a bad one. She turned away from him with a sullen move.

"I told you not to stay with me," she said hoarsely.

He frowned at her, at the thin sheen of perspiration on

her pale skin. The feverish color seemed to have subsided, but it was hard to tell in the firelight. He reached out and touched her forehead.

"It's broken, hasn't it?" she murmured indifferently. "I shall survive."

She was warm beneath his hand, but not burning. He observed her narrowly. "God willing," he said.

"What has God to say to it?" Her voice was weak, but it held a faint sneer. "There isn't any God. The fever's broken. By tomorrow 'twill be quite . . . normal." She closed her eyes and turned her face away. "Nothing will kill me, it seems."

He poured water for her. "Something's come damned close."

She stared at the cup he held out. For a long moment, she made no move. Then, with a weary sound of acquiescence, she lifted her hand. S.T. saw it tremble. He put the cup down and plumped the pillows while she levered herself into a half-sitting position.

She sipped at the water, holding the cup in both hands. Her eyes drifted over the room in a lackluster inspection. They came to rest on him. "You've been stupid to stay."

He rubbed his ear. She watched him over the cup rim. After a silent moment, he took the water before she could spill it in her shaking fingers. "What else was I to do?" he asked.

Her eyelashes lifted. The look she gave him said she didn't believe anyone could be so dim-witted.

He set the cup down and gave her a dry smile. "I live here," he said. "I don't have anywhere else to go."

She closed her eyes and rested her head back on the pillow. "The village," she said weakly.

"And take the fever there?"

She shook her head without opening her eyes. "Stupid man . . . stupid man. If you'd left . . . when first I told you to go. It takes intimate contact to . . . infect."

He watched her without speaking, trying to decide if she was truly coherent and on the way to recovery.

"I hope," she said, "that you didn't stay out of some foolish romantical notion."

He looked down, staring at the tumbled bedclothes.
"Such as?"

"Saving my life."

He looked up again with a grimace. "Naturally not. I
usually throw my houseguests off the cliff."

One corner of her mouth curved faintly. "Then I wish
you would . . . do me the favor." The curve turned into
a quiver. She pressed her lips together.

He sat down on the edge of the bed and smoothed her
forehead, brushing her skin with his thumb. "Sunshine,"
he whispered. "What have they done to you?"

She bit her lip and shook her head. "Don't be kind to
me. Don't."

He cradled her face in his palms. "I was afraid you
would die."

"I want to." Her voice shook. "Oh, I want to. Why
didn't you let me?"

He traced her cheekbones and the curve of her eyebrows
with his thumbs. "You're too lovely. Dear God, you're
too beautiful to die."

She turned her face away. He stroked her skin, feeling the unnatural warmth that still lingered. "Damn
you." Her whisper broke upward precariously. "I'm
crying."

Hot moisture tumbled down across his fingers. He
smoothed the tears away, felt her convulsive, shuddering breath as she fought to control it. She lifted her
hands and pushed feebly at his, trying to evade his
touch.

He moved away, to quiet her. This might be recovery,
or it might only be that last strange moment of lucid
strength before the finish. He'd seen it happen. Standing
there looking down at her pale, finely etched features and
the lifeless desolation in her eyes, he could believe she
didn't have far to go to slip over to the other side.

She was alive in the morning, though. Most definitely
alive, if not more cheerful. Four days later she sat up in
bed, frowning, and refused to allow him to nurse her, but

ate and drank with her own wobbly hands and insisted that he leave her in private for her toilette.

So he did. He went out hunting for Nemo again and came back alone.

The excursion had one success—he took his musket along and managed to poach a brace of royal pheasant, which solved the problem of supplies for the time being. When he returned, Miss Leigh Strachan was sleeping, her dark hair tousled around her face in sable curls, but she woke and struggled up in bed the moment he entered the room.

"How are you feeling?" she asked abruptly.

He lifted an eyebrow. "Considerably better than you, I don't doubt."

"Your appetite is regular?"

"Prodigous," he said. "You're keeping me from my breakfast."

"No febrile symptoms? Or chilling?"

He leaned against the wall. "Not unless my daily sojourn in that bloody frigid stream counts."

"You've been taking a cold bath?" She regarded him with a weak scowl. "That's something then, at least."

"Your orders, mademoiselle."

She lay back on the pillows wearily. "Would that you'd followed them all. I told you to go away, too, but you weren't sensible enough for that. I only pray you won't suffer the consequences."

"I've been drowning myself in rosemary and rue. I'm most delightfully aromatic. Have you noticed?"

She took no regard of the arm he held out for a sniff. "That will be helpful as far as it goes." Her voice was strained, the natural huskiness pronounced, but she went stubbornly on. "I've been considering a further list of herbs you must collect, but you'll have to bring me a pen and paper to write them down." She didn't wait for him to do so, but took a trembling breath and started immediately onto her next point. "In Bedfordshire, they've had some success with washing the walls of fever residences in quicklime. Is there any available?"

S.T. shook his head, watching her closely. He doubted she ought to be exerting herself to this much talking.

Her fingers moved restlessly. "You'll have to make some. I can tell you how. But the herbs should be gathered first; you can brew several necessary decoctions for dosing yourself." She closed her eyes, paused a moment, and then opened them. "You should continue the cold baths. And I'll want to know instantly if you develop the headache or any other of the signs. I'll write them down for you. As for the quicklime, you must gather—"

By the time S.T. had been regaled with the long list of prophylactic measures he was to take for his continuing health, he couldn't decide if Miss Leigh Strachan was truly concerned for him or simply a born drill sergeant. She had that methodical style of categorizing things in descending, ascending, and elliptical orders of priority that he associated with middle-aged spinsters and tax clerks. He began edging out of the room, finally claiming a pot of garlic was on the boil to hasten his departure, and escaped down the spiral stairs.

He got to the armory, tried to remember the first thing he was supposed to do, and shook his head in defeat. "God's blood," he muttered to Charon's portrait. "Quicklime. Peruvian bark. Smoking hell."

He kicked at a ball of dust and shrugged off his coat, electing to clean the pheasant instead. He didn't intend to be hanging about gathering herbs and whitewashing walls anyway—as soon as she could fend for herself, he intended to leave her with some supplies and go looking for Nemo.

When he took her a midday meal of *aigo boulido*, she was sitting up in his chair, wrapped in a bed sheet. S.T. grunted in annoyance. "You'll have a relapse, damn you. Get back in bed."

She merely looked at him coolly, and then at the chipped bowl, full of bread soaked in a broth of sage, garlic, and olive oil. S.T. ate it all the time; it had kept Provençal peasants alive for centuries. Marc even considered the dish particularly suitable for invalids, S.T. knew, but Miss

Leigh Strachan's nose flared delicately as she turned her face away.

"I cannot," she said, turning even paler.

"You can't eat it?"

"Garlic." The single word held soul-deep loathing.

He sat down on the bed. "Very well." He held up the bowl and dug in himself. She watched him with a faint pinch to her mouth. He leaned against the bedpost, savoring the pungent soup. "What would you prefer, mademoiselle?"

"Perhaps . . . some plain beef tea?"

"I heard of a cow in Provence once," he said. "In Avignon. That's about thirty leagues from here." He took another bite. "Lady Harvey had it imported from England."

"Oh."

"She didn't care for goat's milk in her tea."

Leigh bit her lip. "I should like my bread plain, then."

"As you please." He shook his head, finishing off the last bite. "I'll bring some for you before I go."

"Go where?" she asked sharply.

He set the bowl aside. "First to the village. Maybe farther; I don't know. I was going to wait a day or two, but if you're strong enough to complain about the menu, I believe I can leave you to lift your own food to your mouth."

"Certainly I can, but you mustn't leave here now."

He frowned down at his feet. "I won't touch anyone. I'll keep my distance. I just need to—ask some questions."

"Why?"

He glanced down, fitting one fist inside the other. "My wolf . . . he's gone off. I want to look for him."

"He's lost?"

"Possibly."

"How long has he been gone?"

He didn't look at her. "A fortnight."

There was a long silence. S.T. drew a circle, and then a figure eight in his hand.

"It's my fault, then," she said quietly.

He took a deep breath. "No. I sent him. To the village with a note. I didn't have to. You didn't ask."

The bed sheet rustled as she stood up. "Where are my clothes?"

He looked up at her. She swayed a little and held on to the back of the chair for support. "You don't need your clothes. You're going back to bed."

"No," she said. "I'm going with you."

FOUR

LYING with her cheek pillowed against her cloak bag, feigning sleep beneath a pine tree, Leigh watched him from under her lashes. If not for the painting of the black horse Charon, she wouldn't have credited that this man was really the Seigneur.

It was true enough that he fit the physical description. He sat cross-legged in his shirt sleeves, tricorne tossed negligently aside, looking out over the steep-sided valley and chewing on a sprig of wild thyme. His hair was tied back in a careless queue; the sunlight of the south turned it to that shimmer of gold and deep earthen shadow that had sounded so peculiar by report and turned out to be so extraordinary in reality. The black ribbon tumbled halfway down his back. His easy smile and the strange fiendish curve of his brows gave his face a satyric cast, laughing and wicked at once.

But he talked to himself. And though his normal motion was easy and fluid, if he turned quickly, he lost his balance. She'd seen it happen three times now on their hike down along the gorge. At first she'd feared it was an early symptom of the fever, but he seemed unaffected otherwise—save for the way he looked the wrong direction half the time when she spoke to him.

It didn't seem possible that a man with clumsy balance and flawed reflexes could be much of a swordsman, though he wore a rapier at his hip. Or a horseman either—and the Seigneur had been a master of both.

40

But there was the painting of the black horse. And his legendary way with an animal, asking a wolf to do his bidding as if it were a reasoning being instead of a wild beast. And his singular coloring, green and gold and gilded chocolate, which was what had led her to him from as far away as Lyon, where they knew all about the eccentric Englishman with the manner of the true *noblesse,* who spoke *français* so creditably and had unaccountably taken up residence in a ruined pile of stones.

She'd found him. He was the Seigneur du Minuit, without doubt.

He just wasn't precisely the Seigneur she'd been hoping for.

In truth, she could almost feel enough to pity him. To come to this: living in unkempt isolation, grubbing off the barren land with only a wolf and a few ducks for company after what he'd been and done. 'Twas no wonder if he'd gone a little mad.

He looked toward her. Leigh maintained her pretense of sleep, not wanting to speak or move yet. Through the web of her lashes, she watched him use a tree branch for stability as he hiked himself up.

He stood still a moment on the canyon rim, his face half turned toward her but his attention focused intently elsewhere, like someone trying to catch the words of a distant song. The deep sleeves of his linen shirt moved in a faint breeze. It fluttered the simple fringe of lace at his cuffs and outlined his shoulders beneath the fabric. In the back seam of his waistcoat there was a small tear that needed mending before it grew, and his soft leather top boots could have done with a vigorous polish. On his elbow a patch of blue paint marred the creamy white of good linen.

He looked lonely.

Leigh shifted restlessly, turning her face into her arms. The sharp scent of pine needles engulfed her. She closed her eyes. Her body wanted to sleep, to rest and mend, but her soul resisted it. There were decisions, questions, new plans to be made if the old ones wouldn't do. She had nothing to spare for sentiment. If he wouldn't teach her— if he couldn't—she had to go on to another course.

But she owed him something. She'd stay with him until the danger of fever passed, little as he seemed to credit it, and she hoped that a pitiless providence might work one small miracle and return the wolf unharmed.

S.T. had offered to carry her satchel four times, but she'd turned him down. He was miffed about that; she had a way of making a simple gentlemanly suggestion appear to be an immoderate encroachment on her dignity, as if he'd tried to slip a hand up her shirt instead of merely carry her bag.

He would have been happy to slip a hand up her shirt, of course. Or anything else of that nature. He walked along behind her, watching her legs and the swing of her velvet coat over the feminine curves beneath, smiling to himself.

"So," he said, after they'd resumed their pace long enough for the silence to become strangling, "from whence do you hail, Miss Strachan?"

"Don't call me that." She stepped heavily down from a boulder onto the lower grade of a hairpin turn in the path.

S.T. followed, lost his balance in a too hasty rotation, and clutched at a branch to steady himself. This sharp attack of vertigo had begun when he'd woken in the morning and lifted his head. Like the inside of a colorful giant ball, the room had booted into motion, spinning wildly around him.

After three years, he was halfway resigned to the faint dizziness that plagued him all the time, the sensation of disorientation when he closed his eyes or turned his head too suddenly. But the bad spells came on without warning and varied in intensity. Sometimes he couldn't even get out of bed without falling down. Sometimes, he could swallow down the nausea and concentrate on steady objects and move, as long as he didn't move too fast.

Walking downhill was like playing roulette. The slash of leaves from his ungainly stumble brought a look backward from his companion. He stared at her defiantly. "What do you expect me to call you?"

She turned back and kept walking.

"Fred?" he asked. "William? Beezlebub? Rover? No, listen—I've got it. How would 'Pug' suit?"

She stopped and turned, so abruptly that he had to grab a ledge with one hand and her with the other to keep from pitching onto his face. She stood still, her shoulder steady beneath his sudden grip. His instant of dizziness subsided.

" 'Twould be foolish," she said dispassionately, "to dress as a man and be called by a feminine title. Would it not, monsieur?"

S.T. told himself to take his hand off her, but he didn't. It was the first time he'd touched her when she'd been in her right mind, and she wasn't ordering him to let go.

"I suppose that's a consideration," he said, and tried out a smile on her.

For a moment he thought it might actually meet with some success. Her steady gaze faltered, a downward brush of black lashes hiding blue, but when she looked at him again it was with the ice of attack.

"What's wrong with you that makes you so clumsy?" She moved her shoulder beneath his hand.

S.T. let go of her instantly. "A case of general ineptitude, as you see." He leaned on his other hand, bracing against the rock ledge, doing his best to look casual. "Any other complaints, Sunshine?"

"There's something wrong with you," she said.

He tried to stare her down. "Thank you."

"What is it?"

"Bugger off, mademoiselle."

"For God's sake, don't call me so when anyone can hear you."

"Ah, yes—we're all to think you're a great lump of a man, aren't we? Then bugger off, you son of a bitch. Does that suit your masculine sensibilities?"

It seemed impossible to goad her. She merely looked at him intently, and he felt as if he were standing naked in the Champs Élysées. He took a breath, meeting the look, feeling as bullheaded and foolish as he undoubtedly appeared. But he couldn't tell her. His mouth simply would not form the words *I'm deaf. I'm half deaf and I can't keep my equilibrium anymore. I can't hear and I can't ride and I can't fight and I can barely walk down this hill without falling on my face.*

She knew. How could she not? She watched him narrowly enough with those ice-water eyes. Saints, she was so beautiful, and he was a clumsy, stumbling, frustrated shadow man, who would have lied like Lucifer to have her if he'd thought he could get by with it . . . but he reckoned that in the end he couldn't, and so he had nothing but his thick-witted pride to preserve.

"You needn't come along in any case. Nobody asked you," he said—a pretty brilliant sample of school yard wit, he thought in vexation.

Again a tiny falter, an instant's waver of that steady regard. She frowned at his chest, and he could see her thinking, weighing alternatives.

"You need me," she said at last.

Not: *I want to.* Or *I enjoy the company.* Or *I think we could come to admire one another.*

Just a task. Clearly she'd long since decided he was useless for her original purpose. Which he was. But he'd rather have been the one to deliver the snub, thank you.

"Much obliged," he said sarcastically. "But I don't need your help, Miss Strachan—as a matter of fact, you're a hindrance. You may think that outfit will fool a Frenchman, but Nemo won't come near me as long as you insist upon skulking about in the vicinity."

She shrugged. "Tell me when to stay at a distance, then."

"Le diable." He let out an explosive breath. "Do you know nothing of a beast's fine senses? He'll discover me long before I can find him. Stay away, Miss Strachan, if you don't need my nursing. Just stay away from me." He pushed off the ledge and brushed past her. He kept going, down to the next curve in the trail, which he turned with studious leisure, careful to keep his hand on a rock and his eyes fixed on a tree to control the vertigo. He was aware that there was no sound of movement on the path behind him. He managed a quick glance up through the bushes, and saw her still standing there, as if she'd taken him precisely at his word.

Fine. Grand. He'd have let her tag along with him if
she'd shown the least sign of civility. Truth be told, he
could find Nemo with or without her if the wolf was going
to be found. Truth be told, he relished having someone to
be responsible for besides himself—skirt-smitten blockhead that he was—calling halts when he judged she needed
the rest, making certain she paced herself, trying to prevent the crazy chit from pushing till she dropped.

She reminded him of an animal in that way. She kept
on like some single-minded beast, the way a wounded stag
would keep stumbling forward, oblivious of obstacles and
pain and sense. Just moving, as if the motion itself had
some design.

His reason told him to leave it alone, that he'd had
enough of damsels in distress to last any man ten lifetimes.
But his spirit filled him with visions of that nighttime highway, of scandalous glory . . . erotic, heady pleasure, joy
that burned through all his veins, in the saddle or in a
woman's arms.

Love had never lasted; it had all come to naught more
times than he could remember. He gave himself to the
dream, and it vanished in his hands. It had ruined him.

He ought to keep his wits.

But she was like none of the others.

Maybe, this time, it would be different.

Bouffon! He always thought it would be different. He
always thought: *this time* . . .

Ah! but *this* time, this time, this time . . .

Damnation.

By the time he reached the village, his vertigo was abat-
ing, diminishing into the faint disorientation that he'd
learned to tolerate, the sense of being constantly just a bit
light-headed, but he wasn't yet past a stumble. He didn't
know if she had followed him or not—there were a thousand paths she could have taken, splitting off from the trail
to the village and heading north or south or east or west
or any direction a lunatic girl might want to go.

La Paire boasted two bridges over the narrow river, log-
ically enough, and not much else. Marc's tavern clung to

the cliff in between them, a whitewashed, tile-roofed and green-shuttered domestication of the old fort walls, snugged between perpendicular neighbors. The hill town seemed to grow right up out of the top of the gorge and peer over into it, like an upended jumble of child's blocks that managed by some miracle of balance and faith not to fall in.

S.T. had thought the town and the canyon and the pair of bridges arched a hundred feet above the narrow cataracts quite picturesque when first he'd come here. And Marc had laughed at S.T.'s jokes and served good spicy red wine, and there was wild country for Nemo and sunlight like nectar, and it was all a long, long way from anywhere . . . and so he'd stopped running.

La Paire was a border town on the flanks of the Alps, changing hands between Capets and Hapsburgs and the House of Savoy with monotonous regularity. Presently, La Paire stood on the French rim and S.T.'s Col du Noir on the Savoyard side of the border, but any treaty signed in Madrid or Rome or Vienna might change that in a day.

He'd bought the ruined castle by letter from a young chevalier who preferred Paris to rustication. It made a home of sorts, the first one S.T. had had in his life—or the first he'd chosen for himself, at any rate, and one of the few he'd lived in for more than six months altogether. He found he liked solitude. He preferred to go to bed at sundown, he who'd spent all the nights of his past in revelry or scandal or lawless hunting along the dark highways. He painted, slept, and dug in the rocky dirt to grow things, and that had been good enough.

Until now. Until three years of isolation pressed in his chest, a tangle of lust and chagrin curled on top of terror that he would walk across a bridge and see Nemo's skin nailed to the town gate.

He was spared that. The main gate was only a gate, in need of repair as usual, and presently blocked by a coach that had unwisely attempted to cross the river and pass beneath the low portcullis. Since the iron grating had hung at a slant over the cobbled street from some time in the early Middle Ages, there seemed little hope that the com-

bined efforts of the mayor, a dozen townsmen, two housewives acting in an advisory capacity, and a swarm of dirty
little boys were going to straighten it up and free the coach
in the near future. S.T. took the other bridge across.

The guard post was empty, also typically. S.T. walked
from the sovereign territories of His Highness, the King
of Sardinia and Duke of Savoy, across the official border
into France without even a halfhearted challenge. The lack
of ceremony suited him perfectly well, since it saved him
having to hear the sad story of the lieutenant's latest love
affair.

He went into Marc's by the kitchen door, where the
aubergiste gave him no more than a wild glance and rushed
past, carrying a tray up the stairs to the salon. S.T. glanced
at the crowd of spectators pressed around the windows in
the public room and decided to follow Marc upstairs.

He sauntered into the salon as if he were dressed in silk
stockings and Venetian velvet instead of a waistcoat and
stained breeches. Normally he didn't bother to patronize
the upper room, but he could put on his airs with the
noblest of them, as Marc well knew. The innkeeper only
bobbed his head when S.T. commandeered the divan and
crossed his legs in his most elegant sprawl.

Out on the narrow balcony that overlooked the town
gate, a nattily dressed man in a powdered wig sat propped
against the iron rail, swinging an ebony walking stick with
a gold knob and grinning at the commotion in the street
below. His companion, looking bored, slouched at the table where Marc was pouring two generous servings from
a bottle of his best cognac.

S.T. favored the guests with a distant nod and lifted his
finger for a glass. Marc actually looked relieved to hurry
over to him; the tavern keeper left the entire flagon on the
side table, gave S.T. a significant glance and a peculiar
twitch of his eyebrows in the direction of the seated man,
and hastened out of the room.

That was decidedly odd. Normally, Marc would have
required a bit of cajoling and numerous promises before
parting with even a bottle of his Hermitage, much less the
cognac, given the sad status of S.T.'s bill. He took a

thoughtful sip, tilting his head to survey the travelers discreetly.

He found his interest returned. The man at the table was looking at him with insolent openness, one elbow resting casually on his armchair. He wore a gray frock coat, with a thick fall of lace at his throat, and breeches and waistcoat of matching marigold yellow. His weapon was a cane sword, lighter and more convenient than S.T.'s unfashionable but lethal colichemarde.

The stranger's dark eyes moved over S.T. as if he were a horse at auction; the bored mouth curved upward a little when S.T. met his look squarely. Without comment the man turned again to the balcony, stuck his hand into his fair chestnut hair, and rested his cheek on his palm.

"Come and drink, Latour," he said lazily to his companion, "and give me to hope that we won't be incarcerated here for the night."

"I make no promise." The other man straightened and bowed briefly. " 'Tis apparent to me that this execrable hole of a town, she is habited by clowns and monkeys."

"But, no!" Irony dripped from the soft words. "They cannot be so obtuse as this valet of mine, whose unfortunate idea it was to cross the bridge."

The man on the balcony hesitated an instant, and then bowed again more deeply. *"Mais oui,* monsieur le comte. It is as you say, of course."

"Come in and drink, Latour," his master said in a low, silky voice. "Do show some respect. I may be amused to see you drape yourself across the balcony rail when it's between us, but now there is a gentleman present."

Latour obeyed, placing the walking stick carefully in a corner. He stationed himself behind the count's chair and took the glass of cognac offered, but did not drink.

S.T. thought this a queer pair of birds, and rather fancied he'd have done better to stay in the public room below. He'd have learned more there. The shouts and chatter drifted up from the street, echoing in the quiet salon. S.T. sighed and studied his glass. With this turmoil, he'd not get a quite moment to question Marc no matter where he stationed himself.

He tasted his cognac. At least there was no obvious sign that Nemo had been taken or any apparent concern about fever in town. This coach seemed to be the biggest event in La Paire since the Crusades. He glanced toward the table and found the young nobleman watching him again.

"I am bored, Latour," the man said slowly. "Bored. I must do something."

The servant Latour shifted uneasily. "Shall I bespeak a bedchamber, my lord?"

"No . . . in a moment, perhaps. I wonder—dare I be so forward?" He smiled a little. "Could I hope that this gentleman might engage in a small hand of piquet to pass the time?"

S.T. sipped his drink and considered the fellow before him with a professional eye. The man didn't look like a seasoned gambler; he looked like a well-padded aristocrat overcome with ennui. S.T. knew better than to trust that, but on the other hand he hated to pass up an opportunity to fleece a lamb if he had one.

"Nay," he said. "I don't wish to exercise my head so hard, monsieur. And I've no purse about me."

The *comte* sat up straighter. "This cursed place—" He stood suddenly and began to prowl the room. "I cannot bear it! Listen to them down there, the silly dogs; what are they about, to be of such idleness? Inform them I wish to leave, Latour. Go and tell them I cannot tolerate confinement."

The servant bowed. As he left the room, his master pulled out a wallet and emptied it on the table.

"Look, sir," he exclaimed, gesturing toward S.T. "There you are—twenty gold louis. You may count them. Yes—count them! I wager them against nothing, for the sport, if you please. A game, for God's mercy; don't deny me a little diversion!"

S.T. rubbed his ear. He began to wonder about this fellow's wit.

The count swept up his plumed hat from the table and made a deep bow. "I beg of you. The winnings are nothing; they are not of my interest—'tis my mind, you see. I have a lively mind. I'm trying to be good, truly I am, I promise you. But if I have no diversion, there's no saying to what I'll be driven."

Definitely witless. S.T. shrugged and smiled. He could put twenty louis d'or to good use.

The count clapped his hands. "Excellent, excellent; you will play. Come and sit down. Allow me the honor of presenting myself. I am . . . ah—of Mazan. Aldonse-François de Mazan."

S.T. bowed, politely ignoring the little stumble over the name. "S.T. Maitland. Your servant, Monsieur de Mazan."

"Ah. You have an English surname." He stared a moment at S.T. with a peculiar avidity. "I love the English."

S.T. sat down at the table. "Sad to say, then, I must admit that I'm of Firenze. My father was English. I never met him."

"Ah, Florence! The beautiful Italy. I have just left her. You speak French very sweetly."

"Thank you. I have a small talent for languages. Do you have cards, seigneur?"

The count had none—excellent evidence that he was no subtle sharpster. S.T. rang, and they settled down to the fresh deck Marc provided before he hurried back out of the salon without even hanging about to watch the first draw. Monsieur de Mazan was quite a decent player; though S.T. intentionally lost the first two of three deals, by way of keeping the count interested, he didn't have to try all that hard. As the nobleman dealt the third hand, S.T. set about acquiring his gold louis. They came easily enough when he put his mind to the task, sliding across the table to sit beside him with their dull metal gleam of promise.

With all twenty piled on S.T.'s side, the count gallantly offered to quit the table. S.T. gallantly insisted on putting his winnings at risk. He felt the old passion begin to dawn, the pleasure in the gamble.

"Bless you," said the count. "You're saving my life. Here—another five hundred livres against your louis d'ors." He watched S.T. deal. "So you've never been in England, then?"

"Never," S.T. lied cordially.

"Pity. I should like to hear more of it. I've had several English friends to visit my château. Miss Lydia Sterne, the daughter of the distinguished Mr. Laurence Sterne. You've read his *Tristram Shandy?* So droll! I adore the English. And Mr. John Wilkes has told me of his Hell Fire Club—" The count smiled slyly. "That fraternity is of an interest most profound!"

S.T. lifted his eyebrows and shuffled without answering.

"Have you heard of this club?"

He gave the count a level look and lied again. "No, I haven't."

"Ah," the count said, and spread his stock face down. "Pity."

The door to the salon opened again. The valet stepped aside, holding it open, and S.T. glanced up from his hand to see Miss Leigh Strachan calmly enter the room.

All she did was walk past behind him in her blue velvet coat and silk breeches and accept a cognac from Latour, but S.T. found his concentration so suddenly cracked that he neglected to announce his *carte blanche* before he discarded and lost ten points ere the play even started.

Plague take her.

The count seemed equally bemused. He stared past S.T.'s shoulder at her, holding his cards loosely. Suddenly he ran his hand through his light hair. "Latour," he said, "have you a new acquaintance here?"

"Indeed, monsieur—the young gentleman wishes the pleasure of watching the play, if it is *convenable.*"

The count grinned. "A thousand times *convenable.*" He stood up and swept a bow. "Come, come—present the boy, Latour."

The valet made a formal introduction of Mr. Leigh Strachan to the Comte de Mazan. S.T. did not stand up, but only nodded vaguely in her direction. He was determined to be finished with her. Quite finished.

"Perhaps you would permit me to give you my chair," the count suggested, making a move to rise.

"No, *merci,*" she said in her painfully stilted French.

Her husky voice sounded blatantly feminine to S.T., but the other two appeared to accept her for what she seemed. "I prefer to stand."

"But you are not of this country!" The count cried delightedly. "English. You are English. We were just speaking of the English. I forbid you to be anything else!"

She agreed quietly that she was English. S.T. drew a card and turned his head just enough to see her. She looked pale. He had to restrain himself from suggesting that she lie down before she fell down.

"Where are you bound, Monsieur Strachan?" the count demanded. "Where's the rest of your party? Do you make a grand tour?"

There was a short silence, and then she said, "I'm not traveling with a party. I will be returning to England directly. As soon as I secure transportation to the north."

S.T. lost his trick.

"But you needn't seek transport!" the count cried. "I can see that you're a gentleman; you're young; you're alone! You have had misfortunes, perhaps. No, no, you mustn't be left to travel on some washerwoman's ass." He threw down his cards in the midst of the next deal and stood up. "Impossible. You must ride with us. We're for Grenoble, should this ten-times useless valet of mine ever succeed in making our coach free. What news from below, Latour? I'm tired of piquet."

He walked away from the table. S.T. looked down at the half-dealt deck in his hand and tossed it on the table, turning toward the others with a frown. "That's it?" he demanded. "You fold?"

The count waved his hand. "Nay, let us simply forget the game entirely. You won't begrudge my livres, will you, my friend? The louis are yours." He sat down on the couch. "I would rather talk to Monsieur Strachan. We must discuss our travel plans. You will come with us?"

"You are kind," she said in a disinterested tone. "If 'twill not discommode—I shall."

He grinned and leaned toward her. "I look forward to it. We can talk. I have a curiosity about the English." His hand closed on her forearm and his voice rose to an eager note. "The English vice, do you know what I mean?"

S.T. swung around sharply and frowned at him through a surge of dizziness. Just at that moment, a chorus of enthusiastic shouts rose from below. The count leapt up and strode to the balcony.

"*Vive le diable!*" he howled. "We're free! *Venez, Latour*, bring his portmanteau and let us be gone!" He stopped long enough to flip back his coattails in a deep bow in front of Leigh, and then caught her wrist and pulled her bodily to her feet. She made no resistance to this extraordinary familiarity, simply informed him that she had no portmanteau, only the cloak bag.

"Wait a moment," S.T. said. He started to rise, but she walked out of the room without glancing at him. "Wait," he shouted. "You can't just go off with—"

The valet bowed briefly to him, retrieved the count's gold-headed cane and plumed hat, and followed the others.

"—strangers!" S.T. finished savagely. He took a step toward the door, stopped—and sat down again.

He fingered the cards, shuffled and cut and stacked the deck over and over as he listened to the echoing sounds of departure from the cobblestoned street below. The slam of a door, the sharp calls of a postboy to the horses, the cries of advice and warning amid the sound of iron-shod hooves and wheels grating on stone faded into the indiscriminate noise of conversation as the chaise backed from under the portcullis.

S.T. pressed his thumbs against the arch of the deck and sent it exploding across the table with a curse.

He got up and poured himself a drink, staring down at the clutter of cards. Just as the fuss from below was dying away, the street filled again with the sound of horses. He turned toward the balcony, listening with his good ear. He could make nothing of the new shouts and shrill cries of the women, and abandoned all pride at last, striding to the balcony to see if they were returning.

It was not the count's chaise. The steep street filled with mounted soldiers from the other direction, the French side of the border. Cavalry horses milled and reared amid a crowd of townspeople, and S.T. suddenly recognized the French lieutenant from the guard post aiming his musket after the count's coach. The sound of the shot blasted around and around the narrow chasm of the street, and then the whole troop pressed and jostled through the crowd and took off at a gallop across the bridge the way the coach had gone.

Marc burst through the door. "Too late!" he shouted, and ran to the balcony. He leaned out over the rail, waving his fist at the last of the mounted soldiers. "You drunken bumblers! Too late by a trice!" He snorted and pulled back, shaking his head at S.T. *"Zut!* We did our best, did we not? You and I can say so. The cards, that was an inspiration of the finest, *mon ami.* But they'll never catch him this side of the border again. And that poor young fool—the *anglais*—you couldn't stop him going with them? These pups who want to be heroes! God only knows what will become of him."

"Become of him!" S.T. snapped in frustration. "What the devil is going on? They're after Mazan for something?"

Marc gave him a startled look. "You didn't know?"

"Know *what?"* S.T. shouted.

"Ha. Le Comte de Mazan. So he says, eh? Monsieur— he and his valet, Latour, were condemned to the stake a month ago in Marseilles. For blasphemy. And"—Marc lowered his voice to an eager whisper—"sodomy." He shook his head with relish. "And attempted murder of two young girls. He is no comte, my friend. He is Sade. The Marquis de Sade."

FIVE

S.T. had walked the mountain for hours, searching for Nemo far up over the flank until he was almost to the other side, whistling and calling. Now he sat on a lonely hilltop beneath the moon and cursed her.

And himself. His own futile instincts that always betrayed him, that had never earned him anything but misery and a few moments of sensation, come and gone like a winning gamble, the swift thrill that never lasted.

This time, he'd thought, as he always thought: *this time it will be different.* But it was not.

He should never have sent Nemo away, never taken that desperate a chance for the sake of a woman. These grand gestures of his, they never endured beyond the moment of glory before they vanished, and another game had to be played and won again.

And paid for. He'd paid for this one with his last friend. Though he still walked the mountain and searched, S.T. had the news he'd dreaded. He'd come across a Gypsy cutting wood and heard the tale. Two children had seen a monster up on the mountain flanks of Le Grand Coyer, a terrible supernatural creature with the head of a man and the body of a beast. They'd even brought home the wig it had snagged on a bush, and then the Gypsies had made incantations and potions and gone out to draw the beast into a trap, where some Romany witch had turned it back into a common wolf again before they killed it. He could go and see the skin and the tattered wig of the devil's

55

monstrosity if he liked, on display for a small donation in the church at Colmars.

He hadn't gone. He could not. He walked out here on the mountain and pretended there was some mistake, that it was all a dream and he would wake up and find Nemo asleep, curled in a furry, untroubled mound at the foot of the bed.

And her . . . she deserved it, he thought; she got what she was asking for in leaving his protection, which might not rate all that it had in younger days, but was at least more than a match for some popinjay in marigold smalls. She got just what she warranted, running alone about the countryside dressed in breeches: a murdering aristocrat with unnatural tastes to use her and abuse her and leave her body for the birds.

He tilted his head back in despair. A sound hovered at the base of his throat, a low moan of grief and loneliness that swelled into a long note he'd learned from Nemo in the days when they'd lounged on his castle steps hurling wolf music at the moon. He hoped the Gypsies heard it; he hoped the housewives and shopkeepers heard it in the towns; he hoped Sade heard it; he sang Nemo's haunting call as passionately as his human lungs could carry it and hoped they all shivered in their beds, in their carriages and tents and houses and all the places they thought themselves safe.

The wild melody filled him, made him an outlaw again, transmuting his solitude into exile. He sang until his chest ached and the wolf note fell like water into a deep well, cascading down to silence.

He drew a breath. The night was still around him. In the waiting hush, he could hear the blood in his ears, the last faint echo of his wordless lament from the hills around.

And then from far away there came an answer. A single, desolate voice raised the howl again on the night wind, rising up to a peak and sliding earthward. It was joined by a second singer, and a third, until at last it was a chorus: a reckless, savage symphony in celebration of his outlaw cry.

* * *

Leigh had long since grown impatient with this count and his insinuations. He spoke so quickly that she could keep up with only half of his French, fidgeted and touched her arm and babbled on about the English and the Hell Fire Club, staring at her fixedly and then grinning avidly at his valet. She regretted accepting his invitation. Whatever evil he planned could only delay her, and she'd wasted time enough already in this vain journey.

Looking back, she saw that it had been weakness that had sent her here in search of fighting skills she'd never learn. She'd left England driven by a nightmare; clinging to the illusion that she could take revenge as a man would take it. She'd come seeking a champion of justice, a shining, mysterious, half-remembered legend of her girlhood . . . and found that he was human—and lonely—and looked at her as if she could console him.

She would have used that masculine hunger in his eyes, lured him into aiding her in her plan the way a hunter would coax some starving tiger into his baited trap. But when he'd stumbled and held on to her shoulder for support and looked at her with his fine handsome face full of pride and longing, he'd shown her the true extent of his desire.

Something deep inside her had recognized that look. She saw the anticipation in him, and it went beyond uncomplicated lust. Aye, she'd have yielded her body as the price of her goal—she'd resolved on that long ago—but her body wasn't enough. That look asked for more.

So she had left him. She took the first available means, abandoning one more childhood delusion along with all the others. There was no one responsible for justice but herself. She would do what she must alone, in whatever way she could find to do it. She'd hoped to have vengeance with honor, but if honor was not possible, she would have vengeance all the same.

The Comte de Mazan had been in a ferment of excitement all the way from La Paire, where the sound of musket fire had followed them out of town. Apparently the halfhearted pursuit had stopped at the border, since the chaise could have been easily overtaken on the rutted, twisting roads. The track worsened as they went along, reducing them to a pace slower than walking, the wheels falling heavily into holes, bouncing everyone inside, and then climbing out with a creaking groan. Leigh sat silent and tense, clinging to the strap to keep her seat. She judged it prudent to refrain from inquiring into the count's recent past, holding him at a distance with cool replies to his enthusiastic conversation. The valet, Latour, spent the endless time frowning mutely at the road behind them, interposing that with intent glances at Leigh.

"Look at this," the count said, and leaned against her as the coach swayed. He slipped a little leather volume into her hand. " 'Tis in English. Have you read it?"

Leigh glanced down at the spine, barely able to hold the book steady. It was titled *Aristotle's Masterpiece*. She didn't open the cover.

"Have you read it?" the count asked again.

Leigh shook her head.

"Ah, you will enjoy it. Keep it. Mr. John Wilkes gave it to me, and I'll give it to you."

She slipped the book into her coat pocket.

"You do not read it?" He gave her a disappointed frown.

"Perhaps later. It's too rough now."

"Yes, of course. Later." He smiled at her. "We shall read it together. These English words, I was not certain of them all."

The count sat back and began to speak rapidly to Latour. He made several reverent references to a Mademoiselle Anne-Prospère, and Leigh gathered that he was to be reunited with his lover somewhere on his journey, but for now was without companionship beyond the valet. With the aid of a full moon, they traveled on at their snail's pace long past dark, but on the report of a rockfall in the road ahead, Mazan decided to halt for the night at a tiny inn. Leigh swung out of the coach and stood in the yard. While Latour and Mazan followed the landlord inside, she looked up at the steep, moon-drenched valley walls that rose on all sides, throwing the river and narrow road into gloom. She walked a few yards down the roadway. It was wild and empty country, closer into the mountains than La Paire. The sound of the river seemed muffled by the over-hanging rocks, strangely subdued, as if the mass of stone above pressed down on them all. Over the top of the prec-ipice behind the inn, she could see the full moon hanging above the black flanks of a ponderous height.

If she walked away from here, she'd be sleeping on the open ground. They hadn't passed a light for three hours.

"There you are!" The Comte de Mazan gripped her arm. "Come, come, we've arranged a nice bedchamber and a fire for ourselves. Morning will be upon us before you know it." He shivered and grinned at her. "We must put our rest to good use."

He drew her forward with a bit more force than neces-sary. Leigh allowed it. She planned to get her supper out of these two, at least, before fading quietly into the dark-ness.

The inn had no private parlor, only a single bedchamber with two beds and a tiny closet that contained a cot and a window protected neither by oil paper nor glass.

Mazan waved toward it negligently. "We won't even make Latour sleep out there. We can all share." He grinned again. "He's already found us a girl."

This development was a challenge to Leigh's French. Unable to construct a more subtle answer, she simply said boldly, "I don't like girls."

Mazan lifted his eyebrows. *"Mon dieu.* A boy of your age. What does the world come to?" He sat down on one of the beds. "That's all right. I despise women, myself. But wait until you see what I have in mind. Come and be comfortable." He patted the bed beside him.

Before Leigh could marshal her French grammar again to answer, the door opened. Latour pushed a plump, red-cheeked young maid inside.

"My lord," the *fille de chambre* whimpered, trying to set her feet. "My lord—please—I'm a good girl!"

"Nonsense," the count said. "You expect us to believe that in a place like this? You're just trying to raise your price."

"No, sir!" She shook her head. "Ask the hostess; I'm to be married—ow!" She cringed at Latour's hard pinch.

" 'Twas the hostess recommended you," Mazan snapped. "Said you were slut enough to do anything for a guinea, which I don't doubt for a moment. Come now—here it is . . ." His voice changed to gentleness. "Put it in your pocket right now—ah, are you crying, poor child?" He drew her toward him and caressed her cheek as he slipped the coin into her apron.

"Please, sir! I don't want it." She tried to hand the coin back.

He caught her wrist and twisted it. The girl cried out and dropped to her knees.

"Oh, don't," she sobbed. "Leave me alone! Please leave me alone."

"Hold her down, Latour. There—tie her hands, that's it. Oh, yes, do cry, do cry," he crooned, as the valet twisted the girl's arms roughly behind her with a length of linen. With Latour's help, Mazan shoved her face down on the bed, pushed her skirt above her knees and bound her feet to the bedpost while the maid wailed and begged to be released.

Leigh moved toward the door.

"My lord," Latour said sharply.

The count glanced up and saw her intent. He sprang from the bed and stepped forward to stop her, blocking the door.

Leigh met him with the lethal blade of her silver dagger at ready. He stopped, staring at it.

"I've been watching her," Latour said. "She's a woman. I'm sure of it."

Mazan threw him a startled glance, and Leigh took the chance to dive past him. He grabbed at her, roared a curse as she sent a slash across his palm, and brought up his other hand, walloping the side of her head.

Leigh had never been struck before in her life. She staggered against the door, bent over, her head ringing and her stomach wrenched with the unexpected pain. She gripped the knife and dragged herself upright to deflect the next blow, but the sound in her head changed, grew strange and louder—and Mazan wasn't even looking at her; he was standing transfixed, staring toward the window, listening open-mouthed to the deep, inhuman howl that rose slowly to a haunting peak outside.

"What the devil is that?" he cried.

Another wail joined it, and another and another, a sound that made the hair rise on the back of Leigh's neck. It was like nothing she'd ever heard before in her civilized, safe existence—and yet her body knew it, her spine tingled and her throat closed as the low-pitched, throbbing ululation ascended to an unearthly caroling on the night. She closed her eyes and leaned against the door, listening to the eerie concert that filled the air and drowned the muffled shouts of surprise from downstairs.

She felt the closed door shake under the thump of feet in the stairwell. The howling suddenly fell silent.

"*Diable,*" the count muttered.

The door handle turned beneath Leigh's fingers. She instinctively stepped back, waking from the frozen bemusement and aware of a chance to escape. The door swung inward.

From the shadows of the hall, wolf-eyes reflected candlelight with red fire.

"*Jésu Christ,*" Mazan ejaculated.

The wolf's deep-throated growl erupted into a snarl as he spoke; it crouched with hackles raised, staring into the room with bared white fangs. Beside the great beast, half in shadow, stood a man.

The light caught his hair in a shimmer of dull gold. His sword made a graceful arc, flashing as he lifted it. "Monsieur de Sade," he said softly. "As amusing as you appear with that expression on your face, I would advise you to lower your eyes."

"What?" the man who'd called himself the Comte de Mazan demanded breathlessly.

"I do not wish for your blood," the Seigneur said in the same mild voice. "High-minded of me, don't you think? But my friend here hasn't quite mastered his emotions at this spectacle." The rapier made a fluid dip toward the floor. "He sincerely feels he should kill you on my behalf. Look down slowly, if you please, and you will be a small degree safer."

The aristocrat obeyed, breathing in deep, uneven gulps. The wolf continued growling and took a step forward in his menacing creep, spreading one huge paw on the bedchamber's wooden floor. His teeth glittered, sharper than any domesticated dog's.

"*Avec soin,*" the Seigneur commanded in clear, simple French, "Leigh. Untie the girl." Then he added in English, "If she's likely to make a fuss, you'd best use that linen to gag her first. Do not on any account allow her to scream."

Leigh obeyed him, whispering reassurance to the terrified girl. From her position on the bed, the maid had not seen the wolf, but she could hear it. Tears streamed down her cheeks, wetting the linen. Leigh had to lift her bodily from the bed, and her plump legs buckled as soon as she glimpsed the beast.

"Stand up," Leigh hissed. "Stand up, you foolish chit!"

The maid moaned and let her weight fall heavily against Leigh. She staggered under the burden, but supported the wilting girl with an effort, glancing across at the Seigneur in impotent impatience.

He shook his head. "You damsels do choose the most inconvenient moments to swoon." He smiled faintly. "What's your pleasure, Sunshine? Shall we save her or let her lie?"

Leigh stepped back. "Let her lie," she said.

The maid's legs suddenly stiffened as she lost her prop. A muffled "*non!*" came from behind the linen gag as she reached out blindly. The wolf moved, darting foward to snarl malevolently and snap at the nearest victim: the marquis. He swore and the maid squealed. The wolf glided back to crouch beside his companion while the girl clutched at Leigh, squeaking.

"Stand up, then," Leigh said. "Stand up and do as you're told."

"*Oui, madam!*" came the muffled cry. The maid clung to Leigh. "*Mais oui!*"

Leigh looked toward the Seigneur for direction.

He stepped inside the room, fully illuminated now, the candlelight burning cold tawny fire on his hair and long lashes. The wolf moved with him, dashing forward into another savage pass at the marquis and his valet, pressing them up against the fireplace. The Seigneur nodded at Leigh. She grabbed her cloak bag and pushed the maid ahead of her through the vacated doorway.

Outside, she shoved the girl at the stairs. The *fille de chambre* wasted no time in fleeing; she was down the stairwell and gone before Leigh had reached the banister. Leigh heard a vicious burst of snarling from the room behind. As she turned, the Seigneur appeared at the lighted door, raised his sword in a salute, and bowed to the occupants.

"*Bon nuit,* Monsieur de Sade," he said cheerfully. "Do have pleasant dreams."

The marquis cursed. The wolf slid out the door, shrank away from Leigh, and thudded down the stairs with a heavy tread.

"Come along," the Seigneur said in English, turning toward her and lifting his hat from the newel.

She went, crossing the lower parlor without bothering to glance at the paralyzed landlord and his wife where they stood cringing behind a settle. The wolf also ignored them, vanishing silently out the open front door. But the Seigneur stopped, made a polite apology to the mute couple, and helped himself to the bread, salad, and a trio of capons cooling on a tray that had been loaded to take upstairs. He tied the food into a serviette, stuffed the bundle into Leigh's satchel, and packed the wine bottle and cruet of salad oil on top. Assuring them that my lord the marquis would pay for it, he slung the strap over his shoulder and bade the proprietors a civil farewell before he took her arm, pulling her with him out the door.

She could feel the tension in his grip as they strode into the yard. Without stopping, he threw back his head and howled, sending a wild slide of sound into the sky like a song of victory.

From all around came the enthusiastic answer of lupine

voices, a long-drawn serenade of excitement and support. The Seigneur's wolf bounded around them in large circles, stopping to howl with its tail held high and its muzzle lifted. Then it ran behind him, giving Leigh a wide berth, and leaped up to rest its giant paws on his shoulders for an instant before it dropped down and disappeared into the dark trees.

The chorus stopped as suddenly as it had begun, as if the unseen pack had come to the end of its song in prearranged unison. The Seigneur kept his hand on Leigh's elbow, leading her down the road through moonlight and shadow.

"Is that Nemo?" she asked.

"Certainly," he said. There was an undertone of elation in his voice.

"Where was he?"

He looked toward her. There was just enough light to see the way his eyebrow lifted. "With his own kind, Miss Strachan. Haven't you heard them?" His stride lengthened. He still carried his rapier in his hand. It glinted silver as he moved.

She walked with him in silence for a few moments. He tripped on something, and his grip on her nearly pulled them both over as he swayed, a motion out of all proportion to the stumble.

He swore. She set her feet, allowing him to steady himself against her.

He straightened and let go. "Sorry," he said in a tight voice.

Leigh reached out and caught his shirt sleeve as he took a wavering step. Without speaking, she molded his fingers around her arm again: a silent offer of support.

He stood still. Abruptly, he sheathed his sword. "I had an accident," he said. "At times my balance isn't—overly reliable." He kept his eyes fixed on the ground. "Today has been . . . difficult."

"Lean on me."

He slowly lifted his head and stared at her a moment. The moonlight turned the gold in his hair to frost, molded his face in silver and jet.

"I don't care," she said. "I'm accustomed to it."

"Thanks." He moved his hand away. "I don't need your help."

Stupid man. Proud, absurd man. "How did you ever catch up with us?" she asked pointedly.

"The road follows the river. It skirts the mountain flank," he said. "To come over the top is shorter." He shrugged. "I knew you'd be here—there's nowhere else to shelter. I'd already come most of the way, looking for Nemo."

"In the dark? And how did you do it in your condition? Fall down and crawl?"

He took deep offense; she could see it in the way he set his jaw and looked away. She started walking. After a moment she heard his footsteps behind her.

"Really, 'twas nothing," he said dryly. "I've robbed coaches on my hands and knees."

"Just try to plummet in my direction when you stumble again."

"My eternal gratitude, Miss Strachan, but—"

She heard him skid on the rocky track. He collided with her from behind, his hands grabbing for purchase. She tottered an instant, then stood steadily while he held her by the arms and cursed between his teeth.

"I said you needed me," she murmured.

" 'Tis this damned shadow on the road." He righted himself and stood with his hands on her shoulders. "I do well enough when I can see properly."

"You need me," she repeated patiently.

His hands tightened. "I want to kiss you."

She glanced at him sideways. He grinned.

"Please," he said, blowing a soft breath against the curve of her neck. "*S'il vous plaît beaucoup, mademoiselle.* We rescued you and everything."

Leigh scowled, standing stiffly while he caressed her throat. "I agreed to sleep with you if you wished it."

His light touch ceased. He stood still behind her for a long moment, and then his hands dropped away. "I only asked for a kiss," he said tautly. "And I'd rather hoped that you would wish it also."

"I don't. But you may indulge yourself in the matter."
He made a low sound of disgust and pushed her forward. "Never mind. The offer's not that tempting, Sunshine."

It *was* tempting, though. S.T. didn't touch her again, but he was burning up with passion and excitement and temptation.

He'd done it. By God, he'd done it: delivered his damsel from the dragon's lair in spite of his vertigo, in spite of his deafness—with no horse and no mask and no weapon but a rapier.

And the look on Sade's face—*ah, mon dieu*—that sight alone had been worth it.

Sweet fortune, sweet victory: it only needed what Leigh would not give him.

The devil fly away with her. He didn't care.

Nemo came back and padded along at his side, providing a convenient cushion if he fell, but S.T. took heed where he put his feet and managed to stay vertical. It was the moonlight that saved him; if it had been full dark he would have been crawling sure enough. As long as he could focus on a stable object and didn't trip he could keep his equilibrium. This spell was already fading, mercifully shorter than the first.

The wolf pack shadowed them, moving somewhere above along the ridges. He could tell by Nemo's pricked ears and frequent looks and the way the wolf would break into an occasional caper of excitement, bounding forward and twisting back to bow and dance playfully. S.T. headed away from the nearest town, choosing an eastern fork in the road. Some wild cousin had already paid with its skin for Nemo's aborted attempt to make human contact, no doubt trapped and killed and displayed with the wig Nemo had lost so the Gypsies could claim they'd destroyed the devil's beast. S.T. hoped the rest of the pack would return to higher and safer elevations.

A melodic howl drifted from the heights, and Nemo sat down and answered gleefully. He leaped up and mobbed

S.T. again, pushed off and loped up the bank of the road, vanishing into the gloom beneath the trees.

"Will he come back?" Leigh asked suddenly.

It was the first thing she'd said for a quarter hour. S.T.'s elation at rescuing her had been slowly fading, but it lingered still, pumping a low, steady throb through his blood. He was aware of her beside him every instant.

"If he gets lonely enough," he said shortly.

She stopped, looking up the hill. "He won't run away with the others?"

"I don't think the pack's accepted him."

"He didn't come back before," she said. "Maybe you should make a leash."

"A leash!" S.T. swung around and stared at her. "You don't understand anything, do you?"

She met his glare in silence. For a moment he thought the sharp contempt in his voice had hurt her, but she only said, "It seems practical."

He took a deep breath and shook his head. "You don't understand."

"I understand. You're a foolish man," she said. "You live in dreams."

He absorbed that cut, trying to avoid looking at her face in the moonlight, so beautiful and so cold. He looked down at her hands instead, imagined touching one, cupping it between his palms and warming it with his mouth.

Dreams. He lived in dreams.

Too true, he thought, and turned away. "I know a place we can stay the night—if you're planning to honor me with your captivating presence," he said. "It's not far ahead."

She nodded briefly, which perversely cheered him, thereby proving she was entirely right and he was definitely a first-rate fool. He walked along, trying to think of some way to slip past her icy shield.

Nemo came panting out of the darkness, still carefully keeping his distance from Leigh. He seemed calmer, ranging ahead down the road and returning to stick his nose beneath S.T.'s hand. It was comforting, a silent point scored against practicality and leashes. S.T. rubbed the

wolf's ears and smiled to himself. He'd charmed wilder
things than a dour girl, after all.

The steep gorge that contained the road opened into a
little valley, a moon-bathed meadow that stretched away
to the dark hills. He left the road at a ford in the stream.
Nemo splashed through the water and shook himself, scat-
tering shining droplets, but S.T. hesitated. He thought of
gallantly carrying her across and dismissed it as too risky.
Decisive humiliation if he lost his balance. Instead he
pulled the cloak bag and his sword belt over his shoulder
and waded in without ceremony.

"You'll ruin your boots," she said.

"Rehearsing for married life?" He held out his free
hand as cold water swirled around his feet. "Ah, no, forgive me—you're just being practical, aren't you? Step on
this stone here, and I'll give you a boost across."

For a moment he thought she'd refuse the offer. He could
tell she wanted to, but her precious practicality won out.
She made a leap onto the rock, and he gripped her arm
and gave her a propelling lift that landed her safely on the
other side. He waded out, squishing water between his
toes.

"Thank you," she said stiffly.

"Pray don't choke on it," he muttered, rearranging his
sword.

Ahead, he could see the Roman ruins, three pillars that
stood alone in the meadow, dim smudges of white in the
moonlight. He squelched along the path that led to the
remains of the temple and unloaded the satchel on a fallen
block. "We can sleep here." He sat down to pull off the
sodden boots.

Leigh picked them up as soon as he set them down. She
rummaged in the satchel and found the bottle of salad oil.
S.T. slanted a look sideways and watched for a moment
as she pulled off her cravat and used the end of it to begin
rubbing oil into the wet boots.

He wiggled his cold toes. "You don't have to do that."

"They'll stiffen else."

He leaned over and pulled out the bundle of food. Nemo
trotted up and sat, staring. S.T. tossed the wolf a chicken

leg, which disappeared in one bite. He sheared the wax off the wine bottle and pried out the cork, took a savoring sniff, and then offered the bottle to Leigh.

"I don't take spirits, as a rule," she said.

Naturally not.

He swallowed a deep draught and sighed. Nemo inched closer, gazing intently at the capon. S.T. sat up straight and growled. The wolf stopped, his ears dropping submissively, but as soon as S.T. took another drink, Nemo tried to slink forward again.

S.T. waited, setting down the bottle as if he didn't see the wolf advancing one stealthy step at a time. Then suddenly he reached out and grabbed Nemo by the ruff, launched himself on top of the wolf, and gave him a hard shake and a good snarl. Nemo instantly shrank to his belly and rolled over with his tail tucked, whining and wriggling. The moment S.T. let go, the wolf retreated hastily, ears pasted down in dismay. He took up a position a few yards away, put his head on his paws, and stared soulfully while S.T. ate half of the capon.

He looked down at Leigh where she sat cross-legged on the grass, oiling his boots in the moonlight. "Aren't you hungry?"

She didn't even look up. "I'll eat when I've finished this."

S.T. spread the napkin across the antique block and arranged the bread and meat for her. He reached for her cloak bag and dug toward the bottom, intending to retrieve the silver cup and fill it at the stream for her.

"Don't," she snapped. "I don't want you pawing through my things."

"Why not?" He didn't stop rummaging. "One dress with matching slippers, a set of bone stays, one pearl choker, sketchbook, two gold buckles, a lady's fan, some medicinal powders, miscellaneous muslin, cup, spoon, three livres and twenty pence. Estimated value four guineas—not counting the seed pearl on the silk stomacher. I pawed through it all a long time ago."

"While I was ill?" She glared at him. "You are not a gentleman."

"Haven't got a jot of virtue in me." He smiled. "What can you expect? I'm a highwayman." He found the cup and stood up in his stocking feet, picking his way carefully back toward the water. Nemo rose silently and trotted ahead of him, keeping a respectful distance. When S.T. knelt at the stream he looked toward the wolf and called quietly. A soft whine answered him, but Nemo still seemed dubious about his welcome.

S.T. lowered himself all the way onto the ground and called again. "Come on, old chap—you know better than to try to steal dinner. Come here."

Nemo sat down, unresponsive.

S.T. held out his hand. "Do you think I don't love you anymore? What's got into you?"

The wolf tilted his head quizzically, staring into S.T.'s eyes.

"It's her, isn't it?" S.T. sighed. "Afraid she's going to join the pack?" He tugged at a clump of grass and shook his head. "The thing is, Nemo—I'm a blockhead when it comes to women. Can't resist them." He glanced back toward the temple. "Have you looked at her? I mean . . . hell and damnation, do you really blame me?" He put his hands in his hair. "I can feel myself going. I try to stay rational; I know I'm a bloody dunce to fall in love. It never answers. It never comes to anything. I don't even like her. Lord, she's got all the sensibility of a fence post." He closed his eyes. "It's just been so long, Nemo. So . . . damned . . . long."

He sighed again, and drew it out into the canine version—a whine. Nemo pricked his ears. He trotted forward, placed his big front paws carefully on S.T.'s knees, and licked his chin and face in sympathy.

"That's better." S.T. stroked Nemo's ruff and scratched his ears and fussed while the wolf pressed up against him and wagged its tail. "Friends again?" Nemo made a mock swipe and S.T. responded, turning the reunion into a playful tussle on the damp ground.

When they returned, Leigh was still hunched over the boots. S.T. sat on the grass, leaning against the stone. The light breeze fluttered the pages of the sketchbook where he'd left it on the block. He reached up and pulled it down.

"You're an artist," he said, holding it in his lap.

"I merely sketch. And I have not invited you to view my work."

He slid the book back into her satchel, thinking of papa asleep in his library and Anna with her tall captain. S.T. liked the idea of her family. It made him smile, nostalgic for things he'd never actually experienced. He wouldn't have minded looking at them again, but it was too dark anyway.

"Where were you trained to paint?" she asked.

He looked up, surprised by the question. She examined the boot she was holding and set it beside the other.

"You really want to know?"

She stood up and brushed at her breeches. "I was curious—your style is romantic, of course, and you make extensive use of chiaroscuro, but I was unable to identify a particular school."

"The Venetian Academy. I studied under Giovanni Piazzetta." He glanced at her from the corner of his eye to see what she would make of it.

"I see," was all she said.

"And Tiepolo," he added, unable to help himself. "I assisted in Maestro Tiepolo's studio for three and a half years."

She took a helping of food and sat on the ground, breaking the bread in her lap. Quietly, she said, "He would be proud of you, I think. Your paintings are . . . luminous."

S.T. let out a soft breath. He closed his eyes and looked away before she could see the rush of pleasure that made his mouth curve upward without his permission.

She liked his paintings. She thought they were luminous. God.

He yearned to kiss her. He wanted to hold her body close and drown in her. "Let me paint you," he said hoarsely. "Come back to the castle . . . I'd paint you like this . . . in the moonlight, with the ruins. You're beautiful."

She shook her head. "No."

He leaned on his knees and buried his face in his crossed arms. "You're making me insane." He lifted his face. "You want me to teach you the sword? Come back and sit for me, and I'll do it."

She gave him a long, steady look. "I don't believe you can manage it."

He shoved himself to his feet. "Why? Because I can't fight anymore?" He blinked away the dizziness from the sudden move and walked to one of the pillars. He leaned against it. "My fencing master was eighty-eight years old when I began, Miss Strachan, and he taught me to be the bloody best there was."

'Twas true, of course: his master had been the finest teacher on the continent, but there had been a hundred other students and officers and dueling virtuosos at hand to hone S.T.'s skills in practice. But she was looking at him thoughtfully, and he reckoned he could take her through the novice exercises well enough, which were all she could handle and then some. He'd been educated in a formidable school.

"An artist and a blade," she said pensively. "Who are you, Monseigneur du Minuit?"

He shrugged. "I don't know."

"Pardon me." She looked away. "I did not mean to pry."

" 'Tis no great secret. My mother ran away from her husband and produced me upon arrival in Florence. I'm a bastard, almost certainly, but I suppose the dates were doubtful enough for him to acknowledge me. Poor fellow—what else could he do after my elder brother killed his man in eighteen duels and then broke his neck falling out of a whorehouse window?" S.T. smiled. "No doubt the old chap was praying I might display the firmness of character so unhappily lacking in the rest of the family." He tilted his head back against the pillar. "He was sadly mistaken, but I go by the honorable English name of Maitland anyway."

She wiped her fingers on the napkin. "I think you put your Englishness on for me. Like a cloak."

"It's just another language." He massaged the back of

his neck. "I don't belong anywhere particularly. My mother never went back to England. We moved about." He closed his eyes. "Venice, Paris, Toulouse, Rome . . . wherever she could find an English gentleman to provide the suitably desperate romantic entanglement." He paused. "He must be English, you see, so that I should be brought up a proper little country squire. I can be French or Italian—or as beefsteak as John Bull. Whatever you like."

"It sounds an unsteady life," she said.

Cushioning his head with his arm, he leaned against the stone column. "It was rather a lark. Maitland sent money for the fencing and equitation and regular letters about what a devilish mortification we both were to him, and my mother lived off her lovers. 'Twas she who charmed Tiepolo for my place." He smiled into the dark. "We rubbed along well enough, *maman* and I."

He turned and caught her staring at him. Abruptly she drained the silver cup and gathered up the scraps of her meal in her lap. "Should I feed these to the wolf?"

"Aye. Save one of the capons for morning. Throw Nemo the other. He won't come close enough to take it from your hand."

Nemo lifted his head, pounced on the meat that landed in the grass a foot away, and carried it behind S.T. to eat.

"Why are you here?" she asked.

"Here?" He was deliberately slow to understand. "I came to rescue you."

"Here in hiding. Why did you run away? Why are you not in England still?"

"I didn't 'run away,' " he said indignantly. "I merely . . . emigrated."

"You've a price on your head."

"What of it? I'd a price on my head for thirteen years. 'Robbed on the Monday last, by a man wearing a black and white mask, with polite manner, speaking sometime French and riding a tall horse, all black or dark brown.' " He snorted. "I ask you, where's the awful danger in that? If England rejoiced in a secret police and a standing army as France does, we gentlemen of the highroad wouldn't have it so fine, I vow." He looked over his shoulder at her. " 'Tis our great good fortune that no freeborn Englishman will stomach such a womanish tyranny as effective law enforcement. A parcel of country magistrates aren't particularly menacing, provided a man's discreet. Which you may be assured that I am."

"Are you indeed," she murmured dryly.

He crossed his arms. "The real threat's from the thief-takers and fences, and they're no better than thieves themselves. One had better know how to deal with them, or be sorry for it. And sometimes from Bow Street, round and about London. And then, too—'ware the statute of hue and cry. 'Tis raised on occasion, in the county Hundred where the robbery took place." He tilted his head and winked at her. "But it wouldn't be half so diverting if it were too easy, would it?"

"Easy no longer, perhaps. They have your description now."

"Oh, aye," he said savagely, "because a plump and pretty little black-eyed pigeon saw fit to inform upon me." His mouth curled. "Miss Elizabeth Burford." He shook his head. "God, I must have been bewitched—I let her meet me where I was hiding out . . . I let her take off my mask for sport." He sighed. "I'd never done that before. I don't know why I did it then, save that . . ."

Leigh didn't speak into his pause.

S.T. took a deep breath. "Save that it all seemed a shade too tame to be amusing, at the time."

"So she laid your description with a justice? And you fled to France?"

"Certainly not. Must you have it that I bolted like a frightened hare? No one knew my name; I may have been somewhat beguiled, but I wasn't that caper witted. A description's nothing if you move along posthaste and have a persuasive way with your fabrications. No one's going to be hung on the grounds that they've peculiar eyebrows."

"Why, then? Why did you run?"

He frowned. "I had reasons."

"What reasons?"

"You're a pushing sort, aren't you?"

She took the rebuff silently. He could feel her gazing at him. The moon hung low over the mountain, casting long ebony shadows across the silvered grass.

"Why did you become a highwayman?" she asked at last.

He smiled into the darkness. "For mischief. For the thrill of it."

She sat cross-legged, motionless as a statue, still looking at him. S.T. turned on his shoulder and leaned against the pillar.

"Did you think it was for my high ideals?" He mocked her with his voice. "The first time was on a wager. I was twenty. I worsted an excellent fencer, won a thousand pounds and the gratitude of a lady fair. I could see that it was the life for me."

She tilted her head. The moon poured frozen light across her face.

"And what of you, Miss Strachan?" he asked. "What is your story?"

"Mine's simple enough." She unbuttoned her waistcoat and pulled it off, kneeling on the ground to arrange it with her frock coat into a pillow. "I'm going to kill a man," she said. "And I want to learn how to do it."

The breeze rustled in the long grass. Nemo finished his dinner, sighed and heaved himself into a more comfortable position to lick his paws.

"Any man in particular?" S.T. asked. "Or is it just a grudge against my sex in general?"

She stretched out on the grass, propped up on one elbow. Without the tight waistcoat her feminine shape showed clearly, the slender swell of her hips and breasts unbound. She pulled the ribbon from her queue and shook down her hair. "One man," she said. "In particular."

S.T. left the pillar and lowered himself beside her, sitting cross-legged. He leaned toward her. "Why?"

She rested her head back on the makeshift pillow and spread one of her hands, holding it up and watching as she turned it slowly against the sky. "He murdered my family. My mother, my father, and my two sisters."

There wasn't a tremor in her voice, not a trace of emotion at all. S.T. gazed at her cool moon-washed face. She stared back at him, unblinking.

"Sunshine," he whispered.

She lowered her eyes.

He lay down beside her and took her in his arms; held her tight against him and stroked her shining hair.

SIX

"IF you're going to do it," she said in his ear, "go on."

His hand stilled. He took a deep breath, rolled onto his back, and blew out a harsh sigh. "What do you mean by that?"

She didn't move beside him. "I don't object," she said. "I owe it to you."

He stared up at the temple columns, watching the moonlight and shadow. The slender pillars seemed flawless in the dark: cold-white, beautiful. If they'd ever had life to them, if they'd ever echoed to the sound of human laughter, they were silent now. Stone dead and silent.

"I don't want your rotting gratitude," he said.

She lay perfectly still, a mirage of the impersonal moonlight, as lifeless as the ruins. He couldn't even feel her breathing.

"Then I'm sorry." She spoke suddenly. "Because that's all I have to give."

He heard the roughness in her voice and turned toward her abruptly, pulling her close against his chest. He buried his face in the curve of her throat. "For God's sake. Don't build a wall to keep me outside."

"I won't build one," she whispered. "I am the wall."

He cradled her, uncertain of what to answer, how to reach her. "Let me love you," he repeated. "You're so beautiful."

"How easily you fall in love." Her gaze moved beyond

77

him to the night sky. "How many times has that happened
before?"

He tried to marshal his emotions into reasonable order,
but a lock of dark hair fell across her cheek and defeated
common sense entirely. He brushed it away. She made no
resistance as he stroked her skin and kissed her gently.
"Never," he said. "I've had women. Lovers. I've never
felt like this. I thought it was love, but it never lasted."

She smiled, just barely, a grave, mocking curve of her
lips.

"I swear it," he said.

"Foolish man. You don't even know what love is."

He stopped his faint caresses. "And you do."

"Oh yes," she said softly. "I know."

He leaned away, resting on his elbow. "Do forgive me.
I didn't realize there was someone else."

Her smile grew drier. "You needn't poker up, monsieur. I'm perfectly free of that sort of romantic notion."
She shook her head, as if she pitied him. "I'm not in love.
Nor married. Nor even a virgin. So you see—you may ease
your needs on me with a clear conscience."

He closed his eyes. He could smell her; warm musky
female scent that made his body hot.

"I know you want to bed me," she said. "Don't talk
of love. I've more than one debt to you that I can repay.
Let me. Don't suffer for the sake of gallantry."

He closed his eyes tighter. "I don't want it like that."
All along his body, he felt her lithe presence, her legs
beneath the breeches. "To pay off a debt. I don't want a
whore."

"You want an illusion."

He opened his eyes. "I love you." When he said it,
gazing at the perfect lines of her face, it seemed so true.
"From the instant I saw you."

"You want to bed me. I won't forestall you."

"I want your heart—to hold and cherish."

She looked away from him. "You've been wasted as a
highwayman. I believe you might have made quite a torrid
troubadour."

Damn her. It wasn't going properly. She wasn't responding the way she ought at all. He wanted to drag her down into the grass and kiss her until she was beyond mockery. Until she was soft and eager and helpless in her passion, the way a love ought to be.

He set his jaw, staring into the dark. "I'm not a mindless buck, anyway. I don't care to be serviced like one."

She lifted her hand and touched his cheek, drew her finger slowly down his jaw and across his lips. He tasted her and his breath grew quicker.

"Don't deny yourself," she whispered. "Not waiting for some sentiment I can't give you."

Her finger slipped downward, traced a cool path on his throat and chest, drifting to her own neckline. She toyed with the tie on her shirt and pulled it free, exposing her throat in the deep open V.

"Damn." He made a soft, wretched sound. "Damn you." In the moonlight her skin was as cool and white as the stone columns. He ached to kiss it, to press his face in the curve between her breasts and inhale the erotic scent of her.

She tugged upward, slowly pulling the shirt. It was deliberate, a harlot's tease, and he knew it. It made him angry, and it made him desperate. The linen slipped from the smooth swell of her breast. A queer heat seemed to radiate from the back of his throat through his chest and his loins.

She slid her arms above her head. The languid move lifted her, showed him her body like an offering: a delicious waist, the delicate bounce of her breasts as she stretched. He gazed at their tender, curving underside in fascination. Moonlight made her nipples exotic, the color of shadow.

He made a rough sound. "I said I don't want you like this." He felt taut and helpless, refusing to touch her, unable to turn away. "Don't do this to us."

She merely lay still, eyes closed, prostituting herself. Her body gleamed with the pale fire of the moon, as if she were a pagan goddess caught asleep among the ruins. As if in a moment she might wake and rise to dance with

Dionysus, to seduce the reckless god and sink beneath him, entwined in leaves and heathen laughter.

She opened her eyes and stared into his. He felt his soul slipping away, his reason dim in the rising hunger. In the night, amid the fallen columns, he could not think beyond her body. He felt the satyr in him, the elemental power of lust—so aroused he was trembling for her. He'd not had this for too long. He had no sanity left to master it.

She watched him coolly, ice-beautiful and exciting. With a sudden groan he reached for her, slid his palms beneath her breasts and around her. The move made him dizzy. She was warm to touch, as if alabaster had come to life beneath his hands. He pulled her breeches free and felt her legs spread submissively beneath him. She seemed smaller then, so female, fragile and vulnerable and over-powering, swamping him with her compliance.

He kissed her breasts, touched her naked hips and the soft, soft curls between her legs. He spread his hands against the earth and buried himself in her.

He felt as if he'd lost his humanity and gone to the wild god that ruled this place. He saw it as if it were a painting: he saw himself taking her, in the dark grass beneath the moon, two nameless bodies framed by the ancient pillars. He wanted to stop; he wanted to court her and lure her and beguile her into loving him, but it was all lost in this animal burn; the exquisite dance of love reduced to a sav-age, glorious rut upon the ground. She moved beneath him, yielding to his urgent thrusts, driving him past co-herent thought. When her hands came up to touch his shoulders and her legs lifted around his, he exploded.

The deep sound of ecstasy echoed among the stones. His body arched in sensation. He held himself pressed hard within her, panting, feeling his blood beat violently through his limbs. She brushed her ankle along his leg. He cried out, jerked and shuddered in fervent reaction.

Beneath him she lay still. His shoulders trembled.

He let himself sag against her. With his eyes closed, he felt her belly, smooth and soft on his. He pulled his arms in around her and held himself inside. He knew he was breathing harshly, and that she wasn't. He knew that she'd won—she'd only accommodated him, relieved his brute hunger to settle a debt, and he'd been so miserably desperate that he'd taken what was offered as if he were a beggar.

He rested his head on her shoulder, furious and ashamed, and still he didn't want to let go of her.

A lock of her hair curled between his fingers. He rubbed it, feeling the dark silk, trying to slow his breathing and bring it under his control. After a moment, he touched the curve of her ear softly, tracing the shape.

He couldn't look at her, too aware that she made no move to return the tentative gesture, or even acknowledge it. No tender embrace or gentle hand against his back. Her breasts rose and fell in quiet rhythm, a mortifying contrast to his own.

He drew in a long draught, pushed himself up, and rolled off of her. He got to his feet, fumbled at his breeches, and walked through the cool grass to the pillars that stood white beneath the moon. On a crumbling foundation stone he sat down and put his face in his hands.

Some bastard had murdered her family, and all he could do was violate her. He was angry, and humiliated, and lonelier than he had ever felt in his life.

S.T. slept far away from her, with Nemo curled against him in the grass. In the morning he woke to the sound and scent of breakfast. The wolf was gone. Leigh moved about purposefully, without looking at him, even when she brought him a cup of tea and a chunk of bread toasted over the fire she'd built. He accepted it wordlessly and watched her through the steam as he sipped.

She loaded her satchel and carefully folded the packet of tea leaves before she put it back in a pocket of her frock coat. After she'd finished, she walked over to him and set his boots down at his feet. S.T. stared at them glumly.

"They're not quite dry in the toes," she said. "You should oil them again to stop the leather cracking across the instep."

"Thanks." He could not lift his face and look at her.

She stood before him a moment. He gazed intently at her feet and rubbed his morning beard.

"I've been thinking," she said in a quiet voice. "I believe it's best if I return to England now."

S.T.'s mouth flattened. He looked off into the distance, where the morning mist hung about the edges of the meadow.

"It isn't because you can't teach me," she said after a pause. "I've thought about it. I don't doubt you could. But it was an absurd idea, that I thought I could learn to be what you were. Even if it were within my power, it would take years, would it not?"

He sipped the tea and leaned on his elbows. "Is that what you came to me for? To learn to be a highwayman?"

"Not just a highwayman," she said slowly. "The Seigneur du Minuit."

He shook his head and gave a short, dour chuckle.

She stood over him, her face turned at a pensive angle as she watched him.

"You're a legend, monsieur," she said suddenly. "My home is as isolated as this place; the people are simple; we see little of the outside world. You came there three times . . . on behalf of those ill-used and too weak to stand against their tormentors. Perhaps you don't even remember, but we do. The people looked upon you as the final justice, above the sheriff and the magistrates and even the king—above everyone but God himself." She stopped abruptly and swung away, frowning at a temple column. "Now they have another authority, and he's the devil incarnate—but they cannot see it." She took a deep breath. "I thought to resurrect you. To impersonate the Prince of Midnight and send him against this other—Thing—" Her voice held a faint tremor. "This monster who's taken over their hearts and minds. 'Twas all I could contrive, monsieur . . . to make them see again."

He sat back and allowed himself to look at her. She'd put on the waistcoat and frock coat again, and stood in the morning sunlight like a vision.

"Is this the man you want to kill?" he asked at length. "This man you say is a monster?"

"Yes. But merely to kill him—I don't know if it will be enough. I'm not given to flights of fancy. Understand that. Perhaps it's difficult to comprehend, but he's infected their souls. They'll do anything for him. I'll simply kill him if I must, but . . . I don't know . . . what will happen then."

"These are your neighbors you're talking about? You think they might turn on you?"

"On me, certainly. Even on themselves." She blew a harsh sigh and spread her hands. "It seems demented, I know! It is—lunacy. Sometimes I wake in the night and I think it must be no more than . . ." Her voice trailed off. She put her fist to her mouth. "Oh, God . . . how I *wish* I'd only dreamed it all!"

The sun cleared the top of the wooded hills, sending golden light down through the last of the mist. It shone on her hair and caught the color of her eyes.

He watched her turn in a sunbeam. "So you thought to pass yourself off as me?"

"They remember you. They remember that you've always been on the side of truth, and they believe in you. If you were seen to take a stand against this—this fiend who guides them, I thought they might turn away too."

S.T. bent his head, swirling the tea leaves in his cup. It seemed astonishing to him that he could have inspired enough faith in anyone for this implausible plan to occur to her. Oh, he'd known he had a reputation well enough; he'd relished it in his salad days. He'd lived for it. But when he looked back at himself, at his reasons for the things he'd done, it all seemed so far from truth and justice that he hardly knew whether to laugh or to cry.

Truth. They'd supposed him on the side of truth. What if he should tell her that he'd chosen which supplicant to champion as much by the subtle shape of a hip and the charming curl of an eyelash as for the justice of the cause? Perhaps the world had seen only the victimized father or the defrauded brother or the persecuted cousin as the motive of the Seigneur du Minuit, but there had always been a woman in it. A woman . . . and the sweet, stinging flame of a gamble.

"You shock me," he said at last. "I'd forgot I was such a paragon."

She ducked her head. "You deserve esteem, for the things you've done," she murmured, and then her chin lifted. "But my plan—it won't work. I see that now. 'Twould take too much time to learn your skills, even if I could. And you—monsieur—I fear I'm not a good student for you; already you say that I make you insane. You want me, and I was willing to make fair payment in that way, but I see that you truly suffer for it." She regarded him gravely. "I don't wish to injure your peace of mind."

He ran his forefinger along a crack in the carved stone. "I think the damage has already been done, Sunshine."

She bent her head again. "I'm sorry for it."

"Are you?" He snorted. "I think you've a cold heart, ma'am, and a devilish supply of arrogance for a chit your age."

Her head came up. She scowled at him.

"Ah, you don't like to hear that, do you? I'll wager you've had things well enough your way in life until you ran up against this." He tossed the remainder of his cold tea into the grass and stood up carefully. "Aye, 'twas a silly idea that you could play at being me, not least because I've twenty years of hard cuffs and training behind me—with men who'd laugh till they turned blue if they got wind of your aspirations to handle a weapon and a horse." His mouth curled. "You're too old to begin and too weak to succeed and too slight to ever hope to pass as me—even mounted. Even in the dark. You walk wrong. Your voice is too soft. Your hands are too small—and a highwayman's quarry sees his hands, y'know—try slipping a lady's ruby from her finger with leather gauntlets on."

Her lips pursed. "Yes. I said that I was wrong. I didn't think it through."

"Didn't you indeed? You seem an intelligent little witch to me. You mean to claim you traveled all the way here without thinking it through?" He laughed caustically. "Oh no, you thought it out, Sunshine. You thought it all out. I'll wager you had a solution for every one of those problems. You had it all planned. Until you got here and saw

me and realized I wasn't what you'd been led to expect."
He held his arms open and turned his face to the sky.
"God, you must have been appalled. Finding some poor
chap can't even walk down a road without falling flat.
Wouldn't reckon he'd be any use at teaching swordplay,
would you? Wouldn't reckon he could get on a horse, much
less teach you *haut ecole.*" He looked back down at her.
"So you're going to leave—after spouting some noble bosh
about it being for my own good and a dim-witted idea
anyway."

Her eyes narrowed. "And am I wrong, monsieur?" She
took a step away and looked at him, hands on her hips.
"You seem to me like a madman. You talk to the air. You
look off at nothing when I address you, as if there were
spirits speaking. You fight with the wolf over a scrap of
meat like an animal. And yes, you do fall down." Her
voice began to shake. She dropped her hands and faced
him. "You've fallen down three times, and barely saved
yourself ten times that many since I've been with you. Do
you think I haven't noticed? I came to you for help. I can't
change it if you're unfit to aid me. I wish—" She blinked,
and her mouth tightened. Suddenly she turned away,
standing straight and still. "I wish, I wish, I wish," she
said, staring out over the hills. "God help me. I don't
know what to wish."

The echo of her voice died away against the pillars. He
let the silver cup fall from his fingers and laid his hands
on her shoulders. Beneath his palms he could feel her stiffness, feel the taut shift of her whole body as she swallowed.

"Sunshine," he said softly. "Did you never once think
of a different plan?" He reached out and touched her chin,
drew her back to face him. "Did you never think that I'd
go with you if you needed me?"

She kept her eyes lowered. "There's a price on your
head if you return. I wouldn't have asked it of you; I decided that from the first." She bit her lip. "And now . . .
forgive me, I don't desire to offend you, but—"

He cupped her face in his hands. "Now you see that
I'm useless on all counts."

"No." She strained a little against him. "No, I don't doubt you could teach me as much as I was capable of learning, given enough time. But I haven't the time, monsieur—I've taken too much already—"

"You won't need the time." He leaned forward and pressed his lips against her forehead.

"It's hopeless," she whispered.

"Hopeless causes are my calling."

"*You're* hopeless," she said, more coldly. "And mad."

"Not at all. It's just my pride. I can't bear to think of you out there tarnishing my legend with your soft hands and smooth face and puny female efforts with a sword." He stood back. "If my reputation's doomed, mademoiselle, I'd just as soon muck it up myself."

It was harder to leave Col du Noir than S.T. had ever expected. The biggest part of him wanted to stay, to paint and be prudent, the way he'd been since the explosion that had taken his hearing and balance. He'd walked cautiously, moved slowly, taking care to keep himself well within the safe limits of activity that his unstable equilibrium proscribed. On fête days in the village, he never danced or played at *boules,* and he wouldn't have tried to ride even if he'd had the heart to keep another horse after Charon.

Until Leigh had arrived, he hadn't realized how instinctively careful and inhibited his motion had become. He was suddenly aware of himself, not only of the vertigo and ensuing stumbles, but the way he calculated and held back in self-protection.

He had yet to admit his deafness to her. Though he knew she'd noticed some of the signs, she didn't seem to have fathomed the cause. She just thought he was crazy, because he stared at things she couldn't see. So he went on trying to hide it, for reasons he couldn't even explain to himself, the same way he pretended it meant nothing to him to pack up his paintings and his tools and store them under dustcovers and straw.

Col du Noir was his cocoon, and he found he didn't want to leave it.

But there were other passions moving inside him. He kept thinking of Sade and his gold crowns, and the expression on the marquis's face when he'd looked up and seen S.T. and Nemo in the doorway. He thought of Leigh's white body in the moonlight. While he sat by the kitchen fire and worked the blade of his long-forsaken broadsword against a whetstone, he remembered the dark highway and the scent of a hard frost at midnight, and his blood beat harder through his veins.

He would have to mount a horse again. That was the first test. If he couldn't pass that one, she was right and it was all for naught. She tolerated his intention to go with her as a parent would tolerate a child's preposterous fantasy, with grave nods and calm, enraging little smiles whenever he offered an explanation of his preparations. The thought of failure was galling. He ached to stay in his safe cocoon and burned to show her he was still the master of his midnight art.

He wished she'd start wearing skirts. Slender calves, round buttocks that showed beneath her coattails whenever she bent, damn her; she was turning him into a walking bombshell and she knew it. She used it. He wanted love, he wanted excitement and romance; she offered herself with chilly deliberation, as if that somehow protected her from him.

And it did. It was a barrier more effective than stone. He understood the message. He could take her body; he'd never touch her soul.

She read him that well. She offered terms she knew he wouldn't accept. She offered that travesty at the Roman temple. She mimicked a whore on purpose, talked of payments and what she owed him, knowing that the more she debased what he wanted, the safer she was.

In the end, all the power was hers. And they both recognized it.

As he sat honing the spadroon's glittering blade, his eyes drifted to her body. He tried to keep his lashes lowered, his attention centered on the blue gleam of fine steel, but his glance kept returning to the outline of her legs propped on the fender.

He was certain it was calculated, that sultry pose. She might appear indifferent and composed, but she wanted to rub his nose in her ability to affect him. She wanted him to break again, make of himself a goatish fool. And even though he knew it, his heart and his reason kept getting confused. She was female, vulnerable and hurt and alone; he wanted to protect her. His whole body lusted for her. He imagined brushing his mouth against the curve of her throat, breathing against her skin, the cool scent and living heat of her in all his senses. Over his rhythmic work on the sword, he stared at her legs and fantasized until she silently stood up.

She left the kitchen. He could hear her shoes echo on the stone stairs.

He knew where she was going. Where else was there to go upstairs but to his bed? It was an offer as clear as a perfumed whore beckoning on a street corner. It made him furious. He finished the sword in long, savage strokes of the whetstone and stood up, balancing the weapon in his hand. With an inelegant slash, he attacked his shadow on the wall. Then he laid the broadsword across the table and picked up the colichemarde, made a parry and riposte with the lighter weight weapon, watching the tip of the blade catch the firelight like blood.

Sluggish. Far too reserved. His impulse to inhibit his moves maintained him upright and inept.

He closed his eyes and lifted his arm slowly, keeping the sword extended as he raised it. At shoulder level he felt his balance going, felt the weight of his arm and the weapon rock him forward. He held, trembling, trying to find his center within the slow sensation of toppling, trying to ignore that dizzy phenomenon of pitching in endless tumbles and listen to his body instead of his mind.

Inside the reeling spin was his shape, his hand raised before him, his legs spread, his body hot, humiliatingly excited still, his feet solid on the floor and his wrist and back and shoulders accepting the weight of the sword. He lifted it higher, testing for the zenith of the arch. That was easier; he could lock his arm above him and hold his head steady until the sense of rotation settled.

He opened his eyes and lowered the rapier, assessing the same perceptions with his sight: hand there, shoulder and spine there, feet braced, the floor beneath him and the ceiling arched overhead. To think of her in the bed above made him feel raw, embarrassed and violent, perfectly happy to kill anything that came in reach. He let the sword tip rest against the stool. Then he took a breath, brought the sword flat against his chest, and spun.

Instantly, his center shattered. The world gyrated around him. He tried to stop, staggered against something, and clutched the sword while the room went past in a sickening whirl. His knees buckled and he let them, let the rapier clatter against the floor, finding the solid stone beneath his palms the only source of stability. He stayed on his hands and knees, panting and sweating, until the reeling gradually slowed.

Then he stood up and did it again.

A simple surgeon had told him once: make yourself dizzy. Force yourself to do it. Make yourself dizzy, and the spells will go away.

Another charlatan, he'd thought, except the man had refused compensation. S.T. had tried it twice, and it hadn't worked. But neither had all the nostrums and potions pressed on him by more distinguished medical men.

He was down to this. By the third attempt, he'd lost the capacity to pull his shaking knees beneath him and haul himself to his feet. He lay flat on the cold floor, fighting dry heaves, his hand locked around the sword grip and his head aching. He wanted to throw up. He wanted to die. More than anything, he wanted to lie down in his bed and sleep the sickness away.

With a supreme effort he made it upright, using the sword as a support. He careened into the armory and fetched up against the dark stairs with the room spinning around him. He steadied himself and went up, one step at a time, reached the top and hung onto the door. He blinked through the whirling dizziness toward his candlelit bed, and remembered.

"Oh, Christ," he said, and sank to the floor where he stood.

He closed his eyes and let the vertigo have him. She left the bed; he heard the squeak and rustle, but he couldn't open his eyes or he was afraid he would retch.

Her cool hand touched his forehead. "I knew it," she murmured. "The fever."

He lifted his hand, felt her bent over him. He spread his palm against her chest and gave her a ruthless shove, heard a faint gasp and a thump. He opened his eyes and found her sprawled in front of him, struggling up onto her elbow.

"It's not fever," he said sullenly.

The spinning had begun to recede, but nausea floated at the back of his throat. He gripped the sword and stood, trying to breathe through the sickness. For a long moment he stood still, aware of every muscle in his body.

"Get clear," he said, and extended the weapon, lifting it in the same painstaking exercise: out and up, focus on his shape in the space around him, turn his wrist to the side and down, concentrate, refuse the tumble in his mind, collect his attention and fix it on the motion of his limbs, level and turn, steady, watch the point and think of his own form and structure, turn, turn, turn . . .

"You are utterly deranged," she said.

He came around in his slow spin and drifted to a stop facing her. The nausea faded; she only appeared to slide past twice before her image steadied in front of him, her dark hair falling free over one of his voluminous shirts, her skin pale and delicious.

"Your eyes look peculiar." She frowned at him. "Does your head ache?"

"It's not fever," he said impatiently. He came on guard and stepped into a passado, focusing on the axis between his shoulder and knee. The move seemed better, slightly faster, the dizziness a shadow of what he felt when he'd made himself spin. Perhaps this was what the surgeon had meant. Just force it on himself, until standing still was such a relief that it seemed easy in comparison.

He straightened up and took a deep breath. Then he attacked the bedpost, thrusting in *quarte*, opening his wrist and concentrating on how the motion felt in his forward hip when he lunged.

He stepped up and examined the post, pleased to see that he'd left not a mark on the wood.

"Is it still breathing?" she asked.

He looked toward her and gave a slight, mocking bow. "Only because I chose to let it live."

"Fortunately, there were no bedposts lying in wait as you came up the stairs. You weren't in such fettle then."

"A moment of light-headedness," he said carelessly. "I'm all right now."

She lifted her eyebrows. S.T. made a show of examining the blade and tried not to stare at her naked legs.

"I can see that you are," she said. The shirttail just skimmed the top of her thighs. He felt his body begin to betray him again. She added indifferently, "I'm at your disposal, if you wish to please yourself."

He hated to be read so easily. He hated it that she meant to drive him off by beckoning him on. His hand tightened on the sword. "Haven't yet paid off your debts to me?" he mocked. "Perhaps we should just keep a ledger. Half crown a day for nursing. Only a livre a week for bread and garlic soup, since you don't like it. Ten guineas for a valiant rescue from debauched nobleman. Is that fair?"

"Quite fair," she said. "But I haven't the money, as you know."

He scowled at the bedpost. "I don't want money," he said, and then turned to glare at her before she could speak. "Or to be paid in bed, either. Last night—at the ruins— that wasn't what I wanted."

"No." She met his eyes directly. "It would appear that you want more than I can ever possibly give, Monseigneur. I hope you understand that."

He did. It was a challenge, like the fencing and the riding; he'd lost his skill for *l'amour* and would have to restore it. His swordplay was coming back; he could feel it already. He could make her love him if he managed everything properly. He could bring her to her knees. He'd done it a hundred times. He'd botched the thing painfully so far, of course; she'd seen him at his utter worst . . .

but if he kept his head he could pull the fat from the fire. Recoup his losses and win in the end. A hundred times, he'd done it.

He curled his hand around the bedpost and looked at her slantwise. "You may have the bed tonight," he said, as courteously as any ballroom gallant. "We'll leave here at dawn."

SEVEN

THEY left Col du Noir in the teeth of the mistral. It had sprung up in the night, wind howling down through the canyon and around the castle walls like a thousand wolves in full voice. A low rumble seemed to fill the air, a constant grinding sound that could drive a man mad if he listened long enough, sinking into his head and his heart and his bones until he would scream at his wife and thrash his children just for the sound of something human. S.T. felt it in his bad ear as well as his good one; a vibration more than an actual sound, as if some giant inside the earth hummed one constant, ominous note and would not stop.

It made everyone irritable, even on the first day, and the likelihood was that the tempest the French called *vent de bis* would blow for weeks this time of year. Only Miss Strachan seemed unaffected—but then, she'd never lived through it. The mistral was only wind yet to her.

There was no such thing as comfortable transportation out of La Paire, even if they'd had the money. S.T. hoarded his twenty gold louis, only parting with his flock of ducks and thirty livres for a decent donkey that he hoped they could resell for the price of a hired chaise to Paris. The animal carried Charon's saddle and bridle and their small stash of food, another few *sous* worth, enough for the four nights S.T. estimated to see them to Digne. He'd packed four shirts and a pair of black silk breeches, strapped his colichemarde to his sword belt and the spadroon in a halter across his back, and strode out at a good pace on the eastern road.

The trees and mountain flanks gave some protection from the mistral, but it came screaming with icy force down the valleys. He watched as her cheeks grew redder and redder beneath the hat crammed down on her head, but there was no pause in Miss Leigh Strachan's stride as she walked along in the other wagon rut, tugging the donkey behind her.

He was secretly glad she'd been ill—otherwise he suspected that she'd be in far better wind than he. In spite of S.T.'s enthusiastic start, the donkey set the pace for all of them, excluding Nemo, by refusing to break into a trot. The wolf cast about ahead of the small party, stopping to wait and running ahead again, alerting them to other travelers by melting among the white rock and underbrush long before S.T. could hear the sound of approaching humans.

Once, when Nemo's presence indicated they were safely isolated, he said with studied casualness, "I think perhaps we should get married."

She took it rather better than he'd expected. "I beg your pardon?" she asked coolly.

"Someone's going to recognize you for a female. 'Twould draw less comment if you'd just go ahead and dress like one."

"I don't believe it's drawn any comment."

"No. Just wholesome admirers like the marquis."

She transferred the donkey's rope to her other hand and tugged at the straggling beast. "I've thanked you for extricating me from that difficulty. I shall be warned against such things in the future."

"If we're a married couple, no one will bother you."

"I see."

He put his hand on the hilt of his rapier, shaping the cool metal. His face felt hot. He wanted to touch her instead of the sword. "I considered brother and sister," he said, "but I'd rather we travel with some semblance of respectability. 'Twould be remarked upon that you've no maid with you, and we'd be expected to take separate rooms if we can get them. An unnecessary extra expense."

"Yes," she said calmly. "I hadn't been intending to travel with a companion."

He recognized that jibe for what it was, but elected to ignore it. "You needn't worry that I'll disturb your privacy by sharing your quarters." He broke a branch off a bush as he passed and began stripping the leaves. " 'Twill just be for the look of things. I shan't stay there at night."

"I see," she said again.

He kept his eyes on the switch he was stripping. "What do you say?"

"I'll think about it."

He silently damned her stubbornness. He could hardly set her up for a proper flirt while she was dressed as a man. Boy, rather. Nobody could possibly take her for a man. He'd look bizarre in public, trying to romance a pretty youth. As hopelessly debauched as Sade himself.

That didn't stop him for the moment, of course. Nemo's actions told him there wasn't another human being for a long way. He tried to think of something charming to say, but somehow the kind of phrases that had come easily when murmured in a rose garden at midnight seemed a bit more forced shouted into the face of a freezing wind to a girl dressed in breeches and tugging a recalcitrant donkey.

He had to settle for quizzing her. She wasn't overly cooperative with that, either. After getting a few brief replies on the exact location of her home, he dropped back a pace and gave the lagging donkey a light swat with the birch. The creature jogged forward.

"Tell me this—just how did you find me?" he asked.

"I looked," she said briefly. "You're not so difficult to recognize as you may think."

"What, then—did you just start out in the north of England with a thieftaker's handbill, asking for some fellow with outlandish eyebrows?"

"Everyone knows you went to France," she said. "I started asking for a man with green eyes and gold-favored hair in Paris."

"Everyone knows—" He broke off, nonplussed. "Of

all the . . . you mean to say I'm no more private than that?''

'' 'Twas only gossip. In France they know nothing of the Seigneur du Minuit, but they know you if they've seen you. You really are most unusual in your appearance, monsieur—I think perhaps you underestimate it. I kept asking among the *hôtels* and *auberges*, and it led me to Lyon, and then La Paire.''

S.T. shook his head. "Good God, you shouldn't have been straying alone in such places. Haven't you any family left?''

. "Some cousins. I've written to them.''

"And they approve of this expedition of yours?''

"I told them I must have a change of scenery. That I've gone traveling on the continent with a friend of my mother's.''

"Hmmph,'' he muttered sourly, and swatted the donkey again. "So what is his name?'' he asked. "This man we're going to kill?''

She glanced back, and then lengthened her stride to match the animal's new speed. "Chilton. The Right Reverend James Chilton.''

He stared at her. "You're joking.''

She merely walked ahead.

"A reverend,'' he said, and rolled his eyes. "You want to murder a reverend.''

The mistral blew cold silence back at him. It wasn't amusing. He was a tactless oaf.

'' 'Tis not murder.'' Her voice was a hissing whisper that matched the wind. "It is justice.''

"Tell me why you can't go to the magistrate for justice.''

"My father was the magistrate. Mr. Chilton holds his place now.''

S.T. looked up sharply. "And what of the other commissioners of the peace? They let a murderer be entered as one of their number?''

"The others are frightened.''

"Such cowards as that?''

"No." She shook her head, watching the ground ahead of her. "Not cowards. Frightened."

He considered that. It was a telling point, a subtle, crucial difference. Miss Leigh Strachan was no fool.

"Of what are they frightened?"

"Of what happened to my sisters," she said. "They have daughters, too."

S.T. put his hand on the donkey's croup. He watched her back. She walked without faltering in her stride. The wind blew her hair in tangled strands that escaped her queue and whipped against her head.

"Are you afraid to ask?" she said, still not looking back at him. "Do you think I can't bear to speak of it?"

"Sunshine—" he said softly.

"Don't call me that." She turned on him, bringing the donkey to a tripping halt. "I despise you when you call me that. Ask me what happened to my sisters."

He reached for her, but she stepped back, jerking at the donkey's head to avoid the touch.

"Ask me!" she shouted.

The wind blew the words away. She stood glaring at him, gripping the animal's halter with white fingers.

"What happened?" He kept his voice brief and toneless.

"They found Anna at the tarn on Watch Hill, where the lovers go. She was strangled. Her dress was all open and pulled up to her waist, like a harlot." She stared at him, unblinking. "Emily was gone all night. When she came back, she wouldn't speak. Not for weeks. Then she began to be sick, and the doctor came and said she was going to have a child. The next morning she was dead. In the barn. She hanged herself."

He avoided her eyes, looked down at the ground.

"I found her," she said. "I'm *glad* I found her, do you understand?"

He stroked the little donkey's rough flank, watching the wind ruffle the gray coat between his fingers. Then he nodded.

She made a sound; a wordless syllable of derision—

against himself or her memories or what, he didn't know. Perhaps she didn't think he could possibly understand. There was nothing he could say in answer. So he only swatted the little donkey and made it go on, with a pointless comment on the way they still had to travel.

Without bothering to ask if she wanted it, he brought her water when they stopped at the base of a limestone cliff. The mistral roared in the bushes above their heads, tearing at the clumps of wildflowers that grew high up in the vertical crevices. When he took off his tricorne, his hair stung his cheek. He knelt in front of her as she sat on a chunk of pale rock, offering the cup. "The wind's burning your face."

She looked at him, faintly cynical. "It doesn't matter."

"Would you wear a kerchief?"

She shrugged and drank. He still wanted to touch her, to brush his fingers over the flushed skin and cool it.

"Are you tired?" he asked instead. "I can lead the donkey if it's wearing at you."

"That's not necessary." The cool tone informed him that she knew this game and it wasn't getting him anywhere.

He held on to his patience. His own motives for what he was doing were somewhat confused. He wanted to shield her, to comfort her, but it wasn't an altogether saintly impulse. Mostly he wanted to hold her body against his own.

They ate in silence.

"I should tell you everything," she said suddenly. "I can see you would be reluctant to ask more questions."

He carefully rewrapped the bread in a napkin and tied it. "There's plenty of time for that. If it distresses you."

"It doesn't." Her voice was flat. "Since you insist on involving yourself, I'd prefer to tell you the whole at once. Perhaps you will reconsider your decision."

He looked up at her and shook his head.

She held his eyes a moment, and then her gaze slid away. Her hands lay still in her lap, clasped tightly. She stared at a little gray and black bunting that hopped from branch to waving branch in a bush beside the road.

S.T. fiddled with a stem of coarse grass, pulled it loose, and chewed the end. He could see her rocking, a faint motion back and forth like the bushes in the wind, her elbows pressed close to her body as if she wanted to make herself as small as possible.

"Tell me why," he said gently, when it seemed she couldn't bring herself to speak. "Why do you think he hurt your sisters?"

"Oh, it wasn't *him.*" The words came out in a rush. "I don't say he did it himself."

"He has accomplices."

She tilted her head back and looked at the sky. "Oh, God. Accomplices." She drew a deep breath, let it out harshly. "The whole town are his accomplices. All he had to do was stand up in his pulpit and say, 'She's fallen, her flesh is weak, she tried to seduce me and I'm a man of God,' and poor Emily was damned. They all believe him. Or they're afraid to speak out if they don't. My mother spoke out, and look what happened." She lowered her face and stared at her hands. "He made an example of us. And then he cried." Her mouth curled into a sneer. "The evil beast. He cried at my sister's grave."

S.T. picked another stem of grass and knotted it. "What of the one who actually killed her? You don't want justice there?"

She bit her lip. Her face was strained. "I don't know who killed her. I don't care. Whoever it was, they weren't themselves when they did it." She hesitated, and looked up at him. "That must seem queer to you."

He frowned, slowly knotting the next stem onto his chain of grass. "I had a friend once, in Paris . . . my closest friend out of a pack of schoolboys." With careful precision, he slitted a stem and strung another piece through it. "The whole parcel of us came across a wounded bird in the street once. Just a pigeon. Broken wing, flapping around on the pavement looking awful and silly and sad. I was going to pick it up, but the biggest fellow started to kick it about. They all laughed. And then the rest of them started to kick it and step on its wings to make it flutter." His fingers stilled. "Even my best friend." He stretched out the chain between his hands.

She looked up. "Did you hate him for it?"

"I hated myself."

"Because you didn't say anything."

He nodded. "They would have laughed. They might have turned on me. I went home and cried on my mother's lap." He smiled slightly. "She wasn't much of a religious scholar. I think it took her four days to find a Bible and another three to get the right page. But she found it." He dangled the circlet of green grass from his fingers. " 'Forgive them, Father, for they know not what they do.' "

"Platitudes," she said viciously. "They don't change anything. My father was always—" She stopped and shuddered. "But that's of no moment." With a sudden move she came to her feet. "Chilton came four years ago. He started a religious society. My father held the regular parish living . . . he was ordained right out of university, you see—he'd never expected to inherit the earldom, and he just kept on with the parish work after he did. He wasn't a forceful man. He was shy, really. His sermons put everyone to sleep, but he liked to write them. And then this Chilton came into the neighborhood and began to hold evangelical meetings. He started a school and a home for poor girls."

She put her fist to her mouth and began to pace. The slender, strong legs passed out of S.T.'s line of vision and came back again. This was the first he'd heard of her being an earl's daughter. He deliberately didn't look up, but turned his head to hear better, pretending to gaze beyond her at a silvery-gray mound of wild lavender.

"What church does Chilton represent?" he asked.

"He calls it a Free Church. I don't know if it's even real. I doubt it. I never attended his services, but I think he made everything up. He'd try to say it's the same as a Methodist society, but we had John Wesley to preach, years ago, and my mother said Chilton is nothing like. It's true that everyone is required to confess openly, in front of the

others, and then they all decide on the penance together.''
She stopped and turned and looked directly at him. ''But
if someone doesn't confess, they decide on a punishment
anyway. He takes in these destitute females, and gives them
bed and work, and bids them not walk out with any man,
nor marry nor think of it. He says women have no souls,
and can only hope to be born again as men by submitting
to higher authority in this life, like the plow horse submits
to its master. In my neighborhood, there hasn't been a wedding in nigh two years.'' She paused, her color high. ''Sometimes, when Chilton permits it, there are—arrangements
made—to please the men, and instruct the women in
obedience.''

''God,'' he said. ''I follow your drift.''

''My mother stood against him. She was always an ad-
vocate for the education of women, and she said his views
were barbaric. She laughed at him, at first. He called on
my father in public to bring her in hand and put a stop to
the 'study of wickedness' that she imposed on my sisters
and me.'' Leigh clasped her hands and held them to her
mouth. ''She tutored us in mathematics and Latin and
physicking—that's what Chilton calls 'wickedness,' Monseigneur—and wrote pamphlets refuting his sermons.'' She
sat down again. There was a rhythmic shudder in her
shoulders as she hugged herself. ''He began to stand at
our gates with a crowd of his followers and demand that
my mother give her daughters over him before it was too
late. We couldn't go out freely; he made us prisoners in
our own home. My father—'' Her body grew tense, her
dark brows drawing downward. ''He did nothing, just
prayed and gave us little gifts and said 'twould pass over.
That's what he always did. 'Twas my mother, you see—
all my life, she took the real care of us. She was so good
and clever. Everyone admired her. She always knew what
to do when my father got muddled.''

S.T. watched her teeth work savagely at her lower lip.
He clamped one hand inside the other against the urge to
reach out to cradle her. It tore at him, the way her voice
stayed cold and steady while her body shook as if the wind
had hold of it. He wanted to make it easier for her, and

he didn't know how. "What did your mother do about Chilton?" he asked in a flat tone.

"She had him arrested. We didn't know then—we never suspected . . . he frightened my sisters, but Mama and I only thought him an evil nuisance. Papa was the justice of the peace, you see—our family always held that place— but Mama did all that sort of thing for him, kept the county tax rolls and listened at the quarter sessions and wrote Papa notes on how to adjudicate and what the Poor Rate ought to be. Everyone knew she did it, and no one objected. She sent the constable to have Chilton arrested, and the people at our gates disappeared."

Suddenly she lowered her face, bending forward into her knees with her hands locked across her head, rocking and rocking. "My papa," she said in a muffled cry. "My papa said, 'There, you see, it's all right now,' and he went out, and when he was too far away to get back . . . they stoned him in the street." She began breathing in frantic gusts, still bent into her knees. "From the houses and behind doors and carts; they were all silent—you could hear him calling out for them to stop. Please stop." She made an inarticulate sound. "My mother went out; she told us not to go, but I went too—he was already insensible—maybe he was already dead . . . they didn't throw stones at us; they threw refuse and horrid stuff . . ." She lifted her face and looked blindly into space. "Oh, Papa . . . oh, Papa . . ."

She wasn't crying. She was shaking in every limb. S.T. made a slight move, shifting his hand, and she jerked to her feet.

"Don't touch me," she cried. "Oh, God, don't touch me!" She spun away and went to the donkey, working feverishly at the pack straps, unbuckling them and buckling them without reason.

S.T. stayed where he was. Nemo walked up behind him and sat down, the wolf's furry weight resting heavily against his spine. Nemo sniffed at S.T.'s ear and licked it.

"No one would act after that," Leigh said, staring down at the packsaddle. "Chilton preached in the street about the wages of sin. My mother couldn't even form a grand jury for my father's murder—the gentlemen refused to hand down an indictment. They said 'twas a mob had done it; no one could be singled out for blame and she was overstepping her bounds to demand more, as if she was a justice herself. They said—'' Her jaw worked sharply. ''They said perhaps Mr. Chilton was *right*, and women in our county should study their proper place.'' Leigh made a sound of anger and despair. She tugged at the pack strap over and over. ''Mama wrote to the lord lieutenant, but never had an answer. I doubt the letter ever got past Hexham. That was when Emily was—punished. But of course there was no proof, no way to show Chilton had made it happen. Oh, he knows how to frighten them. He knew how to keep them from speaking out. Mama thought if she could just make them see—she went to all the magistrates and tried to convince them to act against Chilton. Then Anna was found, and people looked at us as if we carried the plague. The servants left. The jury met, and called it another suicide. The next we heard, 'twas Chilton's name on the list, to be appointed a clerical magistrate in my father's place.''

She lifted her face to the wind. S.T. watched her pure profile.

'' 'Twas too much for my mother,'' she said quietly. ''Even Mama wasn't strong enough to take it all on herself. She told me to pack for my cousin's in London. She shut up the house. She put the horses to the chaise herself—we didn't even have a coachman! I sat inside while she drove.'' Her voice drifted as she looked around at the sky and the hills. ''She really wasn't in her right mind. I suppose I wasn't either, or I would have stopped her. I don't think Mama had ever handled a team. They bolted before we reached the bridge.'' She shrugged and said, ''My mother fell off the box.''

He put his arm around Nemo and stroked the wolf's thick fur.

''You see, Seigneur,'' she said bitterly, ''if you come with a price on your head to England and take a stand against Chilton, you'll have every hand against you from the Crown down to the parishioners. It's not one man alone who will try to destroy you.''

S.T. stood up, steadying himself with his hand in Nemo's deep mane. A certain black elation had begun to uncurl in him, the potential of a gamble still too distant and elusive to chance. There was the little glimmer of menace that fanned the flame, the sharpening of thought and emotion, the keen sensation of coming alive.

He wanted it; ah, he wanted it again. He felt as if he'd been asleep for three years.

"I'll come," he said. "I'll do anything for you."

She looked at him, off guard, as if it startled her, and then her face grew indifferent and her mouth set in calm irony. "They'll eat you alive, monsieur."

"They'll not even get close."

She gave him one of those infuriating little smiles, composed again, cool—rejecting everything he offered.

"Damn you," he said under his breath. He took a step too quickly, brushed his leg against Nemo, lost his balance, and landed on his knees with that sudden blur and rush of the world tilting around his head.

She stood looking down at him, expressionless. "I've warned you," she said.

Nemo held steady, the way he'd been taught. S.T. gripped the dark fur. He felt himself coming apart, pride and shame and anger and all the things he wanted wrenching him in different directions.

The wolf licked his hand and leaned against his leg. S.T. took a deep breath and pushed himself to his feet. "I'm coming," he said stubbornly. "You need me. I'm in love with you."

The words had a power of their own. His limitations vanished and his old world opened up as he said them— the excitement and glory of it, the passion. To be alive that way, to hazard fortune for the sake of love . . . he wanted it again. He wanted all of it.

"You're a fool," she said, and turned away.

EIGHT

THE Seigneur began to ask after a horse and vehicle in the town of Digne. Leigh watched him inquire at every village and crossroads, but it was ten more days of walking beside the donkey, with the mistral driving them ahead in cold fury, before any such thing could be discovered.

Then it was only an old two-wheeled cabriolet, in a dusty street that felt hot after the sudden lapse in the north wind. The blessed end of the mistral came as suddenly as it had begun, leaving the atmosphere to settle to crystal clarity and the colors to brighten into intense blue and dusky green, with the limestone houses shining white against the shade in the narrow street. In two weeks they had walked into the heart of Provence, from alpine foothills into a land that might have been Spain or Italy from its aspect: a land of olives and fruit trees, warm and baking beneath a cloudless sky.

Leigh leaned on a wall in the sun and listened to the Seigneur haggle over the chaise. She couldn't follow the rapid argument, half in French and half in Provençal, but there was a hint of angry desperation in his voice as he bartered.

She waited. The street was empty of life, except for the donkey standing patiently under their baggage, its eyes closed. The wall rose above her to a great height, ascending to the crown of the village: a grand, crumbling Renaissance château that towered over the tiny town huddled

105

around its flanks. In the warming air, the scent of lavender enveloped her, drifting from the wild bushes that grew along the edges of the street and up the decaying wall.

The Seigneur's hair burned in the sun, gold and shadow, like the bright walls shining against the charcoal depths of the shade. Next to the somber little villager he was a flash of sunlight itself, an exasperated Apollo, his voice ringing fluently in the vacant street.

Leigh caught herself staring at him, lowered her eyes, and looked away.

She thought again that she ought to walk on and leave him here, as she'd thought it a thousand times since La Paire. He'd be no help to her; he wasn't the champion she'd come searching for; she should go on alone and do what she must herself.

But she didn't. She lingered, uneasy and sullen, finding no logic in it and tarrying still.

He turned away with the villager and glanced over his shoulder at her. "Wait here," he snapped in English, an order that elicited a sulfurous glare from her as he walked off still contesting vocally with the other man. The worst of it was, she did wait; she and the donkey, equally docile, standing as if they were tied in the street the same way that Nemo had settled, whining unhappily, under a bush outside the town—all of them bound by some implausible magic, some strange inertia that would only dissipate when he returned with a soft word and a caress, a handful of forage and a whisper in a furry ear . . . and for Leigh, that smile slanted from beneath his devilish eyebrows.

He'd embrace the animals, put his arm around the donkey's neck and scratch it under the chin, tussle with Nemo on the ground, sleep with the wolf curled at his back. He never touched Leigh. She thought that if he had, she would have felt it like a shock of light all through her.

She wished he would never come back. Implausible, romantical, air-dreaming idiot.

When he had disappeared around the corner, she sat down against the wall and pulled the little book out of her pocket, the one with the English words the Marquis de Sade had not been sure of. Leigh was not perfectly certain of some of them herself, but if she hadn't understood a syllable of the text, the detailed illustrations would have made the point quite clear.

She wondered, archly, if the Seigneur would look exactly so undressed. Men looked more or less the same—all of them, one presumed, although these pictures appeared to somewhat exaggerate the matter. She examined them critically. Her mother would have said any knowledge was valuable, even such stuff as *Aristotle's Masterpiece*. It was rather mortifying to Leigh to find just how little she did know of the subject.

She scanned slowly through the book. Some of the plates seemed ludicrous; some made her wrinkle her nose and some increased the sense of disquietude in her, bringing an unwelcome warmth as she studied them. She stared at the erotic illustrations and thought of the ruined temple in the mountains . . . and the Seigneur.

She'd had only one man before him; one boy, who'd been clumsy with excitement and pledged eternal love, who'd seemed infinitely younger than herself, even though he'd been seventeen years to her sixteen. He had wished to elope. She had not. Their short affair had ended when Leigh desired to end it.

That had been a sinking moment—when her mother discovered what Leigh had done. All of Leigh's explanations had seemed to come out as defenses; all her grand theories of seeking knowledge wilted before her mother's grave stare. She knew better, Mama said. She knew that what was between a man and a woman was blessed, or ought to be—Mama had hoped that Leigh could observe her own parents and understand that.

And Leigh had been ashamed, and felt very young and careless, because she'd lost something her mother thought precious.

She was older now. Even the shame seemed innocent, remembering. How scandalous she'd felt, how stained and tarnished by an adolescent mistake, how chagrined and utterly humiliated by the lessons Mama had decreed from the local midwife on things Leigh had not comprehended.

She'd always been the strongest, the oldest and most

clever, growing up capable and admired like her mother.
She'd given away her virginity because she'd wished to do
it, because she was curious, because there was a part of
her that sometimes, fitfully, rebelled against the narrow
course of her breeding and life and consequence. At sixteen, she'd not realized the risk of such an experiment.

The midwife had taught her that, and a few other things
besides, which Leigh suspected even Mama had not
known. Leigh hadn't forgotten; she had the proper leaves
and powdered herbs to protect herself in her satchel. She
was no longer so naive. Nor would she let herself be at
the mercy of a man like the Seigneur, who made such easy
promises of love and radiated sensual hunger in every move
and glance.

The little donkey lifted its head, releasing a raucous
bray, awakening rasping echoes in the street. As the bois-
terous noise died away, Leigh heard the sound of slow
hoofbeats. She pocketed the book swiftly and stood up.
The Seigneur and the villager turned the corner, leading a
roan horse between them.

. Leigh looked skeptically at the thin mare. The Seigneur
met her glance and shrugged. "We'll not do better," he
said.

"She's moon-eyed," Leigh pointed out.

"Aye, I know it." He still sounded nettled. "She's got
a little sight left."

"And the price?"

He scowled at her. "Four louis for the chaise and the
mare. Do you try to chaffer him down yourself, if you
please."

Leigh turned away from him. " 'Tis no concern of
mine."

He was silent a moment. Then he spoke to the villager
briefly in patois. The little man led the mare to the cabriolet and backed her between the traces.

S.T. drove. He kept his eyes locked on the ground
ahead, determined not to display any sign of the queasi-
ness that he felt in the swaying chaise. Leigh sat beside
him, gripping the side of the cabriolet against the bumps,

wincing every time the blind horse tripped. S.T pretended not to notice.

Across the Rhône at Montélimar, through wave after wave of the strange hills of the Ardèche, volcanic rock and black promontories, the blind mare took her stumbling passage on a road that was sometimes little more than a stony track. As long as S.T. concentrated, and didn't relax or allow the vehicle to pitch him about, he kept the discomfort under control. More than once, he got out and walked, leading the horse over the roughest stretches.

For distraction, he began to work the mare while he drove the chaise, both reins gathered into his left hand and passed between his fingers so that the lightest squeeze sent a signal. He murmured to her, a soft, tuneless rise and fall of tones, using his voice to precede the cues of the reins.

The little sightless mare was smart; after taking some time to accept the sound and smell of a wolf as Nemo trailed behind, she started to settle down and to respond quite readily: to turn slightly left in answer to a low tone, to the right in reply to a higher one even before he tightened the rein. He was pleased to find that it seemed to help her move. Instead of being pulled off balance by the reins in order to avoid rocks and obstacles, stumbling when she reacted too slowly, the more subtle cue of his voice brought an instant response that allowed her to evade the impediments before she tripped over them. By the time they'd traveled half a day, the horse was walking bravely on long reins, her ears flicked back to catch the signals and her stumbling infrequent. When the road widened into a smooth, new-built stretch, she picked up a willing trot.

Nemo jogged along behind the cabriolet, looking purposeful and content now that they were covering ground. It was for the wolf's sake that S.T. had chosen this secondary road instead of the frequented highway through Lyon and Dijon. The memory of the man-eating Beasts of Gévaudan, blamed for killing threescore human victims only a decade ago, was fresh all over France. Nemo wouldn't show himself if he could help it, but the more lonely the country they traversed, the easier for him to find cover.

What would come of taking the wolf into the belly of populated France, S.T. had not yet brought himself to face.

By evening, he judged they had traveled nearly three times the distance they might have made on foot. His back hurt from the tension of sitting forward and resisting the motion of the chaise. His head ached. Just outside of Aubenas, he stopped the cabriolet and looked at Leigh through the chilly evening air. "Would you like your supper served on a table tonight?"

Her eyebrows rose. "What a novel idea."

He hiked himself out of the chaise, calling Nemo. The wolf came panting up from some side trip, leaping over a clump of broom and greeting S.T. fervently. S.T. led him up off the road into the pines, casting about until he found a promising fallen log. He knelt down and pushed at the pine needles and dirt, scooping a wolf-shaped bed. Nemo joined in, circling and pawing until he finally flopped down, satisfied, and curled his tail over his nose, looking up at S.T. from behind the furry brush.

S.T. made the signal to stay. Nemo's head came up. As S.T. walked away, he knew the wolf's eyes were on his back. He wasn't absolutely certain Nemo would remain there until he returned, but he hoped the wolf's training would hold in the absence of some intense distraction like the pack that had lured Nemo away from Col du Noir.

He returned to the chaise, dusting the dirt off his sleeves. Inside the vehicle, he took a deep breath against the queer sensation that gripped him as soon as the cabriolet lurched forward. Leigh looked at him sideways.

"How do you feel?" she asked.

He wasn't going to admit it. Not to her, oh, no. He pasted on a confident smile. "Voracious. There's bound to be an inn at Aubenas."

She gazed at him intently. S.T. set his jaw and drove on.

Like all French inns, dim and dirty as it was, the Cheval Blanc laid a decent table. Leigh did the ordering: *soupe maigre,* carp and roasted partridge with fresh lettuce, chard, wheat bread, and mounds of butter. He could see that after weeks of dry black bread and cheese, she found the fare very pleasant.

S.T. was not so cheerful. The travel sickness was slow to leave him. He sat quietly, eating only the soup and the dessert of biscuits and apple, taken along with some wine. Even the bill of nineteen livres—a ruthless extortion equal to all they'd paid for food since La Paire—hardly seemed worth the trouble of disputing. He paid without a murmur and then sipped his coffee, gazing out the window into the dark.

"Are you quite well?" Leigh asked suddenly.

He glanced at her, and then away. "Yes."

"Perhaps we should put up here for the night."

"If you like," he said indifferently.

"I think I should prefer a bed to the ground. Was your wine drinkable?"

He looked toward her again, this time with a little more consciousness, a slight lift of his eyebrow. "Very adequate, thank you."

"I wonder if they have a chess set?"

"A chess set." He sat back and gazed at her. "Your disposition becomes friendly."

She avoided his direct look. "Merely a thought," she said.

He turned and spoke to the landlord in patois. The variation in dialect caused S.T. some trouble in communicating, but after a long bout of questioning, with recourse to French and much hand waving and repeating of *"Échiquier, monsieur?"*; *Mais oui, échiquier!"*, a badly faded chessboard was finally forthcoming. As he debated with the landlord, S.T. began to feel better. By the time he procured the box of game pieces and a smelly candle, he settled in his chair across the table and looked up at her with a grin.

"Will you trounce me in white or black?" he asked, holding out his closed fists.

She hesitated, and then chose the left. He opened his hand on a black pawn.

"Very sinister," he said. "I'm winning already."

"Many a gentleman would give up the opening move to—" She stopped herself.

"A novice?" he supplied innocently, knowing she'd been about to claim her perogative as a lady.

"A younger person."

"I suppose I'm perfectly primordial."

"You're far older than I am."

"Thirty-three. On terms with Noah." He dropped a white knight in its place. "For that impudence, I'm afraid I shall be forced to deal with you as you deserve." He sorted the other pieces and began to place them. "You needn't worry that anyone here understands English, by the bye. They barely understand French."

Leigh watched him open with the queen's pawn. She stared at the board, settling into intense concentration. It took little time to recognize that she'd challenged an experienced player, but his moves were so unfathomable that she couldn't really judge his ability. The rest of the inn grew dark and empty as they played; only their single candle shed a halo of light on the table, the pieces casting long shadows across the board. The Seigneur lounged back in his chair between moves, his hands folded across his waistcoat, his face composed. She began to feel they were fairly matched. As she closed in with her purposeful strategy, his play quickened, becoming even more haphazard, a sure sign that he was floundering. She kept on until she had him trapped.

"Check," she said.

He sat forward and leaned on his hand. "Checkmate," he murmured, moving his bishop.

Leigh slumped in her chair.

"We doddering ancients must take our victories where we may," he said apologetically.

She bit her lip.

He looked up at her, still leaning his cheek on his hand, and smiled. "You're only in need of wider experience, Sunshine. And a bit less predictability."

Leigh met his eyes. Like an instant flame, it was there— the powerful awareness of his physical presence: of his body relaxed in the chair, his arm resting easily on the table. The candlelight caught and emphasized the upward curve of his eyebrows and sprinkled gilt on his lashes.

After the concentration of the game, the intimate glance took her by surprise. For a moment it seemed to rush in her blood. She felt strangely fragile, felt how it might have been in another time and place, how he might have turned and caught her with a look: across a gay ballroom, a silent invitation amidst the polish and refinement, a temptation to reckless things.

Forbidden worlds. Wild joy and romance. A midnight ride with an outlaw prince, and life, and life, and life. He burned with it.

And she would have gone. Her throat grew thick with longing. She thought: *you should have come sooner. You should have come when I could feel.*

He sat silently. His faint smile pierced her, wounded her in its tenderness, like a sweet note vibrating on the evening hush, a joy too intense for the heart to bear.

It terrified her. She felt the cliff, the crumbling edge—how easy it would be to fall. Her back grew stiff. She sat up straight in the chair, her mouth curled into scorn. "What will you have for a prize then, monsieur?" she asked.

S.T. did not immediately understand her. He'd been gazing at her, watching her droop in the chair, smiling at her chagrin over the loss. She'd really thought she was going to beat him, little tigress, settled over the chessboard with that fierce scrutiny and charming frown.

He would have grinned and said, "a kiss"; he almost did—and then the cool, contemptuous way her lips curved as she spoke struck him with abrupt and vicious effect. The moment of affinity evaporated. He saw himself manipulated again, set up and mocked, what he felt perverted deliberately into what she chose to make it.

A mercantile transaction. A profanity, a desecration, a conscious attack.

His mouth tightened. "Nothing." He pushed back sharply from the table and stood up. "Hire yourself a room," he said, low and hostile. "I'll sleep outside."

Leigh watched him use the door frame to catch his balance as he pivoted. The door slammed behind him.

She bowed her head. She stared at the table, hardly able to breathe.

Let him trifle with her. Let him flirt and romance her, use her as a whore . . . anything. Just let him never look at her with that open tenderness again.

Not now. Not yet. Not ever.

The moon-eyed mare stood quietly in her stall, her nose in the empty trough. By the light of a tallow lamp S.T. fondled her ears, leaning his shoulder against the lava wall. She nodded gently beneath his touch, lipped the trough and sighed.

He passed his hand over her cloudy eyes, trying to make her blink. He thought she could still see a little; in a month or two the progressive moon-blindness would render her completely sightless.

He ran his hand along the top of her neck. "What's to become of you, *chérie?*" he asked softly. "Who'll take a blind mare?" He massaged her thin withers. "Damn . . . damn . . . damn . . . who'll take a sorry relic of a highwayman? Not she. Oh, no." He leaned on the mare's shoulder and put his arm across her neck. "It's hard, *chérie*. I wish to cherish her, and she spits on me. She doesn't believe in me."

He scowled, stroking the unkempt roan coat. The mare rubbed her chin on the edge of the feed trough.

"What shall I do about it, eh?" he muttered. "Shall I show her?"

Carefully, he set his hands on the mare's back. With one swift move, he hiked himself up and swung his leg over, grabbing at her mane as his balance whirled. He almost went off the other side. For a long moment he hung onto her neck like a child with its first pony, his face buried in the long mane.

The mare stood steadily, braced on all four legs against his awkward position. Slowly S.T. pushed himself upright.

"Quite the *cavalier*, no?" he murmured. "What do you

know of the high school, madame? Can you show me the *courbette?* The *capriole?''*

He stroked her neck, smiling grimly to himself at the thought of this angular mare suddenly rearing up and leaping on her hind feet, rising free of the earth in the *courbette.* Or more absurd, perform a *capriole,* spring into the air to thrust forward and kick out with her hind legs in the most spectacular and difficult of all the airs above the ground.

"Ah, would that you had seen my Charon before you lost your sight," he told her. "You would be in love, little peasant. A handsome stallion he was; all black as pitch. A great one for the ladies." He leaned over and slapped her on both sides of her withers. "I miss him. My God, look at me, Charon, my friend. Look what it comes to. I've lived too long."

Experimentally, he pressed his leg against the mare's left side. The horse ignored him, snuffling in the trough after stray corn.

"What a sad ignoramus you are, *chérie.*" He tugged at the base of her mane. "You came along smartly enough today—I shall have to teach you something else. What should a blind mare know, hmm? Perhaps you would like to learn a proper curtsy? Shall we cultivate your manners and see you fit to make your bow to the king?"

She blew out a noisy breath against the wooden box.

"*Mais oui.*" He braced himself on her neck and carefully dismounted. Untying the lead, he backed her out of the stall and began the first stage of the lesson.

By the time he was finished, the lamp had long since burned out and they both worked blind. He thought that fair: it gave him a better notion of what the mare's world was like. Since she'd already done a full day's labor, he didn't try to finish the trick in one session, but only taught her the signal to place her foreleg. Then he gave her another half measure of corn and tied her in the stall.

He slept in the stable yard, sitting up in the cabriolet with the leather hood raised to keep off the dew. Sometime very late in the night, the chaise rattled and bounced wildly. He woke to find Nemo trying to crawl into his lap.

S.T. grunted and shifted while the wolf sprawled heavily across his legs. Nemo licked S.T.'s chin, sighed, and settled himself, bushy tail and one hind leg hanging off the cramped seat.

Just at dawn, the wolf woke suddenly and pushed upright, digging clumsy paws into S.T.'s stomach. S.T. groaned sleepily and shoved, but Nemo was already jumping down.

A female sceech rent the morning quiet. S.T. jerked awake, thrusting himself forward, catching the dashboard and stumbling down from the vehicle. In the half light, a dark-eyed barefoot girl was at the stable door, shrieking in patois, *"Wolf! Father, come! Help! Father, Father, it's a wolf!"*

S.T. grabbed her around the shoulders. "Hush!" He bent his mouth to her ear. "Hush, hush—be quiet; it's nothing; you're safe."

"I saw a wolf!" She whimpered, clinging to him. "Here in the yard! A wolf!"

"Non, non, little foolish one." He cradled her in his arms. "You dream. *Le bête noire, oui?* A nightmare."

He could hear the commotion from the main house. The landlord came pelting around the back of the inn, followed by a fat woman brandishing a broom.

"C'est bien," S.T. called, still holding the dark-eyed girl. "Only a fright."

She leaned against him. "I saw it," she cried. "I saw it! Father, a wolf!"

S.T. patted her cap and kissed her forehead in urgent reassurance. "There was no wolf. I'm certain. I was out early, to see to my horse." He looked up at her father. "A witless little sparrow, eh?"

The innkeeper relaxed. He regarded S.T. and the girl, apparently not displeased with the arm S.T. had around her waist. "Witless," he agreed gruffly. "Don't pester the man, Angéle."

The fat woman broke into voluble patois, called Angéle an idle hussy, and gestured with the broom toward the barn. S.T. gave the clinging girl a squeeze of encouragement. He chucked her beneath the chin.

"Do your chores," he said. "There's no wolf, I promise you, sweeting."

She loosened her hold reluctantly. Her parents went back around the house, but Angéle adhered to S.T., holding his coattail in her fist, her black eyes round.

"I saw it, monsieur," she insisted. "I saw a wolf, big as life. Beside your chaise!"

"No—you're mistaken—"

"I *did!*" Her voice grew shrill. "I did, monsieur!"

"Silly child; just forget it!" By way of distraction, he drew her back, tilted her chin up, and kissed her mouth.

Angéle's body went rigid. After an instant, she softened against him, and seemed willing enough to pass over the incident in those circumstances. She stared up at him as he lifted his head. "Monsieur!" she murmured.

"Would I could stay another day," he teased.

She ducked her head. S.T. let her go. She looked up at him beneath her dark lashes, the tip of her tongue just peeking between her lips. Then she giggled and dashed into the stable. S.T. watched until she slipped inside, and began to walk toward the inn.

Leigh stood in the doorway, leaning on the frame.

Merde, S.T. thought.

He stopped and smiled tentatively. "No wolf."

"Only a two-legged one," she said, and turned her back on him.

NINE

A WEEK beyond Aubenas, in the dismal flat heath of the Sologne, Leigh sat crammed beside the Seigneur, forced into intimate proximity by their baggage piled into the cabriolet instead of tied on the rack behind. After the upheaval at the Cheval Blanc, he'd surrendered to the inevitable and ordered a crate built to hold Nemo. The wolf now rode behind bars on the baggage rack.

The blind mare pulled the extra load patiently. The bright winter of the south had fallen behind, yielding to low clouds. Rain set in, and the folding leather hood of the cabriolet afforded only slight protection.

Leigh drove much of the time, using the Seigneur's voice commands and trusting to her growing faith in the blind mare's native surefootedness. The Seigneur slept whenever he wasn't driving, having worn himself out, Leigh didn't doubt, in making love to the tap maid he'd found so enchanting and talkative at supper in Bourges last night.

Sometimes amid the bumps and rocking, his body grew heavy against hers and his head came to rest on her shoulder. And sometimes she just let him stay there, while she stared into the cold drizzle, listening to the carriage creak and the mare's hooves slap in even time through the puddles, feeling his breath warm on her neck.

She drifted into a reverie, dreaming that they traveled to some unnamed place, some home she'd never seen, where her family waited . . . New Year's Eve, 'twould be, and everyone gathered with the hot spiced ale and mince pies and plum pudding, with the bells ringing all through the sky at midnight. Her papa would be mumbling the important lines of his New Year's sermon, so that he wouldn't forget them, and Mama would supply the proper word when he faltered—at the same time that she handed out noisemakers and coaxed everyone from their games at the stroke of the clock to greet the first visitor to step over the threshold in the New Year. And what a splendid First Footer the Seigneur would make, to bring in the traditional New Year luck: handsome and male and unmarried, with his remarkable coloring and fine height, as auspicious as could be desired. And surely nature could not have been so cruel as to make him flat-footed. By unchangeable superstition that flaw would be ill fortune indeed for the coming year. Leigh caught herself glancing speculatively at his feet in the worn pair of top boots.

Reality revived. She frowned and gazed ahead, feeling numb still after all these months, yet unable to believe it was true, wanting to lift her face to the leaden clouds and shriek and scream that it wasn't, that it could not be, that she would not allow it. That so much love and life could not just . . . vanish, into nothing, as if it had never been. That they must be alive and snug and happy somewhere, waiting for her.

The Seigneur turned his head into her shoulder. *"Qu'est-ce que c'est?"* he mumbled sleepily.

She shoved at him, blinking hard. "Get off me."

He lifted his head and peered at the landscape without sitting up. "Have we passed La Loge yet?"

"No." The tears menaced behind her eyes. She could not look at him.

He nestled back into place, his cheek turned into her body. "I'd rather stay here," he murmured.

"Get you off," she snapped, pushing him desperately. "Get off, get *off!* Don't touch me!"

He struggled upright. His sleepy, confused look only made her angrier. She turned her face away, toward the puddle-marked ditch beside the road.

"It's time for lunch," she said sullenly.

He rubbed his palms over his eyes. *"Eh bien."* His voice was quiet. "Pull up under that chestnut."

Leigh directed the mare into the shadow of the tree, where the yellowing leaves and outstretched branches created something of a shelter from the cold drizzle. He pushed himself off the seat and stepped down from the chaise, leaving a chill where his warmth had pressed up against her.

He walked to the mare's head. "Hungry?" he asked the horse.

The mare lifted her nose high in the air and nodded up and down in a perfect imitation of a positive answer.

Startled, Leigh looked from the horse to him. He patted the mare's neck, not meeting Leigh's eyes. She scowled. After a moment, she got down from the chaise. She stretched and turned her back on him and began to search for provisions.

Their midday routine was well established. After the Seigneur spread a rug over the horse, he went around to the rear of the cabriolet to release an urgently impatient Nemo. The wolf did a dance of excitement and then raced along the empty road, sending showers of water out of the puddles. He came flying back at a whistle, and leaped into the air as the Seigneur raised his arm, coming down with a splash and then whirling around to leap again the other way.

Involuntarily, Leigh found herself watching them as they moved slowly away along the road playing catch with chestnuts. The wolf was a glorious sight, vaulting into the air after the targets, showing his incredible long teeth in a gape that ended with a snap Leigh could hear even from a distance. Several times, the Seigneur made a motion with his hand, and the wolf dropped onto its belly. They would stare at one another for long moments, and then the Seigneur would tilt his head left or right and Nemo would go racing off in that direction. Once, the wolf disappeared into the bushes, and the Seigneur walked casually on down the road until Nemo erupted from his cover, yelping and cavorting delightedly at his friend's melodramatic whoop of surprise.

Leigh leaned against the chaise. She squinted at the mat of wet yellow leaves on the ground. She swiped angrily at her eyes and rummaged in her satchel for her medicinal wallet, taking out a vial of eye bath she'd prepared from a powder of lapis calaminarius, rose water, and white wine. She walked to the mare's head and pulled back the blinkers, applying two drops with a glyster pipe to each of the horse's eyes. When she saw the Seigneur turn back, far down the road, she bundled up her medicinals and prepared to stuff the wallet away.

The corner of her sketchbook stuck out from beneath the flap of the traveling satchel. As she tied the wallet, she looked at the worn cover of the book. She glanced again at Nemo, watched the wolf spring into the air, all muscle and rippling fur and wild joy, with the Seigneur flicking a chestnut off one thumb.

She fingered the sketchbook. She chewed her lip, and then suddenly pulled the book free. He had charcoal and pencils at hand for his own little drawings that he never bothered to finish of houses and trees and old peasant women they'd passed. Leigh sat against the footrest of the chaise and opened her book, flipping quickly past the watercolors to the last blank pages. She grasped a pencil stub between her fingers.

She stared at the creamy page. There was an old smudge on it, the print of her own thumb, left from some other day—some other scene that had caught her heart. Some forgotten, never recorded occasion . . . a birthday, an afternoon's teatime, one of the small things that she sketched when she wanted to crystallize a moment in time and take it with her into the future.

She held the pencil. She put the point down on the paper. For a moment she thought of the wolf, the outline of it, the proper shading—she never got it right, really she was only a dilettante . . .

She pressed her trembling lips together. Suddenly she gripped the pencil in her fist and tore it across the page with a violent move; gritted her teeth and pressed the point down hard, scrubbing it viciously into the book, scrawling a black jagged scribble of nothing over the paper.

Her hand seemed to move of its own will, not drawing, attacking—battering and violating the empty page, tearing through the paper with slashes of dark and gray and white. She could hear herself breathing, dry sobs as she bent over the book, squinting down at the work, not stopping until she'd torn the page into ugly shreds that hung from the binding like old clothes.

She looked down at it, at the pencil and her smeared hands. Then she stood up and threw the book away from her as far as she could throw it.

She turned around to the scratched and faded sideboard of the chaise, panting as if she'd been racing: as if she'd climbed and crawled to the top of a mountain. She pressed her palms together and held them to her mouth while her whole body shuddered. She swallowed, and swallowed again, and slowly her breath came back to her. The force that gripped her muscles let her go; she could move again, and think.

She closed her eyes for a long moment. She heard the wolf go panting past her, and looked up to see the Seigneur. She wanted to turn away, but she watched as he walked over to a puddle in the road and picked up the open sketchbook that lay half in and half out of the skim of muddy water.

He didn't look at Leigh. He brushed away the wet leaves that clung to the book and then separated the pages, drying the corners with his coat sleeve. The copy of the thieftakers' bill lay a few feet away; he dried that too, and with his stiletto, he stood in the road and painstakingly cut away the tatters of the mutilated page.

He wadded up the torn pieces and tossed them in the puddle. Then he walked to the chaise and packed the book in his own bag, sliding it carefully between his shirts, slipping linen shirttails between the wettest pages and padding the book's corners before he closed the valise again.

He never looked at Leigh. He said nothing. If he had, she would have disintegrated into a thousand shivering rags of mad anguish.

But he didn't, and she held on.

They ate without talking, the way they did almost everything. Leigh sat in the chaise, while he leaned against the trunk of the chestnut with Nemo at his feet. It was peaceful and cold, the road vacant of any other traffic. Nemo put his head on his wet paws and napped.

When the Seigneur finished his lunch, he went to the mare's head, removing her nose bag. "Was your meal perfectly satisfactory, madame?" he asked.

The horse nodded extravagantly.

"You've taught her that," Leigh said, making her voice curt, so that he would not think her disarmed by such a child's trick.

The mare nodded again.

"I don't perceive how you're doing it," she said.

He stroked the mare's forehead. "Oh, once I learned she spoke English, 'twas easy enough to strike up a conversation."

"How droll," Leigh said sarcastically.

He smiled a little. "I'm pleased to hear you like it," he said, and folded back the blanket.

Five more dreary days to Rouen, where Leigh went quietly out to the stable just before she retired to her chamber at the Pomme du Pin. She took her medical kit to bathe the mare's eyes, even though after a fortnight she doubted the treatment was having much result. She'd not really thought it would, but she looked ahead and thought of what would become of the faithful creature when they reached the coast.

She was a little later than the usual hour of her evening visits. Normally she only waited until the Seigneur had occupied himself with whatever flirt he'd discovered for the night, and slipped out just after supper. The drops only took a moment to apply; then she went directly upstairs to her room.

This night, after supper at the common table, the twelve-year-old son of an English family staying at the Pomme du Pin had engaged her in a game of chess—the Seigneur having been so kind as to promise the boy that Leigh was monstrous good at the game, and to issue an extravagant challenge on her behalf: a sack of bonbons to the Seigneur's jar of pickled cherries from Orléans. Leigh had lost, but at least it had been by design.

The Seigneur himself had long since disappeared, of course, out seeking his pleasures according to habit.

She'd borrowed a lamp from the inn, but she could see a shaft of light pouring across the cobbles from a crack in the door. Beyond the roofs, the asymmetrical towers of the cathedral showed black and gothic against the sky, their bells pealing an echoing call to late mass. Her breath frosted around her as she reached for the door.

Laughter and voluble French drifted out of the stable. Inside, a little group of stable hands clustered in the open area outside the stalls, gathered around the roan mare, who sat on her rump in the center.

Quite literally sat, her forelegs splayed out in front of her and her tail spread on the clay floor.

Leigh stopped in the doorway and put down the lamp. No one noticed her, least of all the Seigneur. One of the grooms asked a loud question, and the mare nodded vigorously. The little audience roared with laughter, which spooked the mare, but before she gained her feet the Seigneur was tapping her rump with a whip, murmuring, *"Non, non—à bas, chérie!"*

She sank back with an equine grunt. He rubbed her ears, feeding her a biscuit and calling her sweet names in French. Then he stepped back. *"A-vant!"*

The mare heaved herself to her feet and received another warm cherishing. In the midst of interested comments from the bystanders, the Seigneur looked up and saw Leigh.

He grinned and turned the mare toward her. The blind horse struck out with a foreleg and lowered herself onto one knee in an impeccable bow.

All the ostlers applauded.

Looking at their delighted expressions, Leigh suddenly realized what he'd done. He'd trained the sightless mare into value, given her a solid worth, made her an asset when she'd been only an encumbrance. While Leigh watched, the mare stood up and stuck out her nose, nibbling at the Seigneur's tricorne, then taking the brim in her long yellow teeth and pulling the hat off. She shook it up and down, while the ostlers screamed with mirth.

Leigh lowered her eyes. She couldn't help the way her lips curled upward. "Good," she said softly.

The Seigneur bent his head. He rubbed the mare's ears vigorously, slanting Leigh a sidelong smile as he took his hat and settled it on his head again. He handed the mare's lead to an ostler.

"And what brings you out so late?" he asked, coming toward her. "I thought you snug in bed."

Leigh shrugged. She leaned against the door and held the wallet behind her. "I wished for some air."

"Come here," he said softly. He walked past her out the door. "I want to show you something."

He moved off into the shadows. She hesitated, and then followed him. In the darkest corner of the yard, beneath the alley wall, he stopped and turned. Leigh ran up against him and he slipped his arm around her, his hand closing on the medical wallet.

For an instant she resisted, out of instinct. Then she let go. "I've been bathing the mare's eyes," she said, feeling somehow even more defiant for it, now that he'd produced a more eligible remedy.

He took the wallet gently. "I know." She couldn't see what he did with her kit. His arm came around her again. *"Ma bonne fille,* I know."

Leigh began to breathe faster. "Hush!" she whispered harshly. "I'm not your good girl, I assure you."

"Kind and sweet," he said, bending closer. "So sweet." His lips drifted over her temple. "So very sweet."

"Don't," she said, appalled that her voice quivered. She could feel his body close to her, without seeing him— as if he were the darkness made real and warm. "Not now."

His hands tightened on her shoulders. "Leigh . . ." He kissed the corner of her mouth. "My beautiful heart . . ." His lips closed over hers, coaxing rich pleasure from the cold black well inside her. For an instant she leaned into him, let him hold her; for an instant she let him prevail in all his hunger and heat.

His arms slipped downward, pulling her into him. *"Je t'aime,"* he groaned, kissing her hard. "I need you. I want you. I adore you."

Her passion and anger and pain rose to a pinnacle as she stood trembling in his hold. She put her arms against his chest and shoved, tearing herself away. He caught her elbow. "Unhand me," she said through her teeth, "or I'll kill you."

"Pistols at dawn, monsieur?" His voice was low. "When are you going to buy a dress and put an end to this farce?"

"At my pleasure." She jerked her arm away. "Not yours."

He made no move to catch her back. She stood with her hands in fists, her legs braced, struggling with the sensation that burned behind her eyes and in her throat.

"Leigh," he said out of the darkness. "Don't go."

Her spine stiffened. "Could you find no other willing game tonight? I suppose if you must gratify yourself, I'm—"

"No, don't say it!" he uttered fiercely. "Just don't." He pushed past her—then stopped and turned. "Your medicines," he said, shoving the wallet into her hand. "Perhaps the eye bath helps."

"Perhaps," she said. And then added, in a stifled voice: "But . . . 'tis nothing . . . to what you've done for her. Teaching her the tricks." She put her hand on his arm. "Thank you."

He stood still, only an outline against the lights of the inn, his breath frosted and bright around his head. He was silent. She couldn't see his face.

"God, you'll drive me mad!" he said at last, and expelled a harsh laugh as he walked away.

They reached the coast at Dunkerque, and sold the mare. S.T. spent a few days investigating the town and prospective buyers. When he'd given the horse over to her proud new owner, an elderly tinker with a spotted dog and a merry eye, he felt hopeful that she'd be esteemed and kept fed for her talents.

Leigh didn't take the parting well. She'd quit trying to doctor the horse's eyes after Rouen, and stopped the surreptitious treats that S.T. knew she'd been slipping to the animal. Those extra favors of an apple or a sweet, given for no reason, hadn't helped his training program, but he'd let her do it. And when she stopped the treats, when she left off patting the mare, or speaking to it, or even looking at it very often, he almost wished she'd go back to disrupting his carefully disciplined methods with her unthinking indulgence.

The morning he gave over the mare to the tinker, Leigh claimed with a frown that she had better things to do with her time, and left S.T. on Dunkerque's dockside, holding the horse's bridle. She never even looked back.

When he'd seen the mare to her new stable, S.T. went into a free port shop, taking care of errands of his own. He glanced out the door at the dockside. Water glittered cold and bright against the dark interior of the shop. A small cart drawn by a dog passed the door. There was no sign of Leigh yet. He looked down at his palm, considering the silver locket that had caught his eye. It was shaped into a delicate star with a tiny paste diamond at the center. He rubbed his ear and eyed the shopkeeper.

"Cent cinquante," the man said in Flemish-accented French.

"Le diable!" S.T. laughed and let the locket slide back onto the counter. *"Cinquante,"* he said firmly. "And I'd expect a ribbon with it at that."

"Vhat color?" the shopkeeper asked, switching smoothly to English. He opened a drawer and pulled out a rainbow of satin ribbons. "I don't see such a locket go for below a hundred. Silver metal, yes? *Regardez* . . . vhat color be her eyes, monsieur?"

S.T. smiled. "The southern sea. The sky at sunset. Fifty-five, *mon ami.* I'm in love, but I'm poor."

The man held up a swath of ribbons in sapphire hues. "Ah—to be in love! I understand. Ninety—and I gif you the riband as a token."

S.T. chewed his lip. He had one hundred and twenty livres left—five English guineas, after changing the money the blind mare had brought. But there was lodging still to be paid—and for the channel passage, some smugglers' palms to be greased into silence.

"Eighty-five, monsieur," the shopkeeper offered. "Eighty-five, and a riband in every color to equal all her pretty dresses."

S.T.'s mouth flattened. One pretty dress was more than he'd been privileged to see in the past weeks of traveling north across France with Leigh Strachan. He shook his head reluctantly. "I can't afford it. Just give me the razor."

"Sixty, m'lord," the shopkeeper said quickly. "Sixty for the locket, the razor, and the sapphire riband. No duty. A free port, Dunkerque. It is all I can do."

S.T. glanced outside again. He tapped his fingers on the counter. *"La peste."* He sighed. "I don't know. All right. Give it to me."

"Her blue eyes, they will sparkle like the star, monsieur. I promise you."

"Certainement," S.T. said dryly. He paid, got a receipt against the French duty, stuffed the package into his waistcoat pocket, and walked outside. He stood for a moment, watching the water and boats sway dreamily in front of the neatly painted shops and houses with their arched Flemish gables. He shuddered in the cloudy northern chill. The memory of his last channel crossing haunted him. He turned back inside and asked the direction of an *apothicaire.*

Leigh met him a quarter hour later, just as he was stepping out of the pharmacopoeia. He could not imagine why everyone on the street didn't stop and gape, she looked so clearly to him like a lovely woman dressed up in men's clothing. Her hair was pulled back in its queue and powdered, which made the blue of her eyes seem intense. She walked with more grace than any gawky youth of sixteen had ever managed. She'd wanted to carry his rapier, but he wouldn't let her. She didn't know how to use it, and he saw no sense in making her a fair target for a fight.

She looked at the paper packet in his hand. "What did you buy?" she demanded in her husky counterfeit voice.

She had the most annoying talent for putting him instantly on the defensive. "Some dried figs." He fiddled with the ring on his sword belt, adjusting it unnecessarily.

"Oh. Figs." She shrugged, and then actually favored him with a small smile. "I was afraid you might have bought something medicinal from that quacksalver."

S.T. frowned. "A quack?"

"I went in earlier, to replenish my stock of savine. The digitalis was mislabeled as magnesia, and his plantain is molding. It's that sort who gives a patient deadly nightshade when they meant to administer the common variety. But the fruit seemed well enough. May I have one?"

S.T. bounced the packet in his palm. "Well, they're not precisely . . . figs . . . exactly." He squinted at her. "You're sure he's a charlatan?"

"You did buy medicine, didn't you?"

"Did you purchase some proper skirts?" he countered.

"That's neither here nor there at the moment. What did you buy in there? I don't want you dosing yourself from that shop. It's not safe."

"Careful, Sunshine. You'll make me think you give a damn about my welfare."

She snorted delicately. "I wouldn't treat a dray horse from a pharmacy like that."

"Ah. Thank you. For a moment there my head was swelling." He turned and started to walk down the street.

Leigh was right beside him. "What do you need medicine for? You should have asked me."

"Where are your new clothes? I don't see any packages. No dresses, no hats, no reticules. That damned frock coat's getting a little threadbare, don't you think?"

She frowned and didn't answer. He knew she wanted to berate him for mentioning female articles here on the open street, but she didn't dare. There were enough outsiders in Dunkerque to render English a comprehensible language, no longer so safe and useful for private communication as it had been in the tiny villages of France.

S.T. let her stew. He waved at a dairy cart and tipped the farmer a sou to carry the two of them out of town with the empty milk pails. The ride passed in stony silence, barring the pass through the customs as they left the city, where he produced his receipt and murmured to the officer. S.T. wouldn't have disapproved entirely of a bodily search, on the chance that Leigh might stand revealed as a female for once, but they escaped without that adventure.

A mile from Dunkerque on the coast road, where the white sand blew off the dunes and splayed in pale fans across the raised roadway, he slid from the tail of the cart. Leigh slipped down and walked back a few paces to meet him. The ox and farmer plodded onward, oblivious.

A dog began to bark as they walked along a dike toward a neat cluster of house and outbuildings set a little back from the road. Moments later, a young boy in baggy trousers and long, striped stockings raced out to meet them.

"The wolf's awake, monsieur!" The boy danced backwards in front of them as they walked, speaking rapid French. "He waits for you! Maman gave me a mutton bone to feed him, but I didn't put my fingers through the bars, monsieur, I promise! Will you take him out now? Will you allow me to pet him again? I think he likes me, do you agree?"

S.T. pulled at his lip, pretending to give the question deep thought. "He licked your face, yes? He wouldn't lick your face if he didn't admire you."

The child giggled. Then he cast a sly look at Leigh. "But he doesn't lick Monsieur Leigh's face."

S.T. bent down and whispered loudly, "That's because Monsieur Leigh is such a giddy puss. Never stops laughing. Haven't you noticed?"

He glanced at her as he spoke, but couldn't tell if she followed his French or not. The boy stuck his finger in his mouth and laughed. He regarded her with wide eyes and took S.T.'s hand. "I think Monsieur Leigh more scary than the wolf," he confided shyly. Then he brightened. "Maman says that my father left a message of importance. He is to send the boat for you at high tide, so you must be waiting at the *Petit Plage* with all your things. Beyond the last dike—I'm to show you where."

"When's the tide?"

"After dark tonight. Maman said she would tell you when to go. You must eat first, she said. We're to have a *hochepot* with pig's ears and mutton. She made that specially for you. And she packed a ham and baked some raisin buns for you to take on the boat. Do you think the wolf might like a raisin bun?"

"He'd like some of your mother's exceptional sausage much better."

"I'll tell her," the boy exclaimed, and ran ahead into the farmyard.

"No doubt you'll find a pound of it wrapped up in Brugge lace on your pillow," Leigh murmured in English.

"Jealous?" He grinned. "She's a pretty little housewife, isn't she?"

"I only dislike to see poor trusting *père* grow a cuckold's horns while he's out at his trade."

"Perhaps he shouldn't be so trusting. Perhaps he ought to come home more often, and not stink of fish when he does, hmm?"

She lifted a dark eyebrow. "You've no scruples about it?"

"About what, Sunshine? Kissing the hand of a sweet *femme* for her kindness to us? That's all I've done, I assure you."

"She's half in love with you." She kicked a muddy pebble out of the path. "Well enough the wind's turning. We've only been here two days. I shudder to think if we were to stay a week."

He stopped and looked toward her, his mouth curving faintly. "I'd no idea you accorded such potency to my charm."

"Oh, I've no illusions on that score," she said. "You've been breaking hearts from here to Provence."

"I can't touch yours, it seems. What's left to me but flirting with a *demoiselle* now and again? 'Tis harmless enough."

Her eyes met his directly. "I think not, when you stay with them all night."

"Ah." His jaw hardened. "Really, do you think you ought to take the high ground with me on that subject?"

"You know my position on the matter," she said stiffly. "I'm accessible for you to satisfy yourself; I see no need for you to make all these young ladies fall in love merely to prove that you can stir them to it."

"I'm not trying to prove anything. What damned business is it of yours where I sleep?"

"I feel that I'm responsible for you."

He stared at her, astonished and incensed. "I beg your pardon, mademoiselle. But I'm a man full grown; I don't need an impertinent chit of a girl claiming responsibility for me."

"Do you not? Then who do you expect will be accountable for this foolish wife when her husband tosses her out for sleeping with another man? They're a family! 'Tis something precious, what you're playing with. You haven't even any discretion about it. I expect it makes no difference in a public inn, and I've said nothing every night since we left Aubenas, but in a private home like this when you claim to go for a walk after supper and then come back at dawn, there's some notice taken, I assure you."

"Is there indeed! Notice taken by whom? The boy? He's long asleep. Her husband? We haven't seen that mullet-monger in person yet, have we? He's too busy netting smelt to have a care for his poor lonely wife. 'Tis you takes notice! A precious family, is it?" He gave an angry laugh. "I bow to your greater experience—I don't know much of that! So what's my punishment to be? Another six weeks of bad humor and cold shoulder? Is that what you're pleased to call 'accessible' to me? God, I don't know how I'll bear the delight!"

Faint color rose in her cheekbones. She turned her face away. "I pity the woman. Yes, she is lonely. She's weak. Why must you take advantage of her?"

"I made her laugh. I called her pretty. I kissed her hand at the kitchen fire. That's the sum of it. As to all these shameful, wanton hours after midnight, it's Nemo I spend 'em with, not some willing female—much to my regret! I take Nemo out and let him run free while he has the chance, when there's less prospect he'll be shot by some stalwart village knight with a notion to protect the populace. I hate it that he has to go back into that damned kennel box we had built for him. Can you comprehend that? Lord, did you truly think I've slept all day in an open chaise just because I've been debauching myself beyond bearing every night? If you're going to spy, you'd best go a little further with the effort and get your facts straight before you make your accusations.''

She stood very still, staring at him, her figure silhouetted in deep colors against the dingy sky.

''Not that bedding her isn't a perfectly splendid notion,'' he added wildly. ''She's got warm blood in her in place of ice water, which is more than I can say for you.''

Her shoulders lifted. She held them back, rigidly straight.

''Does that offend you?'' he sneered. ''Good.''

The color in her cheeks had become a blaze. She moistened her lips. ''I beg your pardon,'' she said in a deathly hollow voice. ''I have been mistaken.''

His harsh breath made the cold air frost around his face as he watched her walk away from him. He twisted the paper package and crushed it in his fist. When she was almost to the farmyard gate, he called her name.

She didn't turn. The chained dog began to bark again, but she ignored that, too. S.T. took a deep breath and strode after her, but by the time he reached the yard, she had disappeared into the gabled farmhouse. The boy was just running out the door toward him, begging to pet Nemo and give the wolf a handful of smoked fish.

S.T. stared past him at the farmhouse. It took a conscious effort to force his hands to relax. He was a brute; a bastard; he well knew why she had no warmth in her. But the way she treated him, the endless cutting snubs in spite of every attempt to win her admiration—it drove him beyond endurance. After a long moment, he turned on his heel and followed the boy into the barn.

TEN

S.T. had thought he was prepared for the channel crossing.

He wasn't.

All those queasy weeks of bouncing along in an open chaise, where at least he could focus on stable landscape, were nothing to the reeling horror of a ship's berth in a heavy sea.

While he could still reason, he wished he'd taken the powder he'd purchased at the quack *apothicaire*. If it had killed him, so much the better.

He couldn't see; his vision swung and pitched if he opened his eyes, amplifying every lurch of the ship until his insides seemed stuck in his throat. His hand clenched on the wooden rail that edged the berth. He kept swallowing, trying to draw breath enough in his lungs to think. It seemed that a massive hand throttled him, pressing down with unrelenting force. He'd lost what little he'd eaten before they'd even left the shore boat to board the smuggling lugger, and now he had nothing but sick agony squeezing his stomach and chest and head.

He heard the slide and rattle of the curtains drawn back from across the berth. A soft touch pressed against his cheek and temple, sweet-smelling release from the dank odors. He turned his face into it, tried to speak and only managed a choked groan.

"You're breathing too quickly," Leigh said. She braced

against the bulkhead and sponged his face with the scented water. "Try to slow down."

He gripped her hand so hard that it hurt her. She held steady while he panted against her skin. He was trying to obey her: a harsh exhalation, a suspended moment, and then another desperate rush.

"Slower," she said softly. "Slower than that."

"Can't." He swallowed convulsively. His breathing went back to the quick and shallow pants.

Leigh bit her lip, knowing of nothing more to do for him, even out of all her mother had taught her. Earlier, she'd tried to coax him to take an infusion of boiled fern root, prepared on deck with great difficulty over an iron pot full of charcoal, but he could not keep the first swallow down.

Heavy boots sounded in the passage. The captain of the little smuggling vessel came up behind her, peering over her shoulder into his berth. "Bust me," he muttered. "I seen 'em in rum case in my time, but I hain't never seen nobody took this bad before. Sure it's only the seasickness, are you?"

The Seigneur opened his eyes. He seemed to be trying to focus, but his head moved with the motion of the ship and instead of fixing on Leigh or the captain, his line of sight swung as if he were watching a fly circle their heads. She stroked his damp forehead. "Don't try," she murmured. "Close your eyes, monsieur; you needn't talk."

He made a sound, a low-pitched whimper that was almost lost in his labored breathing. He was quiet compared to the crying and moaning crowd of seasick passengers Leigh had seen aboard the mail packet on her first trip across the Channel to France; very quiet and far more ill. It was the same way he'd looked with his dizzy spells on the road north—his skin sweaty and white, his jaw clamped against the sickness—only on the lugger's deck it had gone on and worsened until he'd seemed to lose command of his very limbs and sunk slowly down onto one knee, slumped against her leg. Taking him below to the captain's berth hadn't revived him; he'd only lain panting and ashen, driving to empty heaves if he tried to keep his eyes open.

"I don't know why he's in such extremity," she said, still stroking his face. "I understand this sort of thing varies with the individual sufferer."

The captain snorted. "There's a passle o' fancy words. You're an educated young gentleman, then, are you?" He watched her hand a moment and then grinned. "You his mollie-cull?"

Leigh paused in her stroking. The Seigneur turned onto his side with a heavy sound.

"No need to frown. 'Tis no nevermind to me," the captain said. "Live and let live, says I. I think I could like a pretty rogue, myself." He lifted a lock of hair that had fallen over her ear. "I like a soft cheek, I do."

Leigh put her hand on the dagger beneath her coat, but before she could draw it, the Seigneur made a sudden move. The captain lurched in the direction of the berth, his waistcoat caught in the Seigneur's grip.

"Mine," he snarled, his voice hoarse and frightening between violent pants. He'd hiked himself half up in the berth; his teeth showed white in the dimness as he twisted the waistcoat in his fist. A button popped free, bouncing against the rail and then the deck.

"Here now," the captain said. "You're a sick man."

"I'm not—dead," the Seigneur growled.

The captain pulled free with a grin. "Couldn't 'a proved it by me. You bloody well look like a corpse."

"Don't touch . . ." the Seigneur said shakily, his eyes shut. "Cut . . . y'r heart out."

"Aye, I'm a basket o' nerves, I am." With a good-humored chuckle, the captain bent down to search for his button. "Got no time for it anyhow. We're within sight o' Cliff End." He straightened up and stuffed the cracked pearl button into his waistcoat pocket. "I'm not going any closer. You two chaps and your circus beast can lighter ashore with the goods as best ye may."

When finally he made the beach, S.T. dropped to his knees and put his head between his legs. He could hear the voices around him: the smugglers' soft calls and Leigh's quiet instructions about Nemo and their baggage, the rattling chunk of the waves as they broke on the shingle. Somebody threw his two swords down next to him; he heard the metal sheaths ring against the cobbles, but he could not bring himself to turn his head.

He just wanted to stay perfectly still. It was lovely, this solid ground. It had saved his life. He pressed his forehead to a cold stone in desperate gratitude.

A quiet voice spoke above him. "Monsieur, they say there's a cart here. We can ride with our baggage closer to town."

He tried to bring his sluggish brain to attention. "Town," he managed to say thickly. "What town?"

"We've landed off Rye."

He stretched himself full-length on the beach, ignoring the discomfort of the shingle beneath his chest. "Let me sleep," he muttered. "Just let me sleep."

"They'll leave without us. They won't dally for the revenue officers, monsieur."

"Sunshine." He found words in the weary stupor. "I can't . . . get on that cart."

He was vaguely aware of an enormous defeat as he said it. She would leave him now; she'd never wanted him to come and it was beyond him to move. She'd leave him for what he was, an impotent fool facedown on the ground and unable to get up.

He was trapped in England now. Nothing would make him board a ship again. Nothing. God help him, he'd swing at Tyburn first.

"Damn you," she said softly. "I don't want to wait."

Damn me, he thought in dull surrender. He closed his fist around an English stone, smooth and round. *What am I doing here?*

The noises went on around him, but he could not summon the energy to think. He drifted in and out with the crunch of cobbles beneath smugglers' boots and brandy kegs, the whiff of horses on the cold sea breeze. He woke once and they were growing distant, woke again and they were gone. There was only the endless chunk of the little waves breaking on the shingle.

A star hung like a lonely lantern on the horizon. He

blinked, trying to hold his eyelids open, but the lethargy swallowed him in its effortless void.

When he opened his eyes again, in the very first faint dawn, he could see the outline of Nemo's cage. The wolf stood inside, watching him.

So—she'd left Nemo, at least—although that was no surprise. Short of making a few crowns by selling him into a traveling fair, a tame wolf would be of even less use to her than a spent highwayman.

He lay with his cheek resting on his arm, utterly cheerless. Away down the empty beach, he could see a white headland shining subtly between the pearl gray of the sea and the sky. The tide had fallen. A black-headed seabird came skimming along just above the cobbles, a flash of white against the dark stretch of stone.

Hesitantly, he risked lifting his head. He focused on the distant cliff and raised himself on his hands.

Nemo whined. He pawed at the slats on the cage.

"Calme-toi," S.T. muttered. "Keep your fur on."

He levered himself into a sitting position without any ill effects. It seemed almost strange, to have a steady head after the prolonged misery of the Channel passage. He pushed himself to his feet, the kind of move that always sent his balance spinning, and found even that was not so bad. In fact, in comparison to the agony he'd just endured, the world seemed to stay perfectly constant around him.

The morning mist sent a shiver through his spine. When he turned his good ear away from the sea, the sound of the surf grew suddenly distant. He looked to see if they'd left him a greatcoat and found Leigh sitting against a boulder in the shadow of the cliff.

She was awake; she watched him with her knees drawn up and her chin propped on her crossed arms. Her hat lay on the shingle beside her. She didn't smile or say good morning—not that she was prone to such pleasantries at any time—but only stared at him balefully.

"Now what?" she asked.

Her dark hair flowed down the back of her shoulders,

loose. The dawn light softened her cheekbones to a delicate creamy pink.

He couldn't help himself. A slow grin curved his mouth. "You waited for me."

For a long moment, she looked out to sea without answering. Then she shrugged. "You have the money."

He tried not to let it nettle him. He remembered, vaguely, a soft voice and scented cloth amid that swimming nightmare aboard the lugger.

She pushed herself upright and walked toward him. "What shall we do now?"

It might have been deferral to his authority, or it might have been a mocking challenge. He preferred the former, and chose to take it that way.

"Walk. Find transport. Take ourselves off to London Town."

Her brows lifted. "London!"

Nemo scrabbled furiously at his cage and whined. S.T. walked over to it and sprang the lock. The wolf came bounding out, leaped up to greet him passionately, then loped to the base of the white cliff and began to mark new territory.

"It's too dangerous," she said. "What if you're recognized?"

He snorted. "Aye—informed upon for a fine three pounds. That doesn't worry me, milady." He reached down to retrieve his swords, buckling the rapier around his hip. "I believe I'm going to become a wealthy eccentric. On a walking tour." He looked around at the sea and sky, leaning elegantly on his spadroon as if it were a gold-knobbed cane. "To view the terns."

"What of Nemo?"

"Nemo?" He acquired an imaginary quizzing glass, lifted it, and peered at her. "Oh, do you mean that picturesque hound of mine? He is a quaint monster, isn't he? Half Russian. The czars hunt wolves with them, don't you know." He whistled, and Nemo came racing up, curvetting playfully at his feet until a faint hand signal sent him into a whimpering, eager crouch. S.T. pulled an invisible handkerchief from his cuff and sniffed at it stylishly.

"Would you care to pet him? He's quite harmless. A little shy of the ladies, I fear."

"No one will swallow that. You've maggots in your head."

He dropped his hand. "I daresay if you can pass as a male, I can certainly pose for a mere odd character."

"And what else should I be? Your 'mollie-cull'?"

Leaning on the spadroon, he stared at her blandly. "Do you even know what that means, Sunshine?"

"I'm not a complete green-head." She made a careless gesture with her hand. "That captain saw through my costume. He took me for your mistress."

"Ah." He smiled. "Not precisely."

He saw that she wouldn't give him the satisfaction of showing curiosity. That was well enough. If there were depravities she didn't know about, he wasn't going to engage her in an improving conversation on sodomy. She looked so young, standing there in her man's clothes, her legs braced: so wide-eyed and frowning and virginal.

"Just don't throw the title about intemperately, *ma petite,*" he said at last. " 'Tis a hanging offense."

She frowned slightly, a betrayal of confusion that he found endearing. The entire topic was apparently beyond her ken. Whatever she thought she'd learned of worldly wickedness, and wherever she'd learned it, the schooling hadn't been so sordid as she appeared to want him to believe. He began revising his original plans, thinking of where he could safely leave her while he made a prowl of his old, wild haunts in Covent Garden.

"How do you do?" she asked abruptly. "Are you feeling better?"

"Quite well, thank you." In the relief of standing on ground that didn't reel beneath his feet, he didn't even feel unsteady in the way he usually did. "Excessively well. I believe I'll stay off the water for the remainder of my natural life."

She tilted her head, a faint frown between her brows, very serious and beautiful. "Was that what you wanted with the apothecary? If I'd known how ill you'd be, I would have compounded a powder for you to take beforehand."

S.T. called Nemo to him and knelt on one leg to caress the wolf. Devise a powder, would she? It wouldn't work. He'd had enough drops and pills and electuaries to reckon on that by now. What he really needed was something else entirely—an aphrodisiac, a love philter—a powder that would melt her ice down into sultry emotion before he lost his mind.

He thought it was there. He caught her sometimes, looking at him.

If he could be what he'd once been, he wouldn't need love potions.

He stroked Nemo's thick ruff. "Powders don't work."

"Are you certain? Perhaps—"

"Do you think I haven't tried them? Do you think I've not seen a hundred physicians? They don't know what's wrong—half of them never heard of such a thing, and the rest try to dose me with asses' milk and tar water, and say 'twill go off in a few weeks. Well, it hasn't gone off, not for me. It's been three years."

"Three years!" she echoed softly.

"Aye.'Tis worse and better, in spells. Sometimes I almost feel all right—the way I feel now . . . as long as I'm careful. Then I turn my head or make a quick move, and the world goes round like a top." He shrugged. "And I fall down. As you've noticed."

She gazed at him. Behind her, seabirds soared along the chalk cliff.

"And that's why, isn't it?" she said slowly. "That's why you ran."

He laughed bitterly. "Oh, aye, you ought to have seen me when I crossed to France!" He blew out a harsh breath. "They had to carry me ashore, and I couldn't stand up for two days. There wasn't even any bloody wind that time— the water was like glass. Never again will I board a ship. Never."

"How did this happen to you?" she demanded.

"You needn't look at me as if I ought to know better, damn it," he snapped. " 'Twas in a cave. I got myself cornered by the militia that Miss Elizabeth turncoat Burford set on me, and they exploded a heavy charge at the entrance." His mouth tightened. "Killed my horse. Nothing hit me. Just the sound." He bent his head into Nemo's ruff. "Just the noise. It *hurt*. It hurt my brain. It made me dizzy to stand up or walk or move my head at all. My ear bled." He took a deep breath and lifted his chin. "Can you repair that? Can you make a powder and give me back my hearing?" His voice rose, in spite of his attempt to keep it casual. "I'm deaf on the right side, did you realize it yet?"

She stood frowning at him. He saw her finally put the signs and the truth together. Her expression went from discovery to shock to a furious frown.

"Hell and the devil," he muttered, and looked down, gripping the wolf's thick fur between his fingers.

"You didn't tell me!"

"Come along," he said defiantly. "You didn't see it for yourself—why should I?"

She stepped back, her hands spreading. *"Why should you?"* she cried. "I don't understand how you suppose to go on with this! What else is wrong with you that I don't know? For the love of God—you'll be no help to me. None!" She flung out her hand. "Why did you come at all? Go away! 'Tis nothing but a mockery!"

S.T. stood up. His back was rigid. "You want to be shut of me?" He cast the spadroon at her feet in a ringing clatter. "Fine. You've been asking to carry a weapon since we left Provence. There it is."

She looked down at the sword and up again.

"I'll leave it with you if you want it," he said roughly. "See how it fits your grip."

For only a moment, gallingly short, she hesitated. Then she knelt down and clasped the hilt, letting the sword slide from the sheath. She lifted it in one hand and steadied it between both.

"Le voilà," he snapped. "The Prince of Midnight."

" 'Tis not as heavy as I expected." She swished the blade experimentally through the still morning air.

"Think you could kill a man?"

She met his eyes coolly. "The man I wish to kill. Yes. I can do it."

S.T. drew his rapier with a snap of steel and in a single pass stepped forward, came under her wobbly guard, and disarmed her. The spadroon went clanging onto the stones. He pressed the tip of the rapier into the thick folds of linen at the base of her throat. "No," he said gently. "Not if he's got a sword, you can't."

She took a prudent step backward.

S.T. lowered the colichimarde and sheathed it. "I'm half deaf, mademoiselle. I'm not crippled."

The seabirds swooped and cried in the silence. Leigh stood with her chin lifted, her hands tight. "I apologize." There was a clear tremor in her voice. "I see that I have misjudged you yet again."

He turned his back on her. He was angry with himself for allowing his emotions to seize him. It had been dangerous, that move, a showy circus trick on bad footing; he was rusty, with no call to pretend otherwise.

But he hadn't lost his balance. He realized it only as he thought of what might have happened if he had.

He hadn't lost his balance.

He had not lost his balance.

He stood still, suddenly afraid to move.

That fencing attack, that abrupt drive forward . . . he should have lost his balance. For three years, no matter how stable he felt when he was motionless, a move like that had sent the universe careening.

He put his hand on the hilt of the rapier. He shook his head from side to side and then even tilted it back until he was looking at the sky. He drew the sword and lifted it slowly in front of him, holding it steady at shoulder level, waiting for the slow reeling sensation to take possession of his head.

"It's gone," he whispered. "Oh my God . . . it's gone."

For the first time in three years: in thirty-six months, two weeks and four days—he'd kept count—he moved freely in a fixed universe, without his senses betraying him whenever he turned his head.

"Oh God," he said, throttled beneath his breath. "I don't believe it."

He whirled around, facing the cliff. Nothing happened; no crazy pitch, no wild swing of the horizon.

An awed smile spread across his face.

He felt as if he'd been freed of fetters that he had not even known bound him. Normal felt so normal that he'd not even recognized it. Like a headache, the constant and unpleasant sense of instability had evaporated at some unknown moment when he wasn't thinking about it, the exact instant obscured in the contrast between the heaving ship and the solid ground. He didn't know when it had happened: he'd just fallen into harmony with himself.

The ship. Could it have been the ship? Maybe that bloody surgeon had been right—maybe it had just required such an extremity of disequilibrium that he'd never been able to carry it far enough of his own will.

Part of him was terrified. What if it came back? He shook his head again; closed his eyes, and waited for any trace of disequilibrium.

The world stayed firm beneath his feet.

He wanted to run. He wanted to dance. He turned suddenly to Leigh and grabbed her hand, sinking into a deep formal bow. "I'm at your command, mademoiselle. I beg you won't send me away while I have the power to serve you."

"Don't be a nod-cock." She pulled her hand free. " 'Twould appear that I haven't the power to send you away even if I wished."

He straightened, frowning, hardly able to comprehend that she could not see the difference in him. It must be obvious, it must be—and yet he had not even perceived it himself.

He could win her now. No longer was he the stumbling buffoon. He could ride, he could use his sword; he could do anything.

What if it came back?

Don't let it come back. For the love of God, don't let it.

He stared at her, wanting to hide it, wanting to tell her . . . if he told her, and it came back . . .

"I'll go away," he offered slowly. "If that's really what you want.

Her eyebrows lifted above those skeptical aquamarine eyes. She turned and walked away toward the cliff.

"You came to me for help!" he shouted after her.

She whirled and looked back. "Aye. I rubbed the bottle, didn't I? And freed a genie. One wonders what you will do next."

He couldn't restrain it; he met her scowl and felt his face break into an exhilarated grin. He was free, and nearly whole; he owned himself again. He laughed and swept the blade in an arc and circle above his head. It sang a lovely high-pitched note as it cut the air descending. He stood with the sword in his hand, his legs spread in easy balance. "Who knows what I'll do? Depends on where I spring game, Sunshine."

Leigh walked behind the two of them over the downs, holding her hat on her head against the wind, watching as the Seigneur knelt once again to unsnarl Nemo from a difficulty. He had finally submitted to putting a rope on the wolf, but though he'd surrendered to the idea that Nemo would be safer leashed in the daylight, he wouldn't allow a shorter length than the full ten feet of line that they'd salvaged from the bindings on the cage. The wolf didn't seem to mind at all, beyond getting constantly tangled in bushes and wrapped around trees.

Leigh felt unsettled. She felt precarious and tormented, unable to concentrate on the future. Whenever she looked at the Seigneur, she thought of him with the bared sword shimmering above his head, the morning light liquifying the blade into a runnel of silver as it moved. It was as if the image had gotten etched somehow on the back of her eyes, like a bright flash, overlaying all the other things she saw or remembered of him.

His endless patience with the animal made her miserable and weak inside. She had to set her jaw to keep her lower lip from trembling at the most preposterous small events. She wanted to snap at him to stop this maudlin nonsense and simply keep the animal close at his side.

Nemo had never accepted her. He was beautiful; fluid and quick and shrewd, but he was a royal bother—and inseparable from the Seigneur.

At his decree, they walked toward Rye. Leigh didn't care which way they went. She stared out across the high chalk downs and desperately wished she were alone.

This was not why she'd traveled to France, not to come back shepherding an erratic Robin Hood half as wild as his wolf. He'd been bad enough with his romantic mooning about and making up to anything in skirts. But there was a new anticipation in him now, an intensity shimmering just behind his satyr's grin. Her hands still stung from the jarring impact of his blade against the sword she'd held.

That had been an extremely enlightening moment.

With the sword in her hand, she'd felt . . . effective. She'd known she wouldn't shrink from killing Chilton, and for an instant, just an instant, she'd had the means to do it. She'd held a blade, honed and balanced to kill.

And then he'd taken it from her.

There were moments of humbling in life that one did not soon forget.

She felt bleak and afraid. Not for herself, but for making a mistake, a fatal overestimation of her ability to carry out her chosen course. For death she cared nothing—'twas failure that she could not contemplate.

All along the road through France, she'd known she should leave the Seigneur behind. She thought about him too much. She hated finding herself tangled in his frivolous little peccadilloes. She hated worse than anything moments like that one at the French farmhouse—finding herself mistaken in her presumptions, in matters that were none of her concern.

And then the way he watched her . . . as if everything inside him were at a slow boil.

She doubted if he was quite rational. Truly, she'd thought he'd have given up on the journey long since. Between the dizzy spells and the risk of returning with a price on his head, she'd been certain he'd turn back at the Channel. And then, after the crossing itself . . .

That was why she'd waited for him there on the shingle: it had seemed only fair to make that small gesture, because she'd been certain he'd give up after that.

And see what that moment of sentiment had gotten her. She watched his back moodily. 'Twas maddening, the way he could draw her into things that she didn't want to be drawn into, make her find herself offering to treat his dizzy spells, or boiling fern root for him, or giving her opinion on whether a senile old tinker was capable of managing a blind mare with a small repertoire of silly tricks. The thought of the mare brought on that dangerous hot sting behind her eyes, and he made it worse by stopping again for the thirty-second time to tolerantly unwrap Nemo from around a tree while the wolf leapt all over him and licked his face.

"We haven't any money left, have we?" she snapped.

Nemo took off in a lope forward, pulling the Seigneur along. He set his feet, hauled the wolf back, and said, "Two guineas."

His calm answer just aggravated her more. "Veritable nabobs, in fact!"

He shrugged and ducked a branch as Nemo tugged him along.

It was worse when he wouldn't rise to her baiting. With silky mockery, she said, "Perhaps you should hold up the next coach."

"Oh, aye!" he said. "I had my eye on that haycart we outstripped a mile back. Couldn't make up my mind between that and the brewer's wagon."

"So you helped push him out of his mudhole. Quite the scourge of the hightoby."

He hiked the pack and saddle higher onto his shoulder. His tricorne was cocked rakishly down over his eyes, while the hilt of the broadsword slung across his back glinted in the weak December sun. He looked like a hell-born rogue.

"At least the man showed a grain of common gratitude," he muttered. "You didn't have a *sou* when you came to me; I don't know why you're on about it now as if I'd gambled away your entire dowry."

"I'm being practical," she said, in a tone she knew would provoke him.

He slanted her a hot glance beneath the golden satanic brows. Nemo entangled himself in a hedge. She felt better—colder and steadier—satisfied to build a wall of annoyance between herself and them.

She followed the two of them down the slope of the hill, walking on the grassy hump between the wagon ruts. Below lay the marshes and Rye—a medieval pile of gray walls and patchwork roofs perched on high ground overlooking the spread of wasteland. The marshes stretched toward the sea from the very foot of the city, scintillating with bright, icy ponds amid the winter's drab.

At the foot of the slope, a slow river flowed between banks laden with long grass. The road widened at a stone bridge, blocked for repairs, and on the other side a ferry rested against the bank under the bare branches of a large tree. The ferryman began poling the barge off with one hand and hauling on the cable with the other.

Leigh and Seigneur boarded as the ferry touched their side, Nemo for once drawn close to the Seigneur's legs. The ferryman gazed at the wolf warily.

"It don't bite, do it?" he asked.

"Certainly not," the Seigneur said, and grinned. "Only on order."

"Huh. Looks like a blinkin' wolf."

The Seigneur leaned against the rough-hewn wooden rail and laid his hand on Nemo's head. "Aye. Rather daunting, don't you agree?"

"Huh," the ferryman said again, thrusting the pole into the Seigneur's hands and taking hold of the cable.

The Seigneur put his weight into the rod, his shoulders flexing powerfully beneath his buff-colored coat. When they pulled up to the bank, Leigh stepped ashore, leaping over the muddy spot, and turned in time to see the Seigneur press one of the two guineas into the ferryman's hands.

"Good God," she exclaimed, "are you—"

"Yes, yes, I'm coming!" He broke into her furious protest, giving her a sharp quelling glance. "Here—take the cloak bag, will you?'' He stared to hand the traveling case across to her, but the ferryman hustled forward.

"Allow me, m'lord! Here now, watch your feet in the mud.'' He hauled the bag across the low spot and dumped it unceremoniously in Leigh's grasp. "I'll give you me arm, sir—watch your step. There you are, m'lord, safe as houses. Thank ye, m'lord. Thank ye!'' His face could barely be seen for the forelock tugging.

Nemo had already bounded past Leigh and hit the end of the rope. The Seigneur was apparently ready for the jolt, for he only set his feet and endured it before turning back to the ferryman. "Maitland,'' he said, with a slight nod. "S.T. Maitland.''

"Very good, m'lord. I'll remember, I will. Lord bless ye, sir. I wish ye luck with the wolf-dog.''

The Seigneur relieved her of the satchel. He slung it onto his shoulder with the saddle. The ferryman followed them halfway up the bank, still tugging reverently at his forelock.

"You're mad!'' she hissed, as soon as they were out of earshot. "You gave him a guinea! You told him your name!''

"There's nothing wrong with my damned name. Did you ever see a handbill with my name on it?''

She gritted her teeth, glaring at him. "Why on God's earth did you give him a guinea? We've hardly enough to fetch dinner as it is.''

"We might pass this way again.''

"That's all very well, but I'd like to know how we're to go on!''

He only smiled that seductive, unholy smile of his and walked ahead. Leigh watched him move—all the promise of easy grace fulfilled, no more little stagger or hesitation or quick reach of a hand for balance as he turned his head. He seemed tougher . . . more distant . . . transforming right before her in ways that she couldn't seem to fathom.

ELEVEN

ALFWAY up an ancient side street in the walled and
cobblestoned city of Rye, the sign of the Mermaid
hung over a half-timbered inn nearly choked by
vines. Without an instant's hesitation that Leigh could see,
the Seigneur strode up the steps and ducked into the low
doorway of the venerable edifice, bade a skittish Nemo to
sit himself down, dropped the saddle and baggage in the
middle of the hall, and asked a passing waiter to see if the
landlord could spare him his usual room.

The man paused for a moment, staring, and then his
face brightened with recognition. "Mr. Maitland! We ain't
'ad the honor for some time, sir!"

The landlord himself appeared, and it was quickly apparent that at the Mermaid Inn they had not the least objection to sinister guests and their ill-assorted parties. Mr.
Maitland received the warmhearted welcome accorded to
a familiar and gratifying visitor. The innkeeper only
glanced at Leigh and Nemo, and made no protest at all
about the animal as he led them along a bewildering maze
of corridors to the Queen's Chamber, where a tremendous
dark four-poster dominated the tiny room.

The place smelled of age and beeswax, pleasantly
musty, with a new fire laid ready in the grate. Green-dyed
light from the window streaked the polished, uneven
planks of the ancient floor. Nemo immediately leapt into
the middle of the bed and lay down. The Seigneur made

a sharp move with his hand, and the animal stood up obediently and jumped off, its nails clicking on the bare wood.

"I'd best warn the maids," the landlord said benignly.
"We wouldn't want them to think a wolf's got in."

The Seigneur looked over his shoulder. The half light
of sunset through the leaded window emphasized the upward curve of his eyebrow, casting him in dramatic glare
and shadow. To Leigh he seemed positively Machiavel-
lian, like a Renaissance prince, a subtle assassin considering his prey.

"But that's why I bought him." He leaned against the
windowsill. "Shame he's such a pudding-heart! Paid a
pretty penny for him, too. I thought I'd try to breed the
devil and see what I got." He looked down at the wolf
affectionately. "Do you think he'll pass along his yellow
eyes?"

The landlord considered. "What of those tall Irish
hounds with the rough coats? Ye might try that cross."

"There's a notion. You don't object to having him inside?"

The landlord didn't seem to notice the faint smile. "Not
a'tall, sir; you should know we don't mind the dogs, sir,
if you can vouch for he's house-trained. Will your man be
staying belowstairs?"

"My man? Oh—you mean this fellow here, do you?"
The Seigneur's face grew rueful. "Rot me—does no one
at all see through her? That's my wife, old chap. I've gone
and got myself leg-shackled."

The landlord's mouth dropped open, quite literally. He
looked at Leigh and blushed crimson.

She glared at the Seigneur and flung herself into a chair.
"You faithless brute!" she said viciously.

He turned away from the window and held his hat behind his back, giving an excellent imitation of staring
bashfully down at his toe. "We've only been married a
week." He looked up with a moonling smile. "She still
calls me 'Mr. Maitland.' "

"Toad!"

"Well, sometimes she calls me 'Toad.' " He put his

hand over his heart. "You're charming, my love. Adorable."

The landlord had begun to grin.

The Seigneur winked at him. "We had a wager," he said. "She claimed she could come all the way from Hastings without anyone the wiser." He gestured grandly with his hat. "We're on a walking tour. I wished to view the terns."

"A walking tour," the landlord said faintly, and nodded in Leigh's direction. "You're very intrepid, ma'am."

"Pluck to the backbone." The Seigneur slapped his hat on the bedpost. "You should see her handle a sword."

"Indeed, sir." This news seemed less astonishing to the innkeeper than the wedding itself. "You will have that interest in common, then. Please accept my sincere congratulations, Mr. Maitland, and every best wish to your lady. Will you be needing anything else?"

"M'lady's gown is in that bag. Take it away and have it pressed, will you? We'll both want a bath and a tray—cold meat will do. And a spot of the Armagnac, if the Gentlemen brought you anything worthwhile on their last run."

The landlord nodded and picked up the cloak bag. "Will you want the boots, sir?"

"Aye, send him along. My coat could use a brushing—no, wait, you've a decent tailor hard by, don't you? Take this to him and see if he's got something fit for town made up in my size. Velvet or satin." He unstrapped the broadsword from his back and shrugged out of his buff coat. "I dare swear m'lady's had her fill of terns for the moment. We'll let her promenade about Rye on my fashionable arm a while, shall we?"

The landlord took the coat and bag and bowed himself out. Leigh sat staring at the Seigneur. There was an uncomfortable sensation at the base of her throat. She thought of that single remaining guinea, and the cost of all the services he'd ordered.

He was taking off his waistcoat. As he pulled it free of his broad shoulders, a small package dropped from the inner pocket. He smiled as he picked it up. "I've never had a wife before."

"You don't have one now," Leigh said inflexibly.

In the shadowed room, the evening light seemed to gather around him, shining dull gold off his hair and his lashes, giving his full-sleeved shirt a pale glow. He broke the string on the little packet and opened it, held out his hand and asked gravely, "Would you do me the honor of wearing this anyway?"

She looked down at the delicate silver pendant that flashed in his palm.

"What is that?"

He met her eyes. "Something I wanted to give you."

She frowned, and tightened her hands. "Is it yours?"

"I didn't steal it, if that's what you mean."

She stared at the necklace. It was pretty—dainty and feminine, like something her father would have chosen for her. A peculiar burning tightness in her chest made her breath grow harsh.

"I bought it for you," he said quietly. "In Dunkerque."

"Dunkerque!" She seized on that fact and propelled his hand away furiously. "Of all the shatter-brained, sap-headed, romantical foolishness!" She thrust herself out of the chair. "How much did you spend?"

He took a step back. His expression made her turn away, unable to bear it while her lower lip trembled so painfully.

"Never mind," he said, and she heard him move across the room.

She turned back abruptly. "We've a guinea!" she cried. "One single guinea, and you bought a silly necklace in Dunkerque that's worth three pounds if it's worth a penny!"

He sat down on the bed and glanced at her slantwise, his green eyes shuttered beneath the golden demon's brows.

"You're going to rob a coach, aren't you?" she demanded. "Oh, God—we've barely landed and you're going to go right out and risk it."

The ghost of an ironic smile touched his mouth. "Now, why the devil would I want to do that?"

She looked around the private chamber. "Perhaps to pay for this!"

He shook his head. "Really, you disappoint me. Where's your practicality? What if I could take a coach—even without a mount? I don't have a fence here for jewelry, and we wouldn't want to risk spending any cash we'd just prigged in the neighborhood. On the whole, I think it far more prudent to make a withdrawal from the bank."

"From the *bank!*"

"Well, it's not that shocking, after all. It's really considered quite the thing." He dragged up the jack with his toe and began to pull off his boots. "You just go in, tell the fellow you wish to withdraw a reasonable sum, and he's most honored to obey."

"You're going to rob a *bank,*" she cried.

As he bent to yank off a boot, his burnished queue and its long black ribbon curled together, falling over his shoulder against his shirt. In his stocking feet, he lay back on the pillows with his hands beneath his head. "I hope it won't come to that," he said, gazing at the canopy. "I'm sure I've at least a thousand quid here. I never let the dibs fall below nine hundred on any of my accounts."

In the quiet room, Nemo stretched out on the wooden floor and put his head on his paws with a sigh. Leigh stared incredulously at the relaxed figure on the bed. "Do you mean to say you've an actual balance in a Rye bank?"

He rolled over onto his elbow. "Yes."

She wet her lips. "So you won't have to—steal anything to pay for all of this?"

"No."

The threatening weakness quivered behind her eyes. "Curse you, then!" she snapped. She strode to the window and thrust it open, staring past the leaded green glass into the stable yard below.

"I beg your pardon," he said dryly. "I didn't realize your heart was set on it."

'It's not," she said. "You may believe me, it's not."

There was silence behind her.

"Could this possibly be concern for my neck?" he asked softly.

She turned away from the window, ignoring that. "We should have a plan, should we not? You arranged this. Why are we here? If you have a plan I want to hear it."

His gaze rested on her for a long moment. "Close the window," he said.

She looked at him sharply, and then obeyed.

"Come here."

Drawing a deep breath, she sat down on the edge of the bed, so that he wouldn't have to raise his voice for what he had to tell her.

He held up his hand, the silver pendant dangling against his palm. "It's been six weeks," he murmured. "Six weeks I've wanted you. I know how you move, and how the sunlight makes a shadow on the curve of your cheek, and the shape of your ear. I know what you look like under that bloody waistcoat."

"What has that to do with a plan?"

"Nothing," he said. "Not a damned thing." He chuckled harshly, then turned his head on the pillow and looked at her. "I'm dying," he said. He dropped his fist against his chest. "Right here, you're killing me."

"That's not my fault," she said stiffly.

He closed his eyes. She suddenly realized that his body had grown ready for her, that he lay with his shoulders taut, breathing deeply. *"Merde,"* he said in a low, impassioned voice. "Tell me, Sunshine. Do you still have any debts to me outstanding?"

"Is that all you want?" She tilted her head back and sighed angrily, feeling shaky, all nerves, staring up at the red damask folds of the canopy. Her fingers curled into her hands until her nails cut into her palms. She was afraid he was going to reach for her, and she didn't know what she would do then.

He lay like a lion stretched on the bed, tawny and masculine. The silence grew. He made a moody sound, staring at the pendant.

"I thought it was beneath you," she said. Her voice

came out wrong, too husky, a little fractured. "You've hardly touched me since the first time."

"Aye," he said bitterly. "I've wanted you to ask."

She would never give him that. She wouldn't stumble into the kind of absurd emotional maze he lived in. Daft, he was. Sentimental, daft, devastating. She could imagine him with her sisters. He would laugh at Emily's jokes even when she couldn't remember the punch lines. He would tease Anna into tantrums. He would . . . no, not *would* . . . would have, would have . . .

Sometimes she thought she heard them, heard their voices, somewhere just beyond sight. Just beyond reach, fading into dreams.

But all that was gone.

Gone, gone, gone . . . as if it had never been.

Reality was an unfamiliar room and a highwayman. He was magnificent, his green eyes, gold dusted; his knee lifted and his body relaxed, as beautiful in its own way as the wolf's. She knew the strong shape of his hands and wrists and the sudden, beguiling shock of his devil's grin.

It felt like drowning, to be this close to him. It felt like pain: the deep ache and anguish of heat applied when all her limbs were frozen. She didn't want it; she couldn't survive it.

"I won't ask," she said. Her voice sounded crystalline, brittle in the silence. "I need nothing of what you call love. What you want is your own affair."

He looked away with a grimace. He held up the pendant and watched it twist in the light.

"Did I speak of love?" His jaw was set. His mouth looked forbidding. "I thought I spoke of debts." He opened his hand and allowed the pendant to slide slowly from his fingers, one silver loop after another. "My bed. My food. My money," he said softly. "Ever since La Paire." There was just the faintest trace of scorn in his voice. He lowered his hand and rested it against hers. "What of that? You'd have it all business between us—so you've told me."

Leigh grew taut. She remembered him, again, with the

sword on the beach—the rapier's wicked song as it cut the air.

He slipped his fingers about her wrist, sliding his hand up her arm and slowly down again. The twist of his mouth held a sardonic challenge. "So . . ." he whispered. "Pay me."

She breathed deeply, like a deer frozen in alarm.

Did he think she would shy from it now? She stared at him, at the moody smile, the lowered lashes that hid his intent.

Her eyes narrowed.

Let him. Let him believe it was in his power to move her in any way.

He shifted his hand to the buttons on her waistcoat and began to flick them open, one by one, deliberately. He reached the last. "You're strangely passive for a whore," he said. "Don't you know your business?"

She felt a flush rise in her face. But she wouldn't give him anything, not even shame.

Without lifting his head, he caught her chin between his fingers, caressing. There was still that scornful curve to his mouth. "If I'm buying this, I don't expect to undertake all the exertion."

"There'll be servants coming."

"Turned up shy?" he murmured. "They won't stay long."

She fought the alarm, sought for the shield of resentment. She thought of the way he'd struck the sword from her hands as if her fingers had no strength in them. She wanted redress for that, and for other things: the way he drew her in and made her afraid for him and what he might do.

She thought of the scenes in the marquis's little book, the erotic stories. Her lip curled.

Let him think he could shake her this way.

She turned her head and brushed her lips over his hand. Delicately, she closed her teeth on the tip of his finger and lowered her eyes. "I'll bathe you then, monsieur."

* * *

S.T. lay on the bed as the maid finished pouring the last pail of hot water into the bath. Rye's preeminent tailor had not been behindhand in offering his wares. S.T.'s new coats, brought by the shop boy, were spread for inspection on the clothespress amid their paper wrappings: bronze velvet trimmed with dark green frogging, midnight blue satin decorated in gold, along with a hopeful offering of matching breeches, heavily embroidered waistcoats, and fresh linen shirts that dangled discreet lace at the cuffs.

The maidservant gathered her empty pails and left on the heels of the dismissed shop boy. S.T. sat up on the edge of the bed. He reached for the platter of cold meat and ate a slice of beef on bread, tossing another portion to Nemo, who consumed it in one swallow.

All the time, he watched Leigh.

Her hair was tied back again, revealing tender skin, snowy and silken. He kept his lashes lowered, kept a check on himself, just watching, like a hunter in the trees.

She moved around the room—arranging towels, laying out soap, and making little feminine sorts of preparations, the kind of things he'd never seen her do before.

It made him hot to watch her in the boots and breeches, her head bent in quiet attention to the tasks. The effect was maddening, sublimely exotic. She was doing this for him, all these little meek rituals, these maidenly things, while he wanted to rape her—she'd driven him that far.

He'd not intended it this way. He'd tried to impel her to refuse him, to shame her into it.

She won. He lost . . . lost the bluff, the whole stake, the entire war, every scrap of conscience and restraint— and took painful, inglorious, mortal pleasure in it.

He sipped at a glass of brandy, feeling it warm his throat and chest. He was disturbed to find that his hand wasn't steady. The drink did not blunt the hunger in him, or the self-contempt.

She moved to the bath, tested the water, and turned to him. "Monsieur?"

Her eyes were lowered, her tone polite and reserved, as if she were a docile servant. He felt bound; unable to stand up and take her in his arms in the usual way of things. He just sat there, violent inside, his hands shaped to the edge of the bed.

She came to him, stood beside the bed. "You wish me to undress you, my lord?"

His lips parted a little. The husky voice was seductive, her manner grave. He thought she must be mocking him, calling him by a deferential title, as if she were truly a servant. She dropped her eyes in a sort of courtesy, her dark lashes curving against her cheek, inflaming him beyond logic with this offer of service.

"Yes," he said hoarsely, surrendering to the erotic promise of it.

He'd been attended by servants a thousand times. He'd never thought about it in his days of living high. He was a gentleman; he had a valet when circumstances permitted. But not this. Not this tantalizing female who lifted his shirt, trailing her hands over his torso and chest, touching him in places he had not been touched in three years.

Her fingers stroked him, moved up his ribs and outlined the curve of muscle on his chest. She caressed his nipples until he lifted his chin and drew in a heavy breath. She pulled the linen over his head, moving away to lay the shirt across the chair as if everything were commonplace routine. Then she came back and paused in front of him, her gaze still lowered modestly, like an attendant awaiting his pleasure.

He stood up. She touched him without hesitation. The back of her hand pressed him leisurely as she unbuttoned his breeches. He was having trouble breathing. He wet his lips as she pushed the material aside and released him.

He felt as if he were sinking into a dream.

Her fingers closed around him intimately, warm and stroking. He sucked in his breath, put his hand on her shoulder, and arched his head back. His whole body seemed to reach for her, to fuse and center on that touch.

She slid her palm down the side of his hips, bent to unfasten the buckles at his kneebands. He stepped to one side, freed of breeches and stockings, standing naked and aroused while she made a neat pile of the clothes and tested the water again.

"Monsieur," she said gravely. "Your bath is at a pleasant warmth."

He looked at her. His brain did not quite accept this scene: his own nakedness; her demure downcast eyes, her figure in the provocative breeches, the shirt, all covered and all flagrantly in view. His mind disowned it, but his body beat a hot and ready song.

He stepped into the bath. The steamy water flowed around his calves. On his bared back, he could feel his queue brush softly when he turned his head, like cool silk while he simmered all over.

She held a washcloth and soap, waiting, but somehow he could not bring himself to sit down. His knees would not bend, his shoulders would not relax. All his muscles seemed taut with pleasure. He flexed his hands as he stood with the warm water caressing his feet.

She waited a moment, her gaze steady at the level of his chest. When he made no other move, she folded back her sleeves to the elbows, knelt, and doused the washcloth and soap in water. She was so beautiful, she made every move delicate, gracious. He wanted to hold her face between his hands and drive his tongue deep into her mouth. As she rose, she drew the scented bar and cloth up the back of his leg, up his thigh and his loins, cascading warmth down his body.

He bit the inside of his mouth and tilted his head back, feeling her hand move on his skin, slowly massaging.

She began to soap his chest. The water ran down in heated rivulets. He heard himself breathing, rough and uneven, the only sound beyond the swish of water in the tub.

She knelt again and brought a fresh soapy flood of sensation, washing his throat and his shoulders, taking each of his arms in turn and working gently down to his fingers. Her skin felt slick and hot against his; he caught her wrist, but it slipped from his hand as she turned away. She filled the pitcher and lifted it above his shoulders to rinse.

He closed his eyes as the water poured down over him. She knelt again and began to soap his legs, running her hands over the hard muscle of his calves, and then upward.

She stroked the back of his thighs and caressed him provocatively. He could not believe it; he couldn't speak; there was a sound caught in his throat, a blocked whimper of ecstasy. He touched her hair, thrust his fingers through it, and held her head between his hands as if she could keep him standing when his braced legs felt as if they would give way.

She let the cloth fall and brushed the inside of his thighs with satin-slick fingers. Then, while he stood trembling, she slipped her hands around his hips, leaned forward as she knelt, took him in her mouth and kissed him.

His back arched; he clenched his teeth and panted through them as she stroked the most unbearably sensitive part of him with the tip of her tongue. Sweet flashes of agony sent tiny spasms through his frame. He began to move; he couldn't help himself, his hips pressed forward into the rhythmic strokes and his hands slid down to her shoulders to lift her.

He wanted to drive her backward onto the bed, to bury himself in her instantly. But she slipped from his grasp, twisting free with a shrug.

His eyes opened. She stepped back as he reached for her. She had a faint wry smile, a strange brightness to her eyes as she surveyed him.

"You're a very beautiful man, monsieur," she murmured. "But I think our ledger is in balance for now."

Before he could adjust to the sudden change in the direction of events, she pulled down her sleeves and slipped out the door, leaving him standing alone and soapy in a hip bath.

He heard the latch clunk. For a long moment he simply stared at the door, confounded. He sent a wild look around the room, breathing fiercely.

He could not believe it. His body rejected it entirely, demanding completion. He let out a shout of rage that sent Nemo scrambling under the bed.

The door stayed closed.

"*Leigh!*" he roared.

There was only the sound of the slow, worried thump of Nemo's tail.

"Jesus," he said. "You little bitch. You vicious little
. . . *God!*" He broke off, beyond words. An inarticulate
snarl was all that passed his throat.

He shoved one fist into the other. His body ached and
burned. He stared again at the door, had a wild thought
of snatching one of the coats and going after her; realized
what an unutterable ass he would look if he tried.

"God damn you, *what do you want?*" he shouted.
"What do you want; what do you want? Cold-blooded
bitch—is this it?"

No answer.

With a furious splash, he sat down in the tub. He put
his hand over his face and chewed his fist. He was breathing hard, panting through his nose in harsh gusts. Over,
he thought. Over. That's it. No more.

He grabbed the extra bucket and poured ice-cold water
down on his head.

Two hours later, he stood before the mirror on the dressing table, glaring at himself. He wore the bronze velvet,
because that was the first thing on top of the pile, with
blond lace and a waistcoat of gold tissue embroidered in
green silk and silver thread. The whole rig gave him a
metallic shimmer, picking up the gilded gleam of his hair,
which he left unpowdered for just that reason. He thought
he looked well. He hoped he looked damned good. He
snarled at his image and saw a golden satyr sneer back.

He drew in a deep breath. He swung off the stool and
kicked the damp towels out of the way, banged open the
door, and signaled for Nemo, who came reluctantly, his
tail between his legs. S.T. took an extra minute to get
down on his knees and reassure the animal, but although
Nemo licked his face and put his paws on S.T.'s shoulders, he still moved with the half-creeping posture of a
worried wolf as he followed S.T. down the corridor—
another crime to place at Leigh Strachan's door.

When he reached the front hall, the landlord looked up
from his ledger and smiled. S.T. had a notion that the
state of his marital tranquillity was known throughout the
inn, but the man made no sign, simply directed him to a

private parlor, where the innkeeper said Mrs. Maitland was awaiting her husband.

He stepped inside the opened door. In a pleasant salon warmed by candlelight on rich linen-fold paneling, a young woman sat by the fireplace, reading.

He hardly recognized her. She rose as he entered and curtsied to him, bending low, spreading a fan and the skirts of her gown, so that the familiar Prussian blue birds showed clearly. Her hair was dressed and powdered to the palest hint bluer than her pearl choker, falling in short ringlets against her throat and curling gently around her face. She wore a tiny beribboned flower in it. Even her brows were different, plucked into perfection, with an arch that seemed unnatural and delicate, like the tiny black patch placed at the corner of her lips.

He looked at the exquisite sable kiss against her soft skin and felt crazy, all the heat coming back in a rush.

She closed the fan with a skillful snap as she rose and held out her hand to him. Fully aware of the landlord still standing in the door behind him, S.T. allowed her to pose there for a noticeable moment before he turned around and shut the door in Lady Leigh Strachan's face.

TWELVE

H E rode under the stars, fast and hard, on a horse
he'd stolen right out of the stable yard. The wind
beat his eyes; blew the moisture from them, so
that he saw nothing clearly. He'd walked out of the Mermaid and seen the animal standing there saddled, grabbed
the reins, and mounted it.

He didn't know where he was going. He didn't care.
The devil had him, the old devil that drove him to act on
the razor edge of chance. He rode in a fury, intoxicated
by the feel of a galloping horse beneath him, enraged with
himself, with his needs and his weakness. He left behind
him all the indignant shouts and civilized rules, plunging
down a road too dark to see.

A shadow hunted beside him, a dark shape that made
the horse snort and shy when it drew too close. Without
deigning to use some unknown gentleman's absurdly short
stirrups, he rode out the fitful bucking, relishing the sensation, the ability to find his center and hold to it. All
those nights when he'd painstakingly mounted the blind
mare were nothing now, all that light-headed, cautious
practice rendered immaterial. Without the dizziness, the
skill was simply there, the way it had been all his life that
he could remember, ingrained in him as deep as simple
breathing.

He urged the animal on through the night. The elation
of the race consumed him, fueling the fury, burning it up
until he was a bonfire. The direction meant nothing, the

pounding gallop was all that mattered, until in the blackness ahead something flickered—a smear in his blurry
eyes.

He pulled up the horse and stared. The light glimmered
and swayed, moving slowly downward. He passed his hand
over his eyes and blinked to clear them, turned his head
to listen with his good ear. Above the horse's rhythmic
blowing, he could hear the sluggish thunder of a trotting
team and the creak of wheels.

Close already. Nemo had disappeared into the gloom.
He felt the horse draw a breath and lift its head to whinny
a greeting. He used his leg to push it violently to the side,
off the road. The horse lunged up a low bank that he hadn't
realized was there.

As the carriage lantern came into view, he broke into a
ruthless grin. His elevated position gave him an unexpected advantage, putting him above the unsteady pool of
light that wavered along the road.

He reined the horse around, facing it the way the carriage was coming. He drew his sword and bent deeply over
his mount's neck, clamping his free hand across the animal's nose to catch a whinny before it was born. The horse
sidled beneath him. Over his shoulder, he could see the
murky bulk of the team, catch the scarlet of the driver's
liveried arm and the glint of lantern light off harness brass.
He refrained from looking directly into the lantern itself,
to keep the light from dazzling him.

The slowly trotting team rattled toward him, the leaders
passing with their heads at the level of his mount's belly.
They could smell his horse; he could see by the way they
lifted their heads and blew nervously, but the blinkers kept
them uncertain and silent. The coachman spoke softly to
steady them as he passed.

S.T. lifted his sword.

"*Stand to!*" he roared, and drove it into the lantern,
shattering glass and plunging everything in darkness. He
spurred his horse down the bank, shouldering into the off-
side wheeler to slow it, and then grabbed in the pitch black
for the leader's rein with one gloved hand. In the bruising
tangle, the driver was shouting and S.T.'s own horse was

attempting to plunge right past the team without his restraining hand on the reins. In desperation he threw his weight back and down in the saddle as he hauled on the leader's rein, hoping against hope he had a well-trained mount.

It worked. Whether by training or a desire to stay with the other horses, his mount thudded to a halt as the team did. The coachman's whip cracked, stinging S.T.'s arm and cheek. He grunted, lashing out instinctively with his sword arm. He couldn't see, but he felt the thong curl around his wrist above his glove. His body reacted before his mind formulated the plan: with a quick jerk, he sent the whip flying into the night.

He groped for his reins and legged his horse around in front of the leaders. "Stand to!" he yelled again. "I've a pistol primed and ready!"

This was a blatant lie, but safe enough in the ink-black circumstances. Someone inside the coach had lighted a taper, which cast just enough glow to show him the coachman's silhouette frozen on the box and the equally immobile outline of a footman perched up behind. S.T. had thought someone might produce a blunderbuss, which was why he'd stayed close to the team for cover, but the men seemed unwilling to risk such a move.

A sudden silence descended, with only the metallic jingle of the harness to break it.

"Very good," S.T. said, in a congratulatory tone.

He urged his mount back up onto the bank, careful to avoid even the dimmest glow of light.

"Come down off the box," he said to the driver. He watched as the coachman dropped the reins and slowly obeyed. "Get inside. Your footman, too."

A low sobbing broke out in the interior of the coach. S.T. bent a little as the driver opened the door. He caught sight of a white-faced couple of middle age and a young woman with her face bent into her hands before the taper was snuffed.

"Light it again," he said. "I don't want to kill your servants. If they stay where I can't see them, I will."

The sobbing increased. After a little shuffle, the taper

flickered again. The servants climbed inside. S.T. sat leaning on the pommel of his saddle, studying his huddled victims.

They were clearly returning home from some party. Diamonds flashed at the neck and wrist of the younger woman while she bent her head into her palms. The man wore a fine watch fob and huge ruby stickpin; his wife had a set of matching rubies in her hair and draped around her plump neck. They weren't driving far; they'd never have risked such jewelry with so little protection on a ride of any distance.

He nearly let them go. There was no reason—no justice to take, no downtrodden soul to reimburse. But the young woman lifted her face. Tears were streaming down her cheeks; she was crying as if her heart would break, and he thought of Leigh suddenly—who never wept.

"Bring me the diamonds," he said.

She let out a wail of despair and bent over, shaking her head.

"Coachman," he said. "Take them from her."

"No!" She scrambled back, her hand at her throat. "Thief!" she cried. "Horrid thief!"

"Give them up, Jane," the older woman said in a low voice. She fumbled at her own necklace. "For God's sake, give him all of this jewelry—'tis nothing but stones."

"I only want the diamonds," S.T. said. "Keep your rubies, madame. I compliment you on your wisdom."

"You're only going to take my diamonds?" the girl cried. "Oh *why*? That's not fair!"

"Do you care so much for stones, my lady?" He tilted his head. "Were they a gift? A lover's token, perhaps?"

"Yes!" she said, staring blindly toward the sound of his voice. "Have mercy."

"You're lying."

"No—my fiancé—"

"What's his name?"

She hesitated, just a beat. "Mr. Smith," she said wildly. "John Smith."

He chuckled. "Pretty feeble, m'love. I find I'm not in a romantic mood tonight. Bring 'em here."

She shrieked and pushed at the coachman as he reached toward her. S.T. spurred his horse right up to the door, staying above it on the bank. He extended his sword with a shift of his wrist, palm downward, and then slowly turned it until the point came up into the open door. He held the blade there, allowing the dim light to slide up it and down.

"Diamonds aren't such a terrible thing to lose, my lady," he said softly.

She stared at the sword, and broke into sobs again. He waited silently. After a few moments, she fumbled at the clasp. He saw what she was about and shifted suddenly, catching the necklace on his blade as she threw the diamonds toward the door.

He lifted the tip and let the jewels slide down to the hilt. *"Très charitable, mademoiselle."*

With a flick of his wrist, he tossed the necklace into the air and caught it in his other hand. Then he drove his heels in, sending his horse in a lunge forward and a great bounding leap off the bank. He bent his face into the stinging flare of its mane and let it carry him at full gallop into the dark.

The horse sprinted for a spell, and then, having no idea it was now a fugitive from the king's law, began to slow. S.T. allowed the pace to ease to a canter and then a trot. Jogging along alone, he sheathed his sword and slipped the necklace inside his glove. He set his back, and his mount obediently dropped to a walk. It shied a little as Nemo loped up behind them, the sound of his panting loud in the quiet night.

S.T. halted the horse and sat considering.

He frowned pensively as he lengthened the stirrups to his own measure and took them up.

Slowly, a smile of awful mischief spread across his face. He couldn't stop himself. He turned the horse around and began to post leisurely back toward the scene of his crime.

He halted frequently and turned his head, listening intently. Long before he heard anything, he could feel his mount's head come up alertly. Though he couldn't see it, he knew the horse's ears were pricked toward the sound and scent of its erstwhile companions. He allowed his

mount to walk slowly ahead, until finally he caught the
furious voices and sharp slam of a coach door.

Knowing his own imperfections, he judged that the
coach must be quite close, though it sounded a good distance away to his attenuated hearing. He held up his fist,
chewing on his glove and grinning. When he detected the
sound of the coachman's bark and the rumble of the wheels
and hooves, he set his horse along, following his agitated
victims at an innocent distance all the way to the town
gate at Rye, delighting in the farce of it.

When he was close enough to see a few late lanterns
burning in the cottages at the edge of town outside the old
walls, S.T. turned off into a sidetrack and threaded his
way through the empty alleys to the gate he and Leigh had
entered that morning. The brewer's dray he recalled was
still there, loaded with empty kegs. He stopped his horse
and leaned over, opening taps experimentally until he
found one with a few dregs left in it. Having anointed his
neckcloth with the unmistakable aroma of stale beer, he
began to lean heavily on his horse's mane and sing a
drunken little song.

By the time he reached the stable yard of the Mermaid,
he was so sloshed that he lost his stirrups as he tried to
dismount and fell off, hanging with his arms around his
patient horse's neck. His feet slipped out from under him
as he swayed, and he landed with a gusty *whoof* at the feet
of a stable boy.

Nemo whined and licked his face.

"Oops," he mumbled, staring up from his back at the
ostler. "Los' m' reins, shir. Gi' me back m' reins, will-
ya?"

"Yes sir," the boy said. "But this ain't yer horse, sir."

S.T. rolled onto his elbow, pushing Nemo away. "Yes,
i'tis. Jus' got off it."

"No, it ain't. Belongs to Mr. Piper, sir."

"Pi—Pi . . ." S.T. dropped his head back on the pavement. "Dunno th' shap."

"Well, ye took his horse, sir, right enough."

"Lis'n," S.T. said. "Lis'n here—you got somethin' for

a man t'drink?'' He sighed deeply. "M'wife don't like me.''

The ostler grinned. "Yes sir, Mr. Maitland. They got punch an' beer and an' anythin' ye want inside.''

S.T. held up his arm. "Fine thing, when a man's . . . bloody . . . wife . . . don' like him. Damn fine thing, I sh-ay. Calls me 'Toad,' does she?'' He waved his hand slowly back and forth in the air, staring at it. "Wha' d'ye think o' that, hmmm? Bloody . . . bitch.''

"Aye, Mr. Maitland. Look here—we're gonna take ye inside now.'' The young ostler grabbed S.T.'s arm at the same time another groom grabbed the other. Together, they hauled him to his feet. He hung heavily on the shoulder of the nearest.

"Eggstra oats,'' he mumbled, and gripped the ostler's arm. He put his face against the stable boy's neck and fumbled for his purse. "Rub 'im down, you hear? Good ol' horse. An' give him a' egg . . . eggstra measure. Here—thas f' you, m' fine fellow.'' He put the whole purse in the ostler's hand. "Take whatever ye want.''

"Yes sir. But he ain't yer horse, I'm sorry, sir.''

S.T. lifted his head. "Yesh he is.''

"No, he ain't, sir.''

S.T. stared blearily at the animal in question. "Yesh he is. Best ol' horse I ever . . . had.''

" 'E ain't yours, Mr. Maitland.''

S.T. pushed himself off the stable boy and swung around to face him, with both hands on the youth's shoulders. "How d'ye . . . know he ain't m' horse?'' he asked earnestly. "How d'you know?''

"Ye don't have a horse, sir.''

S.T. considered that. He stared into the ostler's face. swaying slightly. "I 'us ridin' him, washt I?''

"Aye, ye were ridin' 'im right enough. Took 'im without even a by your leave, sir. Put us all in dustup, ye did. Rode right off in the dark on Mr. Piper's horse so fast we didn't even know which way to go after.''

"Did?'' S.T. hiccuped and frowned. He closed his eyes. "Must'a been . . .''

He reeled, and put his arms around the ostler. "Must'a been . . ."

He groaned into the ostler's ear, breathing hard.

". . . *drunk,*" he proclaimed, and slid down into a senseless heap on the ground.

Leigh started up at the heavy pounding on her door. She'd been listening to the thudding commotion in the corridor outside, expecting it to pass by. After a long evening of trying to soothe the hapless Mr. Piper, making endless promises of restitution and agreeing wholeheartedly with his every muttered curse, she opened the door with considerable trepidation.

The sight that met her eyes did nothing to reassure her. Behind the landlord, who carried a hat and a damp cloak over his arm, two puffing stable boys held the Seigneur hung between them. The one in front dropped his feet, and the one in back tried to haul him up by his armpits. He mumbled unintelligibly, sliding back down to the floor.

She closed her eyes, able to smell the alcohol from inside the door. "For God's sake." With a furious shift of her skirts, she stood back. "Bring him in," she snapped.

The ostlers picked him up again and waddled forward with their burden swaying between them. Nemo slipped past them and jumped onto the bed. They shouldered the limp body up onto the mattress beside the wolf, and then the younger of the two put the Seigneur's purse on his chest. " 'E said to take what we wished, mum—but I don't think maybe he might mean it in th' mornin'."

The Seigneur held out his arm, and let it drop, hanging off the side of the bed. "Give ish—" he muttered, and lifted his arm again, groping with his gloved hand at the purse. He spilled Rye banknotes all over his fine velvet coat, and closed his fingers around a thick roll. "Vela good . . . fellow . . ." He held out the notes toward Leigh. "Give ish—plenty . . . madam."

She plucked the money from his slack fingers. "Good God—where did all this come from?"

The landlord smiled amiably, hanging the hat and cloak in the wardrobe. "I advanced him a bit from the till this evening, 'ere he could make a call at the money shop. 'Tis all in order, Mrs. Maitland. Would you like me to send someone to—ah—ready him for bed?''

"No," she said, and began to rummage in the purse. "He can sleep in his boots, for all I care."

"Fishteen," the Seigneur mumbled. "Fishteen . . . pounds. Fine fellow." He lifted his lashes. "Shtole his horse."

She blew out an explosive breath. "You besotted ass."

He started to giggle. "Fishteen pa—pounds . . . madam!"

She pressed a half crown apiece into the stable boys' hands.

The Seigneur rolled onto his side, still giggling. He listed an instant at the edge of the bed, and then fell over with a crash. He lay on the floor, glaring fuzzily at her. "Gish 'im fishteen . . . y'silly bitch."

"Oh, certainly, you drunken cod's head." She turned to the first ostler and counted out the extraordinary fortune of fifteen pounds in a loud voice. "You may split it and retire in luxury," she snapped, and looked over her shoulder. "Satisfied?"

The Seigneur didn't answer. His eyes had closed. One hand twitched, and he emitted a soft snoring sound.

Leigh looked up at the landlord. "That will be all," she said with magnificent stiffness.

"Certainly, madam." He hardly cracked a smile as he made a deep bow. He turned away and shepherded the ostlers out of the room. She heard them break into whoops before they were halfway down the stairs.

She put her hands over her eyes and lifted her face toward the ceiling. "God, how I hate you!" she cried. "Impossible beast! Why did you come back at all?"

"I had a mind to finish what you started," said a soft, lucid, and perfectly distinct voice.

She jumped back, dropping her hands and staring down at him.

He pushed up on his elbow and lifted a finger to his lips. "Don't screech, if you please," he murmured.

It was almost as startling as seeing a corpse rise up and

speak. She stood with her hand over her breast, her heart pounding.

He hiked himself to his feet, quite steadily, and motioned Nemo off the bed.

"What are you about?" she hissed.

He pulled off his neckcloth, sniffed at the linen and grimaced. "Alas! I smell like the parlor carpet in Mother Minerva's bawdy house."

"For the love of God—where have you been? What's the meaning of this?"

He tossed the offending fabric on the floor and reached out to catch her elbow in one gloved hand. He drew her to his side and bent his head near her ear. "Why, 'tis a gift, *ma petit chérie.*" His voice was low and mocking. Turning over his hand, he slipped a finger inside his glove and drew out necklace that flashed and shimmered in the candlelight. "You didn't care for the expense of the first one," he said against her ear. "So I've brought you another . . . with a price more to your taste."

The magnificent jewels dangled, shedding prisms of diamond light.

She closed her eyes. "Oh my God," she said softly.

"What think you, my lady?" His breath caressed her throat. "Have I pleased you at last? I was told it was a lover's bauble, worthy of a lady's tears." He lifted his hand and traced his forefinger in a curve beneath her eyelashes, as if to brush away a drop. "Will you weep for me?"

"All too soon, I'm afraid," she whispered. The glove felt hot and supple, heated by his hand. The suspended stones grazed her skin. "When you hang for this."

"Oh, no," he murmured. "Have a little faith." He passed his other hand beneath the nape of her neck and spread his gloved fingers on her cheek, pressing her to turn her face toward him. "Weep for delight." He smiled darkly and kissed the corner of her mouth. *"Ma perle. Ma lumière. Ma belle vie.* Weep because I've made you happy."

"You have not made me happy." She bit her lip and turned her face away. "You've made me afraid."

His hand tightened, drawing her back. She resisted, but he had somehow caught control of the moment. His suppressed energy seemed to inflame the quiet room. She couldn't defend herself; couldn't find the antagonism amid her dismay. He moved behind her, pulling the gauzy lace fichu from her bodice, baring her shoulders.

"I don't want it," she exclaimed. "I'll not have it."

He slipped the necklace around her and clasped it. His hands cupped her throat, slid upward, holding her steady as he kissed the nape of her neck. "Do you spurn the Seigneur's token, sweet?" he breathed. " 'Tis a gift. An emblem of my passion for you." His touch compelled her; his soft voice smoldered with an uncanny force. "Take pleasure in it with me."

"No. Remove it." She put her hands to her mouth.

"Non, non, petite chou—why should I do such a foolish thing? I brought it for you. I love you. I wish to see you admired and beautiful. But you tremble, *chérie.* " He caressed her leisurely, nibbling and playing, touching her with his tongue. "Of what are you afraid?"

You, she thought. *What have you done?*

What are you doing to me?

The heat of his kisses went through her in little jets of sensation. She bent her head. He caught her around the waist and pressed his mouth to the slope of her bared shoulder. His hands pulled her back into him.

She bit hard on her lip. "You're a reckless fool."

He shook his head against her throat. "My absurd chick—I am the Seigneur du Minuit, am I not? To delight you I would hazard any peril."

"They'll catch you," she whispered.

He laughed softly. "Not this time." He began to work at the ribbons that laced the front of her bodice. "And why should you care, cold heart? I thought you wished me well gone."

She held herself stiff. " 'Tis not your neck that concerns me, but my own," she said cruelly. "I'll not swing with you. Not for this."

"No—I wouldn't like that. Love me instead." One by one, without letting go of her, he pulled off his gloves and dropped them. With experienced assurance, his fingers worked open her embroidered stomacher. All the time, he kissed and fondled her, his golden tinged head bent to her shoulder and her throat, his black ribbons trailing down between them. The gown drooped off her arms. He pushed it down and pulled the shoulder ties and eyelets on her corset free.

Leigh breathed in agitated gusts, unnerved, standing powerless amid the ruins of her barricades. She'd allowed this too far; let him take her by surprise; propel her uneasy balance into a tumble of confusion.

"Je suis aux anges," he said reverently as the rigid garments fell away, leaving only her petticoat and a sheer chemise that the landlady had provided for her. He made a low sound and pulled her back against his chest, enfolding her breasts in his palms. "Leigh," he whispered. He gave her throat a silken kiss. "You make me insane."

She tilted her head back against him. He stroked her nipples and her lips parted. With a faint, hopeless murmur, she said, "Clearly I do."

He laughed low in her ear. The stolen necklace seemed to burn where it lay against her skin.

He knew how to undress a woman. Her stiffened petticoat presented no puzzle; deftly he released eyelets and allowed the linen cage to fall as her skirt sighed into a pile of silk around her feet. He drew her back against him; she could feel the buttons on his waistcoat and the velvet of his cuffs, the drift of his lace over her exposed shoulders.

"You're trembling still," he said. "Are you cold, *mignonne?"*

"I'm afraid," she cried softly. "I'm afraid!"

"We're safe here. There's no one coming." He rocked her gently. "Perhaps tomorrow there may be questions, but I've answers ready enough."

She pushed away desperately, retreating to the other side of the room, holding her arms crossed, shivering in her chemise. "You've changed! I don't like it."

"I'm myself. The Seigneur du Minuit." He stood watching her, all bronze and shimmer in his embroidered velvet. His green eyes lowered. He smiled slightly. *"C'est possible* . . . you like it too much, mmhh?''

She leaned against the bedpost, breathing deeply. He came toward her, and she backed up to the wall. His hands hit the oaken panels on either side of her head, trapping her there. He bent and kissed the base of her throat greedily, searing her skin against the diamond necklace.

A feeling rolled through her, a deep thumping pleasure. She had experienced this before, felt the rising excitement as she'd bathed him, the desire that threatened to drown her reason.

It was too much. She shook her head, pressing back against the wall. "I can't," she said. "I can't, I can't."

"Why not?" He leaned his shoulder against the paneling beside her and drew his finger up the curve of her breast, watching intently as he stroked the tip. "Because it isn't 'business'? Because you're not so cold as you'd have me think?"

She tried to shove away, but his arm came up beneath her breasts, an inflexible barrier.

"Oh, no, my little tease. Your reckoning is upon you now."

Her breath came in uneven gasps; her chin lifted and her back arched as he held her, pushing her into the wall, pressing his lips to her bare skin. He seemed larger than he'd ever seemed before, stronger than she'd understood. She strained to break free and could not do it.

"I loathe you," she said.

"Eh bien. I can feel that you do." His hand cupped her breast, his thumb teasing the nipple. "In truth," he purred, "it's remarkable, this loathing you have for me."

"Bastard!"

He only smiled at her vicious epithet. "Aye, *ma pauvre,* of course I'm a bastard. I've said so all along, haven't I?" He stroked her cheek very gently, kissed her temple softly. As he gazed down at her, the mockery faded from his smile. "But I'm at your feet," he whispered. "My life is yours."

Some protective shield snapped inside her. Her eyes watered. He gathered her up in his arms, holding her hard against his chest. For a moment her breathing was beyond her control, almost a sob. "I hate you," she said plaintively, her face in his coat.

"Then come hate me in bed." There was new tension in his voice. "I want you, Leigh. I can't—I've got to have you now."

She shuddered, with his mouth on her chin and her throat and her breasts. He lifted her, took her to the bed, pushing her down before she was halfway on it. His breathing was husky and uneven, brewing passion. His hands fumbled, slid the chemise up above her waist.

"Leigh," he whispered hoarsely, moving his palms up and down her naked hips. He stood between her legs, leaning over her, still fully dressed: gold and velvet and emerald, masculine and elegant; his face like something from an ancient dream, like a warrior prince from a forest kingdom. He bent his head and kissed her belly. His fingertips seemed hot; she let him touch her and didn't pull away.

He scooped her up, put his knee on the bed, and lifted her; and she realized that he wasn't going to wait, wasn't going to undress himself or put out the candles or be civilized; he was kissing her fiercely and loosening buttons at the same time, and then he was on her, shoving into her with his hands at her hips, pulling her toward him; breathing hard and raggedly and saying her name over and over.

She put her arms around his neck. His kiss was wide open against her mouth as his body drove into her. The sensation engulfed her: the force of him, his hands pressed into her buttocks, pulling her up into him in his own impassioned cadence.

She wanted to cry out; she couldn't seem to breathe deeply enough for the sensation that dilated and spread inside her. She pressed upward and he drove over her, harder and harder, his thrusts pulling something impossible from within her, something crazy and frightening that she could not defend against.

He gripped her to him. She heard him making low sounds as if words were throttled in his chest, as if he were crying. A deep tremor passed through him and into her, a powerful instant of suspension, with his face pressing into the curve of her shoulder.

Then, with a harsh rush of air between his teeth, he relaxed. He rested his forehead against her breast, breathing deeply, pulling back a little to put his weight on his hands.

She felt him trembling with the awkwardness of the position, and it dawned upon her with a shaky, hysterical little spurt of humor that he still had one foot on the floor.

"What the devil's funny?" he muttered between his teeth.

She didn't know what to do with her hands. Tentatively, she touched his hair with fingers that felt weak and clumsy. "You still have your boots on."

He slid his arms beneath her. "Bastards never take their boots off," he said, his voice muffled against the mattress beside her ear. Then he pushed up, away from her, and stood.

He tilted his head. Faintly, he smiled at her.

Leigh felt precarious, painfully shy, sitting up and fussing at her chemise to cover herself. But he reached over and took it by the hem, pulling it over her head in one sweep.

"Under the bedclothes, *chérie*," he ordered, kissing the top of her head. When she hesitated, he flung back the sheets, picked her up bodily, ignoring her faint squeak, and deposited her in a heap upon the pillows. Then he stood back and began to undress, taking no trouble for modesty.

She watched him pull off the velvet coat, hang it up, and shrug out of his glittering waistcoat. The full-sleeved shirt fell into a white puddle on the floor. He dragged the ribbon out of his hair. In open breeches and bare chest, he stood over the jack, pulling off his boots, looking utterly heathen with his loose hair in a gilded tumble of chocolate shadow across his shoulders.

Nemo got up and snuffled at his stocking feet. He knelt beside the wolf and embraced and stroked it: long, hard strokes that made the animal lie down and roll over and wriggle with delight.

Leigh bit her lip. Her lungs felt queer and trembly. She drew a deep breath and pulled the sheet up to her chin.

As the Seigneur stood up, Nemo bounded to the door, sticking his nose to the crack and then looking over his shoulder hopefully.

"We've had our hunt for tonight, old man," the Seigneur said. "Time to bask in our well-deserved glory."

Leigh put her hand to her throat, recalling the stolen necklace with a jolt.

"Leave it on," he said, as she reached for the clasp. He strolled over to the bed and sat down, teasing the sheets away from her. "It's most becoming," he murmured, lifting the jewels with his forefinger.

"Oh, yes. A most flattering noose. I don't know why you're so proud of yourself."

He traced a line down to the tip of her breast. "Ah, but look what it won me."

She dropped her eyes. "You are mistaken."

"Am I?" The devil's brows cocked in interest.

"Yes. I didn't—I wasn't impressed by your so monstrous wonderful necklace. That wasn't why I let you—" She pushed his caressing hand away. "That wasn't it."

"Oh? But what else is a man to conjecture? Your sex is beyond our poor male powers of logic."

"Forgive me, but I find discussing logic with a madman to be a futile exercise."

He smiled. "Perhaps more useful than discussing it with a woman."

"You didn't buy me with a diamond necklace!"

He leaned over and kissed her cheek gently. "No, did I say so? You are a silly *enfant*. You understand nothing."

He left the bed and snuffed the candles. She heard him move around the room. When he came back and slid under the sheets, she turned away, but his arms enfolded her, pulling her against him. He was naked and warm, a startling sensation—luxurious, his body as smooth as the velvet of his coat.

It was all a dream, she knew . . . she'd finally let herself fall into the dream world that he built and lived in.

I am the Seigneur du Minuit, am I not?

Absurd man.

Charming, witless, dangerous lunatic.

His breath ruffled her hair. She thought of pulling away, but it seemed fruitless after everything else. There was fear waiting out there in the dark, fear and memories and feelings that she could not bear, but here in his arms 'twas as if her mind had separated from her body, and she did not think farther than physical awareness, the sensual heat of his embrace.

She didn't care. She could not think. Dreams were enough for the night.

THIRTEEN

S.T. made love to her again, just before dawn. He woke up enfolded in warmth, with Nemo lying heavily against his back and Leigh's body soft and luscious in his arms, all in a heap as if they were a pack of wolves curled together on a snowy night. For a long time he just lay there, enjoying the sensation.

His own little family, he thought.

The notion made him amorous. He brushed back her hair and put his arm across her, tasting the bare, cushioned skin of her breast. She turned her head quickly toward him, and he realized that she hadn't been asleep. She shoved at him a little, as if in protest, but he moved on top of her and pushed easily inside, working slowly, kissing and caressing her throat.

He came in a rush of pleasure, holding her face between his palms, savoring her mouth. When it was over, he wanted to do it again. He didn't want to move away, so he lifted himself on his elbows. *"Bonjour,* mademoiselle," he murmured. "I trust you slept well?"

She didn't answer. He could feel the small shudders that flowed through her body, the way she shifted and pressed him restlessly. He smiled into her shoulder.

Ah, the things he had to teach her.

In the first blush of dawn, the diamond necklace cast a shower of tiny sparks around her neck. He remembered his own business and worked at the jewels until the clasp came open under his fingers. He pulled the necklace free and rolled over, trying to sit up, battling Nemo for space on the bed while the wolf tried to lick his face.

Nemo won. S.T. finally lay back, sputtering, while the wolf straddled him, holding down his shoulders with huge paws and subjecting his face to a thorough wash. Then Nemo began play biting at S.T.'s nose and trying to dance around on the bed, which included a heavy strut on S.T.'s stomach. He grunted and shoved, Leigh sat up, and Nemo started back at the sight of her, recoiling as if she were a horrific monster rising out of the sheets.

The wolf retreated to the end of the bed, standing on S.T.'s feet. For a full minute, Nemo stared at Leigh. It was his thoughtful look: his ears pricked, his yellow eyes holding a penetrating, quizzical stare, his head tilted slightly in concentration.

She didn't move. S.T. wondered if she was afraid. That unblinking gaze conjured up the primeval night, eyes glowing in the shadows, all the human dread of what was wild and dark. He wasn't certain himself what Nemo might do—he never really was—but he contained any move that might frighten or annoy the animal. She made Nemo nervous, and an anxious wolf was an unpredictable one.

Nemo's head lowered slightly. He sniffed at S.T.'s leg, and then took a step up the bed. The wolf tilted his head again, staring into Leigh's eyes. Then he dropped his nose, and with a brute's complete lack of reserve, began to explore carefully at the sheet over her, paying particular attention to the interesting scents between her legs.

"You bloody *voyeur,*" S.T. muttered. "Have a little delicacy."

But Nemo wasn't to be disturbed. He examined Leigh painstakingly, moving farther up the bed, his big paws spreading for balance as the mattress sank beneath him. He looked deeply into her eyes again. Tentatively, he touched her chin with his nose.

"What should I do?" she whispered, so low that S.T. could barely hear her.

"Pet the pushy devil," he said.

She lifted her hand and stroked Nemo's ears. He licked her face, and she winced and drew back. Nemo leaned forward and made a little dance on his front paws, tucking his chin against his chest as he lifted his forefoot and started to paw at her in wolfish enthusiasm.

S.T. reached over and cuffed the wolf's nose, growling a warning. Nemo quailed back instantly, his tail flagging. He gave up on his short-lived romance and sank down contritely, crawling over to S.T. for reassurance. S.T. stroked him and scratched his ears. The wolf sighed, pressed up against him, and gently took his hand between its teeth.

"Trying to steal my lady, are you?" S.T. cupped Nemo's head and gave the wolf a playful shake. Nemo flopped down between them, rolling over as far as he could in the narrow space, his eyes closed in ecstasy as S.T. scratched the furry belly.

Leigh slowly put out her hand. She rested it on the wolf's thick ruff, and Nemo stretched his head back and licked her wrist, his long, ardent tongue curling around her arm.

S.T. looked up at her. "Now you have a pack," he said simply.

In the early light, her face was still. She stroked the wolf. When S.T. took his hand away, Nemo scrabbled over toward Leigh, looking for attention where he could get it. At a pause in the rhythmic movement of her arm, he put his paw on her stomach, fixing his solemn, expectant eyes on her.

She gazed down at him. Her mouth worked. She bit her lips and turned away, flinging back the sheet. "Damn you! Damn you both," she said, and got up.

It was almost seven o'clock when the inevitable knock came. The Seigneur turned over in bed and pulled a pillow onto his head.

Leigh took a deep breath. She'd dressed and finished breakfast hours ago, while he lay abed like the great bag of moonshine that he was, dozing as if there were nothing in the least amiss. With her heart thumping in her throat, she picked up her skirts and turned to the mirror on the dressing table, leaning on her elbow in a negligent pose. "Yes? Come in."

It was the landlord, with Mr. Piper at his heels.

"Forgive me for disturbing you, madam," the inn-keeper said, "I—"

A groan from the bed interrupted him. They all looked toward the lump amid the bedclothes, where nothing showed but a broad back, one slack hand, and a tangle of brown and gold hair.

The hand moved, groping. The Seigneur lifted one corner of his pillow and said, "Ummmpf."

"Forgive me, sir, for the imposition, but—"

"Ale." The voice from the bed had a sepulchral ring. "For God's mercy."

"And put some arsenic in it," Leigh suggested, smiling sweetly at the landlord. Then she peeped behind him. "My dear Mr. Piper!" She stood up. "You wish to speak to my husband, of course. It's so excessively mortifying, but I'm afraid he's not yet up to snuff. I apologize with all my heart. You can't possibly know what a painful trial he is to me."

Mr. Piper, a small, barrel-chested gentleman with a voice very like a frog, gave a bobbing bow. "Indeed, ma'am," he said in his low grate, "I do most sincerely feel for you. But I believe I'm owed some restitution, ma'am—I really must insist on indemnification—especially now, when they're saying 'twas my horse that—"

"*Ale,*" the hollow voice repeated. "Oh, God . . . who the devil's that . . . croaker?"

"That, my darling ass, is poor Mr. Piper. You stole his horse."

"Aye, and near ran the poor creature into the ground, too!" Mr. Piper's rumbling voice rose in indignation. " 'Tis by nothing but the grace of God that he didn't bow a tendon. I've had the groom poultice him, just in case, and walk him gently for an hour this morning. They tell me he's sound, but I've a notion there's a little weakness in that nearside hock."

The Seigneur groaned and peered at his accuser from beneath the pillow. "A regular jaw-me-dead," he mut-

tered, and pulled the corner down. "Go away, before you
. . . kill me."

"I will not go away, sir. I've been waiting since five
o'clock to speak to you—I have business elsewhere, and
the constable wants to impound my horse!" Mr. Piper's
color rose. "I've been interviewed this morning as if I
were a common criminal, and I did not like it, sir! Not
one bit did I like it!"

"Oh, dear—of course you didn't like it," Leigh said,
in the same soothing tone she'd used all the evening before
with him. "Whoever had the impudence?"

"The constable, ma'am! There was a coach robbed on
the Romney road last night, and the culprit rode a horse
with four white stockings, so what must they do but send
out the town crier, and look out every unfamiliar nag with
white stockings in the neighborhood for to interview the
owner! As if a poor honest businessman had any notion
to go out robbing coaches after a hard day's work. They'll
be wanting to speak to your husband, too, ma'am." He
bobbed stiffly toward her again. "Since I don't scruple to
say that I told them he was out on my horse, which is
nothing but God's truth, and I hope for yourself's sake,
ma'am, that he can say where he's been!"

Leigh's heart was beating so hard she felt sure that her
voice must shake, but before she could speak, the Seigneur dragged himself up from the depths of the bed and
sat looking at Mr. Piper with revulsion. He ran his hand
over his face. "What," he said, holding back his hair,
"must I pay to have you thrown bodily from my room?"

"Thirty guineas," Mr. Piper said promptly.

The Seigneur sputtered. "Thirty guineas." He swung
his feet to the floor and sat with the sheet pulled across
his lap, leaning on his knees with his face in his hands.
The queasy groan that leaked out of him made even Leigh
feel a little anxious.

"That's the value of my horse," Mr. Piper said stubbornly. "They're threatening to impound him."

"Don't even remember . . . your bloody horse," the
Seigneur mumbled, spreading his hand on his abdomen.
"Ah damme, but I'm queer."

"I have witnesses, sir. Willing to speak! I must insist
on restitution. I've no wish to bring a formal charge, but
I—"

"Take it." The Seigneur swallowed several times.
"Take it. Take it." He gulped a deep breath and waved
one weak hand. "Just . . . go away and leave me in
peace."

He looked toward Leigh with a helpless appeal that was
outrageous in its credibility. What an amazing fraud he
was! She half believed in his morning-after agony herself.
As he sat there, drooping in his misery, she searched in
his purse with shaking fingers, right past the incriminating
diamond necklace itself, and gave Mr. Piper enough Rye
notes to equal thirty-one pounds, then scrupulously
counted out four crowns in silver.

"And keep your damn nag," the Seigneur muttered.
"Don't want the . . . spavined beast."

"I'm so sorry for the inconvenience, Mr. Piper," Leigh
said, and meant it. "Have they really taken your horse?"

He tucked the notes into his coat. "Not yet, ma'am.
They'll want to speak to *him* first, I warrant." He gave
the Seigneur a lofty glance. "I advise you to do your best
to bring him to a rational state in preparation, ma'am, and
I hope he hasn't been out cutting up stupid larks on honest
gentlemen's horses."

The Seigneur bent over, with an ominous gagging
sound. Leigh moved instinctively toward him, and the
other two men moved instinctively away.

"I'll have a tonic sent up," the landlord said hastily.
"Come along with me, sir—if you're satisfied here."

"Bring the ferryman—" the Seigneur croaked, barely
lifting his head. "I 'member now. Last night—just a little
. . . jollity with the ferryman."

"Very good, Mr. Maitland. I'll have him brought round,
then, to vouch for you to the constable—if such a thing
proves necessary."

The door closed on the pair of them. Leigh stopped,
with her hand on the bedpost. All her limbs felt precarious, as if they might give way with her. The Seigneur lay

back on the bed, his arms behind his head. His mouth curved with immoral humor.

"How tiresome," he murmured. "To choke down a tonic, when I'd far rather have a pork sausage. I don't suppose you thought to save me one off your tray?"

She took a deep breath. "Were you drinking with the ferryman?"

"Sadly, no. I was terrorizing the highroad on a horse with four white stockings all last evening. An unfortunate setback, those stockings. Let us hope my largesse has been well placed."

Leigh bent her head. "And if not?"

"Then they hang me, Sunshine."

She pressed her hand to her temple.

"Don't concern yourself overmuch," he said easily. "I'll attest your innocence to my last breath."

Pushing away from the bedpost, she walked to the window. "I find I cannot—take it all so lightly."

A moment of silence passed. She stared down into the stable yard. Behind her the bed creaked.

"Don't get up," she said sharply. "The tonic—what if someone comes?"

"So they'll see that I've made it to my feet, *chérie*. Cultivate a somewhat more indifferent manner, if you please. You put me all in a flutter."

She closed her eyes, listening to him move about the room and dress, resting her closed fists on the windowsill. Her mind played over and over the coming disaster. Would they burst in and take him by force—or come politely, asking sly questions, expecting to trap him in his story? She imagined him in manacles and had a wild thought of throwing the necklace out the window as far as she could hurl it.

Chains. 'Twould be like the wolf on a leash . . . wrong, wrong, wrong.

He came behind her. She whirled on him, flinging his hands away. "Don't try to touch me! Don't come and say you did it for me."

He went down on one knee with a gallant flourish. "What else am I to say, my love?

"I don't understand why!" she cried softly, looking
down at his familiar full-sleeved shirt, at the gilded hair
retied in black satin. "There was no reason for it."

He turned his face up to her, smiling faintly. "I can't
help myself."

"Nonsense," she snapped. "You're preposterous."

The slight, coaxing smile faded. At a scratch on the
door, he came to his feet and disposed himself in an af-
fecting slump against the post. As soon as a curtseying
housemaid had left his tonic and gone, he opened the window, checked up and down the yard, and poured his morning bracer into the gutter below the sill.

An hour later, the innkeeper came up in person again.
Leigh gripped the arms of her chair. She sat immobile as
the Seigneur bade the landlord enter—with the message
that Mr. Maitland's alibi had been quite confirmed by the
ferryman, Mr. Piper's mount released, and a proclamation
posted with a reward for any information on the missing
horse with white stockings.

"And a pinch-penny reward it is, Mr. Maitland," the
innkeeper said carelessly. "Five pounds!"

"Dog cheap, in fact," the Seigneur said, sitting down
in his riding boots and shirt sleeves at the dressing table.
He folded a piece of paper around some money and rummaged in the stationery box for wax. "Ask one of your
excellent ostlers to carry this to the ferry, will you? Con-
vey my solicitations to the ferryman, and I hope his head
doesn't ache like mine."

"With pleasure, Mr. Maitland." The innkeeper took
the fat envelope and bowed out.

Silence fell. The Seigneur sat looking at himself in the
mirror. He met Leigh's eyes in the glass.

He smiled at her . . . a slow, wicked grin that trans-
formed his face into the devil prince of the green forest.

She stood up. "Iniquitous enough that you've got away
with it," she said, not quite able to keep her voice steady.
"You needn't relish it quite so immoderately!"

"Relish it! That bauble's costing me a fortune, my girl.
Ten pounds to our quick-minded ferryman—and well he

deserves 'em—which brings the sum to . . . let's see . . .
good God, over fifty. I wonder if you're worth it.''

She looked up at him. He appeared to quickly decipher
the expression on her face, for his eyes slid away and he
turned back to the mirror with a demeanor reminiscent of
Nemo sidling cautiously into a corner out of harm's way.

"No doubt you are," he murmured. *"Dolce mia. Car-
issima!"*

"Italian now?" She sat down and laid her head back on
the chair. "A fool in three languages."

"Che me frega," he said in a velvet undertone, flicking
his fingers against the underside of his chin.

If her French was shaky, her Italian was nonexistent.
The words might have been a gutter curse or a lover's
compliment, but the little mocking gesture of those fingers
was as eloquent as any thumbed nose.

He leaned his elbow on the dressing table, toying with
an ivory comb. She frowned at his reflected image, at the
gilt eyebrows with their singular curve that was fiendish
and cheerful at once. His easy speech in an alien tongue
made him seem even more exotic—beyond mere common
humanity: something mad and mercurial, able to conjure
diamonds out of the dark.

He'd his full balance back, she was certain. Since they'd
left the ship, he'd moved easily, confidently, with a freedom and boldness impossible to disregard. The medical
enigma intrigued her. The alchemy of his character fascinated and alarmed her.

Outside in the stable yard, there was a sudden crash.
He turned his head alertly . . . the wrong way, toward the
door.

It was nothing, an upset haycart or some such incident.
Through the open window Leigh could hear voices yelling
in irritated retort, but she was watching the Seigneur. He
stared expectantly at the door for a moment, and then his
mistake dawned on him.

He glanced at her. A dull flush crept up his neck to his
hair.

"Oh, yes," she agreed softly. "You're a sham, aren't
you?"

His mouth grew hard. He stared at the tip of his boot without answering.

" 'Twas not your prowess—'twas nothing but devil's luck got you through this silly trick, was it?"

He brushed his finger back and forth over the feathered tip of the quill in the inkstand.

"I'm not deceived," she said. " 'Twas luck."

"I understand a horse fair begins today at the market," he said stiffly. "Perhaps you would like me to help mount you, mademoiselle."

It felt strange to be female again, to be led around puddles and supported up steps. Between the skirts and borrowed muff and high-heeled shoes and steep, cobbled hills, Leigh found she had to lean on the Seigneur in spite of herself.

She submitted to a sedan chair, more to save herself the threat of a sprained ankle than to avoid the foggy chill. They had shut an unhappy Nemo in the room, and the Seigneur walked beside her, carrying his hat and acting icily polite. Misty sunlight gave his coat and hair a soft gleam, made him a golden idol amid so many dusty chimney sweeps.

One of the ancient fortified gates loomed up like a black cave in the vapor. They passed by it, then wound through the narrow streets into the market square. She lowered the window. The horse fair was in full voice and pungent odor, the square crowded with animals standing in uneven lines for inspection or being trotted out by hand to show their soundness.

"Do you like anything?" he asked, as they moved slowly among the horses.

She tapped the front glass on the chair, and the attendants stopped in front of a pretty bay mare. The Seigneur opened the door, bowing with an excess of formality. One of the chairmen rushed to help her forth.

Several shirt-sleeved men had been eyeing Leigh and the Seigneur as they passed; instantly one of them took the mare's halter and led her out. Her snowy white stockings flashed as she trotted quietly up and down amid the confusion, away from them and back again. She came to a smart halt and stood still under the man's light hold. The Seigneur looked her over critically.

"First rate," he said, bending slightly to speak into Leigh's ear. "Fine points, adequate bone, superb manners. You won't get her for under fifty."

She frowned.

He gave her a sideways glance. "Insufficient funds, Sunshine?"

"As you are quite aware," she said stiffly.

"Pity," he said. "She's a nice little piece."

"I shall sell this dress," she said, keeping her voice low.

"That's won't bring much, I'm afraid."

"You said yourself it was worth four guineas. That will get me to Northumberland. And there are my pearls."

"I said everything in your satchel might bring four," he murmured. "You could get—perhaps fifteen shillings, if you pawned the shoe buckles with the dress, and a good three pounds for the pearl choker. Shall I put 'em on the shelf for you?" he asked ruthlessly. "There's a broker just along the street."

She said nothing, but her eyes dropped.

"You could trade your diamond necklace," he said in a normal tone. "That ought to suffice."

Her head came up sharply. "Are you mad?" she hissed beneath her breath. "Don't speak of that!"

He smiled. "Oh, do you care for it so much?" He took her hand over his arm and patted it. "Never mind, my dear. I can get you another where that one came from."

"No!" she said, digging her fingers into his arm. "Stop it!"

He glanced at the man holding the horse, gave the faintest shake of his head, and walked on. The disappointed horse coper bowed and led the mare back into position.

The Seigneur dismissed the sedan chair and kept her arm. He stopped several more times, causing other animals to be paraded with merely a glance. In velvet and silk, Leigh knew that she and her escort were by far the most expensively dressed of the shoppers. The copers began to go to lengths to attract their attention and jockey potential purchases into good view. The circus atmosphere of the fair heightened in their vicinity, with horses wheeling in circles and being forced hurriedly into their best paces like troops of jugglers preceding a king and queen.

At least one animal registered violent objections to this sudden activity. A few yards ahead of them, just beyond a tall black gelding, a handler was swearing at a big gray with a coat pale enough to be almost milky. The horse lashed out with its forefeet as soon as it was asked to move forward. The Seigneur stopped, applying a light pressure to her arm.

She was glad enough to stay at a safe distance from the battle that suddenly erupted. The gray tossed its head savagely, hauling the handler right off his feet. A circle opened around them. The horse fought, alternately trying to bite and rear, while the handler hung on, yanking at the halter with what Leigh thought was rather foolhardy enthusiasm, until she realized that there was a chain looped over the horse's nose and through its mouth. Traces of blood speckled the animal's lips and chest.

The handler danced out of the way of the well-aimed snap, and just at that moment another man brought a bat down across the horse's nose. It squealed and jerked around, eyes wild. Its head snaked out, and its teeth clamped with deadly ferocity on the culprit's shoulder.

The man screamed and dropped the bat. Amid shouts and bedlam, the horse shook its attacker as if he were a rat in a terrier's mouth. The man staggered as the animal let him go, gobbling incoherently and clutching his shoulder while he stumbled to safety. The handler had managed to knot the lead around an iron ring in the wall and scramble out of range while the horse was occupied. As soon as everyone cleared back, the gray horse stood still, sweating and swishing its tail angrily. Bright blood ran down its nose.

The Seigneur moved forward, walking slowly around the horse in the open circle that had formed surrounding it. The gray swiveled its ears back, following his movement and breathing gustily, blowing cloudy vapors in the cold air. It swerved away from him and cocked a hind leg dangerously as he bent to examine its underside from a yard's distance.

"Recently cut?" He looked at a coper who was standing impassively by.

"Aye. Ye can see why. Rogue stallion—Spanish, if I was to judge." He turned his head and spat. "Dunno where he come from, but he's made the rounds of every stable in the countryside. Wasn't a stall that would hold him, and he ain't never been backed. Tossed 'em all what tried." He nodded toward the man who'd been bitten. "Poor old Hopkins there's trying to fob him off now—fool thought maybe gelding would take care of it, but as you can see, it ain't. He'll be off to the knacker's yard—nowhere else to go after Hopkins. Nice pair with that black, though, ain't he? They been the rounds together."

"Very pretty," the Seigneur said, looking at the second horse. "Perhaps Mr. Hopkins will speak to me when he recovers."

The coper spat again and chuckled. "Oh, he'll recover quick enough when 'e hears that. Jobson, say! Tell yer master to get on his feet and wait on me lord!"

Poor Hopkins obeyed with as much alacrity as he could muster; his rather bull-like face was chalky as he made his way toward them.

"I'm interested in the black," the Seigneur said, nodding toward the second horse of the pair. "You will kindly show me his teeth."

Hopkins snapped at a hostler, and the Seigneur was given the opportunity to view the horse's teeth, to run a hand down each of its legs and watch the handler pick up its feet, to view it trotting away and back on a long lead, to see it take a bridle calmly over its ears, and in short, have most of his commands fulfilled with delight.

"I would like to see him ridden," the Seigneur announced.

"Surely, m'lord. I'll get a saddle fetched an' you like,

m'lord. But I'm an honest man, by the Bible, and I'd be lyin' an' I didn't tell you that this 'ere animal, I've schooled 'im to be driven to a carriage. If it's a riding 'oss your lordship be desirous of, I've got—''

"Never mind. I'll give you ten for him as he stands."

"Oh, sir, m'lord—'' Hopkins began to swing his broad shoulders reluctantly. "I didn't never think you 'us a man to be wastin' me time, m'lord. You're a 'orseman, sir, so's I see. You know 'e's worth a century an' 'e's worth a groat."

The Seigneur smiled gently. "Nothing of the sort. Particularly since I'll have to take that evil beast that savaged you along with him."

A general chuckle broke out at this. Hopkins scowled around at the rest. "I can see no need for that m'lord. By goles, I tol' ye I do be the honest 'un, 'oo stands up by his mis-culculations. You could not give me no hamount o' money, no sir, to let some poor innocent creature take on that rogue. I'll be seein' to 'im, never fear."

"No doubt you will." The Seigneur shrugged. "Very well—I'll give you a hundred for this one, then . . . on the condition that I see you take him out of the square alone. Without the rogue, my good man."

This simple request seemed to leave Hopkins at a stand. Then he said huffily, "Do you think I'd cheat you, sir? Ye'd see me damned first! I do be 'appy to take fifty now and fifty 'pon delivery. You just go on along to your tea, and this 'ere 'oss will be baited at the stable of your choosin' afore dark."

"Mr. Hopkins," the Seigneur said patiently. "I've no interest in that. You and I, and I daresay every other local man here, are quite aware that this horse will not leave the vicinity of the other animal without creating an excessively unpleasant scene. If I want the one, I'll have to take the other. I'm willing, You'll won't get a penny on the pound from the knacker."

"Give over, Hopkins," someone said. "The man's got 'is eyes wide open."

"I do, you know," the Seigneur said kindly. "There's no hope of passing your flummery off on me."

"Well," Hopkins sputtered. "By the Lord Harry!"

"I'll give you twelve for the two," the Seigneur said, "just because you're an honest man."

Hopkins looked sullen, but he nodded. After a quick darting glare in the direction of the bystander who'd spoken up, he stuck out his hand. The Seigneur barely touched it for an instant and paid in Rye banknotes from his own purse.

"I'll send you word where to take them," he said, and offered his arm to Leigh again.

"Awake upon every suit," she said tartly as they strolled away. "Quite the horse trader. If the pair truly won't be separated, what use is the one you bought?"

"I know horses," he said briefly. He was watching another two men arguing over a leggy chestnut with a white blaze. It appeared that the gentleman holding the horse's lead wished to return his purchase to the coper, vehemently complaining that it refused to cross any body of water under any kind of duress whatsoever—not to mention the flighty beast had backed his new curricle into a tree in an attempt to avoid the ferry. The coper was equally vehement in denying any intention of taking the animal back. As the level of their voices rose, the chestnut horse danced uneasily, its ears pricked and its head lifted.

The Seigneur looked down at her. "Do you fancy him for yourself?"

"Not at all. I fear there are a few streams between here and the north."

"I can take care of that."

She glanced at him, hardly knowing whether to believe in such simple confidence or not.

He was watching the horse. "I like his lines. He'll carry you north, and no mistake. That poor coxcomb who bought him's in a desperate lather. I can get him for a whistle," he said.

Still she hesitated. The owner of the chestnut was shouting at the dealer. It was quite apparent that the seller had no intention of taking the animal back at any price. "Perhaps I'll ride the stage," she said warily.

He looked down at her. "You don't believe me," he said.

"I think you're monstrous full of yourself."

He lifted one eyebrow lazily. "Would you like to place a wager on it, madame?"

Fourteen

L EIGH stood beside an oval paddock, shivering a little
inside the Seigneur's old buff coat, back in her
breeches at his personal request. She felt more conspicuous than before when no one had guessed she was
female. But if she got numerous interested glances from
the small crowd of horse copers and farm boys who ranged
around the paddock ready to watch the show, it was worth
the freedom of wearing boots.

No one would touch her or make a rude remark, that
she knew by now. The eccentric Mr. Maitland, with his
sword and his odd starts, seemed to have a certain reputation in the neighborhood of Rye: a smuggler's town,
where audacity—and money under the table—spoke far
more loudly than the law.

In the cold air, the sound of hooves beat a low, excited
thud, interspersed with the shrill call of the black that the
Seigneur had purchased that morning. It cantered recklessly back and forth in the oval paddock, neighing frantically in the direction of a distant pasture, where the
Seigneur's rogue and the blaze-faced chestnut tore along
the fence line with their tails in the air.

The Seigneur stood in the center of the little paddock
with a long driving whip. He was in his shirt sleeves in
spite of the chill; his velvet coat and embroidered vest
reposed safely in the arms of a wide-eyed dairymaid sitting on a stump. The horse completely ignored him, flinging clods of earth as it arched its neck and dashed at a

197

high-stepping trot from one end of the enclosure to the other in its desperation to rejoin the other horses. It skidded to a halt at the fence, hurled itself around, and galloped the other way.

"Look at this," the Seigneur said quietly. He addressed himself to Leigh, disregarding the horse as wholly as it disregarded him. "Do you think this animal's paying any attention to what I want?"

The horse chose that moment to pound past within a foot of him, snorting and blowing frost in the frigid air.

"No," Leigh said. "I can't say that I do."

"Watch, then. I'm going to teach you something that's not *luck*, Sunshine."

She leaned on the fence. Nemo bumped his nose at her waist, and she rubbed his head. He sat down next to her and leaned on her leg.

"The first thing I want this chap to know," he said, "is that he's not alone in here." He lifted the whip, which had a long, stiff shank doubled by the length of its lash, and gave it a sharp crack. The horse flinched at the sound, glanced at him, and continued to canter around the paddock.

He cracked the whip again. This time, when the horse came barreling around the pen, the Seigneur took a few steps sideways, as if to walk into its path. The animal skidded to a wild-eyed stop, turned tail, and went the other direction around the ring. After one revolution, the Seigneur stepped forward, cracked the whip, and changed the gray's direction again. The horse circled the paddock, then threw its weight on its haunches, as if to stop and call out to the others, but the Seigneur moved behind it, brandishing the whip and making a chirruping noise, driving on the horse without ever touching the animal or even coming close.

"Now does he know I'm here?" he asked.

Leigh watched the horse's high head carriage and plunging gallop. The sound of its blowing was loud in the quiet air. "Barely," she said.

"Right. Watch him looking off over the fence all the time while he goes. He's not thinking about me; he's thinking about having a champagne punch and a rubber of whist over there with the other fellows.'' He stepped again to the side and turned the horse with a cluck and snap of the whip. ''I don't want the fence holding him in—I want his attention keeping him here. How am I going to get that?''

She frowned a little. ''Are you going to whip him?''

''My sweet love—that's a stupid guess. Is he going to stay here if I hurt him?''

She pursed her lips.

''Not if *I* hurt him, no,'' he said. ''But if something else hurts—if his lungs hurt, and his muscles ache—and I'm the agreeable fellow who lets him rest . . . then we open a negotiation, hmm? We begin to communicate.''

He flourished the whip and took a step, forcing the horse to turn. She could see the relaxed concentration in his face, the way he never took his eyes off the horse as he spoke, the familiar way he handled the whip. Every motion he made was smooth and deliberate.

''For now, I just want to control one thing—the direction he's going,'' he said. ''These are the lessons for the present: he can run like the devil, the faster the better . . . but he has to run the way I want him to go, he has to turn when I ask, and he can't stop unless I let him.''

He pushed the horse on every time it showed any slight inclination to slow on its own, popping the whip and forcing the animal to turn around and run in the opposite direction whenever its attention strayed over the fence, which was frequently. Over and over, he repeated the sequence, until the horse began to breathe in heavy gusts.

Its shrill calls for the other horses had stopped: the black had no time for that now. It gradually became too distracted by the whip and where the man in the paddock might step next. Within a quarter hour, the Seigneur had only to hold up the whip and point it toward where the horse was headed to make the black slide to a stop, whirl around, and run the other way.

''Watch the way he turns when he changes direction,'' the Seigneur said. ''See—it's always outward, away from me, toward the fence. He'd still rather not be in here with me. I want him to start to turn inward, with his head toward me. I want him to learn that it's more pleasant to pay attention to me than to keep running around like a fool.''

The next time he stepped in the horse's course, he kept his shoulders relaxed and the whip lowered. The black skidded back on its heels and turned tail, swinging its head outward again. The Seigneur's whip came up and drove him on with that insistent pop.

''No luck that time. I'll ask him again,'' the Seigneur said. ''I'm giving him a chance—do you see what I'm doing?'' He lowered the whip and stepped toward the horse's path. ''I'm quiet; I'm not clucking, I'm not using the whip. I'm offering him a pause.''

This time the animal hesitated for an instant, flinging its head in his direction before it scrambled around with its rump toward him once more.

''There,'' he said. ''He's thinking about it. He's got his brain working now.''

He dropped the tip of the whip again as he moved, and amazingly, the sweating horse did swing its forefeet inward and its rump to the fence, giving the Seigneur and the whip a good swift look before it trotted off the other way.

There was a faint murmur of appreciation from the audience.

The Seigneur drove the horse around the ring a few times with the whip, then relaxed his arm. The black turned instantly inward—and this time it stopped, staring at the Seigneur, its flanks heaving.

''Clever fellow,'' he said caressingly. He took two steps to one side. The animal's head swung, its large dark eyes riveted to him. The Seigneur walked the other way, with the same result. He kept walking, and the horse's head followed him, turning so far that it had to shift its hindquarters in a circle around its forefeet as the Seigneur walked, until the animal was facing exactly the opposite direction from where it had been before.

''Now is he paying attention to me?''

Leigh couldn't suppress a smile. ''Yes.''

A distant whinny brought the horse's head up and around. Instantly, before the animal could respond to the call, the Seigneur cracked the whip and sent the horse back into a canter around the ring. After a number of revolutions and turns, he gave it another chance to stop. The horse halted facing him, blowing hard, and took a few steps in his direction.

Another faint call came from the distance. The panting black lifted its head as if to answer, heard the Seigneur's chirrup, and abruptly dropped its nose, staring at him. It seemed to be weighing its options, daring another glance toward the far pasture. The Seigneur clucked again and lifted the whip a fraction. The black jerked its head slightly at the warning, and then the taut muscles in its neck relaxed. It ambled over to the Seigneur, the picture of total surrender, and stood with its head lowered next to him.

He scratched its ears, murmuring softly.

A ragged round of applause made the horse lift its head for an instant, but then it dropped its poll again and pushed gently at the Seigneur's arm. When he walked toward the fence, the black followed him like a huge puppy, ignoring the repeated whinnying from the far pasture.

Leigh felt a strange tug in her chest at the sight. What an extraordinary man he was.

The horse took an introduction to Nemo with complete aplomb, giving the wolf no more attention than a barnyard cat. After that, it seemed only reasonable that the Seigneur could quite easily introduce a saddle and bridle, and mount while the black stood quietly. Before noon, he'd ridden it in the paddock, and then outside, heading away from the excited calls of the other horses until he was completely out of sight.

When he'd returned and dismounted, he took a deep swig of water from a long-handled cup that someone offered. There were plenty of volunteers to take the horse and tend to it; everyone was waiting, hoping he'd tackle the rogue next.

"The Mermaid packed us a basket," he said to Leigh. "You'd best eat." Then he turned to the horse coper Mr.

Hopkins. "Go ahead. Bring the devil over here—any way you can manage it."

While Leigh and the Seigneur ate a silent lunch beneath a tree, half the crowd of locals tramped down the road to watch the new show. The rogue was moved into the paddock by creating a human chain to block the lane and chasing both horses out of the pasture, down the little road, and into the paddock. Then someone caught the more docile chestnut and led it back out to wait with the young black.

The rogue danced along the edge of the paddock for a few minutes, sending spectators back off the fence, then dropped its head to graze. Its ears flicked back and forth furiously as it tore up the grass in quick, ripping grabs.

The Seigneur stood and held out his hand to Leigh. She allowed him to help her to her feet, feeling his fingers warm and strong beneath her elbow as he led her a little distance from the spectators ranged along the fence. She waited while he frowned intently at the gray rogue. It was a magnificent horse in spite of the bloody scars on its face; as pale as moonlight on ice, with a flowing, tangled mane and a tail that dusted the ground. When it flung up its head at some disturbance, the great brown eyes showed white and its neck arched, so that it looked like some fierce, noble mount in a painting of a soldier king.

"Just remember," the Seigneur murmured, "he's frightened of you."

She turned her head. "Of me!"

"Aye. You saw what I did. You can do the same with this one."

"Are you mad?" she exclaimed.

"Not at all. I showed you how." His lips curled a little. "It's not *luck*, after all."

"For God's sake. I won't go in there with that animal."

He gave her a slight frown, as if he was surprised to find he didn't quite approve of her. "He's frightened," he repeated.

"He savaged a man."

"What would you do if somebody held you down and beat you across the face?"

She drew in a breath and gave a shaky laugh. "I know I've insulted you." She looked at him. "You want me trampled to death in return?"

"You're afraid!" he said, in a voice of soft astonishment. "The girl who plans to murder the Reverend Mr. Chilton."

She was stung into turning away from him. "It's not the same thing."

"How do you know?" he asked. "When it comes to the breach, do you think you'll have it in you if you don't have it now?"

She whirled back. "It's not the same!" she hissed. "I *hate* him!"

"It takes more than hate to kill a clever man, Sunshine." His hard words cut the clear air. "It takes brains. I'm trying to teach you something you can use. That horse is a weapon, if you have the nerve to master it."

Her jaw worked. She turned her head, staring at the untamed beast trotting boldly around the paddock. "I thought you meant the chestnut for me," she said at last.

He moved his hand impatiently. "The chestnut will do for a cover hack. But this fellow here—God, look at him! Show him some courage and confidence and he'll take you straight into hell if you ask it."

Just then, the horse bunched its muscles with awesome power, kicked out, and squealed and took off along the length of the paddock, its tail flying. Leigh felt that painful, trembly sensation rise in her chest again at the rapt look on the Seigneur's face. She bit her lip.

He wanted this horse.

And he was forcing it on her. He looked down, his mouth set, his green eyes intent and challenging.

She felt suddenly helpless, that shaky weakness inside trapping words and arguments in her throat. Her cursed lower lip kept threatening to tremble. He lifted her hand and laid the long-handled whip across it, closing her fingers around the braided leather stock.

"I'll help you," he said. "I'll tell you what to do."

She looked at the ground, trying savagely to suppress the telltale quiver of her mouth. "I really don't care if the damned horse kills me," she muttered. She rested the butt of the whip on the springy turf, and then lifted her face to the magnificent devil that pounded down the paddock. She tossed her head. "I don't give ha'pence what happens."

S.T. watched her climb the gate and walk out into the center of the pen. He hardly knew why he'd insisted on this. He could work the horse faster and better; he itched to do it, to help the belligerent, brutalized animal learn that a man was something it could trust.

But she thought he was a sham. She thought it was all luck. Too easy to just go out there and tame this rogue for himself—he wanted her to experience it right down to her toes. He wanted her to fail. And then he could show her.

He wasn't afraid for her safety. The "rogue" wasn't past reclaim. It wasn't heart-deep vicious—just a smart, hot-blooded stallion that had been badly mishandled and discovered every trick to thwart anyone who'd tried to master it. Gelding the animal had been a crime and an abominable waste, but these phlegmatic British never could seem to deal with stallions. They had to cut every animal in sight and harness it to a carriage.

At least Hopkins or some other fool hadn't docked its tail. Likely couldn't throw the beast down long enough.

There was no threat now in the horse's pricked ears and rhythmic snort as it stared at Leigh. It felt itself free—or free enough, for the moment—and warily curious. There was still dark, dried blood smeared on its face and flecked across its chest. It looked as if it hadn't been groomed in weeks; mud spatters and grass stains marred the pale coat, but for all that, it was still the loveliest brute he'd seen since he'd lost Charon. It had stood out in the fair like a grubby Galahad amid the rabble.

S.T. spoke to Leigh in an even tone. "You want to stay a little behind him when you make him move." The horse flicked an ear toward the sound of his voice. "When you ask him to turn, take a step into his path, use the whip and your voice, but give him plenty of room. If you fear he's going to run you down, get out of the way. Don't corner him. And don't just stand there as if you've been planted. Move him on, now.''

She was awkward at it, getting her feet tangled in the whip for a moment before she managed to make it snap. The horse jumped and stood its ground, still staring at her.

"Move him," S.T. repeated. "Show him the drill sergeant's got here now: he can't just slouch around and do anything he likes. He's got to move, and you've got to tell him which way."

She took a step toward the animal's rump, snapping the whip with a motion that didn't quite result in a real crack. But the big gray got the notion. He gathered his haunches and took off running, careening around the paddock at a breakneck pace.

After several minutes of this pounding gallop, S.T. realized she wasn't going to do anything. He raised his voice over the pumping sound of the horse's breathing.

"Make him turn. Just hold out the whip if you're afraid he'll run you down."

"I'm not afraid," she said instantly.

"Then do it, Sunshine."

She took a large step sideways. He thought she looked luscious, spread-legged in her breeches and boots. The gray skidded to a stop as if a nightmare had suddenly materialized in its path, hauled around, and galloped the other way.

"Good," S.T. said. "We're not here just to wear him out—you have to convince him that you're worth listening to. This is a lesson. Turn him again. Keep on until I tell you differently."

She did it, getting tangled in the whip again as she transferred it to the other hand. The gray broke to a wild trot, and her chirrup drove him back to a canter without S.T.'s prompting.

Her face had grown absorbed as she watched the animal move and tried to anticipate its attempts to evade her. The whip seemed to fit more naturally into her hand. She repeated the turning exercise once more, and then again and again.

S.T. watched the horse critically. It took far longer to work the powerful rogue than the black—this animal had a true mind of its own, and convincing the beast that it was responding to direction rather than just desperately escaping a threat was a long, slow process. For a solid hour, he said nothing, just let her turn the horse and turn it again, drive it on and turn it, until the animal's pale coat had gone dark all over with sweat and the sound of its breathing was like steam exploding from a boiler.

"Can't I let him stop?" Leigh cried at last. "This is going to kill him."

Perspiration trickled down her own face. Her cheeks held a bright flush, but she never took her eyes off the circling horse.

"Sweeting, that horse could run for the next three counties. See the way he scrambles around when he turns? He's still convinced you're the devil himself." S.T. squinted at the winded gray. "But he's thinking about it. There—did you catch the way he looked at you instead of stargazing off at the countryside? Next time he does that, lower the whip, relax your stance, and offer to let him turn toward you."

S.T. watched patiently as she missed the first half dozen chances, overlooking subtle changes in the fatigued horse's posture that were as clear as a shout to S.T. The animal gave her every opportunity, dropping its nose and flicking its ears slightly back and toward her as it cantered recklessly along.

S.T. began to feel a twinge of affection for the gorgeous, muddled beast. He always did as his horses approached this point, getting exhausted and earnest, blowing hard with each stride, looking around like confused children for somebody to take charge. Somebody to say it was time to stop running.

"Lower the whip," he said quietly. "Give him a chance to look toward you."

Leigh's mouth was set. She gripped the whip even as she lowered it, her knuckles tight. She stepped forward to turn the horse—and the gray still scrambled around with its rump defiantly toward her as it turned. Its flanks were heaving, sucking air with every desperate breath, but the animal would not surrender to her.

She tried twice more, without S.T.'s encouragement. Both times the horse turned tail, declining to swing its head inward as it changed direction. He could see her frustration in her back, in the way she carried her shoulders.

"I can't do it," she said, without looking away from the horse.

"You're losing your temper," he said.

"I'm tired!" Her voice was quivering. "I don't want to do this. You can do it, if you want."

This was where he had intended to take over. To stride out and assume control and prove his competence.

Instead, he heard himself say, "Try again."

She tried again. It didn't work.

"See?" She glanced at S.T., defiant and vulnerable.

"See what? Don't tell me you're tired; that breaks no squares with me. You're telling him you're angry with every muscle in your body—do you think he's going to stop and ask you why?"

She wiped at a trickle of perspiration with her sleeve and looked away from him with an irritated move. The horse cantered relentlessly on, its shoulders and flanks dark with sweat.

She lifted the whip again, asking the rogue to turn. Once again it spun away from her. Three more times, she repeated the attempt, and three times failed to coax the willful, weary horse to yield her its head. The fourth time the gray showed her its rump, she gave a harsh, defeated sigh and threw down the whip, turning to the gate.

And the gray came to a complete halt, its head hanging, facing toward her at the center of the paddock.

"Hold up," S.T. said instantly.

She looked back.

"Just stand there," he said.

She stared at the blowing horse. They both looked bewildered—a little amazed at the sudden stalemate.

"Let him rest. Let him stay there as long as he will, but the minute he takes his eyes off you, drive him on."

Someone coughed, and the gray jumped, swinging his head toward the sound. Instantly, Leigh's whip came up, and the horse scrambled into a canter.

"Give him another chance," S.T. said after a moment.

She lowered the whip and stepped toward the horse's course. The gray swung its head inward and bounced to a halt, staring at her.

"Good," S.T. said. "Good. Drive him on if he takes his attention away."

But the rogue had made a choice. He stood with his nostrils flaring, drinking in air frantically, his eyes locked on Leigh. She stayed still, the tension in her body gone at last.

After a few minutes, S.T. instructed her to walk in a slow arc around the horse. The animal swung its head as if magnetized, shifting its hind legs, turning in a complete circle around its forefeet in order to keep her in view.

"Take a step straight toward him," S.T. said softly. "If he starts to back off, don't chase him. You walk away before he does."

She obeyed. The horse lifted its head suspiciously. She took another step. S.T. tensed as the horse did, but she caught the signs in time and turned away. The gray lowered its head and walked a few steps after her.

She stopped. The horse stopped. Once again, she took a few steps toward it. The gray looked nervous, moving its head away, and then snapping its attention back to her when she clucked quietly.

"That's it," S.T. murmured. "That's the trick."

In small increments, the horse allowed her to come closer. When she was within a yard, S.T. told her to walk away. The gray followed her.

She faced it again and took a few slow steps forward. Several times the horse almost turned away to run, indecision in every trembling line, in the way it lifted its head and twitched its nose an inch away and then back again at her soft warning chirrups. He could see the horse trying desperately hard; scared of Leigh and tired of running, working to conquer its own fear.

"Let him come," S.T. said quietly. "Let him make the choice. Turn away."

She turned her shoulder to the horse. It took a step, gazed at her doubtfully out of one eye and then the other. And then, with a great sigh, it dropped its head and ambled forward to stand with its poor battered nose a few inches from her sleeve, asking for rest and comfort in the only way it could.

"Very slowly," S.T. murmured. "See if you can touch his face."

She lifted her hand. The gray's head came sharply up again, and the animal watched her with liquid brown eyes. She dropped her hand, and the horse relaxed. She lifted her hand again, and this time the gray didn't shy, only raised its nose a little. She touched the blood-spotted forehead lightly. The horse's ears were flicking back and forward anxiously, its nostrils still swelling with the quick pants. But the animal stood its ground.

She moved her hand down, barely stroking its nose. She touched its ears and ran her hand down its neck as S.T. had done to the other horse. The rogue stood steady, its sides heaving. She rubbed its poll. The horse turned its head, pushing upward into her hand a little, as if to ask for a harder massage.

"Oh, God," she said in a cracked voice. "Oh, God."

Her mouth opened, and she put her hand over a sudden, wrenching sob. She took a step back, and the gray threw up its head in startlement. Then the horse turned, following her. It stood with its nose at her waist, breathing more steadily.

Suddenly she turned and began to stride away. Her face was white, as if she'd just seen a terrible accident. The horse trailed behind her. She stopped and turned. The rogue stopped beside her.

No one spoke.

"Oh, *look* at you," she cried in a broken voice. She put her hand over her mouth again, and reached out with the other. As she rubbed the horse's ears, it bobbed its head gently. "Look at you!" Tears began to tumble down her face. Her expression seemed to crumble, to lose its substance and shatter into something wild and awful. She stood there with silent sobs racking her body, massaging the horse's poll.

S.T. felt as if the breath had been knocked out of his chest. He almost went over the fence.

But he didn't. He was paralyzed. He whispered, "See if you can put your arms around his neck."

She did that, breathing in distraught hiccups. She bent down when he told her and picked up one of the rogue's forefeet. It stood peacefully, only turning its head to nudge at her as she bent over. She was crying all the time as she went around the animal and handled each of its feet. He told her to walk away again, and the gray plodded along at her side.

She looked at it as if it were something terrible, some strange and terrifying vision as it came to a placid halt beside her. Her face was wet, splotchy with tears. She swallowed painfully. "Oh, how did this happen?" She stroked the animal's face again, its neck and ears, making little whimpering sounds. "Oh, God, you're so beautiful; why are you coming to me?"

She wiped the tears away with her arm. The horse nudged her. She shook her head and sobbed frantically.

"I didn't *want* this!" She shoved at the animal's head, as if to make it move away, but it only shifted around and faced her again. "I don't want it!" She put her hands over her face. Her shoulders were shaking. The gray pushed its nose against her body and tried to rub its face on her coat.

She sank to her knees, her face buried. S.T. moved at last, hiking himself over the fence, savagely curbing his impulse to run, moving with slow deliberation to reassure the horse.

The rogue's head lifted in startlement at this new intrusion. It took two steps backward, and he jerked his chin up and spoke sharply to drive it on. He reached for the whip where Leigh had dropped it and sent the animal cantering around the paddock.

"I had to make him go," he said inanely to the huddle at his feet. "You've got to stand up, Sunshine; it's too dangerous.'' He caught her arm, tugging gently. ''Stand up, sweeting—you can't lie down here.''

She lifted her face, and he felt a shaft of pure agony at the dazed misery in it. He pulled her up, allowing the whip to fall. The gray instantly dropped to a trot and turned inward, walking toward them. When she saw that, another huge sob welled up, and she turned her face into S.T.'s chest, holding on to his coat.

''Damn you!'' she shouted into his shoulder. ''Why did you do this to me?'' She curled her fist and smashed it against him. *''Why—why—why?''*

He stood there helplessly, holding her close with one arm and stroking the horse's offered head with the other. The gray seemed to take her hysterical voice as a matter of course, adjusting to it as quickly as to S.T.'s presence. ''It's all right,'' he murmured. ''It's all right.''

''It's not all right!'' she cried against his chest. ''I hate you!'' She gripped his coat in her fists. ''I don't want you. I don't want this.'' She was breathing as if she couldn't get enough air. ''I can't—*bear* it!'' she cried, with her voice breaking in a shrill whimper like a frenzied child's.

He didn't answer. The three of them stood there in the middle of the paddock, with twenty pairs of yokels' eyes on them. He kissed her hair, said incoherent soothing things, blew a loose lock of his own hair out of his face. She felt soft and shaky against him, as if she'd lost the ability to command her own body.

''Do you want to sit down?'' He stroked her back. ''Do you want me to finish this?''

She shoved away from him. ''I want to be free of you!'' Her cheeks were flushed, her voice high and strident. ''You importune me. You inconvenience me. You're a fraud. I wish you gone.''

''Leigh—'' he said, but she went on speaking, glaring at him, her voice rising.

''You're *deaf,* cocksure dolt—*deaf*—and bungling, and trying to be what you aren't any longer! Do you think you impress me with this?'' She flung up her chin. ''Do you think I want your help or your horse or your bloody bribes to make me sleep with you?''

He felt himself growing cold.

"I'm just waiting for you to fall flat on your face," she cried. "You're so proud of yourself because you can stand up and walk instead of reeling like a drunkard. But you'll never know if it's to last, will you?" she sneered. "And neither will I. I can't trust you. I can't depend on you. You've run entirely mad and useless."

In public. In full view and hearing of a crowd of fascinated bumpkins, she said these things. She paused in her abuse and caught her breath in a sob. Her eyes glittered, swimming blue with tears as she stared at him defiantly.

"As you will, madame," he said, keeping his voice low. He drew a breath of freezing air. "I will not importune you any longer, that's certain."

Leigh whirled away, wiping fiercely at her eyes with the back of her cuff. The cold air made her damp cheeks feel icy. She stalked across the grass, trying to get her breath, still hiccuping with every inhalation.

Before she reached the wall, she heard the sound of slow hoofbeats behind her. She glared at the men standing beyond the gate, hating them for their shocked and curious faces.

"Go away!" she screamed. "What are you staring at?"

They gawked at her. The gray came up behind and nudged at her with its nose. Leigh put her elbows over her face.

"Go away!" she shouted. She dropped her arms and hit wildly at the horse.

It shied off, trotted in a small circle and came to a halt, looking at her. After a moment, it took a step forward.

"Go *on!*" She flung up her hands, running toward it. The rogue started to shy and then faced her, backing up as fast as she moved. The instant she stopped, the horse did. And then it came toward her again, closer than before.

"*Don't! Don't! Don't!*" she shouted, lunging toward it, waving her arms frantically. The gray stood its ground, head lifted, nose bobbing with the wild motion of her hands as she attacked. It raised one hind foot, as if to step back, and then put it down in the same place, refusing to budge. Leigh dropped her arms with a cry of frustration.

The horse lowered its head and walked up to her. It stopped with its nose at her elbow.

"Admirable job of sacking him out," the Seigneur said sarcastically. "Care to try it with a blanket?"

She closed her eyes. When she opened them, the horse was still there. The Seigneur was still there. She was still hurting, still alive, still drowning in love and grief and rage.

Oh, Papa. Oh, Mama, I can't do it. I'm not strong enough; I can't hate enough; I'm going to fail.

She looked at the swollen cut that marked the rogue's face where the coper had clubbed it across the nose. There were other scars, older than that one, and the horse's straight profile was marred by an ugly lump from some past concussion.

She was aware of the Seigneur, still standing in the center of the paddock.

"I'm sorry," she whispered to the gray rogue. She put her hand on its shoulder and leaned her forehead against its neck. The horse stretched out its nose and shook its mane vigorously.

She turned away, walking toward the gate, avoiding looking up at their audience. They gray followed her, but this time she didn't stop; she only climbed the gate and passed through the spectators. At the tree where she and the Seigneur had eaten lunch, she sat down, cradling her head on her knees.

For all of the dark and drizzling afternoon, the Seigneur worked the rogue, flapping blankets and banging on tin buckets and creating any other noise and excitement he could manage, until the big gray stood calmly, refusing to even blink.

He rubbed the horse all over with the whip and hung a coiled lead rope on its ears while it followed him around the paddock like a child. Then came the long, deliberate process of saddling and bridling an animal that had known nothing but pain and terror from such things.

The Seigneur had unending patience. It made Leigh want to weep. At times during the endless afternoon, she found her eyes filling again and her breath coming in short sobs. She felt shattered, helpless, as if she should tag behind him compliantly the same way the gray did.

He took exquisite care with the horse. Even when the drizzle started in the late afternoon, he didn't rush. He never tried to force the animal to obey, only set up each situation so that the horse preferred to do what he asked rather than be compelled to keep running around the enclosure. Then he took what was offered, returning praise and friendly scratching.

When finally the moment came and he swung softly and fully into the saddle, the horse stood still, its ears flicked back alertly. In the waiting silence, Leigh could hear the sound of the light rain and feel the expectation from the crowd. The gray had had plenty of time to recover its wind and object to this imposition forcefully.

But the horse just peered around at him from both sides, heaved a sigh, and looked bored.

A loud cheer broke out. The farm boys began to whoop and the horse copers pitched their hats in the air. The gray lifted its head and stared around, but the lessons of the day were not lost. The horse held its place calmly, and then after a moment walked off around the paddock, rotating its ears in casual interest.

The Seigneur was grinning. For the whole of her life, Leigh thought she would remember the expression on his face.

She put her head in her arms.

How can I go on? I'm weak, I'm going to fail, I'm not strong enough; Oh, Mama, I can't keep on with this.

She kept herself buried, not watching anymore, pressing her forehead into her arms and trying to find the bitterness that had sustained her. The evening grew colder as she sat hunched beneath the tree, and finally it was one of the copers who squelched up in the drizzle and timidly said, "Ma'am? Was you wishing to ride back?"

She lifted her head. He stood there holding the chestnut. In the early dark, the rest of the audience had dispersed, and Leigh saw the Seigneur already halfway down the lane, riding the black and leading the rogue alongside.

She accepted the coper's leg up onto the sidesaddle that the Seigneur had insisted upon purchasing for her. The chestnut didn't wait for any signal from Leigh: as soon as the man let go of the bridle, it swung around and trotted quickly after the other horses.

Leigh allowed it, having no better decision at hand. The Seigneur never even turned around and looked at her.

Back in the stable yard, he swung off the black and told the boys that he'd tend to the horses himself. They seemed glad enough to stay clear of the rogue, but there were low whistles and speculation as the big horse stood calmly amid the flickering bustle in the yard.

As Leigh dismounted, the Seigneur caught her bridle. He took off his tricorne and handed her the rogue's lead. "What do you prefer to call him?" he asked shortly.

She gave the horse a weary look. He'd said it could be a weapon. She needed one. Now, more than ever before, she desperately needed a weapon to help her go on. "Revenge," she said harshly. "That's what I'll call him."

He scowled at her. "No. That's a stupid name."

"Revenge." She set her jaw. "That's his name, if you give him to me."

"Right-ho," he said in a low, angry voice. "The way you always call me 'Seigneur.' I'm a person, Leigh. I've got a name. This is a horse, a living breathing animal; he's not a goddamned mission."

She brushed her damp hair back from her face. "I don't even know your name. You only have initials."

"You never asked." He turned to work at the black's girth. "But why should you? That would make me real, wouldn't it? Something more than a tool to get you what you want."

Her throat thickened in that desperate, painful way that kept overcoming her wits. In a caustic voice, she said, "So tell me your name."

He looked back at her sharply. She lowered her face,

staring at the lamplight shining on the wet stone cobbles and the horses' hooves.

She heard the rattle of the girth as he dragged the saddle off the horse's back. She felt bruised inside, unable to look up and encounter his face directly, to see his hair crowned with golden lamplight and rain.

"Sophocles," he said gruffly, in an undertone. "Sophocles Trafalgar Maitland."

He paused, as if expecting her to say something. She couldn't seem to lift her head. He carried the saddle away and came back.

"Well you may stare," he said, and gave a peculiar little humorless laugh. "Silliest name on earth. I've never voluntarily told it to anyone before."

She could see his hand on the reins, sliding the leather between his fingers.

He turned away to the chestnut. "Begotten aboard ship off the Cape of Trafalgar." He unbuckled the sidesaddle's balance strap. "So the story goes. My mother claimed her lover was a rear admiral of the white squadron." He yanked the leather girth straps free. "One might ask how she managed to find herself aboard a navy flagship, but who knows? Maybe it's true." He pulled the sidesaddle off the chestnut and stopped beside Leigh, holding the cantle against his hip. "I go by my initials. S.T. Maitland. And don't bloody well tell anyone the rest, understand?"

She gazed at him.

The truth came upon her with a simple, horrible clarity. *I love this man.*

I love him, I hate him . . . oh, God.

She wanted to cry and laugh at the same time. Instead she only stared stonily. "Why should I tell?" she asked. She flicked the gray rogue's lead. "Where shall I put Revenge?"

He looked from her to the horse, and then plucked the rope out of her hand. "I'll take him," he said. "His name's Mistral."

Fifteen

THREE weeks and three hundred miles, and fifty times a day S.T. thought of what she'd said.

You importune me. You inconvenience me. *You're a fraud.*

With Nemo loping alongside, he rode Mistral from dawn to dusk, alternating every three hours with a lesson on the black he'd named Sirocco. On the road, he taught both horses to give to his hand, to halt with and without reins, to retire backwards, to trot and gallop the Roman S. For three hours in the morning, before they traveled, he worked Mistral alone.

His balance didn't desert him. At first he thought about it, lying warily still when he woke, afraid to move his head. As the miracle held, it became harder to remember, strange to realize in the middle of a school that he'd made some effortless quick maneuver without thinking of the consequences.

When he did recall it, he shook his head vigorously, trying to make himself dizzy as a sort of preventive measure, the way his lowly surgeon had advised. But the renewed feeling of disequilibrium was so unpleasant, the sensation of stability so natural, that he found his efforts growing fewer and farther between.

He had his balance back. It wouldn't leave him. It could not. He concentrated all his mind on the task at hand.

S.T.'s equestrian masters had been Italian, French, Spanish—with one law between them: many horses make

217

a rider; one rider makes a horse. In his life, he'd ridden hundreds, but not since Charon had he found a mount with the natural balance and intelligence of this powerful gray demon. It was a joy and a passion; an obsession; to supple Mistral into the *terre-à-terre* with smaller and smaller figure eights, to begin the *courbette* by teaching him to pick up his forefeet neatly and together, then school him in the *ruade,* asking him to kick out his hind legs with a stroke of the rod under his belly. Mistral had a particular talent for that air, having kicked down more than one stall in his notorious career.

The black Sirocco was an honest, phlegmatic animal, harder to move than to restrain, but Mistral did not suffer a fool gladly. His exuberance and sensitivity required the slowest and most empathetic of hands, the greatest of patience. But the moment that Mistral comprehended a lesson, he was capable of performing it. S.T.'s prime concern was to fight his own urge to bring the horse along too fast. Sometimes, instead of the serious schools, he spent the morning hours in play, showing the gray rogue the same tricks he'd taught the blind French mare, or just standing alongside Mistral and scratching his withers as the horse grazed on winter hay.

It was in those quiet moments that his pride kept tossing up to him the words Leigh had said.

You importune me. You inconvenience me. You're a fraud.

He'd left her stranded in Rye and come alone. It was like a quest: kill the dragon—win the lady.

Damn her, he'd drape her in dragon skin. He'd feed her dragon soup. He'd build her a bloody frigging castle out of dragon bones.

Let her think him a fraud then.

The Reverend James Chilton might call it his Heavenly Sanctuary, but the place had been known as Felchester for more than a few centuries. First a Roman fort on the Pennine Way, almost within sight of Hadrian's pagan wall, and then a stronghold of the Danelaw. The Norman French had not found it worth the building of a castle, but the weekly market and the river ford had kept it alive into the fifteenth century, long enough for a stroke of rare good fortune: a native son, gone to London and come home rich. This proud citizen had seen fit to build a stone bridge across the river, and Felchester's life as a town was assured.

All this, S.T. knew from Leigh. What he had not expected was the charm of it, tucked as it was at the foot of a great, gloomy fell, between the heights and the river. The workaday slate houses of the north were softened, some of them plastered and whitewashed, their formidable outlines obscured by the exuberant twisty lace of bare fruit trees and the reddish winter remnants of creeper. On a clear day in late January, broad patches of sun lay across the wide main street, warm in the sheltered valley.

S.T. felt conspicuous in his point-edged hat and cloak of thick brandy-colored wool. It seemed that the sort of tourists who visited the Reverend James Chilton's model town wore clerical garb and carried hymn books instead of swords.

"You see—I try so very, very hard," Mr. Chilton was saying. After an hour of enthusiastic exposition, his red hair stood out in all directions from his head, heavily powdered, so that the natural color had become a strange shade of pale apricot. "Gentlemen, I'm honest with you. We could not expect a heaven on earth. But now I want you to look around our little home—stop with us tonight if you please, and welcome; any one of the members can direct you to the guest's dormitory."

The visiting clergymen stood around, smiling and nodding. Chilton gave S.T. a particularly friendly smile, offering his hand. His freckles made his face seem young and old at once. For an instant he looked directly into S.T.'s eyes, without a blink. "I'm so glad you've come along," he said. "Are you interested in philanthropy, sir?"

"Just curious," S.T. said, wanting no part of being hounded for a donation. "Is there somewhere I can stable my horse?"

He was the only one who'd arrived mounted. The rest

had come in the Sanctuary's own plain wagonette, met at the front of the church fourteen miles away in Hexham.

"Of course you may take him down to the livery, but I'm afraid you'll have to care for him yourself. As I explained, that is our rule here, gentlemen—responsibility! One stands upon one's own feet. Though you'll find everyone most accommodating and helpful when you have need." Chilton nodded toward S.T.'s sword belt. "I'll ask you to leave that in the stable, too, my dear sir. You've no need for such things here on our streets. Now—I must leave you all to your own devices and see to the preparations for my noonday service. Do come up to the parsonage for a dish of tea in an hour, and then I hope you will attend service with us, and we'll talk further."

As the group broke apart, S.T. gathered Sirocco's reins and led the patient black horse down the high street in the direction Chilton had indicated. He returned a nod and a smile from a shepherd girl as she passed. Her flock of three white-faced sheep gave the scene a pastoral air, like something out of a sentimental etching. A pair of little girls, capped and gowned like their elders, giggled at each other as they carried a milk pail between them.

The females of Heavenly Sanctuary went about their business in buoyant spirits, from what he'd seen. He could hear someone singing from an open doorway across the road.

The stable still held the night's chill, empty of men or beasts but meticulously clean. He put Sirocco in the first stall, pitched hay, and pumped water. The black stuck its nose in the hayrack, only flicking an ear backward as S.T. hung up his saddle. He debated briefly, decided he didn't owe Chilton any particular compliance, and walked out with his sword still on.

He stood at the door of the livery, considering how best to reconnoiter. He wanted this done, and done quickly, but nothing so far was as he'd anticipated. No one in this town seemed downtrodden; no air of evil hung about the place . . . and Chilton—well, Chilton looked nothing more than a bluff and rather boring crusader, if the lengthy

speech on morals and methods with which he'd greeted
them all this morning was any indication.

It might be a little difficult just to assassinate the fellow,
as much as S.T. suspected he'd be happy to do so after
sitting through a Heavenly Sanctuary service and an afternoon of Chilton's prosy philosophy.

He tried to conjure Leigh: her face set, her body shaking as she told him what had happened here. But all he
could recall clearly was the sound of her voice as she re-
viled him with his failings.

He began to wonder if she was rational. Or if he was.
Distress could break a mind. Perhaps it had never happened at all—perhaps there had been no family, no father
or mother or sisters lost.

He knew that he ought to forget about Leigh Strachan.

But here he was.

The high street widened at the market cross, opening to
the bridge on one hand and a wide, gracious avenue lined
with spreading trees on the other. At the end of the avenue, mounting the steep flank of the fell, stood a handsome mansion of silver stone, topped by a copper cupola
and a graceful balustrade.

He stopped.

That, he had seen before. In the background of a young
girl's watercolors, he'd glimpsed that symmetrical facade
with its tall windows, stately and beautiful and warmly
intimate.

Silvering, Northumberland, 1764—

Long grass grew through the magnificent wrought-iron
gates. There at the end of its own fine avenue, with the
neat houses marching up the slope to their crowning gem,
Silvering itself stood alone and unkempt, like a proud old
courtier still arrayed in fading paint and powder.

He felt a sudden hot longing for Leigh, an overwhelm-
ing ache at the base of his throat. To stand here and look
at the place that had once echoed to her laughter—laughter
he'd never heard himself—made him feel supremely alone,
jealously solitary.

They'd been a family here. He'd seen the pictures, wit-
nessed the depth of her grief at her loss.

He wanted . . .

Connection. Kinship. He wanted what that house had been. A home, and something to fill it.

He wanted Leigh, and everything she refused him.

Except it wouldn't work. He saw that, suddenly, standing here beneath the empty mansion. Between her sketchbook and this weed-grown house, there was no human way to repair the broken bond. It had warped her mind and her heart and her memories, this suffering, twisted reality into an obsessive search for retribution that had carried her all the way cross France. Whatever had happened to her family—and he no more thought these cheerful girls had actually killed them than he believed they could be resurrected—the world of the watercolors was gone.

The dragon had turned out to be a puppy, and S.T. could never win her what she truly wanted, which was the life she'd lost.

Which left him with nothing. No way to merit her love, nothing to master and prove himself. He had the weapons honed, his swordplay polished and the gray rogue trained up to the foundations of his art. In three weeks, he'd accomplished it, wanting the victory that badly.

All for naught. He could kill Chilton and go back to Rye with the man's head in a damned basket, and it wouldn't buy him more than a curt thank you. Why should it? She'd got herself convinced she wanted revenge, she'd made Chilton into an evil scapegoat, but she'd find out just how empty vengeance was the moment she had it.

She'd turn from S.T. and go away and leave him as she'd found him.

He crossed his arms, leaned his head back against the carved stone of the market cross, and thought of what a sad coxcomb he looked now, like some eager recruit arrived at the battlefield, only to find no one else there.

Merde.

For want of a better idea, he walked back down the street and smiled wanly at a pretty girl who sat working at a pair of lace ruffles in a bright doorway. He leaned on the garden gate. "Pray—will you tell me where I might find something to eat?"

"Most willingly," she said, laying aside her work and springing up from the stoop. She came forward and nodded up at him. "You must go down the high street—that way"—She pointed, bending her head close to his shoulder as she leaned over the gate. "Then give yourself the trouble of turning to the right, toward the hill, at the first lane beyond the market cross. Be so good as to continue past the infirmary, and in the first house on the left you will find the men's dining hall."

She looked up at him, still bending close. Her plain, tight cap covered every curl on her head, but her blue eyes and fair skin made S.T. envision a cascade of blonde.

He took off his hat with grave courtesy and bowed. "Thank you, mademoiselle," he said. And winked at her.

She stared up at him. "It's no trouble," she said.

"Certainly it has been a pleasure for me." He put his hat back on. "But I'm keeping you from your work."

"Yes," she said, and turned back to the house without another word.

S.T. paused a moment, slightly disconcerted by the abruptness of her withdrawal. Then he turned away and followed her directions, walking slowly down the street the way she'd pointed.

The little black flock of visiting clergy came out of a shop a few yards ahead of him. They spoke quietly together, full of wise nods and thoughtful looks. One of them appeared to be taking notes in a journal. S.T. lifted a finger to the brim of his hat and walked on alone.

At the house that held the men's dining hall, no one answered his knock. Following the scent of food, he found his way to the kitchen, but the aproned cooks were politely adamant that no meal would be put on the table until after the noonday service. They wouldn't even give him a bannock off the tray hot out of the oven. He grinned and talked nonsense and stole one.

They found him out before he managed to sidle through the door, and seemed so genuinely upset at the loss that he confessed and gave it back, in spite of his watering mouth.

Turned out of the kitchen in disgrace, he wandered back down the high street. The same girl was still mending lace in her doorway.

S.T. leaned on the gate. "They aren't serving yet," he said sadly.

"Oh, no," she said. "Not until after noonday sermon."

He smiled wryly. "You didn't mention that."

"I'm sorry. Are you very hungry?"

"Very."

She bent her head over her sewing. Then she looked up and down the street. After a moment, she said softly, "I saved a pork pie from yesterday. Would you like it?"

"Not unless you'll share it with me."

"Oh, no. I couldn't—" She looked down at her lap and up again. "I'm not at all hungry. But you may have it."

She stood up and disappeared into the house. When she returned, S.T. opened the gate and walked up to the door. She handed him the pie, wrapped in a napkin, and he sat down on the step.

She hesitated, and he reached up and took her wrist, pulling her down beside him. "Do have a seat, mademoiselle, or I shall look a pretty rudesby if anyone comes by."

"Oh," she said.

For a moment they sat silent. S.T. bit into the pie. The crust was stale and the pork full of gristle, but he was hungry enough to swallow it.

"Samuel Bartlett," he said, "very much at your service, mademoiselle. What may I have the honor of calling you?"

She blushed and took up her handwork. "I'm Dove of Peace."

Lord spare us, he thought.

"A lovely name, Miss Peace," he said. "Did you choose it yourself?"

She giggled faintly, then pressed her fingers to her temple. "My master Jamie chose it for me."

He watched her as she rubbed her head and then went back to her needlework. "Do you feel quite well?"

"Oh, yes," she said, with a ghost of a smile. "I have the headache, but I always do."

"I'm sorry," he said. "Perhaps you should see a physician."

"Oh, no—there's no need of that." She smiled more firmly. "I'm quite well."

"Have you lived here long?"

"Several years," she said.

"Do you like it?" he persisted.

"Oh, yes."

He finished the pie and crumpled the napkin into a ball. "Tell me—how did you come to be here?"

"I was lost," she said. "My mother was a wicked woman. She took me away from my father, so that I never knew him. I never had food enough or clothes to keep warm, and my mother taught me to steal. She used to pinch me if I didn't bring back what she wanted."

"Did she!" S.T. said mildly.

"Yes, sir," Dove of Peace said. "I didn't know that I was doing wrong, but I was very unhappy. I was like—like nothing but an ant, among all the other ants. I was lonely, and there was nowhere to go, and no one cared." She bowed her head over her folded hands. "And then I came upon some girls who were giving away clothes at the street corner. They gave me a skirt and a cap." She looked up, with a musing smile. "They seemed so merry. So happy. They asked me to be their friend; they took me to the place where they were staying and gave me food. They said I shouldn't go back to my mother. When I told them I'd nowhere else to go, they gave me money enough to take the stage to Hexham, and from there I walked here, and was welcomed just the way that you were. It's a wonderful place. Like a family."

"Is it?" He snorted glumly. "Perhaps I'll join you."

"Oh, do!" she exclaimed. "I wish you would."

He looked at her sideways, his eyebrows lifted.

"You're lonely," she said. "I've watched you walking up and down by yourself. The others—they always stay in their groups when they visit. They don't understand what it's like, to be on the outside. They think the Sanctuary is a good place because we work hard—and we do—but the best thing is that we all love each other, and we're never, ever lonely.'' She glanced at him shyly. "Lots of girls come and join us, but not very many men. Only the special ones.''

S.T. leaned back against the door frame. He tilted his hat down over his eyes. "And you think I'm special, do you?''

"Oh, yes. You have a noble soul. It's in your expression. I knew it the moment I saw you. I don't usually speak to the visitors, but I was glad to talk to you.''

He smiled and shook his head. It was pleasant to be flattered, to have those wide blue eyes fixed on him in admiration. "You've no notion what an agreeable change it is to hear that.''

She frowned a little. "Someone has hurt you.''

"I've been a fool.'' He shrugged. "Same old story.''

"That's because you put your faith in the wrong place. Here we don't despair or feel forsaken or alone.''

"How gratifying.''

"It's warm,'' she said. "People are cold, aren't they? They say cruel things and won't be pleased. Here we care about you as you are, even if you aren't perfect in the eyes of worldly men.''

He sighed, propping his arm on his knee. "Well, I'm far from perfect—in anyone's eyes, I assure you.''

"All of God's people are perfect,'' she said. "And so are you.''

He allowed that to pass without comment. A bell began to ring, and she gathered up her lace.

"That's noonday service. Will you go with me?'' She darted inside before he could answer, and came back a few moments later, closing the door behind her. As he stood up, she took his arm and started down the steps. "Everyone will want to meet you.''

He'd intended to slip away quietly long before this particular threat materialized, but Dove of Peace drew him along with such enthusiasm, and introduced him so affec-

tionately to everyone they passed that he couldn't seem to
find the proper moment to take his leave. He found himself inside the little stone church, seated in the first row
of pews before the bell stopped pealing.

He was in the middle, hemmed in by the prayer rail in
front, a visiting clergymen on one side, and members of
Chilton's congregation on the other—all men in the first
three rows, while the rest of the church was filled with
females, overflowing the seats and standing three deep in
the aisles. He sat with his hat in his lap, looking around
uncomfortably. Dove of Peace had melted back into the
crowd after introducing him to the fellow on his right, who
rejoiced in the interesting name of True Word.

"I'm most impressed, aren't you?" the clergyman murmured in S.T.'s good ear. "It's very moving. Everyone
we met in the street seemed energetic and satisfied."

S.T. nodded and shrugged.

Mr. Word appeared to be disinclined to conversation,
which suited S.T. perfectly. He stared gloomily ahead,
where the altarpiece, the pulpit, and all the front of the
church were hidden behind long lengths of purple silk sewn
together and hung from the roof to form a billowy wall.

The disorder of seating gradually softened to rustling
and coughs, and then to complete silence. A single girl
padded forward and knelt in front of the purple silk, her
face hidden from view by a long white veil draped over
her cap.

S.T. waited, expecting organ music or a choir.

Nothing happened.

He shifted a little on the hard bench. A quick look beneath his lashes showed him that True Word was staring
straight ahead at the purple silk, not blinking or moving.
The clergyman seated to S.T.'s right had his head bowed,
his lips moving in silent prayer.

S.T. closed his eyes. He let himself drift, thinking back
to other churches, the gorgeous Italian cathedrals of his
childhood, the bell-like voices of boys at vespers amid
stained glass and soaring stone. He thought of paintings
he hadn't finished and images he still wanted to try. He
wondered if he could reproduce that incredible awesome

hush, that arc of light and darkness that was the cathedral at Amiens.

Perhaps he'd turn it into a forest, and paint Nemo as a shadow with yellow eyes. Or just the wolf and the horses silhouetted on the open moor, the way he'd left Mistral—free except for Nemo's watchful escort.

Suddenly the church bell began to peal madly, and True Word took S.T.'s hand. S.T. cleared his throat and disengaged himself politely, but amid a general movement of the congregation, the clergyman clasped his other hand firmly just as True Word renewed his grip. S.T. sat with his lips pressed wryly together, entrapped.

Chilton appeared from behind the billow of purple silk, dressed in simple black. Standing at the front of the church, he began another of his sermons, a long perambulation about salvation and his flock. S.T. tried to float back into more appealing thoughts, but the hands clamped to his own bothered him. When he attempted to withdraw unobtrusively, the grip tightened. He tried glaring at the clergyman, but the minister appeared to be lost in Chilton's sermon along with Mr. True Word.

Frustrated, S.T. stared down at his hat. An unpleasant moist warmth grew where his palms were pressed against the other men's. From the corner of his eye, he could see that the whole congregation appeared to be linked, even the girls in the aisles, the nearest of whom held the hand of the man at the end of the row.

Chilton's voice swept on, rising and falling with increasing emotion. S.T. thought the man looked bizarre, with his hair powdered to orange and his wide, childish eyes that moved over the audience with a pendulous rhythm, pausing only to focus on some individual for a moment as he made a personal pronouncement about Sweet Harmony's transgressions or Sacred Light's penitence. He named a large number of the congregation, speaking for several moments of each and receiving heartfelt answers to his urges to acknowledge sin. When he cried, "True Word!" S.T. felt the clutch on his right hand tighten.

"True Word . . ." Chilton's voice dropped to a whisper. "Your master knows. Will you confess?"

"Avarice!" True Word shouted. "Unholy desire and covetousness!"

"Will you let it go?" Chilton asked softly. "Will you bow down in shame and sorrow?"

"Oh, master—forgive me!" True Word bent over his lap. Chagrined, S.T. tried to drag his hand away, but the grip tightened violently. "Don't!" True Word sobbed, shaking his head. "Don't refuse me the healing touch!"

"Bugger off," S.T. muttered, and wrenched his hand free.

True Word groped, caught it back, and lifted it to his cheek. Everyone was looking at them. Under the weight of this collective scrutiny, S.T. drew in a deep breath and suffered the embrace, feeling heat rise fierily in his neck and face.

Chilton stared at him and smiled. He didn't go on with the sermon, as he had with the others. He just gazed at S.T. without blinking.

"I feel the power," he whispered into the waiting silence. "I feel the healing power radiating from you, Mr. Bartlett. Into me. Into the man named True Word. Into everyone here!" He lifted his arms and shouted, "Do you feel it?"

A murmuring started in the back of the church and swept forward. S.T.'s palms began to tingle, a faint itching that grew quickly into a sensation he'd never experienced. His scalp and arms prickled; his whole body felt queer, horribly pulsating, as if all his muscles had gone wobbly and out of his control. Strange patterns began to sparkle and coalesce in the purple silk before his eyes.

He could hear moans and cries around him, Chilton's voice rising and rising, calling him to come, calling him by name. The ghastly sensation intensified. He thought he was going to pass out, that the patterns in the silk would grow and grow and overwhelm him.

"Give it to me!" Chilton cried. "Give it to me—don't suffer; come to me. Let the power come to me!"

S.T. yanked his hand away from the clergyman. Instantly, the deep pulsating feeling vanished, leaving only the prickling of every hair and the pinwheeling sparks before his eyes. He stood up blindly, wanting out of this, but True Word would not let go. S.T. blinked and found Chilton just in front of him as the bright patterns faded from his eyes.

"Pass it to me," Chilton cried, reaching out. "Give your vitality to me, that I may use it as it was meant to be used!"

S.T. lifted his free arm to fend the man off, and between them a brilliant arc of light jumped across a hand's span, from his fingers to Chilton's. The pain made S.T. jerk back, swearing.

The weird prickling in his scalp evaporated. The whole congregation moaned, a single sound, like a huge animal in the last throes of life.

"Dove of Peace!" Chilton thundered.

The kneeling figure at the front of the church rose and came toward them. S.T. saw her pretty young face, her eyes locked on Chilton with awed hope.

"Dove of Peace," Chilton intoned, "you've asked for an end to the terrible pains in your head."

She nodded quickly.

"Come here, my beloved," Chilton said gently.

She moved to him, going down on her knees.

"Take off your veil and cap."

She obeyed, allowing her blonde hair to fall down over her shoulders.

Chilton reached out, holding his hands over her, his palms hovering an inch above her head. S.T. could see the fine golden hair rise up, clinging by single strands to his palms. Dove of Peace gasped softly and lifted her hands, touching the delicate halo that stood out from her head. She brushed Chilton's hand, and S.T. heard a faint crackle. Dove of Peace started and said, "Oh my!"

"This is God's healing power," Chilton said. "God's blessing on you for bringing Mr. Bartlett to us. Is your pain gone, precious child?"

"Yes," Dove of Peace sighed. She sank down onto her heels and looked up at Chilton with wide eyes. " 'Tis gone."

The congregation murmured. People began to stand up

and pray out loud, including the visiting clergymen. True Word kissed S.T.'s hand and started to blubber again.

"The Lord has brought Mr. Bartlett to us," Chilton pronounced over the devout clamor. "Mr. Bartlett"—he looked at S.T.—"will you come? Will you give us the gift that the Lord has given to you?"

S.T. cleared his throat. "For God's sake," he said, keeping his voice low. "Are you—"

"For God's sake!" Chilton cried. "Yes! For His sake!" He held out his hand. "Will you come, then? Mr. Bartlett, don't think you can do this alone. Don't make the mistake of hubris. You cannot go out and perform the miracles that we see here every day—but if you'll join us; if you'll become a part of our family in God, you have the healing power in you, to be used by me to help others. You have it in you, Mr. Bartlett—a power as strong as I've felt in all my many years of service to the Lord. Will you come?"

"I'd rather not," S.T. said. "Thank you."

The moans and murmurs around him sank into silence.

Dove of Peace gazed at him. There was no reproach in her look, only sadness. She stood up and came to the prayer rail, reaching over to take his hands. He felt a tiny snap of sensation as they touched, a pale echo of the painful spark that had crackled between him and Chilton. She had felt it too; he saw her draw her breath sharply, and then gaze at him in adoration.

"Please," she whispered. "Please stay and help us."

Chilton could have preached all day and True Word wept his eyes out, and not had the effect of those bright, hopeful female eyes. S.T. tried to say no: it was impossible, it was preposterous, it was all a sham of some sort—but he could not find words to say so at just that moment.

He took a deep breath and set his jaw. "All right. What do you want me to do?"

"Pray," Chilton said instantly, and the congregation began to kneel. "Come up with me and with your beloved Dove of Peace, and join with us in prayer."

So he had to go and kneel down and hold hands again and listen for an interminable length of time, until his legs were aching and his stomach growled and the sunlight through the stained glass crawled across the floor in ever-lengthening shafts.

For a while he pondered how Chilton had managed the "power" trick. That he'd been electrified, S.T. had no doubt—he'd heard accounts of the sensation. In France it was all the rage: they'd once simultaneously shocked a hundred and eighty of the King's Guards for the amusement of the Parisians, and the news had reached as far as La Paire by eight months later. Just what method Chilton used was mysterious. S.T. thought it needed a machine of some sort, though he didn't see anything that looked likely.

If anyone else doubted Chilton's theory of healing power, they didn't mention it. The service continued until nearly dusk. S.T. was starving. When at last it was over, he stood up, stretching his aching joints carefully. He moved away from Chilton, toward the cluster of visiting clergy.

They all gazed at him, and the one who'd sat next to S.T. blinked and moistened his lips. "I would not have believed it," he mumbled, and made as if to shake S.T.'s hand before he hesitated in the motion, as if he'd just remembered that he didn't want to touch. He turned to his companions. "If I hadn't experienced it for myself, I would have scoffed."

The others looked uncomfortable, but before S.T. could answer, a crowd of Chilton's congregation intervened, swirling around him, all talking at once, welcoming him into their family. True Word shoved his way through the press of females and kissed S.T.'s hand again. S.T. yanked it away, only to have the girls take up the gesture. Dove of Peace hugged him. By the time he managed to work himself free of the hospitality and out into the churchyard, the visitors had all disappeared.

Chilton was on the step, speaking to a little cluster of members. He turned to S.T., catching him by the shoulders. "I'm overjoyed, sir! I bless you for your decision."

"Take your hands off me," S.T. said brusquely. He gripped his sword. "I've changed my mind."

Chilton patted his shoulder and let go. "I'm sorry for that, then." He shook his head. "It happens, sometimes—

commitments made in haste are oft repudiated. We don't
wish for you to stay if you're not fully prepared."

"You're not staying?" Dove of Peace came up behind
him. "You're going?"

"Yes," he said, and only met her eyes an instant before
he looked away awkwardly. "I never meant to stay, you
know."

She put her hand to her lip. "Oh. I'm so sorry." She
looked down at the step. "Thank you—for giving me the
touch. My headache is gone."

"I didn't give you anything you didn't already have,"
he said softly.

Chilton seized his elbow. "If you would be so kind as
to wait a moment, I'll give myself the pleasure of walking
with you and my little Dove to the livery."

S.T. would have gladly foregone that treat, but Dove's
face brightened. For her sake, he waited while Chilton
disappeared into the church and joined them again a few
minutes later. As they walked down the high street and
passed the house where S.T. had met Dove of Peace, Chilton commented that she might consider returning to her
chores.

She obeyed without protest, only taking S.T.'s hand and
giving it a hard squeeze before she turned away and ran
through the gate.

"I'm afraid you may have broken a heart," Chilton said
with a touch of amusement as they walked on. "Foolish
child."

"Very," S.T. said.

Chilton sighed and nodded. "Few are as innocent as
Dove when they come to us from the worst stews of man's
making."

"Aye, I don't doubt that," S.T. said grimly. "I'd never
have guessed that she came off the streets if she hadn't
told me. I'd have taken her for gentle bred."

"I'm gratified," Chilton said. "Highly gratified. Schooling is an important part of our mission, you see. Ah, here is
little Chastity. Is Mr. Bartlett's mount ready, my beloved?"

"No, Master Jamie, sir, 'tain't." The girl who appeared
out of the shadows of the stable shook her head. "That

horse, 'ee 'us going to throw a shoe. Ol' Pap—uh—Saving Grace, I mean, beg pardon—he tooked it away to fix.''

"I hope you aren't in a fearful hurry, Mr. Bartlett? Perhaps you'll dine with us.''

SIXTEEN

IN the neat, plain dining room of what had once been a substantial family home, every man wanted to sit beside his new friend Mr. Bartlett. They loved him in Heavenly Sanctuary; he was one of the ones they'd been waiting for: his "power" brought them one step closer to the day their Jamie would lead them forward into the future where God's world would come to pass.

All traces of decoration had been removed from the room, no paintings, no mantel, no rugs—only the carved plaster on the ceiling remained. Two extra tables were crammed in, although the male members of Chilton's congregation only filled one. When the girls began serving, they had to squeeze between the empty chairs, holding the kettles high over their heads.

S.T. received a huge portion of oatmeal porridge, enlivened by sliced apple and sprinkled with too much salt by an overly enthusiastic neighbor determined to share. He looked at the formidable serving dubiously. They might not eat frequently in Heavenly Sanctuary, but they certainly got plenty when they did.

Everyone quieted, the serving girls lined up along the wall, and all heads bowed. One of the men began a prayer out loud, and when he said "Amen," another began, followed by someone else, all praying in random order and at random length. S.T. sat on a hard chair and watched his porridge grow cold and lumpy. Hunger was beginning to give him a headache.

235

Sometime during the prayer, the front door opened and the visiting clergymen came into the hall. With hushed voices, two of the serving girls ushered them past the dining room with its extra tables and chairs, toward the back of the house.

The prayers droned on. After a while, S.T. caught a tantalizing whiff of meat and warm bread, but no one brought anything else to the dining room. He could hear cheerful voices from down the hall. It slowly dawned upon him that the other visitors were being fed, and they hadn't gotten cold porridge, either.

Finally, a long silence descended. S.T. added his own silent prayer that they could at last begin eating. Twilight was falling, and even lumping oatmeal looked good.

The visiting clergymen came back down the hall, shepherded by Chilton, who bid them a pleasant good night at the front door, assuring them that the wagonette was waiting at the livery, ready to return them to Hexham.

Several of the men at the table grinned. One of them gave S.T. a conspiratorial shove in the elbow. "We don't got to eat with outsiders if we don't want," he whispered.

"How delightful," S.T. said, and picked up his spoon.

He received another jostle in the elbow. "Not yet, not yet," his neighbor whispered. "The girls eat first."

S.T. put his silver down. Chilton came into the dining room and stood at the door, his hands raised in benediction and his head bowed. He said another lengthy prayer, droning on in an affable tone about the weather and the harvest and the amount of lace the girls had made, recommending improvements as if God were a colleague who could stand a little friendly advice. S.T. was beginning to feel light-headed.

"Amen," Chilton said at last. "Share our blessings."

At that, the girls lined along the wall came up to the table. S. T. frowned as each one knelt beside one of the men. His eyes widened when the men took their bowls of oatmeal and began to feed the girls cold porridge by hand, spooning meal into their mouths. More girls filed into the room and lined up behind the ones who were kneeling.

A demure figure knelt beside him. The girl tipped her

face upward. It was Dove of Peace. She waited as if for holy communion, her eyes closed, her hands folded and her lips slightly parted. His patience finally broke. He'd had enough of this place; he really had. S.T. grabbed his bowl of porridge, stuck his spoon in it and held it out. "Here, it's yours. You don't have to act like this, for God's sake."

Her eyes opened. She stared up at him. "You don't wish to share?"

"I'll share," he said gruffly. He had to turn his head to catch her soft voice with his good ear. "But I'm not going to feed you. Get up off the floor. It's idiotic."

The clatter of tableware grew quiet around them. She bit her lip, glancing away. "You shame me," she whispered in sudden silence.

"He does not understand," Chilton said warmly. "You must teach him, Dove."

She swallowed. "I—I don't know how."

"I am with you. The way will come. Have faith."

She nodded and looked back at S.T. pleadingly. "Sharing shows that you care for me. It shows that you will nurture and protect me, as man is commanded to nurture and protect woman, which is the will of God."

"It shows that the woman is joyfully obedient," one of the men added earnestly. "She appears graceful and submissive, as is her nature. Dove is very good; she's happy and meek; you needn't fear anything else."

"This is absurd," S.T. said.

"Please share properly," Dove whispered. "You'll feel better if you do."

"I could hardly feel worse," he said, and shoved back his chair. He put the oatmeal on the floor. "There, Fido. Eat as if you're somebody's pet if you like."

A murmur of disapproval rippled around the room. Dove covered her face with her hands. "Please," she said. "Please!"

S.T. hesitated. They were all glaring at him as fiercely as if he'd beaten her—all except Chilton, who smiled benevolently on the scene.

Dove snuffled quietly and plucked at his leg. S.T. turned

his head again to hear her. "I'm so ashamed," she was mumbling between her fingers. "Don't you love me?"

"Love you!" he repeated dumbly. He looked down at her huddled figure. "Dove—" he said, feeling helpless. "I'm sorry. I don't mean to distress you, but I—this isn't what I want to do. I told you I wasn't staying."

She shook her head without lifting her face. Then she dropped her hands, pulled the bowl of oatmeal toward her, and lifted the spoon to her mouth, eating cold porridge off the floor.

"If this is what you wish, I submit to your will," she said. Tears were streaming down her cheeks. "Please don't go."

"Share with her!" one of the men said urgently.

"Can't you see that you humiliate her by this?"

Another man patted Dove's shoulder. "Aye—why do you hurt her? Poor Dove! Don't cry, darling. Come and let me share with you."

Dove shook her head violently. "I'm obedient," she cried. "I am! I'll do as Mr. Bartlett commands me."

They all watched as she kept on eating, hunched over the bowl on the floor.

"Pride!" It was True Word's voice. "Wicked arrogance, that abuses a helpless female to no purpose."

S.T. pushed his chair aside and went to the door amid a chorus of censure. He nodded to Chilton. "I'm sure my horse is ready by now," he murmured, and caught up his hat and brandy-colored cloak by the door.

Escape to the cold evening air was a vast relief. He strode down the quiet street and around the corner to the livery. In the deep twilight, the dark interior smelled of hay and horses, but he could see nothing. He stopped and listened for Sirocco's welcoming whicker. The place was silent.

For the first time, S.T. felt a little prick of alarm.

He swore viciously and turned on his heel. Temper made his stride jerky. As he turned the corner, he could see the unlit mass of Silvering against the dark rise of the fell. The sight made him pause.

They were all ludicrous: this freckled charlatan with his

electrical card tricks that wouldn't fool a child; these self-righteous prigs and their pathetic girls off the street, begging on the floor for cold oatmeal.

He felt his sword hanging against his left leg, simple and unambiguous. He wanted his horse back—if he had to force Chilton himself to his knees to get it.

The sharing ritual was still in progress when S.T. threw back the front door and stalked down the hall. Everyone ignored him. Chilton was speaking earnestly with Dove, who stood with her head bowed, nodding and weeping. She was the only one who looked up as S.T. stood in the doorway.

A great smile spread over her face. "You've come back!"

"Where's my horse?" S.T. scowled at Chilton.

Dove was already halfway across the room. She grabbed his hands and fell on her knees in front of him. "Forgive me! I've been selfish and disobedient. I'm so unhappy! Please say I'm forgiven, please, my lord!"

"My horse," he repeated, frowning past her and trying to extract himself at the same time. Her hands clung, small and desperate.

Chilton smiled. "I think you must confront something more important before we find your horse, Mr. Bartlett. You've wounded Dove very deeply. Before God, I ask you to apologize to her and to us."

"Apologize for what, damn it? For not treating her as if she's a brainless babe?" He gave up trying to evade her clutching hands. "Where the devil did you dream up this nonsense, Chilton?"

Chilton regarded him calmly. "My word is God's word."

"How convenient!" S.T. said with scorn.

"Please," Dove whispered quickly. She pressed her face to his hands. "You mustn't speak so!"

He gestured violently at the table. "Why not? You don't truly believe this is some order from on high, do you? You don't think there's some God up there who expects you to get down on your knees and abase yourself for a trifling spoonful of porridge? And even if he did, you can't believe he'd confide his wishes to this sack of wind and humbug!''

"Don't say such things!" Dove cried. Hysteria edged her voice. She caught his hand back, and then hugged his legs. He could feel her body trembling.

"Never mind." He tried to soothe her, touching her hair. "I'm not going to be struck dead by lightning, you may believe me."

Chilton chuckled. "Certainly not. But you have not apologized. Your soul is distressed. The true course will be revealed to you."

Several of the men stood up. S.T. watched them as they moved toward him. He couldn't tell what they meant; his hand went to his sword, but Dove's clinging interfered with his reach. "Don't touch me," he said sharply. "Keep your distance."

The nearest one made as if to seize his arm, and S.T. dragged the sword from its sheath. Dove cried out. She caught the blade in her bare hands. "Don't do it!" she shrieked. "Kill me first!"

His instincts betrayed him. In the instant he hesitated, unwilling to pull the sword across her already bleeding hands, they had him. He dropped the blade and swung his fist, but her body at his feet hindered him; he missed, tried to back up, and lost his balance within Dove's squeezing embrace. He fell backwards into the door frame, and they were all on him, holding him down everywhere, fighting like children, suffocating his curses with hands and arms and butting heads.

How long they kept him in the dark, he didn't know. He sat on the floor of a musty room with nothing to lean against; blindfolded, trussed, and utterly furious with himself.

Dove came. She sat on the floor with him and talked for a long time, stroking his hair and his forehead, speaking endlessly of how happy everyone was here, and how much they loved him, and how nice it would be when he learned how to go on; it was a little strange at first; she remembered it had been strange to her, too, but he'd quickly come to see how much better was their way of life than the wicked outside. She wanted him to stay, though of course he could go if he liked; they never forced anyone to do anything they didn't want to do, but she did so hope he would stay and be happy with her. Master Jamie had said Mr. Bartlett might be her own particular spouse, which was a very special favor that was only granted when a girl had been very, very good and Master Jamie loved her very much and thought her wise and agreed with her choice. Dove was really, truly, joyfully obedient.

S.T. said nothing. Dove cried and hugged him and tried to kiss his mouth, but he turned his face away.

Chilton came then, sent Dove away, and walked around S.T. in a slow circle, speaking sometimes in a loud voice and sometimes very softly. S.T. paid the words no attention. A few times, Chilton stopped and stood in one place for a long time, silent, and once or twice S.T. could hear a peculiar soft hissing sound. He couldn't help himself; he turned his face toward it, his nerves stretched taut with uncertainty. Then the long monologue went on, interspersed with the hissing, until he paid neither any attention.

They never left him alone. True Word came in and talked of pride and arrogance until S.T. was ready to kill the man with his bare hands. He pushed off the floor and made it to his knees, but blindfolded, he couldn't even tell which direction to throw himself, and so he just knelt there, breathing hard. Suddenly a quick shove came out of the dark, and he landed back on one trussed elbow with a grunt of pain.

Chilton's voice came from somewhere, softly chiding whoever had pushed him. S.T. lay on the rough floor, his mouth set sullenly. When they tried to make him stand up, he went limp, and they had to carry him. He had that small and bruising triumph until the clumsy devils dropped him, and then he decided he'd rather keep his bones intact and forgo his pride.

It was already mincemeat anyway. He'd not felt so ashamed since that terrible moment three years ago when he'd realized his sweet Elizabeth had betrayed him and he'd walked right into her trap—and lost Charon and his hearing and his last illusion that someone loved him.

His chin lifted. Strangely, he felt better thinking of Elizabeth, dirty little traitor that she'd turned out. To be caught and tethered by a pack of prigs and females was embarrassing, but it was a long way from total devastation.

Damn all women. They turned his brain to mush.

He moved carefully on the stairs. The blindfold brought back a trace of his old dizziness, and the multiple grip on his arms threw him off. Then he was on level ground, surrounded by bodies that packed close, bearing him along out into the frigid night air. He could smell torches, and the gathering murmur of a crowd that followed him and his captors in the street.

More stairs, upward this time. They were in front of the gates of Silvering; they had to be. His body was tight with the desire to throw himself sideways and break free of the suffocating prison they made of themselves, but with his hands tied he couldn't even rid himself of the blindfold.

They turned him around. Metal rattled: the wrought iron gate of Silvering. He felt many hands on his arms, pulling his elbows backward. Something ice cold touched his tied wrists.

Shackles.

He went stiff, and then lunged away without thinking; he fought as he had the first time, only it didn't last even as long as that, with his hands tied and endless arms and clutching fingers to catch him back and push him against the gate until he was driven down to his knees under the soft, crushing onslaught.

No one shouted or hit him. There was talk aplenty; voices telling him to be calm: kind, soothing voices. He would be happy, they said. He would learn the true way. Be good, be calm, be tranquil; it was Master Jamie's wish.

He could hear Dove close by, pleading with him not to struggle, not to shame himself and her. He knelt, panting, the pavement hard beneath his knees. They'd gotten the shackles on him, chained him to the gate, and when he tried to stand up, the fetters held him down.

He wondered if they'd deep telling him how happy he

was while they stoned him, or whatever it was Master Jamie had in mind. His heart was pounding, but he wasn't quite afraid. It seemed so unreal.

Someone took the blindfold off him. He shook his head, squinting at the intense blaze of light from the torches circled close by. He could see nothing but blackness beyond them, but he could hear the crowd. Even that sound was mild, a softer and higher note than any normal mob.

His breath glowed frost, curled in front of his face and drifted away. Silhouettes and dark shapes moved in and out of the torchlight, faces flashed white and then faded into the darkness as the audience jostled. How many could there be? A hundred, maybe two at most—even if everyone in the town was here. Chilton had claimed a thousand followers, but S.T. hadn't seen them in Heavenly Sanctuary.

They began to sing a hymn he didn't know, feminine voices rising sweetly in the night. How had he possibly gotten himself into this, chained on his knees in front of a crowd of schoolgirls? It was mortifying. They weren't going to stone him; they didn't even seem angry.

Chilton appeared out of the blackness beyond the torches and slowly mounted the steps, singing along with his congregation. As the last verse died away, he raised a plain porcelain cream pitcher between his hands and began to pray yet again, asking God to make his will known to Master Jamie and his flock.

S.T. twisted his hands behind his back. The praying in this place was incessant. No wonder they were all balmy.

Dove knelt a few steps below him, her eyes closed, apparently praying with all her might. Chilton's voice began to break and quiver with emotion in another of his one-way conversations with God. The crowd rustled, catching the excitement, even though S.T. could make nothing of Chilton's garbled phrases beyond, "Yes, yes! I understand, I understand. Happiness and peace for your followers. For those who truly love you," and other such profundities.

It was the church service all over again, droning on and on. S.T. shivered in the freezing air. Suddenly Chilton lifted the little pitcher over his head, then lowered it and poured a few drops on the limestone step. It sizzled faintly, bubbling.

"Sweet Harmony," he said. "Do you love your master?"

One of the girls at the foot of the steps hurried forward. "Oh, yes," she cried.

"You have a task. Take this cup. If you truly love your master, you will drink of it. A nonbeliever would be burned. A nonbeliever would feel the fires of hell on his tongue if he drank. But if you have true faith, it shall be as water to you."

He held out the cup. The girl called Sweet Harmony took it in trembling hands. A sound like a sigh came from the invisible crowd beyond the torches. As S.T. watched in helpless horror, she lifted it unhesitatingly to her lips.

As the vessel touched her mouth, Chilton shouted, "Abraham! *Abraham!*" The whisper of the crowd rose to a wail. "I am the angel of the Lord!" Chilton cried, his voice carrying into the night. "Lower the cup, my child. Do not drink. You have proven yourself, as Abraham was tested and proven."

Sweet Harmony lowered the cup, and Chilton lifted it from her hands. Her face was radiant as she watched him.

"Dove of Peace," he said. "Come forward and take the cup."

S.T.'s back grew rigid. He began to breathe harder.

"Your task is more difficult," Chilton said. "You must have faith enough for two. The man you have brought among us is one of the children of rebellion. His soul is the soul of wicked men, which God has said is like the restless sea that cannot be quiet, and its waters toss up mud and refuse."

Dove took the cup from his hands, her head bowed over it.

Chilton put his hands on her shoulders. "It is in you to save him. The faith of Sweet Harmony would have turned acid into water as it touched her lips, because she believed in the word of her master. Do you believe in my word?"

Dove nodded. S.T. wet his lips and swallowed.

"Hear me, then. You must take this cup, and pour the liquid into his left ear, so that the spirit of rebellion will issue forth from his mouth and be gone forever, and he may be at peace."

The shock of it went through S.T. like a great jolt.

For an instant he was frozen, unbelieving. Then his lips drew back. "You bastard," he snarled. "You unholy bastard!"

Chilton stroked Dove's hair. "Only you can give him this gift, my child. Do not hang back from your appointed task."

Dove turned, holding the pitcher in both hands. S.T. couldn't help himself; he shoved back away from her, as far as the shackles would allow him.

"What do you want, Chilton?" he demanded. "What's your price?"

"The Lord saith: 'Listen to Me, you who know righteousness, a people in whose heart is My law,' " Chilton intoned. " 'Do not fear the reproach of man, neither be dismayed at their revilings.' "

Dove of Peace walked toward S.T., her face composed. She knelt beside him."

"Don't do this," S.T. said, breathing fast. "Dove—you don't know what you're doing. Think about it, for the love of God."

She smiled, but he thought she didn't even see him. "I can give your soul peace," she murmured. "I'll make you happy."

"No!" His voice rose. "I won't be able to hear. My other ear's gone—oh, God. He knows it, Dove! He's using you; what does he want? Ask him what he wants."

"We all want you to be happy," she said. "You'll find peace with us when the spirit of rebellion is driven out."

She lifted the pitcher. He shook his head frantically, and then jerked his shoulder, trying to knock the pitcher from her hand.

Someone grabbed his hair, multiple hands, holding him still by force. "You must believe," she said. "You must know I would not hurt you. Have faith."

"Don't do it." His eyes watered. "He's crazy. He's made you all crazy."

She shook her head and smiled, as if he were a small and frightened child. Behind her, Chilton began a prayer. She lifted the pitcher. S.T. fought the tight grip that twisted his head. "Be still," she said. "Pray with us."

"Please," he whispered. "Please." All his muscles shook with resisting the hold. "You can't do this." The pitcher rose and tipped in her steady hands. He squeezed his eyes shut. "You can't; you can't; you can't." He was crying, unable to comprehend it—God, to be deaf, to have the door slammed completely, to be helpless in a silent world . . . the burning cold liquid hit his ear and flooded it, blocking out the sound of chilton's praying, muddling the voices.

The silence became real. They let him go. S.T. bent his head over his knees with a sob.

SEVENTEEN

IT looked the same to Leigh as it always had, this vast and empty country. Desolate. Gray sky and bleak moor, with the backbone of the Roman wall draped across the tops of the long ridges like a serpent. Strange weather rolled over the hills: huge flakes of snow melted when they touched the black ground and thunder muttered above the clouds.

The wind whipped the chestnut's mane as Leigh rode along a muddy track. The horse lifted its head nervously, staring around as if there were tigers liable to leap from the shadowy hollows, alternating a mincing prance with long, impetuous strides as it slogged through the deep footing.

Leigh prayed they wouldn't come to any actual puddles they couldn't go around. The animal's timidity about water had been the plague of her journey, adding a fortnight to what should have been a twenty-day trip. The Seigneur had said he could take care of it, but he hadn't lingered to prove his claim.

He'd left her, there in the dark and drizzle of the stable yard at the Mermaid. Oh, he'd not actually left physically, not at that moment. But he hadn't spoken to her again; he hadn't come to the room to sleep, and in the morning there was only a message. She was to stay until he returned. Her room and board was paid; she could ask for anything she wanted except cash. He took the black and the gray rogue. He left her the chestnut that wouldn't cross a bridge.

247

He'd stranded her there, penniless. Waiting on him like a handmaiden.

It still made her furious, and it hadn't stopped her for half an hour.

The chestnut, however, had slowed her down considerably. She'd tried to sell it in Rye, but they all knew the animal too well, so she'd taken her pearls and her dress to the pawn shop. The broker carried them into the back of the shop to examine the necklace, and then came out and laid ten shillings on the counter, instead of the four pounds that S.T. had predicted. When she'd protested ferociously, the broker just shrugged and handed her a pawn ticket. He wouldn't give the pearls back, and when she threatened to go to the constable, he leaned on he counter and said she could do what she pleased, and see where it got her.

They knew her, that was why; they all knew that Mr. Maitland, with his reputation for liberality and swordsmanship, had left his wife in keeping in Rye. And Rye—unscrupulous smuggler's den that it was—was perfectly willing to keep her, on speculation of the reward.

At tuppence the mile, she'd calculated it would take at least three pounds just for stagecoach fare as far as Newcastle, even riding on the outside. She'd thought she could sell the chestnut once she was out of the neighborhood, but that too had proved impossible. It had been difficult enough just to *get* the horse out of the neighborhood. Once she'd coaxed and tugged and beaten it over the seven water crossings between Rye and Tunbridge Wells, she found that horse copers were a sharp-eyed lot, suspicious, accustomed to sizing up anyone who brought them an animal to sell. The sight of a breech-clad "boy" on a sidesaddle made them jeer, and they recognized the chestnut's failings almost immediately. She'd had to kick one coper in the face, when he put his hand on her thigh under pretense of adjusting her stirrup.

The best offer she got was from a knacker in Reading. Two pounds.

She'd looked at the chestnut. It had refused to approach within ten feet of the knacker; it rolled its eyes fearfully as it sidled against the post to which she'd tied it a few yards away. The bally horse was afraid of everything, she'd though in disgust—they'd have a job just getting it into the slaughtering yard.

She walked over to the horse and it danced around, backing up frantically as soon as she untied the lead. It was trembling, too frightened even to bolt. "So, so, boy . . . be calm," she murmured, the same thing she always said when the horse grew anxious. "Be calm; nothing's wrong. Nothing will hurt you."

As she spoke, it dawned upon her that that was a lie—the ultimate lie—a final betrayal of what little trust the horse put in her.

The animal did calm at the sound of her voice, just slightly, just enough to stop the backing and trembling. It froze next to her, neck stiff, mouth tight, obeying when she asked it to halt—a very small measure of faith in her judgment; a timid, nervous trust that what she asked it to do was safe.

She changed her mind.

The knacker's offer went to three pounds, enough to pay for the stage, but she led the horse to a mounting block and managed to get on in spite of the jumpy shifting and prancing. At the first water crossing she regretted it, and at every water crossing since.

But they had made it to Northumberland. Whatever the chestnut's other foibles, the horse had endless stamina, and the energy to shy and bolt even if they came to a ford at the end of a thirty-mile day of rain and muddy road. It took longer, but they'd made it.

The chestnut stopped suddenly, staring off into the lowering afternoon where the clouds drifted over the moors to the north. Leigh tensed for the shying leap at whatever bogeyman the horse had discovered now, but instead it threw up its head and whinnied shrilly.

An answer came from the distance. Leigh looked up at the gaunt silhouette of the Roman wall, blinking against the fat flakes of snow. Through a tumbled gap in the masonry, a pale horse picked its way, head down as it navigated the fallen stones. The chestnut whinnied again, and the other horse stopped and answered. Then it leaped forward and came plunging down the slope of the ridge toward them.

Leigh dismounted. She let go of the excited chestnut's bridle. She'd ridden the beast long enough to know she couldn't control it, mounted or on the ground—not with an unknown animal at large. The chestnut wheeled toward the approaching horse, galloping to meet it.

They came together halfway down the slope, necks arched, ears pricked.

Leigh stood there in the mud, feeling a sudden tight uneasiness in her chest. It was the gray rogue, she was certain of it: she could see the scars on its face from where she was.

So he had come. He was here. She waited, watching the two horses snort at each other, touching noses. Suddenly the rogue squealed and struck out with its forefoot, and they both took off running.

The horses pounded along the slope, circled away from her and back, and then came galloping toward her, sending mud flying amid the snowflakes. She stood her ground as they tore past, and then the gray seemed to take an interest in her, for it slowed and came prancing back.

The chestnut followed, trotting up to within a yard of Leigh. It dropped its head, snuffling for grass beneath the snow and mud. She moved up slowly and caught it, now that the first ecstasy of meeting appeared to be over. The gray rogue stopped and stared at them, nostrils wide as it drank in the snowy wind. Leigh turned the chestnut and began to walk it along the track. After a moment, she heard the even footsteps of the gray come behind them. The gray hesitated an instant, and then walked up to her, its hooves squelching in the mud.

She patted its neck, and let it rub its face against her body.

"So where is he?" she asked. "Has he managed to get himself killed yet?"

The rogue nibbled at the trailing end of her scarf. Then its ears pricked. Both horses lifted their heads as the long, lonely howl of a wolf came floating over the moors.

* * *

She thought he must be dead.

The rogue might have escaped or been set free, but Nemo would never have voluntarily left the Seigneur to wander alone.

The wolf seemed pathetically glad to see her. She remembered how S.T. had always greeted his lupine friend, and she squatted down and allowed Nemo to lick her face and put his muddy paws on her cloak. She rubbed him and shook his head between her hands, digging her fingers deep into his damp coat to the warm dryness next to his skin. He wriggled delightedly, whining and making half barks of excitement.

The low clouds and winter brought a gloomy evening in mid-afternoon. She led her little band along the wall until the rampart disappeared, broken down over centuries to a level with the earth. She knew this country with all the familiarity of an adventurous child, knew Thorney Doors and Bloody Gap and Bogle Hole, knew better than to stop and ask for shelter at the lonely house called Burn Deviot where sheep stealers took resort.

Nemo ranged ahead, but not far, returning frequently to press up against her and lick any part of her hands or face he could reach. The wind blew hard at their backs. Leigh trudged along in the mud until she found a fallen stone to use as a mounting block.

Beyond Caw Gap the wall rose again, and from the height of Winshields she could peer through the fat snowflakes at the long basaltic ridges of Peel Crag and High Shield, their slopes rising to black cliffs that faced north, sullen and silent, like the shades of Roman sentries.

What if he was dead?

Anger and apprehension warred in her. Stupid man, stupid man! Foolish beyond permission, beyond logic, beyond any sane sense of jeopardy. As if it were a game.

What if he was dead? What if?

Leigh thought of Chilton—what he'd done; what he could do. She put her arms around the chestnut's neck and pressed her face into its mane. The warm, thick smell of horse filled her nose. The heavy scent enveloped her, made her think of the Seigneur's voice, quiet and steady, telling her to touch the battered face of the gray rogue.

Suddenly her mount's head came up, bumping her hard in the nose. She sat back, blinking against the snowflakes and the blur in her eyes. Beside her, the rogue gave a little snort and trotted forward, ears pricked. Leigh squinted along the spine of the wall.

Across a defile, where the stone fortification curved over the next hill, a mounted black horse stood facing them. She couldn't make out the rider. The gray reached the bottom of the cut and broke into a canter, mounting the ridge. Nemo made a curvet of excitement. He looked back at her, his tongue lolling.

Leigh's heart squeezed with sudden premonition. She allowed the restless chestnut to go plunging down the snowy slope.

She thought it was surely the Seigneur who gazed down at her from beneath a moisture-darkened tricorne, though he made no sign of recognition. The rogue scrambled up the opposite hill, stopped, and touched noses with the black. Nemo hung back with Leigh, trying to test the adverse wind, his tail lowered in uncertainty. The horses sidled, and the other rider controlled his mount as the gray danced and blew clouds of steamy breath.

The black sidestepped, silhouetted in profile against the dull sky, and Leigh suddenly realized that it carried two people. She reined in, hesitating at the base of the hill, her heart beating hard.

The foremost rider swung a leg over the black's mane and dismounted, leaving the other a huddled, featureless shape in the saddle. Nemo suddenly loped forward, springing from stone to stone up the steepest side of the defile. At the top, the wolf leaped to greet the man, and then Leigh was sure.

She sat frozen in joy and fury, feeling absurdly defenseless. As if the slightest touch would break her.

The Seigneur held Nemo on his arms, allowing his face to be washed before he pushed the ecstatic animal away. The big flakes of snow tumbled and floated between them on the wind. He stood still, looking down the slope at Leigh.

Alive. Quite alive.

And no doubt as impossible and pleased with himself as ever he'd been. The winter air rasped in her throat and burned her eyes. She clamped her teeth together.

The chestnut carried her up the ridge with lunging steps. When she came abreast of him, he held the black's rein and gazed at her, not speaking.

"Good afternoon," she said coldly. "How very pleasant to meet you again."

His face seemed still. No teasing smile, no cocky lift of those wicked eyebrows. "Sunshine," he said in a strange, flat voice.

The dead sounds of it made her fingers tighten on the chestnut's reins. "What's amiss?"

He stared at her, and then lowered his eyes. "I should have reckoned you'd make it somehow." He swung away from her questioning frown. For a moment he rested his fist on the black horse's shoulder, and then leaned his forehead against it, as if he didn't want to face her.

"Are you a friend?" asked a feminine voice. Leigh's head jerked up. The figure on the saddle pushed back a dark veil. Blue eyes, red-rimmed, peeked warily out.

"Who are you?" Leigh demanded.

"Are you Mr. Bartlett's friend?" the other girl asked again. "Can you help me? We escaped, and I'm cold, and I don't know where we're going. Is there a house or something nearby?"

"What happened?" Leigh repeated roughly.

The girl looked furtive. "Nothing," she said. "Nothing happened. We're looking for shelter."

Leigh ignored her. She slid off the chestnut and grabbed S.T.'s shoulder, pulling him back. "Tell me what happened!"

"He can't hear you," the girl said.

S.T.'s jaw worked, as if he were going to speak. He scowled ferociously, and then suddenly flung off Leigh's hand instead and walked around to the other side of the horse. He pulled a rope from his saddlebag, caught the gray rogue, and looped the lead into a makeshift halter. With an easy spring, he mounted the gray bareback and began to lead the other horse.

Leigh scrambled onto the chestnut and kicked it around to follow. "What do you mean, he can't hear!"

"He can't." The girl wriggled herself into the center of the saddle and looked over her shoulder. "He's deaf."

Leigh sucked in a sharp breath. "Completely?"

The girl nodded. "It wasn't my fault," she said.

"Chilton did it!" Leigh ejaculated.

"Yes." The girl bit her lip. "It wasn't my fault."

Leigh would kill the beast. She would rip him apart, tear his heart out, murder everything he loved in front of his eyes.

"I had enough faith," the girl mumbled. "Truly I did. But Master Jamie's a devil. He made me believe in him because he's a devil, and he made me do the devil's things, and the devil can't turn acid into water."

"*Acid,*" Leigh whispered in horror. "In his good ear?"

"I wouldn't have done it if I'd known. But I couldn't tell. I thought he was holy and wise, and he's the devil."

"*You* did it?" Leigh cried. She dug her heel into the chestnut and lunged, grabbing the girl's hair and dragging at her. "You misbegotten bitch!"

The girl screamed. Leigh leaned over and hit her so hard that a lock of blonde hair tore free in her gloved hand. She heard S.T. raise his voice, but she wasn't listening. She backhanded the screeching girl again.

"Malicious little gutter garbage! Get off his horse!" Leigh drew breath on a furious sob. "Get off!"

The girl was already toppling, and Leigh shoved with both hands. The horses shied at the girl's shriek. She landed in the mud, a sprawl of black veil and white legs.

Leigh circled the chestnut back. She'd have been glad to trample the wretch, but she held the horse and spat on her instead. "I hope you freeze."

The girl lay in the slop, crying. Leigh turned her mount and rode up to the Seigneur. She caught his arm. He looked at her with an alarmed expression. "Leigh," he said, and shook his head. "I'm—"

She leaned over and stopped the confession with her mouth. She held his shoulders between her hands and kissed him hard, as if she could draw him into her and make him whole again.

His skin was cold, his back stiff. He lifted his hands as if to push her away. Leigh wouldn't let him; she gripped his arms and held him as close as the horses would allow.

"You're alive," she whispered against the warmth of his breath. " 'Tis all that matters."

She put her hands on either side of his face and kissed him again. He made a sound in his throat, halfway between objection and surrender. His hands wavered and came to rest at her waist.

The gray sidestepped nearer. The Seigneur's mouth opened to her offer. He responded, tasting her tongue, mixing cold and warmth. His hold grew tight on her body. The wind blew his cloak against her, a heavy dampness that enveloped them together in the falling snow.

He drew back a little and looked at her from beneath his gold-tipped lashes. "Leigh," he said uneasily.

She squeezed his shoulders. " 'Twill be all right," she said. "I'll—I'll make a powder."

He seemed to understand that: his mouth flattened and he bent his head. Then he looked up with a wry smile, a strange tenderness, and touched her under the chin.

Leigh put her fist over her heart and then laid it against his. " 'Tis you and I," she said, slowly and clearly. "Together."

His eyebrows lifted. "You and I?" he repeated. His voice had a husky unevenness in it. She nodded and smiled, because he'd understood.

Tentatively, he leaned toward her and brushed the corner of her lips with his mouth. It was like a question, and she answered, giving herself fully to the kiss. His hands came up and tangled in her hair. He kissed her cheeks and her eyes, savored her mouth, his touch coaxing and sweetly seductive.

"Leigh," he whispered against her temple. He made a peculiar little whuff, like an embarrassed laugh. "I can hear."

She turned abruptly, bumping her chin hard against him.
He sat back and looked at her warily.

She stared at him, speechless.

He flicked his gloved fingers against her cheek. His
smile was the old smile, kindling mischief and flirtation.
"I tried to tell you," he said. "But you were—" He lifted
his hand. "—abstracted."

"You lied," she breathed. "You lied to me."

"Well, I didn't precisely—" He reached out to catch
her as she wrenched at the chestnut's reins. "Leigh—wait;
just wait a moment, damn you—ow!"

He jerked away from her striking hand.

"Why didn't you tell me?" she cried. "Why did you
let me think it was true even for a moment?"

He rubbed his arm over his forehead. "I don't know."

Leigh made a little sob of fury. "You don't know!" Her
voice quavered. "You don't know!"

"All right!" he shouted. "I didn't want to tell you! I
don't want to tell you anything; what the hell are you doing
here? You're supposed to be in Rye."

"You surely didn't think I'd stay in *Rye!*" Leigh bent
forward, shouting herself. "Darning your stockings, I
vow!" She pressed her lips together on a surge of tumbled
emotions. Behind her, the girl was whimpering. Leigh
turned in the saddle and watched her struggle to her feet
covered with muck. "There's a carriers' inn down there.
The Twice Brewed Ale." Leigh pointed toward the south.
"You can walk."

But S.T. had dismounted. He started toward the weeping girl and hauled her up off her knees. She fell into his
arms, whimpering and clinging. "You can really hear?
You're cured?"

"I can hear," he muttered.

"Oh, thank God," she wailed. "Thank God, thank
God!" She clasped her hands together, as if in prayer.

"Save it, if you please." He gave her a little shake and
led her to the black horse. "Get up," he said, offering his
cupped hands.

"Who *is* this?" Leigh demanded, eyeing the muddied
figure.

He didn't answer. After the girl had tumbled into the saddle and arranged her skirts as well as she could astride, he led the black over to Leigh. "Dove of Peace," he said, with a little inclination of his head. "Lady Leigh Strachan."

The girl bobbed and sniffed. "I'm pleased to meet you," she said, as if they were being introduced in some genteel drawing room, and then gave a small gasp. "Strachan? You're not—not from Silvering?"

"Silvering belongs to me," Leigh said. "I intend to have it back."

The girl twisted her hands together. "Master Jamie can make you do things you don't want to do," she said anxiously. "Terrible things."

Leigh gave her a cold stare. "Mayhap he can," she said, "if you're so miserable and weak that you allow it."

Dove of Peace shuddered and began to cry again. S.T. grabbed a handful of the gray rogue's mane and remounted, leading the black.

Leigh moved the chestnut up beside him. "She's one of them." She glanced toward Dove of Peace. "One of his."

"Not any longer," he said.

Leigh blew out a skeptical breath. "Is that what she claims?"

" 'Tis true!" Dove cried. "I've been praying and praying, and the blindness has been lifted from me. Master Jamie couldn't do the miracle after all; he couldn't turn the acid into water. Mr. Bartlett knew. He knew it all along. I should have listened to him instead." Then she frowned suddenly. She looked at S.T. "But now you *can* hear."

His mouth set. He looked out across the landscape. "The man's a charlatan. Can't you see it, Dove? He planned the whole thing. I'd no mind to give him his convenient 'miracle.' "

"But the acid—"

"For the love of God, 'twas no more than ice water in that pitcher. He'd have had the acid somewhere else—up his sleeve, I don't doubt."

Dove stared at him. "But then . . . you were never hurt

at all!'' His forehead wrinkled. "All that time, you could hear! Whilst Chastity and Sweet Harmony and I took such care of you. That was five days, and you never told us. 'Twas unkind, not to tell me! I thought it was my failing. I thought I hadn't faith enough for the miracle.''

"Unkind!'' Leigh cried fiercely. *"Unkind?* Who could blame him if he didn't tell you? Why should he trust *you?''*

"He could have trusted me!''

"With his life? You silly, selfish chit—'twas no nursery game to thwart that pious madman in his den. Do you think your precious Master Jamie didn't know full well that he could hear? That it was a pretense, and only to discredit him! Do you suppose he can let that pass unanswered? He lives off just your sort. Fatuous ninnies, the lot of you!''

Dove stuck out her lower lip mulishly.

"Do you deny it?'' Leigh snapped.

"I'd not do anything to hurt Mr. Bartlett.''

"Only pour acid in his ear!''·

"That was before,'' Dove cried. "Master Jamie had me in a spell! Besides, it wasn't acid, was it?'Twas only water. Perhaps my miracle worked after all!''

Leigh turned her head, beyond the power of speech. She would have happily pushed Dove of Peace right back into the mud, for the good it would have done.

The Seigneur was watching her, with a faint curve to his mouth.

"You got out of there unharmed,'' she muttered. " 'Tis all that's important.''

He grinned at her, his face shadowed by the gathering darkness. "Oh, no,'' he said softly. "I'm going to destroy the bastard. That's what's important.''

EIGHTEEN

HEAVENLY Sanctuary slept, the men in their single dormitory, the women on their mats in the parlors and dining rooms of all the houses along the street. Some of them sat up praying late into the night for the soul of Dove of Peace, who had gone away. Master Jamie had preached a sermon every day on her behalf, and wept, and told them all to forgive her for her weakness. He never mentioned Mr. Bartlett, so they all knew they were not to think of him or of the way his rebellious spirit had been taught to submit.

If some of them disobeyed and spent the midnight hours recalling his face and the way he moved, his outsider's confidence—arrogance, Master Jamie would call it—that had died with his hearing and been replaced by silence, then they had Master Jamie's extra prayers to say.

Sweet Harmony knelt on her mat beside Chastity; they both prayed very hard to be given the strength to forget Dove and Mr. Bartlett, even though it had been their task to help Dove care for him. Sweet Harmony had brought him meals and Chastity had shaved him and kept him neat, and sometimes, as he sat listlessly in the chair staring at nothing, their eyes had met over his head and Harmony had almost cried.

She tried not to blame Dove. Master Jamie had said they must forgive, and certainly Dove herself was distraught. She had wept constantly for the whole time, and never left Mr. Bartlett, and said over and over that she was sure she

259

had enough faith, and there was something wrong, and once she'd even said she wished that Master Jamie hadn't made her do it.

It was the next day that they were gone. Harmony and Chastity had climbed up to the attic room and found it empty. They ran to tell Master Jamie, but he'd only smiled and said it was his will; Dove had suffered enough for her small faith. He didn't say where Dove had gone or what had become of Mr. Bartlett.

Somewhere down in the depth of her heart, where she tried to cover it up with prayers and habits and the old sense of safety and happiness, Sweet Harmony was afraid.

She looked at Chastity hunched on her mat in the dim moonlight through the window and knew that Chastity was afraid, too.

Sweet Harmony moistened her cold lips and lifted her head just enough to see outside the unshuttered glass. In the two days since Dove and Mr. Bartlett had been gone, a hard frost had frozen the mud that swamped the unpaved edges of High Street. The church bell started suddenly, pealed out a loud clamor, ringing on and on in the frigid air. On the mats around her, other girls rustled and dragged themselves out of sleep for the hour of midnight prayer.

A few figures walked quickly and silently down the cobbled center of the road, penitents who'd been required to kneel in the church all evening and pray with Master Jamie. One of them would be his special disciple, Divine Angel, who always did penance, even though she was never obligated by making the little mistakes and failures that haunted the rest of them. Once Angel returned to the house, there would be no sneaking looks out the window during prayers, or somehow Master Jamie would be calling out one's name in the next noonday service and asking for confession.

Sweet Harmony didn't think anyone else in their house had guessed that Angel spied on them. Harmony herself had only been certain of it lately, since Mr. Bartlett and Dove had been locked in the attic and Divine Angel had been so assiduous in her concern and fondness for those whose duty it was to care for the rebellious sinner. Before,

Harmony had only been awed that Master Jamie could see so clearly into her heart and mind that he knew of all her frailties.

She resented Angel a little. It seemed to tarnish what had been glowing and bright. Not that it was her place to question. She loved Master Jamie, just as he loved her, but she would rather think that he didn't need spies. Once the suspicion had come into her head, though, it just wouldn't go away. And the very fact that she carefully didn't betray it to Divine Angel and Master Jamie never called upon her to confess her lack of faith, made it seem all the more real and upsetting.

The church bell fell silent. As the echoes died away against the side of the hill, Harmony became aware of another sound: the slow, even strike of a horse's iron-shod hooves against the cobbles.

She lifted her head openly, peering out the window. It was certainly late for Old Pap—who never answered to the name "Saving Grace" anyway—to be bringing the wagon back from Hexham. She didn't think he'd gone to town at all today, but she'd been kept busy with bleaching the floors in the new Sunday school that was to open next month for the country children.

The brilliant, steady ring of metal against stone grew louder. She saw two of the penitents pause in the street. She forgot her prayers and craned her neck to see. Out of the moon shadows along the road, a pale horse came into view, moving leisurely, its mane and tail like a fall of silver in the night.

Harmony drew in her breath. The rider wore a dark cloak that spread over his mount's back; he and his horse made the somber shapes of the penitent members in the street look small. As he walked slowly past, he turned his face up toward her window, and beneath the rakish shadow of his tricorne Harmony saw the mask.

It was silver and black, painted in jester's patterns, the angles and diamonds and distorted geometry of a midnight Harlequin. There was a luminescence to it, a glow in the tessellated pattern that made the eyes only empty space, only blankness set in the crazy designs that formed half a face: a forehead, a nose, the shape of human cheekbones and the rest lost in shadow. It was as if the night had incarnated itself, moonlight and darkness rode a horse of living alabaster and stared up at her window.

It seemed to beckon, that patterned mask; it seemed to laugh silently, the more terrifying for the humor in the whimsical design. She felt as if she were mocked all the way to her heart, every conviction she lived by laid open to those deep eyes. She clutched her hands together, unable to draw back until the eerie gaze turned from her window and the horse walked past.

"Lord bless us!" breathed Chastity, who'd craned over her shoulder without Harmony even realizing it. "Lord God bless us, 'tis the Prince! That do be the Prince hisself, knock me down if it don't."

"What?" Harmony could hardly seem to get enough air in her lungs to speak. The other girls were shuffling and pushing her back, trying to get a view out of the window. "Are you mad?" Her voice quivered upward. "That's never the Prince of Wales!"

"The Midnight Prince! The French sin-yoor. Old Pap, 'ee said 'ee seen 'im once—'e told me—in that heathen mask, on a horse all black as pitch!"

" 'Tis a white horse," Harmony said.

"What's it for, eh?" Chastity's fingers suddenly dug into her arm. She dragged Harmony back from the window and toward the door. "What an' if 'tis over Mr. Bartlett?" she hissed against Harmony's ear. "What an' if the Prince do want revenge fer that what Dove done?"

The Prince. Harmony suddenly understood who Chastity meant; she remembered newspapers and stories and lessons in French. *Le Seigneur . . . le Seigneur du Minuit*—of course, of course! Her throat tightened with terror and a new excitement. She grabbed at her shawl and fumbled in the dark to find her shoes, stuffing her bare feet inside. Chastity was already stumbling out the door, bumping into the stair rail in the dark.

They ran into the street with the other girls clattering behind them. As if their emergence had broken a spell, from every dormitory came others, some with their skirts pulled hastily over their heads, some still barefoot on the frozen ground. No one spoke; they all trotted quickly toward the church, where the pale horse stood still facing the steps.

Harmony and Chastity were first to catch up. The mounted figure turned his head; the outlandish mask stared at them.

They instantly came to a panting halt. Sweet Harmony pulled her shawl closer, wanting to go closer, torn between fear and fascination.

"Do 'ee be the Prince o' Midnight?" Chastity's demand was bold enough, but her breasts were heaving beneath her woolen gown.

The mask turned toward her. Beneath the painted pattern, he smiled; there was just enough light to see his mouth curve upward.

The gray horse swung around, facing Chastity. It lifted one front hoof, extended the other—and bowed, its fine neck arched and its long forelock dangling to the ground. *"Je suis au service de mademoiselle,"* the rider said in a wonderful low voice.

A shivery, anxious murmur of delight came from the press of girls behind them.

"What's that mean, then?" Chastity quavered.

Sweet Harmony put a hand on her shoulder. "He said he's at your service," she murmured hastily. "Don't talk to him."

"Ah! Cette petite lapine parle français." He sounded amused. The white horse came upright. It shook its head and snorted, dancing on its forelegs. "Why shouldn't she talk to me?" he asked in English. "She's braver than thou, little rabbit."

"Begone!" Sweet Harmony tried hard to keep her voice steady, but the cold made her shake like a leaf.

He put his hand over his heart. "You wound me!" he said dolefully. His black gauntlet glittered, studded with silver.

"Master Jamie won't like you here."

"Then let him come and tell me so himself, *ma petite.* I wish to have the honor of an introduction."

The church door opened; a broad ray of candlelight spread over the steps and then disappeared as Master Jamie let the door fall closed. If the horseman and the crowd surprised him, he showed no sign of it. He stood a moment at the top of the steps. Beneath his hat, his powdered hair looked dusty in the moonlight.

He held up both his hands.

Harmony tensed. She was certain he was not pleased; she was afraid he would call down something terrible on the man and the white horse, require some punishment worse than what they'd done to Mr. Bartlett—for what could be more insolent, what could be more unholy than this ominous, laughing figure that dared stand in silence before him? The Prince of Midnight was a highwayman, an outlaw, a renegade: challenge and discord and defiance; all that Master Jamie said was the wellspring of corruption.

Master Jamie began to pray aloud, and the words chilled her. "The Lord God of Hosts has declared: I loathe the arrogance of Jacob," he prayed. "For behold, the Lord is going to command that the great house be smashed to pieces and the small to fragments."

Harmony could feel the girls around her shift uneasily. Some of them moved back, and they all knew what was to come.

"You have turned justice into poison"—Master Jamie lifted his voice—"and the fruit of righteousness into wormwood, you who rejoice in a thing of nothing." He lowered his hands and stared at the man before him. "For behold, I am going to raise up a nation against you," he said softly, menacingly, and Harmony saw from the corner of her eye two of the others bend down and search on the ground for stones.

She opened her mouth, and closed it. She wanted to warn him, and did not dare. Divine Angel was right behind her, kneeling down to gather a rock. Harmony would be punished if she warned him; she'd be ostracized and unloved. She was shaking all over, sinking to her knees.

"And they will afflict you!" Master Jamie cried suddenly, "From the entrance of Hamath to the brook of the Arabah!''

The pale horse moved, stepping onto the first stair of the church. It leaned forward, pushed out its nose, and nuzzled Master Jamie's face.

Harmony fell on her knees and stared. Everyone grew still except Master Jamie, who kept praying, shouting with his eyes closed as if the animal weren't there. The horse nibbled at his hat brim, took it between its teeth, and pulled the hat away. Then it swung and faced them, dangling the headgear from its mouth drolly. The animal walked over to Divine Angel. She shrank back as it flipped the hat upward, bringing it down to rest on her head at a crazy tilt.

The horse stepped back, tossed its head up and down, and lifted its forefeet off the ground, picking them up together in a neat and elegant advance.

"Most ravishing," the Prince murmured.

The big horse moved forward leisurely, and no one, not even Divine Angel with the hat balanced absurdly on her head, stood firm in its path.

"Au revoir, ma chérie courageuse." He leaned down to touch Chastity's cheek as he passed. "I'll come back for you one night, if you like."

Master Jamie had stopped speaking. In the silence, Divine Angel lifted her hand and threw her single stone, but the horse was already walking away, out of Angel's poor range. The rock hit Chastity between the shoulder blades.

"Here!" Chastity jumped and turned. "Blasted maggoty-head, what'd ye do that for?" She thrust through to Angel and gave her a shove. It landed the other girl on her rump, but Chastity didn't pause to see what came of her wickedness; even as Master Jamie spoke her name, she began to run up the street after the horse.

Sweet Harmony ran, too. The horse and rider had already disappeared into the night. She caught Chastity halfway down the road, grabbed her by the arm, and turned her into their own gateway. That was the only hope now—that Master Jamie might have other things to think of and forget that Chastity had lain a hand of violence on one of the most favored of his flock.

On Divine Angel, who wouldn't let him forget.

"Kneel down, kneel down," Harmony said urgently as they reached the top of the stairs. She could hear the others coming behind them. "Pray for forgiveness."

Chastity threw off her arm and turned sullenly away. But she knelt down on her mat, and when an hour later Divine Angel and Master Jamie came in person, she nodded and cried and asked Angel to forgive her, and they went away, and everything was peace again.

After the church bell tolled the end of midnight prayers, Chastity and Sweet Harmony lay on their mats, close together in the chilly room.

"Harmony," Chastity whispered, barely audible in the darkness. "The Prince, what did 'ee say to me?"

Harmony bit her lip. She didn't answer.

"Please," Chastity whispered. "What do 'sharee' mean?"

Sweet Harmony bent her head into her blanket. "It means 'darling,' " she said softly. "He called you his courageous darling.

"Oh." It was a breath: a faint, awed whisper. "Oh my bloomin' Lord."

S.T. had expected to slip back into the carriers' inn unobserved, but Leigh was waiting for him, out in the cold moonlight, a black shape that rose up from the side of the road and made Mistral shy a bit. Nemo had found her first; he bounded between them, leaping and twisting in excitement at the reunion. She was still the only female that the wolf accepted. Nemo wouldn't even go near Heavenly Sanctuary, and only firm orders would have made him creep inside the Twice Brewed Ale where they'd taken rooms two nights since, so S.T. let him go on running free on the empty moors.

S.T. still wore the harlequin mask, reluctant to relinquish the Prince and become himself again. He loved the mask; savored the fascination it created, relished the astonished faces of the girls in Heavenly Sanctuary. He'd made the mask himself, painted his soul onto papier-mâché the same way he had years ago, the first time, whistling a rigadoon as he worked alone in the empty loft over the stable.

He'd kept his intent to himself, stealing away after the others were abed, but now that things had gone so well he'd no objection to asking Mistral for the beginning of a little *passage*, a few steps of elevated trot, like a victory dance. The horse snorted, unsure of this new request, but the weeks of relentless teaching and practice on the road north had instilled the cues. Mistral tried. He managed one springy stride in his earnest attempt to go forward and stay in one place at the same time, and S.T. instantly allowed him to relax, leaning over to rub his poll in praise. Mistral shook his mane, his ears cocked back questioningly.

"Seigneur," Leigh said with a bow, and he couldn't tell if it was awe or awful sarcasm in her voice—but he suspected, with a little lapsing of his elevated mood, that it was sarcasm.

He removed his hat and pulled off the mask. "Lady Leigh," he murmured, with a slight inclination of his head.

"Where have you been?"

"I've been to visit the Reverend Mr. Chilton," he said, and somehow the announcement wasn't as gratifying as he'd envisioned. He'd get nothing from Leigh, damn her— as if he hadn't known it.

"I thought we'd agreed that you wouldn't do anything alone."

"No," he said. "We agreed that *you* wouldn't do anything. Alone or otherwise."

She stared up at him, her face smooth and ivory in the moonlight. Lovely—so lovely that he felt a sudden twist in his chest and didn't want to argue, didn't want to resurrect the quarrel over Chilton and the danger and the risks. He wondered what it would be like just to talk to her once, just to lie in bed and speak of commonplace things. Insignificant things, like how Mistral had learned to pick up the girth and hand it to him when he asked and whether the landlady would kill the old rooster for stew tomorrow or sacrifice three pullets to be roasted.

He wiped the back of his gauntlet across his cheek and stowed the mask in his saddlebag. "Take you up?" he asked, offering his hand.

"I'll walk." She stood still, and then shivered suddenly, pushing her hands down into the pockets of her greatcoat. "Did you ride Mistral into the town?"

He dismounted and began to lead the horse. "Not very clever, to walk in on foot."

"They'll recognize him. They'll be able to describe him." She fell in beside him. "Did you kill Chilton?"

He could tell that she'd tried to say it casually. But it sounded a fraction out of breath, just a little waver on the last syllable.

He wanted to turn around and hold her close and kiss her forehead . . . just that, as if she were a child—tell her Chilton wasn't her worry anymore. But they'd fought about it for the two days since she'd joined him, fought it to a standstill, mired in a strange suspension at a carriers' lodge in the middle of nowhere, arguing in whispers and behind doors over what came next.

S.T. knew what came next. He had his own reasons for revenge now, and he intended to have it, but she was wavering: she had a dispute with every plan, or she got emotional and bottled up and wouldn't speak, turning away from him as if she had something to hide.

It made him angry: they'd come all this way and now it almost seemed as if she didn't want him to do it, wouldn't break in front of him and wouldn't give it up to him, even once telling him to leave Chilton be, she didn't care anymore, as if it all ought to go away because she'd decided so. Looking at him shaky and furious, as if it was somehow his fault that it didn't.

He couldn't understand what she wanted. He didn't think she understood it herself.

"No, I didn't kill Chilton," he said flatly.

"You should have done," she said. "While you had the chance."

He wrenched down hard on his temper. "My thanks for the advice. But cold-blooded murder is not my way."

"He saw you, didn't he? He'll guess that you're Mr. Bartlett. He'll be prepared now. He'll be afraid. He's dangerous, you reckless blockhead—haven't you learned that yet?"

Mistral twisted his head and pranced, protesting the sudden drag on his bit. S.T. eased his hold. He strode forward, keeping his eyes on the shadowy ground. "I've learned it. We've had this conversation before. Several times. It begins to grow tedious, you may believe me."

"Don't play with him," she said. "It's not a game."

"Oh, but it is." He stopped and faced her. "You want revenge, madam, you want justice—there's no measure in skewering the fellow from behind. I want him to know who's killing him. I want him to see his malignant little kingdom smashed to nothing. I want to pull it down piece by piece around his ears before he dies." He stared down into her face. "Perhaps you've forgotten what he's done to you. I haven't."

She didn't flinch. "And then what?" she hissed. "Then I fall down on my knees and say I adore you? Don't hope for it."

That wounded. He felt embarrassed and furious, the worse because it was halfway to true. He still had hopes which he hadn't realized until he heard her say it.

God alone knew why. She was fine enough to look at, the condescending shrew, but hardly cordial company. He could do better. Far better, curse her if he couldn't.

Just one small part of him held on, kept going back to the memory of that moment when she'd put her hand against his heart.

Together. You and I.

The rest of him said: certainly . . . and no, the sun won't come up tomorrow, either. Fool. He had his faults, but he'd never been feebleminded.

Together. You and I together.

No one had ever said that to him before.

They'd said, "I love you." They'd called him handsome and charming and devilish exciting, and couldn't he stay longer and come more often and bring some pretty bauble they might show to their friends and whisper who it came from, because it was all so exotic and exhilarating and they'd never felt such passion, not with anyone, never known this fervent devotion that would live on forever, and did he love them truly?

He swore he did, he brought the gifts, he stayed as long as he judged it safe, sometimes longer than was sane, because he believed in it all. But somehow that was never enough. Somehow there was always soft coaxing that turned to pleading and then to tears.

"There's no use in this silly swashbuckling of yours, do you understand?" she was saying belligerently, as if he'd been arguing with her. "I don't want you on my conscience."

He didn't answer her, didn't see any use in it. He just put his hand on Mistral's neck and walked silently on, all the elation of his encounter in Heavenly Sanctuary drained out of him.

Dove was wide-eyed, dewy, her blonde hair waving freely down her back in public in a way that Leigh had been brought up to think vulgar, if not promiscuous. "You've been out." Dove put her hand on the Seigneur's arm. "Lady Leigh was right . . . you went there?"

The Twice Brewed was still noisy, the hall packed with a caravan of carriers that had arrived late. All the carters at the table stared at Dove between gulps of ale and huge bites of roast beef.

"Shall we retire upstairs?" S.T. grabbed Dove firmly by the elbow and turned her around. Leigh went up behind them. He headed for the little chamber Dove shared with Leigh, which put her in a worse temper than before.

As soon as the door closed, Dove took both his arms. "Lady Leigh was right, wasn't she? You went back to the Sanctuary!"

He gave Leigh a sour glance. "I'd not thought to have it common knowledge."

"You truly did!" Dove exclaimed. "What did Master Jamie say? Did he see you?"

S.T. tossed his hat and saddlebags on a chair and stripped off his sword belt. "I trust he didn't recognize me, in any case."

"Oh." Dove sounded a little disappointed. "You stole in?"

He drew the mask out of the saddlebag, dangling it from his fingers. "Not precisely."

Dove put her hand over her mouth. "You wore that? Oh!"

He smiled and held it up to his face. Even in the candlelit room it changed him, made him mysterious and strange, his face impossible to focus upon beneath the intricate patterns that danced on the mask. His eyes glittered faintly in the depths; he might have been watching either of them, or no one. It was impossible to tell.

"I've seen pictures of that. 'Tis a highwayman's mask," Dove whispered.

He lowered the camouflage. "Not just any highwayman's, love. Mine."

Dove absorbed that, standing with her lips in an "O" of wonder. Leigh had no great opinion of her wit, but the truth appeared to dawn upon her with surprising promptness. "The Seigneur du Minuit! You're *him!* Oh, are you *him?*"

He swept a bow.

"I had no notion," Dove cried. "And you've come to punish Master Jamie? You planned it all along? How brave you must be!" She sat down on a chair and gazed up at him. "How wonderful and brave to do that for us."

"Wonderfully ill-advised," Leigh murmured.

He gave her a brief glance. Then he smiled at Dove. "Honored to be of service, fairest."

Dove slid off the bed onto her knees. She took his hand and kissed it, holding it against her mouth. "Thank you," she whispered. "Oh, thank you. You are so good."

Leigh thought that at least he would look chagrined at this outburst, but instead he allowed Dove to cling to his hand. He actually seemed gratified; he chuckled complaisantly and even reached out to touch her, brushing her long hair back from her face.

Leigh wet her lips and turned abruptly away. Silly man!
Let him wallow in brainless adoration, then. She crossed
her arms tightly over her stomach and leaned against the
wall, staring out the window.

"When you are quite finished," Leigh said, "may I ask
if Your Highness has given a thought to the king's men in
this scheme?"

He caught Dove's arms and raised her. "Chilton won't
call on the Crown."

"Won't he?" Leigh watched Dove look up at him shyly
through the shining curtain of her hair. "You can't be
certain of that."

"Soldiers? That would be the last thing he'd care for—
a power above him in his own kingdom. You needn't worry
for my neck on that score."

Dove still held on to him. She brushed back her hair
and clasped both hands on one of his. He glanced down,
gave her a faint, indulgent smile, and squeezed her fingers.

Leigh found herself turning scarlet. It wrenched something deep inside her to see him touch Dove in that gentle
way, as casually as if they'd been lovers for years. But
Dove was what he wanted, of course—all that breathless,
unconditional admiration; no matter that a week past she'd
been pouring what she'd thought was acid in his ear. Coxcomb! Bloody stupid coxcomb.

" 'Tis late." Leigh walked over to the candle and blew
it out. The smoky scent of tallow enveloped the room.

"And I perceive that I'm desired to go away," he said
in the darkness. "Give you good night, *demoiselles.*"

After the door closed on his back, Leigh shrugged out
of her waistcoat and got into bed in her shirt. She held
onto the bedpost, facing the window, making sure that she
didn't touch Dove at all when the other girl climbed onto
the mattress.

For a long time Leigh clung stiffly to the edge of the
bed, feeling Dove wriggle and shift at intervals until at
last her breathing settled into the even rhythm of sleep.
The moon hung low, shining in Leigh's eyes through the

window, setting slowly over the northern moors where Nemo hunted alone.

Leigh turned her face into the pillow. She bit her lip and squeezed her eyes shut, and tried to make her heart into stone.

NINETEEN

A
T the sound of footsteps outside his door, S.T. sat
up among the bedclothes and dragged his arm
across his face. The carters had long since gone
to bed, the noise from the taproom subsided into silence.
He'd left the bed curtains tied open, and strong moonlight
frosted everything in the room to black and silver. He
squinted, listening.

The latch rattled, sounding distant to his good ear. He
rolled over in bed and put his hand on the hilt of his sword.
He hadn't locked the door, having no key—and abruptly
all of his blood was alive, singing danger through his veins.

The door creaked open. A pale figure, barefoot, stood
uncertain on the treshold.

"Leigh," he said hoarsely.

For an instant his grip stayed tight on the sword, as it
took his muscles a moment to react to the message of his
mind. Then he relaxed, leaning over to prop the weapon
back into position within easy reach.

"Confound you, woman," he muttered. "You're like
to have a rapier through your belly, creeping upon me that
way."

She closed the door behind her.

S.T. hiked himself up onto his elbow. "What is it?"

She didn't speak; to his astonishment she came forward
and sank to her knees beside the bed.

"Sunshine." He sat up in dismay. "What the—are you
ill?" He reached out to touch her forehead.

274

She caught his hand. A peculiar sound escaped her, like
a small and miserable laugh. She pressed her lips against
his skin, shaking her head.

"What is it?" he whispered. "What's wrong?"

"I want to tell you something," she said. Her voice
was trembling. As he spread his hand against her face, she
pulled away, the voluminous shirt flowing around her.

Awareness of her flooded him, the shape of her body
beneath the linen as she stood. He tossed the bedclothes
back and came to his feet in the cold room, uncertain and
aroused. "Tell me what?"

She made that queer small sound again, facing away
from him, her hands over her mouth. "You'll think me
mad," she said dismally.

In the moonlight, he could see that she was shivering.
"You're cold." He moved without thinking, almost taking
her into his arms. Then he hesitated, unable to draw her
against his nakedness, hoping the shadow hid the way his
body revealed him.

She turned suddenly and put her hands against his arms,
shaking her head, moving into his embrace silently.

"What is it?" He cradled her against him, trying to give
warmth to her shivering softness, his hands exploring her
back and her hair. On his bare shoulder he felt her cheek
wet and cold. "Sunshine," he said painfully. He hugged
her hard against him. "Are you crying? *Mon ange; ma
pauvre petite.*"

Her fingers closed on his arms, clutching as if he might
disappear. He held her steadily, enfolding her, stroking her
hair while she wept soundlessly, the tears slipping down
his shoulder.

"Little love, little lost one," he soothed. He rocked her
gently, laying his cheek against her hair. "All's well. I'll
not leave you alone."

Her fist curled; she struck it softly against his arm.
"Liar," she whispered. "Liar."

She bewildered him. He bent his head, nuzzling her ear.
"No, you've naught to fear."

She didn't answer, only stood with her face hidden in
his chest. He could feel each smothered breath she took.

Then she raised her eyes to his in the moonlight.

And he understood. Oh, he understood; he didn't need words to interpret the direct look, the slight lowering of her lashes, the way her hands kneaded his arms in an unconscious rhythm.

"Leigh . . ." he breathed. "My God."

She burrowed against him, her shoulders hunched, as if she wanted to hide in his embrace. She had to know the state of his desire; she pressed herself against the whole length of his body.

He took a deep breath and made the sacrifice: held her off a little and cupped her face between his hands. "Think a moment. 'Tis that you've came back to this place. You've—memories. You're unhappy. You're mourning. You don't truly want . . . this." He kissed her forehead and then added tentatively, "Do you?"

She lowered her eyes. He thought she would speak: she wet her lips and stared at the base of his throat. The silver trail of tears glimmered on her skin.

"You don't want this," he repeated heroically.

Her eyes squeezed closed. Lightly, purposefully, she began to draw him toward the bed.

He surrendered then, tossing scruples to the devil. He wanted to make her one with himself, shelter and solace and protect her. He wanted to drown in her body. He cradled her in silence, undressed her in silence, kissed her bare shoulder and her throat and bore her down on the bed without words.

"What did you come to tell me?" he whispered against her ear.

Her lips moved; he felt it on his skin, but he could not hear the words, too soft for his ear or never spoken aloud at all.

"I love you, too," he whispered.

She lay her head back with that aching sound between a laugh and a sob. "Oh, you are cocksure, are you not?" she said in a small, shaky voice.

He kissed her temple. *"Chérie,"* he murmured, brushing his lips against her cheek. "Tell me what you came here to say to me."

Leigh gazed up at him. "I don't know," she whispered. "I don't know what I came for." By the light of the moon, she watched his body: unmarked, strong, with no visible sign of the injuries he'd suffered.

Alive. Burning like a golden flame in the dim room.

Fear and despair welled up once more. She thought him beautiful enough for tears.

He kissed her eyelids as the moisture leaked from beneath her lashes. "Don't," he said, as if it hurt him. "Don't."

She reached up. She wanted him inside her, for proof of something: that he was vital and warm and living. The slide of his skin on hers made her shudder. His weight pressed her into the bed, his arousal stiff and responsive to every touch. She opened to let him take her as he had before, in impetuous thrusts, but instead he touched her nipple with his tongue, drawing a sharp breath from her throat.

She'd thought herself experienced, having lain freely with two men. But he began to do things he had never done before, and she found that she'd only been initiated into a world that her lover had long ago mastered.

He knew things about her that she hadn't known herself. Her heart began to pump harder. She arched her head back as he caressed her breasts, circling the tips with his tongue and his forefinger while his hand drifted downward, made a feather stroke up and down the inside of her thigh and tangled in the curling hair there.

He slipped to the side and pressed against her, gently urging her to turn over away from him. With his chest against her back, his hardness pressed into her buttocks, he leaned over her and nibbled at the tender skin beneath her arm, then bent to suckle and tug at her breast. He enfolded her, encompassed her with himself, hugged her close and drew his thigh up between hers to make an erotic cradle of his body. His hand moved; his fingers slipped deep inside her.

The sensation was exquisite, a heavy penetration in time to the warm tugging pull at her nipple. Leigh pushed back against him mindlessly, lost in the feel of him all round her, moving in the rhythm he established. She heard herself; from somewhere in the depths of her came small gasps of helpless pleasure.

He shifted, nuzzling upward, and bit her neck lightly. "I love you," he whispered fiercely. "I love you, I love you, I love you."

He pushed his body against her back in slow cadence. With each move, his arm brought her closer and his breath came in a rush on her skin.

She could not contain it; she turned toward him and wrapped her legs around his, pulling him urgently toward her. He moved with a low, masculine sound, mounting her quickly, as urgent now as she. His hair had fallen loose from the black ribbon; it spread over his shoulder; she scooped it up in her fist, tangled her fingers in it, and pulled him down to kiss his mouth.

His body seemed heavy within her, deep and powerful. She arched beneath him. He shoved slowly, pinning her with each aching, deliberate thrust, using himself to pleasure her. Her head fell back and her breath came harshly. He kissed her exposed throat, sucked the sensitive skin, his whole weight pressing her against the bed. His rhythm compelled her, pushed her, driving harder into her center. She met him and matched him, and passion burst over her, blowing and shattering and throbbing through her body in waves and waves.

She only realized that she'd slept when she drifted awake. The moon still burned white, casting icy shadows across the plastered walls and low beams. She could see him clearly; he lay on his side with his arm across her body, his face turned a little into her.

She thought he was asleep. His chest rose and fell gently.

Without moving, she gazed at him. It felt strange and raw, this terrible love, this wobbly sense of possessing a measure of joy. She feared it, and yet she could not give it up. Worse, it left the rest of her spirit in shambles; she could not seem to resurrect the grim determination that had carried her so far. She hated Chilton, but the emotion seemed academic, distant and illusory in comparison to her intense awareness of the man who lay beside her.

And when she lost him . . . when he went away . . . what then? She was afraid; the terror of it lay waiting somewhere ahead, cold and implacable, real and not quite real, like childhood monsters in the dark beyond the bed. They can't be there, the child cried plaintively. 'Tis only shadows.

Oh, but they are.

They're there. They exist. Only the fairy-tale princes fade, like shadows, when daylight comes at last.

She studied the arc of muscle along his outstretched arm, the shape of his jaw, the way the fingers of his other hand curled in the glimmering tangle of his own hair.

Painfully, beneath her breath, she whispered, "I love you."

He opened his eyes.

A slow smile curved his mouth. He reached up and spread his hand over her temple, smoothing a lock of her hair between his thumb and fingers.

She saw he was going to speak, put her hand to his lips, and shifted back a little. "No. Don't say it."

He raised himself on his elbow. Moonlight fell across his face, highlighting the upward curve of one eyebrow, making his smile seem gently wicked. "Foolish Sunshine—don't say that I love you?"

"Don't say that you love me. Don't say you've never felt this way before. Don't say . . . just—don't say any of those things." She bit her lip. "I could not bear it."

His eyes dropped. His mouth hardened a little. He moved his fingertips across the skin of her shoulder, down to her breast, barely brushing. "You leave me speechless, then."

She stared upward. The light touch drifted over her skin, drawing circles, spirals, hearts.

"All I wanted was Chilton," she whispered. "I wanted your help; I didn't want a lover—I wanted justice for what's been done to my family. That's all I asked of you."

"You'll have it," he said.

"Oh, aye!" She laughed hopelessly. "You are the Seigneur, are you not?"

His hand stilled.

"The great highwayman," she said. "The Midnight Prince. The legend, the hero, the myth." Fear made her ruthless. "I threw your diamond necklace in a millpond."

She felt the way his body altered, a subtle shift, a tightening of every muscle. He gripped her shoulder, leaned over her, and kissed her mouth, rough kisses at the corners of her lips and in the center, sweet with the heat and scent of him. "What do you want?" The space of a breath separated his mouth from hers. "Do you want me on my knees?"

She gazed up into his face. "I want to be left alone."

"You come to me." His mouth lowered, but he didn't quite kiss her.

"To forget. To not hurt any more—" She bit her lip. "To hurt all my life."

"I won't hurt you," he whispered.

She closed her eyes. "You tear me apart."

"Leigh," he said, "I love you." The intensity in his voice made her turn her face away.

"Leave me alone," she said.

He drew back, pushing up on one arm. "Leave you!" he echoed, the words etched in frustration.

"I can't bear it, why can't you understand that?" Her voice began to break. "Why can't you have mercy and leave me in peace?"

He rolled away and stood up, naked and splendid, his hair free and his body cast in shadows. "Why did you come to me?"

She pressed her face into the warm place where he'd lain. "Leave me alone."

"Tell me why you came, Leigh."

She crushed the pillow to her.

"Only let me love you," he said. "Just let me—"

"Love!" She threw the pillow aside and sat up, pulling the beclothes around her. "You hypocrite. 'Tis nothing to you to say that, is it? You prate about love and roses and devotion, but you don't know the meaning of the word. You never have, and I doubt you ever will.''

He let out a harsh breath. "I don't understand you. How you can say that, after—'' He spread his hands and made a baffled sound. "After *this.*''

"This! This is fancy, 'tis infatuation, 'tis a dream. Maybe you love your horses, maybe you love Nemo—all you require of me is a reflection of yourself. You and your bloody mask!'' She was crying openly now, her head tilted back, her eyes shut against the tears. "Don't keep trying to dress it up as love, because I know what love is, and it hurts, it hurts, it hurts.''

"Aye,'' he said quietly. "This hurts.''

She felt him come closer. The bed sagged beside her with his weight. He touched her face, and she pulled away.

"Don't,'' she said. "You've had what you want from me tonight.''

"That isn't all I want.''

"Oh, indeed,'' she said bitterly. "How could I think it enough? Just my whole self, every inch of my body and soul, that's what you want.'' She opened her eyes and stared into his. "It is not me who demands a lover on their knees.''

He lowered his gaze, his face sober, troubled. "You said it was you and me, together—and I . . . it felt so good. I want it that way.'' He looked up at her from beneath his lashes and said in a low voice, "I think I know what love is, Leigh.''

"Go away!'' She hugged the pillow to her. "Go away, go away, go away.''

" 'Twas you who came to me,'' he said softly.

"I . . . hate . . . you.''

He bent, resting his forehead on her shoulder. "You cannot,'' he whispered. "You can't hate me.''

For an instant she sat with her lip trembling, her whole body cold except where he touched her. "How many love affairs do you have to your credit, Monseigneur? Fifteen? Twenty? A hundred?''

He did not look up. " 'Tis no matter.''

"How many?''

"Some. I never gave my heart, not this way."

"I have had one," she said. "His name was Robert. How many can you name?"

He blew out a breath and drew back. "Why?"

"Why not? Name me the last five."

"What is your point?"

She lifted her chin, looking down her nose. "Poor ladies, can you not recall them?"

"Of course I can recall them. The last one was named Elizabeth, and she was the bitch who turned me in."

"That's one." She watched him. "Who preceded Elizabeth?"

He frowned and shifted, pushing away to arm's length. "I don't see that it's important."

"You've forgotten."

"I haven't forgotten, damn it. Elizabeth Burford, Caro Taylor, Lady Olivia Hull, and—Annie—Annie, uh—she was a Montague, but she married twice—you'll forgive me if I can't recall her married name, and Lady Libby Selwyn."

She lifted her eyebrows. "You move in elevated circles."

He shrugged. "I move where it pleases me."

"You were in love with all of them."

"Ah. Is that the point? No, I was not in love with any of them. It wasn't at all the same. This time—" He stopped, with an arrested look, and then his gaze evaded hers. "It's different this time," he said.

"Certainly. Do you propose to set up a nursery? Build you a fair manor house upon a hill? Give up your—occupation—and settle in to be an honest country squire?"

He stared into the shadows, brooding. "I've a price on my head. You know that."

She thrust back the blankets. "How fortunate for you."

He looked at her sharply. "I don't find it fortunate at all."

"Do you not?" Leigh groped for her shirt, pulling it over her head.

"Wait." He reached for her. "Leigh! Don't go like this."

"I've no notion to stay." She turned away for the door.

"You're not the same as the others," he exclaimed. "I love you. I *love* you! You're—God, Leigh, you're like the sun, you burn so bright it hurts me. The rest . . . all the rest, they're candles to it."

She put her hand on her heart. "A nicely turned gallantry, ready primed," she murmured. "I said you should have been a troubadour."

"Plague take you!" His feet hit the floor with a thump. "Why won't you believe me? I love you!"

She snorted. "Decidedly! Which plague will you have dispatch me?"

He gripped the bedpost. "Leigh—listen to me." His voice gained force. "I've never felt like this."

She laughed outright.

"It's true," he shouted. "I've never felt this way; *never;* I love you! For God's sake, tell me how I can prove it!"

She stood with her hand on the door, staring down at the latch.

"Tell me how," he said.

She hugged the shirt around her and shivered. "Leave Chilton alone," she said slowly.

"What?"

She turned to him. "Stay out of Felchester. Forget Chilton. Leave it be."

"Forget Chilton," he echoed. His arm stiffened against the post. "What do you mean?"

" 'Tis plain enough, I think."

He shook his head in frustrated bafflement. "Not at all." He shook it again. "No. This is how I'm to show my love? By failing you?"

"I don't care anymore," she said steadily. "It won't bring my family back. It won't change anything. I've known that . . ." She took a breath. "But it seems to have come clearer lately."

"And so I'm to abandon it."

"Yes."

He was silent for a long time. She leaned against the door, holding her arms around herself against the cold.

"I can't," he said at last.

She lowered her head.

"I can't!" he said, louder. "And it makes no sense, anyway. I don't understand you."

She closed her eyes. "Do you understand fear, Seigneur? Have none of these ladies of yours ever dreaded to see you put on that cursed mask and ride out to hazard your chances?"

"None that ever said. Do you doubt me? How would slinking off like some man-milliner prove aught of what I feel?"

"Perhaps it might prove that you think of what *I* feel," she said fiercely. "But that's no part of your love, is it?" She shoved the latch open.

"I think of what you feel! You'd not have me walk away from this; that can't be love, that can't be what you truly want of me! To be some spineless—nothing!"

"As well if I did," she said scornfully. "Nothing is all you give of yourself. Hide behind your mask, then, if you will. I'll none of it."

"Leigh," he said, with a faint, desperate edge in his voice. "What if you're wrong about me?"

She stepped into the hall and closed the door gently behind her.

S.T. bowed his head and pressed the heels of his hands over his eyes. Curse her, damn her, how could she know it wasn't love he felt? She was so sure, so resentful, she twisted his intentions around so far that she made him doubt himself.

It *was* different this time. He loved her courage; he loved her when the freezing rain dripped down off her hat and her hair was plastered against her throat and she never once complained; he loved her in her breeches, he loved her when she snarled at Dove and when she made an eye bath for a blind mare. He loved her because she'd followed him; he loved her because she never cried and then he loved her to the deepest raw center of his soul when she did. He wanted to hold her and protect her—and he wanted her respect more urgently than he'd wanted any prize in his life.

He should have told her. He'd mismanaged it; he should have put everything differently. But how could he say such things? Not to a woman, to *her*, not when she sneered at him. Not when she doubted him. It made him burn with shame to know she'd so little regard for his skill that she was afraid for him. All the arguments and wavering over Chilton fell into place and made mortifying sense to him now.

But she came. Why had she come, ah, God, and let him love her, and then told him what she thought of him? A failure, a fraud, so bumbling that she dreaded to see him ride out into danger.

It always happened this way. One instant of balance, a moment of union, and then everything was fragmenting. This time was different, different, different, and yet it was going to be just like all the others; slipping away into time and memories. He felt frantic at the thought, threw himself facedown on the bed, and clutched a pillow between his hands as if he could strangle it.

I love you, he thought ferociously. *I'll show you it's different.* He sat up with the pillow and socked it against a bedpost. *It's different!* He gritted his teeth and hammered it back the other way. *I love you . . . I'll show you . . . I love you . . . I'll show you . . . it's different, it's different, it's different . . .* he kept on pounding until the feathers exploded and fluttered around him, impossible to catch or combat or master.

TWENTY

A T twilight Sweet Harmony heard it and straightened up from her sewing. Her eyes met Chastity's.

The sound echoed in the quiet street: horse's hooves
chiming against stone in a solitary rhythm.

It had been four days. Chastity's hands were pink and
bleeding, swollen from the nettles that she had to carry
everywhere as a symbol of her contrition for pushing Divine Angel. The nettles lay in her lap now, dried to winter
stiffness, their stinging hairs rubbed away by hours of contact. In the morning Angel would go with her to the mid-
den to see that she cut a fresh bouquet of penance.

Harmony lowered her eyes, afraid to betray the frantic
leap of her heart. He was back; he'd said he would come
again and he came—and Harmony could see the scarlet
color flood Chastity's face.

Don't get up, Harmony wanted to cry to her. Don't
move, don't speak.

But she dared not acknowledge the sound in the street
while Divine Angel sat with them. She held her breath and
went on sewing, thrusting her needle through the linen in
jerky moves.

"I hear Master Jamie calling us," Divine Angel said,
setting aside her work.

Harmony heard nothing but the sound of horseshoes on
the cobblestone.

286

"Come." Angel rose. "You must bring the nettles, Chastity."

Harmony stood up. Chastity made a little sound as she came to her feet, but whether it was pain or anger or fear or protest, Harmony couldn't tell.

"Did you speak, our dearest sister?" Angel asked kindly.

"No, Angel." Chastity lowered her face.

"Your time of affliction will soon be over. You must bear it with grace and submission in your heart."

"Yes, Angel," Chastity whispered. "I do be very sorry."

"Master Jamie wishes us to join him in destroying the evil that threatens," Angel said serenely, and waited for them to go ahead of her out the door.

In the deep evening shadows, others were gathering, lining the street near the piles of stone they had collected. It was to defend themselves, to crush the devil's influence. This time they were ready, and down the street the devil came, riding on his pale horse, masked in dazzling mockery.

"Go away," someone cried, a shrill, single voice in the silence. "We don't want you here!"

The horse walked ahead, drawing slowly nearer. Harmony wished she could cry out the same thing, to make him go away, to stop what was going to happen. He must know, she thought frantically. Surely this time he must know.

The church bell tolled once. Master Jamie appeared around the corner of the churchyard, carrying his Bible. It was time for dinner; every evening he made this passage at precisely this moment, to say his blessing over the ceremony of obedience in the men's dormitory.

He halted at the top of the street, facing the approaching devil.

Harmony looked away from him, back toward the advancing rider. One of the men picked up a stone and threw it. He missed, and the gray horse suddenly wasn't walking anymore; it moved at an easy, collected canter, past Harmony and Chastity before Divine Angel even had time to take a rock from the nearest pile.

Stones fell in the street, most of them thrown lightly, an instant too late. Harmony realized with horror that she hadn't even picked one up; she glanced at Angel, and stooped quickly to grab the nearest as the men moved into the street, brandishing larger rocks. Some of them had pitchforks, and one even carried a blunderbuss. The girls threw weakly, without their hearts in it, but for days the men had scowled and talked and promised what they'd do if the intruder came again.

She glanced desperately back toward Master Jamie as the horse and cloaked rider cantered down on him. Someone shrieked. Harmony sucked in her breath, frozen in place as Master Jamie lifted his Bible in both hands.

"Stone him!" he cried in a mighty voice that echoed all the way to hill. *"Cast out the devil!"*

The big rocks came hurtling past. But none of them touched the target; the horse was well beyond range and had gone right past Master Jamie.

He lowered the book and yelled, "We are triumphant! See how he flees from the righteous hand of God!"

The men raised an uneven cheer, but Harmony stood silent with the others, watching as the white horse halted just behind Master Jamie and came sidling back, moving sideways with one hoof crossed over the other.

It stopped behind him, close enough to touch, with the rider's boot just even with Master Jamie's back.

The man in the mask stared at them all over Master Jamie's head. Harmony couldn't see his mouth in the shadow beneath the harlequin design, but she was certain he was grinning.

Master Jamie didn't turn. He must have known what was there, but he stood straight, beginning to walk toward them as if he was continuing on his way to the dining hall.

The white horse came right behind, prancing sideways. Every two or three steps it bumped into Master Jamie, sending him stumbling. He stopped, and the horse nipped his hat away and shook it up and down.

Someone giggled. The men stood with their rocks lowered, unable to throw them without the risk of hitting Master Jamie. Suddenly the man with the blunderbuss lifted the weapon to his shoulder.

The Prince drew his sword instantly, dropping the reins. He held the blade against Master Jamie's neck.

"Throw it down," he said, in that low, carrying voice.

Evening light seemed to pulsate along the steel. Harmony realized with deep shock that Master Jamie was shaking, his face white and red.

The horse moved sideways again, bumping up against his back. He lurched forward, and then turned, grabbing the sword. "Fire!" he shouted. "Kill the devil!"

His fingerless mittens closed around the blade. It swept upward; Harmony saw blood, heard screams and Master Jamie's own screech as the cutting edge swept across his fingers.

The sword came up, free. The Prince leaned over and caught Master Jamie around the chest with one arm, dragging him halfway up into the saddle as the big gray rocked back on its haunches and reared.

Master Jamie's feet dangled off the ground. "Fire!" he shrieked. "Fire!"

"I can't!" the man shouted. "I can't—Master Jamie—get back; get away!"

But the Prince gripped him while he kicked and writhed like a madman. He made squealing sounds every time the horse reared.

The man dropped the blunderbuss. "Put him down! Let go of him!" He was almost sobbing with frustration. "Leave us alone, you fiend! Why don't you leave us alone?"

The Prince let go. Master Jamie fell to his knees and scrambled upright. He started to move rapidly away, but the white horse shifted around and caught him by the collar of his coat. The horse began to back up, and Master Jamie stumbled and fell on his rump.

"Poor fellow," the Prince said. "It's not such capital fun on the other side, is it?"

Master Jamie pushed off the frozen ground and rolled onto his knees. He gripped his hands together. " 'O Lord, thou hast seen my opression! Judge my case! Thou hast seen all their vengeance, all their schemes against me. I am their mocking song. Thou wilt recompense them, O Lord; thy curse will be on them. Thou will pursue them in anger and destroy them from under the heavens of the Lord!' ''

Divine Angel dropped to her knees and began to pray aloud with him. One by one the others followed. Harmony looked around at them and at Chastity standing with the nettles in her arms. Chastity was staring up at the Prince. Her body shook; suddenly she threw down the nettles and ran forward toward the horse.

"Thee said—" She stopped as Master Jamie lifted his head. He never paused in his praying; he just looked at her with an unblinking gaze. She crossed her arms over her breast, staring back like a bird frozen before a snake.

"Chérie." The Prince held out his black-gloved hand, his voice a vibrant undertone to the march of Master Jamie's prayer. "Do you wish to come with me?"

Chastity whirled toward him. "Yes!" The word was a quivery piping. "Thee said I could, afore! 'Ee said! Please!" She reached out, and then gasped with an audible whimper as his gauntlet closed over her swollen fingers.

He let go, but she clung to his arm. Harmony saw him lean down and take her hands gently on his open gloves. Then the mask came up; the deep eyes stared past Chastity at Master Jamie.

Harmony swallowed. She saw the wrath in that look. Even the pinwheeling black and white patterns on the mask couldn't hide it.

"Aye—you'd best pray for all you're worth, Chilton," he said. "Because I'm not nearly finished with you."

In the early morning light beneath a dirty window of the Twice Brewed's taproom, Leigh bathed the girl's hands in Gilead oil and wrapped them in lint.

"Nettles, was't?" The landlady had brought a tray herself, her sleeves rolled up to her freckled elbows. She set it down with a clatter. "Fell doin's, that is," she said forbiddingly. "Dinna care for it, that thy laddie gaes pokin' aboot that place o' night. We bide nae trouble here."

Chastity looked at the woman with terror in her eyes. "Please, mum—will'ee turn me out?"

The woman crossed her arms. "Dinna hold wi' turnin' out. 'S only this, nae good weel come o' stirrin' that cauldron, an' if the laddie do't mair, ye ken there be nae welcome here."

"I'll speak to him," Leigh said quietly.

The landlady frowned out the window, where the Seigneur worked with Mistral in the stable yard. This morning, like all the others, he was up at dawn and training the horse, riding it in circles and figure eights and serpentines; mount and rider quiet, intent on the task, with only the rhythmic snort of Mistral's breath for tempo. Dove of Peace stood by huddled in her cloak, the Seigneur's dogged shadow, always willing to fetch or carry or help in any way.

"Aye, speakit—for the good 'twill do." The landlady shook her head. "I've haird ye scold an' fume, miss, an' still he gaes, dinna he?" She trod heavily to the door and turned. "He's a bonnie, skellum lad, good for no but blethering and fechtin' and wooin' yon silly lassie wi' his airs. Ye speakit to him!"

The door slammed, leaving them alone in the empty taproom. Chastity sat with her head bowed. "I do be that sorry, mum, t' make trouble for 'ee."

" 'Tis not your fault," Leigh said. "But you must listen to me." She lowered her voice. "You've seen him in that mask—and if you have a care for his neck, or mine, or yours, you won't ever mention it to anyone. They don't know who he is here. Do you understand?"

"Yes, mum," Chastity said in a tiny voice. "I do."

"We'll change this dressing in the afternoon. Try not to scratch at your hands." Leigh poured out a spoonful of medicine. "Take this."

Chastity swallowed it. "Thankee, mum," she whispered.

Leigh gathered up the cloth and balm, and set the tray near Chastity. "Can you use your hands to eat?"

"Yes, mum."

The front door opened. The Seigneur ducked through, dressed in leather coat and black top boots, with Dove at his heels. He ignored Leigh as if she weren't there, pulling off his fingerless mitts and stuffing them in his pocket. For four days he'd not spoken directly to her, only worked Mistral all day and then disappeared into his chamber. Leigh had begun to believe he might not go back to Felchester.

But he had, of course.

She saw Chastity look up at him. The girl's eyes fixed on his face with unblinking devotion; she didn't touch her food or speak or look away.

"Tu va bien, petite courageuse?" he asked her cheerfully.

Chastity turned scarlet. She worked her hands in her lap, plucking at the lint and gazing at him mutely.

Leigh contained a sigh. "She's in a little pain, I think," she answered for the speechless girl. "I gave her a light dose of laudanum."

He gently flicked Chastity's cheek and sat down on the high-backed pew near the hearth. Dove settled beside him, close enough to touch his sleeve. She slanted a sideways glance from beneath her lashes, full of admiration and promise.

It wasn't precisely as if he demanded it. He never did more than smile and accept what was offered. But Leigh could see how it pleased him, the silly block, to be fawned upon and cooed over and doted on.

"The landlady has warned we're not welcome here," she said coldly. "Not if you go back again."

He took a deep breath and leaned back against the settle. "Ah. That's difficult."

"Only if you insist on continuing this madness."

He bent to unbuckle his spurs. "And if I stop? We'd as well pack up and go anyway."

"She's afraid of what you'll bring down upon them." Leigh stood up, unable to sit quietly. She faced the small morning fire that smoked and sputtered inside the huge hearth. "You should have killed him right away," she said in a low voice. "What do you think, that you can steal his converts one by one until you've freed them all? Some may not want so badly to go."

Chastity said timidly, "Could 'ee jus' go back for Sweet Harmony? I do be afraid . . ." Her voice trailed off.

The Seigneur looked up at her. A subtle shadow hardened his jaw. "Afraid of what?"

"Of her—of her punishment. Sweet Harmony, she didn' heave no rock at 'ee—an' she still 'us standin' up; not kneelin' down when Master Jamie prayed. And Divine Angel, she seen it." She worried her lip. "They'll be wicked cross, 'cause I'd ride off wiv'ee."

"You see?" Leigh said sharply. "They'll persecute this girl Sweet Harmony now."

He stood up, dangling the spurs. "And what would you have?" His steady gaze pierced her. "Do you say I should have left Chastity there? You doctored her hands—you saw what they did, just because I singled her out."

"Of course I saw it! Why don't you see it?" Leigh gripped the high wooden back of the settle. "You *know* what he's capable of doing, and yet you go in and stir them; you rush ahead with no more sense than a horse that's bolted. Chastity said one of them had a gun." She pushed off the wood. " 'Tis luck you weren't shot before ever you saw Chilton's face."

He leaned toward her, scowling, his shoulder against the settle. "But I wasn't, was I? I know what I'm doing, damn you. I've faced far worse than a broken-down blunderbuss."

"And completely forgotten the consequences, I see!"

He straightened up as if she'd struck him. "Oh, no," he said softly. "I haven't forgotten."

"Think on it, then." She walked to the front door and dragged it open. "While I leave you to the enjoyment of your seraglio."

Chill morning air hit her face. She slammed the door behind her and walked past Mistral, who stood in halter with the lead trailing down to the ground. The horse watched her cross to the stable yard, but didn't move. He wouldn't, unless Leigh were to pick up the lead. Another dumb beast caught in the Seigneur's spell.

The stable smelled of frost and hay, lit by shafts of thin, dusty sunlight that brought no warmth. Nearby lay the Seigneur's sheathed rapier, balanced across a bucket, with the sword belt dangling where he'd taken the weapon off temporarily while he worked Mistral from the ground. She propped back the door with a stool to let in more light and reached for a grooming box.

A human shadow fell across the floor. The Seigneur stepped inside, pushing back the door. He grabbed her by the elbow. "Seraglio! Is that the burr under your saddle?"

She felt heat flood her face. "Let go of me."

He didn't. He pulled her closer and shut the door, sealing them into the dusky stable. "You're jealous."

"You're an insufferable peacock."

It sounded childish, and she knew it. He released his tight hold. Something changed in his face, an unexpected softening, a perceptive half smile. "Am I?" he asked in a low voice.

Leigh wanted to fling herself away. Instead she stood frozen, encumbered by her weakness, paralysed by his light hold. "I thought you weren't going to go back," she said painfully. "And then you do worse yet. You tease Chilton into madness, you bring that girl; what are we to do with her? What are we to do with both of them?"

His hand moved up and pressed her arm gently. "There's a stage leaves Hexham on Thursday," he murmured. "I've already looked into it. The girls will be on board."

"To where?"

He moved his head casually. "I don't know. I'll ask. Wherever they came from." The stroke of his hand worked up to her collar. One finger slipped inside, between the linen and her throat. "Does that please you?"

Leigh stood still, feeling the coax of his hand on her skin, the warmth of his body close to hers. He was going to kiss her. She saw the relaxing of his face, the downward brush of his lashes lit by the faint light from the hayloft.

"I don't know," she whispered.

"Tell me what I can do." He brushed his lips against her temple. "You know I'd do anything you asked."

She closed her eyes. "Then I'm asking you again. Don't go back to that place."

His fingers tightened cruelly on her shoulder. But he kissed her eyes and her cheek, his breath a subtle caress. "Don't fear for me, Sunshine. I know what I'm doing."

She shook her head slowly back and forth.

He pulled her into his arms and leaned back against the partition of an empty stall. "I can destroy Chilton for you. I can turn the town against him. That's why you came to me, Leigh—have you forgotten it? I can give you your revenge; 'tis what I've spent my life at doing."

She started to pull away, then gripped his coat instead and pressed her forehead against his chest. "I tell you, I tell you—'tis no longer the same. I don't want . . ." Her throat closed.

I don't want to lose you to him, she thought. She clenched his coat until her fingers hurt. *Damn you, damn you; I just could not endure it.*

He stroked her hair. Feathered kisses drifted down her cheek and jaw. His breath was warm in the freezing air, his body solid and close beneath the leather coat, scented with hay and horse and his own male essence.

He twined a lock of her hair around his finger and kissed the top of her ear. "What don't you want?" he whispered.

She pulled back sharply. "I don't want revenge! Everything's changed. He's driven out everyone I ever knew or cared about. There's no point in it anymore." She let go of his coat. "I don't need vengeance. I don't need you to do it."

He caught her shoulders, but she resisted.

"Do you understand?" She met his eyes. *"I do not need you!"*

His hands tightened. The golden, mocking brows drew down.

"Forget about Chilton," she said. "Go back to France. I don't want you to do anything for me. Take yourself off to your castle and your paintings and your garlic."

He let go of her. For an instant he stood against the

stall, very still. "Garlic," he said, as if the word were a mortal affront.

Leigh closed her eyes and tilted her head back. "Do you understand me at all?"

"I understand." His voice was low and violent. "You think I can't do it."

She turned away and slumped down onto a trunk, holding her head between her hands. She stared at the dirt floor in despair.

"I can," he said, the words bruised with bitterness. "I can and I will, devil take you; I've done it for years. I never got caught, not even the last time. I know what I'm doing; I have the best horse I ever set eyes upon; I have my sword and my balance—I can do it. Blast you—don't *doubt* me."

She shuddered, pulling her arms around her knees. "I don't want you to do it."

"Aye, you'd have me go back to my garlic, would you? I'm to think you don't give a fig for Chilton anymore, or your family or what you've lost."

"I don't!" she cried, pressing her hands to the sides of her head. "I don't."

"Rot!" The stable reverberated to the sound of his boot heel as he smashed it against the partition. Two stalls down, her chestnut's head came up in alarm. "You'll turn me into a madman."

"Kill yourself, then!" she said violently. "Go on and kill yourself!"

He stared at her a moment, his mouth set. Then he slowly shook his head. "You just don't believe I can manage it, do you?"

She didn't answer. The chestnut moved restlessly in his stall, rolling his eyes and trying to see over the partitions.

"Infinitely obliged," the Seigneur said, softly and sarcastically. She heard the grating drag of the stable door. The wide shaft of sun flashed and dimmed and brightened again as he passed beyond it.

He left her alone.

She sat on the trunk and toyed with a grooming brush,

turning it over and over in her hand. Then she stopped, listening.

From far away, muffled by the stable walls, came the low-pitched moan of the wilderness. Nemo's call began in a deep chord and slowly rose, swelling to a rich, plaintive peak, a loneliness that shivered in the empty air. It was the first time he'd howled since they'd been at the inn, and the melancholy sound seemed to pull at her with a physical force.

Leigh stared at the Seigneur's discarded sword. It was the lightweight weapon, the one he called a colichemarde, meant for fencing with the tip instead of cutting sideways in a murderous slash like his flat-bladed broadsword. She reached for the weapon and drew it across her lap.

The hilt was plain, unlike the beautiful and complex interweave of the broadsword's basket hilt. The narrow hand guard of the colichemarde gleamed with a dull rainbow of metallic green and red and blue on steel, the decoration on the hand grip worn almost smooth by constant use.

She stood up, propped the tip on the ground, and buckled the belt around her waist as she'd seen him do, dragging the leather thong up three holes to keep it on her hips. The blade felt awkward, far too long, sticking out behind her and bumping against the walls when she turned.

Leigh went to the anxious chestnut, pulled off his rug and set to work with furious strokes, brushing him down in the half light. He sidled and quivered, catching the heat of her emotions. By the time she heaved the sidesaddle on him, he was tossing his head in agitation.

She mounted off the trunk, struggling to control the ungainly scabbard and the horse at the same time. She ducked wildly as the chestnut shot out the stable door. If the Seigneur was still with Mistral in the yard, she didn't know it; she didn't look, but gave the chestnut a kick that sent it cantering recklessly out the gate, across the road, and toward the barren moors.

Clouds moved in from the north, swallowing the sunlight ray by ray. They spread low over the wild and empty landscape, sullenly familiar in their dismal chill. In her childhood, she'd loved the Roman wall, loved it even in this mournful, freezing weather when the stones stood black and eerie against the sky. When she was small, her mother had taken Leigh on winter outings bundled to the ears, allowed her to scramble over the fallen masonry, and told her stories of the pagan days when Caesar's cavalry held the rampart against the barbarians of the north. She'd dug for coins, and found a tiny clay lamp once, and a lumpy, discolored piece of metal that her mother had carefully scraped clean to reveal as a pair of bronze tweezers.

Leigh took the covert way to the place that had once been home, crossing by the drove road that cut the ancient wall and skirting along in the northern shadow of the cliffs. The chestnut moved in its long, pushing strides, head up and blowing nervously as they neared the open gap where the wall curved down between two hills. In the cold air, faint steam rose from the horse's sweaty coat. The sword hilt lay at a difficult angle across her thigh, never meant to conform to a female on a sidesaddle.

On the north side of the gap she reined the chestnut to a halt, faced into the wind, and lifted her chin. She gathered all her breath into her lungs.

She howled. It was a sad imitation of the full-throated cry she'd heard from the moors, but she raised her voice to its limits in spite of the horse's uneasy sidling beneath her.

Before her breath had given way, Nemo answered. His deep harmony rose with hers, far closer than she'd expected. The chestnut shied in agitation. Leigh grabbed its mane and broke off her cry. She dismounted, the sword banging her calves, and held the frightened horse as a gray shadow came bounding down from the trees atop the cliffs. Nemo leaped across a frozen puddle, his mouth agape, uttering little wows of excitement.

Leigh lifted her head and howled again, and the wolf stopped a yard away, raising his chin to join in ecstatically. The caroling drowned out her own, loud enough to hurt her ears. His rich, wild note surrounded her, shivering into her skull as she fought to hold the chestnut under control.

Nemo left off his cry and leaped up to greet her, his teeth colliding with her chin in a painful blow. She tottered, scrambling to hang onto the reins and stay on her feet as Nemo planted his huge paws against her shoulders and washed her face with his tongue, a coarse and ruthless laundering that stung where he'd cut her.

She pushed him off, a rebuff that sent the wolf into a wallowing bask at her feet. As Nemo fawned, the horse settled down to restive strutting, staring dubiously at the wolf.

Leigh reached up and stroked the chestnut neck. "What a brave fellow," she murmured, knowing she was fortunate the horse hadn't bolted for a mile. "Brave, clever fellow."

One ear flicked toward her, and then pricked back anxiously, riveted on the wolf. Nemo rolled over expectantly. Leigh bent, keeping the reins in a firm grip, and rubbed the wolf's belly until Nemo wriggled and squirmed, trying to lick her arm and wag his tail at the same time.

Her chin throbbed and stung where his teeth had grazed it. She pressed the back of her hand to her jaw and came away with bright red blood on her skin. But Nemo was licking her hand as if he'd never loved anyone more. When she stood up, he rolled to his feet and pressed against her legs with enough affectionate force to send her toppling again. She only saved herself when the tip of the sword caught against the ground, providing an instant of stability.

Nemo bounded away on stiff legs, his ears flattened to the sides, his eyes wide, inviting her to play. His comical expression took all the menace from his clear yellow eyes; his tongue lolled, tempting a frolic. Leigh had seen the Seigneur respond to that, run and roll and play tag, and sometimes come back with a bleeding scratch like her own from Nemo's strenuous wolf games. The Seigneur played, but he never quit until he was on top, refusing to surrender his sovereign position even in fun.

But Leigh could not take time for amusement. She had

a goal. Dove had been quite specific in her description of
the rigid routine at Heavenly Sanctuary. In the late morning, Chilton would be found at his preparations for noonday service, working alone in the church.

Leigh remounted, turning the chestnut east. Nemo fell
in behind. He trotted in single file after the chestnut, just
far enough back to avoid a stray hoof.

Leigh kept her bare hand on the sword hilt, warming
the frigid steel. She'd gone to France to find the Seigneur
with no family and no future and no fear, with a wellspring of hate in her heart. But now she was afraid. Now
she was cornered and desperate. Now she had something
to lose.

TWENTY-ONE

S.T. didn't discover that she'd taken his sword until he broke for the midday meal and brought Mistral into the stable. It must have been her—the potboy that the Twice Brewed's landlord was pleased to call an ostler hadn't been near the place. S.T. cleaned up the stalls, dressed Mistral, pitched hay, and spent a quarter hour searching through the stable for a sword he knew he'd left in plain sight.

He'd seen her ride off like the devil to go; who could miss it? Nothing in creation would have made him trail after her, playing the groveling pup. Dove had been waiting, anyway, with a pint of small beer for him and a lump of sugar for Mistral, and Leigh could go to hell.

The silliness of the theft roused his temper. Steal his sword, would she? Perhaps she thought the lack of it would be enough to send him back to France and his garlic. Mayhap she really thought him that much a humbug.

He swept up a bent horseshoe and hurled it into the wall. The metal rang against stone, and Mistral lifted his head from his oats as the shoe bounced to the floor. The horse looked around, blew out a long breath, and began munching again. S.T. shoved back a loose lock of hair and retied his queue with a jerk, planting his hat on his head as he stalked out the door.

The potboy was just leading a newly arrived pair of job horses inside as he left. S.T. glanced at the animals, judged them well above the standard of horseflesh normally to be

301

expected at a carters' inn, and gave one an acknowledging slap on the rump as he passed. A weathered black traveling chariot stood outside the stable, mud splashed, its empty shaft propped on the watering trough. He tucked his gloves under his arm, breathing clouds of frost in the glacial air. The door to the Twice Brewed stood open; inside he could see the dark outlines of the newcomer and the landlady.

He pulled off his hat and bent his head to enter.

"Harkee," a cordial voice said. "What have we got here? By my soul—that can't be S.T. Maitland!"

S.T. froze with one foot over the threshold.

There was no hope of evasion. Slowly, he put his gloves inside his hat and lifted his head.

The gentleman in the pink lace coat and steep macaroni wig stood beaming at him. "By God if it ain't. How d'ye do? Haven't set eyes upon that remarkable phiz for years. Bob Derry's Cyder Cellar, was it?"

S.T. reluctantly inclined his head. "Lord Luton," he murmured.

"Did you ever see the like?" Luton rolled his pale eyes toward Dove and Charity, who stood together near the fire. "Couldn't find better in London, could we?" He tapped his tassled walking stick against S.T.'s shoulder. "What're ye doing here? I've just got in, and cold as hell it was to drive in that wind. Sit down by the fire and share a bottle of Toulon, and tell me what dissipation brings you into the outlands."

S.T. saw no help for it. Luton was as wild as he was depraved; he disposed himself elegantly on the settle, one leg propped up, displaying the high red heels and ribbons of his Italian shoes. He arranged his cuffs, staring openly at the girls while he talked, a faint curl at the corner of his aristocratic mouth.

"Where are you bound?" S.T. asked, taking the bottle from the landlady and pouring for them both.

"I'm in no hurry to go anywhere." Luton sniffed at his wine and wrinkled his nose, never taking his eyes from Dove and Charity, who kept their faces shyly averted. "Perhaps I'll put up here for the nonce."

S.T. snorted. "You'll rue it," he said. "It's naught but a carters' lodging. Not a'tall in your style."

Luton smiled and held up his glass. "To auld lang syne," he said dryly, and watched as S.T. met the toast and drank. "Do you wish me out of your way, old friend?"

S.T. cast a meaningful glance toward the girls. "And what do you think, *old friend?*"

Luton tipped back his head and laughed. "That you're a selfish bastard, you scaly dog. I'll not go."

S.T. stared at him darkly. For a moment Luton's smile wavered, and then he swigged down his wine.

"No, no," he said. " 'Tis no use giving me that devil's gaze of yours. Call me out if you wish; I won't go. I've business here." He paused, peering down at his glass, and then suddenly slanted S.T. a thoughtful look. "Perhaps we're about the same project, eh?"

"Perhaps," S.T. parried.

"Dashwood sent you?"

S.T. was suddenly on crumbling ground. Luton's arrival had unsettled him; Sir Frances Dashwood's name was a pure jolt. Coming from a rake like Luton, it conjured the noble hooligans of the Hell Fire Club and the unholy monks of Medmenham.

"I came on my own," he said.

"Did you indeed?" Luton's tone gave away nothing.

"I heard a rumor," S.T. said, hazarding a chance. Luton was preposterously out of place here; S.T. wanted to know the reason. "I'm interested in your business."

Luton had pale blue eyes; he gazed at S.T. without blinking. Then he lifted one white hand and placed his finger against his lips pensively. The ruby on his forefinger gleamed.

"You might need a friend at your back," S.T. said, nodding toward the jewel. "There's a highwayman at work in these parts."

That got a start out of Luton. He sat up. "The devil you say."

"Aye. And you with your gems all about you."

Luton swore. "A highwayman. It only needed that."

S.T. smiled crookedly. "My hand is yours," he said "I'm passing fair at swordplay."

"I know it. I saw you fight poor Bayley on Black- heath." The other man took a deep breath. He kept turn- ing his glass in his hand. "So . . . Dashwood has been talking to you, has he?"

"A rumor," S.T. said. "Only a rumor. I thought it—" He paused, and then said carefully, "worth my time."

The look Luton gave him was enough. S.T. knew he'd struck close to a powerful secret. Dashwood and Luton and Lyttleton; Bute and Dorset and the rest of them—for three generations they'd pleased themselves to the limits of civilized vice. S.T. wasn't entirely innocent of that par- ticular brimstone himself. In the earliest reckless days of his career he'd watched Dashwood's black mass in the chalk cave at West Wycombe: twenty years old and law- less, hot to prove his mettle, ready to use Dashwood's blasphemous "nuns" and relish the theatrical obscenity of the rites.

Very brash. Very young.

He wondered if Luton remembered.

He wondered what Luton's business was now. What would it take to amuse a man after that many years of debauchery?

"Come," Luton said. "Walk outside with me."

S.T. stood up. He pulled on his gloves and watched Luton help himself into his own greatcoat. The mere fact that a man of Luton's elegance was traveling without his valet or groom was curious.

Outside, Luton picked his way over the stones of the yard in his high-heeled shoes. "Tell me," he said calmly. "Where have you been these few years?"

"Traveling." That answer was easy enough. S.T. turned deliberately away from the stable and Mistral. "Let us walk this way. The pavement's cleaner."

Luton followed willingly enough. "You've been on the continent?"

"Aye. France. Italy. A spell in Greece."

"I'd have thought you long lost. No one mentions your name in Paris."

"I prefer to rusticate. I'll take the south of France to Paris."

"Lyon? Avignon?"

S.T. kept an indifferent face. "Both, at some time."

"I've toured Provence." The tassled cane tapped a quick rhythm on the pavement. "There is an interesting village near the Lubéron. Lacoste. Perhaps you've heard the name?"

The carefully casual tone brought S.T.'s senses to full alert. "I've heard the talk," he lied.

The cane came up, hesitated, and then fell. Luton leaned on it. "What talk?"

S.T. searched wildly for an appropriate guess. He squinted out across the moors. "Of uncommon things." He looked at Luton, assessing the man and his reputation and what was like to lure him. "The gossips call it . . . unnatural."

The icy pale eyes held his. Luton smiled. "And you don't?"

S.T. decided he could only bluff so far. "I simply have my rumors." He suddenly remembered a name, a man who might have the acquaintance of an aristocratic English traveler with Luton's tastes, and tossed it on the table as a wild card. "The Marquis de Sade spoke of intriguing things. You know him?"

It took the trick.

Luton shot him an piercing, eager look. "You've talked to Sade?" Relief and excitement shivered through his voice. "When?"

"I believe it was November." S.T. had his companion's full attention now. "He was sharp set upon when last I saw him."

"Set upon! By whom?"

S.T. smiled. "The French militia seemed to have taken him in dislike."

"The deuce go with it all! Did they catch him?"

A memory of the marquis backed up against the wall, with Nemo snarling in his terrified face, made S.T. look away. He gazed out over the landscape. "Milord was safely on Savoy's side of the border when I left him."

"My God, I'm glad to hear it. We've had no word for months. It was like to tear my nerves to pieces. I thought he'd lost his stomach for the thing—after it was his notion to begin with. But he's still in it with us, is he?"

"I can swear it." S.T. perjured himself without compunction.

"And you." Luton gave him a curious look. "You fancy your scruples can bear it, going the full distance? I don't know much of you, Maitland. Your brother was as hot at hand as ever I saw a man, and game for any outrage, but you seem to come and go in a pretty queer fashion."

S.T. shrugged. "My brother was a lunatic."

Luton cleared his throat and frowned. "Apologies," he muttered. "I should not have mentioned what would distress you."

"It's nothing to me," S.T. said, leaning against a low stone wall. "The whole world knew him for a murderous blackguard, and he ruined my father to boot. If a whore hadn't broken his neck, the hangman would have." He grinned. "What of it? I never set eyes on father nor son."

A faint smile played about Luton's mouth. "You're damned cold about it."

"Perhaps I'm a little mad myself."

Luton nodded slowly, still smiling. "Good," he said. "I like a madman. I liked your brother. A fine untamable animal, he was. 'Twas a pity that he couldn't keep his reason about him."

"A pity. Mayhap the whole family's blood cursed. A Gypsy warned me I'd be lucky to end on the gallows myself." S.T. crossed his arms and tilted his head back to the sky. "But I intend to enjoy myself in the meanwhile."

Luton touched his arm. "Join us. We have the ultimate pleasure in mind, my friend. The final act."

S.T. lowered his head and gazed at the other man.

"Have you imagined it?" Luton murmured, staring into his eyes with a weird intensity. "The last violation. The final sin against God and man. We've done all the rest, and now we're ripe for the pinnacle of excitement. Think of it, Maitland." His mouth curled in a glimmer of a smile.

"Have you ever dreamed of what the climax would be like, with the girl beneath you in her death throes?''

Leigh paused at the crest of the fell. Below her, a pair of well-kept wagon tracks followed the bank of the river. The burn tumbled down the valley, frozen now, opaque white where it spilled over rocks in summer, and a darker color in the deep pools, translucent frost over ale brown.

At the end of the glen, she could just see the ford where the wagon road crossed the river. The hills still hid the town from view, the place that Chilton called Heavenly Sanctuary.

A single rider moved along the road on a horse Leigh recognized even at a distance. Anna's black Friesian mare with its long wavy mane and feathered hooves had been an Epiphany surprise two years before, presented proudly with a bridle Mama had trimmed in silver and red ribbons that Leigh and Emily had braided through its silky mane and tail.

Now the gift they'd given in love and simple innocence trotted ahead with Jamie Chilton on its back.

Leigh remembered how to hate.

She remembered her family like a blow, like waking up from a dream. Her breath grew quick and uneven; she could hear herself on the edge of a crazy sob as she clenched the sword.

He'd taken everything she loved; she would not let him have more.

Beside her, Nemo seemed to catch her frenzy. He settled on his belly, his ears alert and his golden eyes fixed on the figure that moved toward them. She let the chestnut start forward, and the wolf shifted instantly into a swift glide alongside her. Halfway down the hill the chestnut began to trot. Nemo broke into a long lope, his jaws gaping, sweeping wide across the slope as he gathered speed.

Leigh dragged the sword free of its dangling sheath. The chestnut fell into a canter, plunging down the hill in a charge straight for Chilton. She saw him look up toward her. The wind beat her horse's mane into her face as she leaned forward; the air seemed to grab at the sword, pull-

ing the point upward while the chestnut's motion pitched
her arm. She could see Nemo from the corner of her eye,
racing in a deadly blur of cream and shadow to cut the
quarry off.

The ground went past in a smudge of grayish green.
Her eyes stung with cold and speed; the reins seemed a
tangle of confusion in her left hand, useless, and her ears
were full of the sound of wind and her horse's hooves.
Chilton stood up in his stirrups. His mouth was an open
darkness, but she couldn't hear him. She came off the
slope at a pounding gallop. He kicked the mare. The horse
jumped forward and shied off from Nemo's attack, and
she had a moment's terror of cutting the mare.

Then she was there, the sword whistling through the air
at Chilton's head.

He ducked away, wrenching at his reins. The mare
reared and came down an inch from Nemo's snarling teeth.
The wolf dodged her hooves. Leigh flashed past, missing
her target by a foot, powerless to coordinate the jumble of
her reins with one hand. She dragged the chestnut to a halt
and scrambled for one loose rein, pivoting the horse
around with the Seigneur's sword pointed toward the sky.
Nemo had circled to the mare's flank, pinching the target
between them, leaping toward Chilton's leg with a savage
growl.

He caught Chilton's boot, but the man never made a
sound. He fought in silence, slashing at the wolf with his
riding crop. Leigh kicked the chestnut at him again. She
aimed the sword with her trembling arm. Everything
seemed to go too fast and too slow: she could not control
the chestnut, she couldn't keep her hand steady, she could
see Chilton's mouth set hard and his eyes rolling as he
fought, spurring his horse for the opening between her and
the wolf and the river.

The sword whistled through the air, a violent hum of
sound above Nemo's snarling. It caught in Chilton's coat;
she felt the sudden drag at her grip, and pulled back desperately to save her hold. She jerked the sword free, but
he was moving; there was nothing she could do but make
a wild swing. The rounded blade slid harmlessly across

his neck, and only a wrenching lunge brought the point upward, dragging the tip over his cheek.

Blood spilled from the cut, rolling down his face, but still he never made a sound. He looked like a wildman, with his hat gone and his hair springing out from his head in an orange cloud.

The mare bounded forward, out of reach. Nemo had his teeth sunk into Chilton's ankle, half running, his hind feet bouncing off the ground. The crop cut downward again, and the wolf let go. Nemo sprang into the mare's path, but Chilton reined her hard sideways and gave her his spurs. Leigh lunged forward over the chestnut's shoulder, stabbing the sword at his back. She felt resistance, but she was too far away to thrust the point home.

The chestnut shied away from Nemo's snarling. The sudden swerve jolted Leigh off her seat. She grabbed the horse around the neck and clenched her legs on the sidesaddle's leaping tree, hanging on with all her strength. By the time she'd regained her balance and found the reins again, Chilton had driven the mare into a gallop.

Leigh propelled the chestnut forward, joining Nemo in the chase. The terrified mare's tail floated behind her like a flashing black banner. The Friesian was fast, but Nemo and the tall chestnut gained on her, pounding along the frozen track. Leigh threw a wild look to the side and realized they were heading back toward Heavenly Sanctuary. She kicked the chestnut again, leaning over his neck, the fingers of her sword hand tangled in his flying mane and the blade pointed upward.

Ahead, she could see people standing in the road. Their figures were a smear. She gulped air, panting for strength, hearing nothing but hooves and her heart thundering. Above it, she caught a faint pop, and saw Nemo falter. The wolf went head over heels in a flash of pale fur, and leapt to his feet as she thundered past.

The mare veered ahead of her, swerving toward the river ford. Chilton's arm came up and the riding whip slashed downward. The mare took a huge leap, as if she could clear the river. It landed her in the middle; Leigh saw her crash through the ice, saw Chilton topple in over his shoulder, saw the mare regain her footing, and then the chestnut was at the bank. Leigh shouted in vicious elation, leaning back for the jump, grappling at her sword with her enemy trapped in her grasp.

The chestnut gathered himself. He lifted his front hooves in the air.

Water.

With a powerful coiling leap, he refused—twisting sideways, sending her forward in a somersault that yanked her free of the sidesaddle.

She pitched. The world spun. *Water.* It flashed in her vision. Ice and agony hammered into her like an explosion. *Water, water, water, water . . .*

Dove sat down on the bed in S.T.'s chamber. "I'm not going," she said placidly. "I'm staying here with you."

He ignored her, opening his wallet. "They've got the dogcart ready to take you to Hexham. Stage fare's paid as far as Newcastle. How much money do you think you might need between you?"

"Charity may have it," Dove said, pushing away the purse. "I won't forsake you, not after all you've done for us."

"Nay, you needn't feel you're forsaking me," he said impatiently. "I want you and Charity away, where you'll be safe.

"Mr. Bartlett," Charity said in a small voice. "I ha'n't nowhere t'go."

He took a deep breath. "Where did you come from?"

"Hertfordshire, sir." She bobbed her head. "But me pap 'ee be long gone away and me mum wi' no work, I'd be on the parish there, sir." Her bandaged hands worked and squeezed together. She wet her lips. "Oh, please, sir—I don't be wantin' to go back in the poor house!"

S.T. put his hand on her shoulder. "You stay together. Stay with Dove. I'll give you money enough to find work."

"We've no references," Dove said amiably. "No one will hire us."

"For God's sake, I'll write you a reference. You have to leave here. I want you out of Luton's sight."

"I've no fear of him." Dove smiled mistily at S.T. "Not whilst you're at my side."

"Nor me, neither," Charity said with resolution.

"Well, you can't stay here!" He strode to the window and looked out. "I've things to do; I can't be playing nanny. And damn, where the devil has Leigh got to with my rapier? There's no time left now for games, plague take her!" He turned around and took Charity's arm, giving her a little push toward the door. "Come along, and be good girls."

Charity turned into him and threw her arms around his waist. "I do be beggin', sir—don't sendin' me off! Dove's kin, they woan' take the likes of me; great people, they do be—"

"Charity!" Dove said shrilly. "Don't speak nonsense."

Charity let go and whirled on Dove. " 'Tis the truth, and 'ee do know it! A great big house, ye got, a mum and a pap—'ee do be a fine lady—"

"That's not true!" Dove came to her feet. "I'm an orphan. I am precisely the same as you."

S.T. looked up quickly. Dove's modulated speech struck him with sudden and momentous effect. "The devil you are," he said incredulously. "You never learned to talk that way in Chilton's school."

"I *did!*" Her lower lip puckered. "My mother made me steal in the streets!"

"Nonsense." S.T. crossed the room and took Dove by the shoulders. "What's your real name?"

"I've forgotten."

He gave her a shake. "Listen to me, you little dimwit— if you've a family to take you in, I'll have you tell it!"

"I'm an orphan!"

"A lady, 'ee be!" Charity cried. "Ye and Harmony and Angel and lots of the others—'ee be fine, wi' gentle airs; us all knew it, and that Master Jamie loved 'ee best. 'Twas always the fine girls would be chose for ascension."

"That's not true—there was Eternal Light.'' Dove glared at Charity. "She was chosen, and she came of a mending stall in Covent Garden.''

"There 'ee be; she didn' ascend proper, then, did un? She be back a'crying the next very morning 'cause she 'ad the French disease and weren't yet suited. Them that do ascend proper don't *never* come back to this worldly vale o' tears.''

S.T. forgot Dove; he dropped his hands and stared at Charity.

"She was chosen, though,'' Dove insisted.

"She come back!'' Charity countered stubbornly. "When Master Jamie took Holy Faith to ascend, did 'er come back next mornin'? Did 'er? Nor Zion, nor Bread of Life, and they all been gentle-bred girls.''

"Oh my God,'' S.T. whispered. "They didn't come back?''

Charity shook her head. "Master Jamie chose them to ascend.''

"And they never came back? You're certain?''

"They went up to heaven,'' Dove said. "That's what Master Jamie told us.''

S.T. turned to the window. It was late afternoon; Luton had left the inn, mounted, half an hour ago. The suspicion that had formed in S.T.'s mind seemed so preposterous that he hardly credited it. Luton and his friends, they might have their black fantasies, they might speak of them to make them seem more real, they might even commit an isolated murder if they thought themselves secure to do it—but S.T. hadn't even speculated on more. He'd wanted Dove and Charity gone, out of Luton's sight: the man was an immoral animal on any count, and he might, if he excited himself enough, if he felt safe enough, if he saw opportunity, be capable of playing out his imagination in reality.

But that there could be more to it than that; more than the threat of a spur-of-the-moment isolated crime . . . it seemed incredible.

He looked at Dove. "These 'ascensions' of his. Anyone might be chosen?''

"Yes. It comes to Master Jamie in a vision."

"Are the men ever called?"

"Oh, no. They're already chosen; they needn't be born again." Dove's eyes widened eagerly. "Is ascending something wicked, do you think? He belongs to the devil— it must be monstrous sinful. You'll kill him now, won't you?" She smiled up at him. "How wonderfully daring you are!"

TWENTY-TWO

SWEET Harmony clung to the girls' hands on either side of her and watched as Master Jamie walked stiffly to the purple curtain at the front of the church. Her heart beat quickly; she could not seem to get her breath under control.

Soon . . . soon . . . as soon as this service was over she was going to do it.

She didn't dare glance to one side or the other, or catch anyone's eyes. Master Jamie was changing. He looked about him often, as if he knew. As if he truly could see right into their hearts. When his eyes found hers, she trembled down in her throat and her belly; she couldn't even swallow. He stared at her a long moment, the scratch on his cheek a lurid pink and red in the candlelight, and then raised his arms.

His right hand didn't quite reach as high as the left. It shook, his fingers spread wide, white and trembling against the glowing, violet-shadowed background.

"Hear my cry, O Lord!" he shouted. "Hell's agents have come; they hound us; Lucifer sends she-devils to prick us and demon beasts to rend us, but You have caused a horse—a dumb animal, one of your humble creatures— to deliver the witch into our power. You have shown us that all nature is on our side; all God's creation will rise against this curse! We shall not succumb to fear. The witch shall not escape our vengeance, done in Your holy name!"

"Holy vengeance!" someone cried: Divine Angel's

314

voice. Some others moaned and muttered, but there was not the great cry that once would have arisen in unison.

Harmony knew they were all remembering the bruised face of the witch who'd assaulted Master Jamie with a sword. It was a familiar face. An unnerving face. Harmony had seen it when they carried the terrible limp figure, bound and insensible, into Heavenly Sanctuary.

There were things that were past; things no one spoke of anymore—but the white, vulnerable face of their dazed captive brought it back.

Other people had lived in Heavenly Sanctuary once. Evil people. There had been things that Master Jamie said his flock must do, and they'd done them. The unbelievers had been driven away, and Master Jamie's peace settled on the town.

This witch had been one of the unbelievers. Harmony remembered her, and so did others. They had whispered among themselves this afternoon, behind Master Jamie's back.

Behind his back.

And now Harmony was going to leave. She was not going to obey Master Jamie anymore.

She was terrified.

It was the Midnight Prince who'd given her this much daring. Some of the others felt it, too, she thought. It was the Prince who'd made Master Jamie look a clown, made him rage impotently and fall on his rump in the icy street—but the Prince wasn't here now, and there was no knowing when he'd come back.

Master Jamie was still master, more master than ever, with his kindness all twisted into rage, with Divine Angel and the men to do his bidding to anyone who wavered.

So it was necessary to profess faith.

It was necessary not to shake or hesitate in prayers or waver from what was asked.

That was why she had to leave now. There was no hope for the witch—she was doomed—but Harmony could not bring herself to help Master Jamie punish her. Or dare to refuse.

She had only to live through this endless service. Then

she would simply move into the shadows of the church as everyone was leaving and wait there until the street emptied. She would walk away. It would be after the midnight penance before Divine Angel would return and find Harmony gone.

So simple. She could have done it anytime these two years.

Tears of grief pricked her eyes. It seemed impossible, that everything she loved was crumbling. Without Master Jamie, without her friends, without Heavenly Sanctuary, she had nothing. Her other life was like a dream. She didn't know where she would go, what she would do, but she could not stay. It was as if she'd been living with scales on her eyes, the way the Bible said.

They were torn away now—but how could something that had seemed so wonderful and safe be horrible? Like turning up a shiny stone to find worms and corruption underneath.

"Sweet Harmony!"

Her head jerked up.

*"Sweet Harmony—*I call you!"

Master Jamie stood with his eyes closed, his arms spread wide, his hands clenched into fists.

"Sweet Harmony . . . oh, Sweet Harmony." His voice dropped to a caressing whisper. "The time of your blessed ascension has come. Rise up. Rise up and follow me!"

She sat, frozen in terror.

Master Jamie began a hymn, and the others took it up, swaying in the pews. As they sang, he kept calling her name above the words. The girls next to her let go of her hands, leaving her palms cold and clammy.

Divine Angel came up the aisle and stood at the end, holding out her hand. Everyone seemed to be looking at Harmony, their mouths moving in a song she couldn't even comprehend.

Slowly, she rose. The others stood up and let her pass. Most of them were smiling, believing: an ascension was a happy occasion. Harmony remembered that she was supposed to be joyous at being chosen. But she could not make her mouth obey her and produce delight.

Angel's hand closed over Harmony's. She counted every step to the front of the church, watching her feet carry her forward over the gray stone. Master Jamie lowered his head and opened his eyes. He took her hands in his, gazing at her avidly. The cut and his freckles stood out, sharp and shocking against his bleached skin.

He hates me, she thought wildly, suddenly. *He hates all of us.*

She knew the simple ritual. Her knees collapsed of their own accord. She stared at his waistcoat as he bent over and laid his hands on her head, then kissed her hair. The sound of the song rose around them, echoing in her brain.

He raised her. She knew he must feel how her hand was shaking; the shudders were coursing through her whole body.

She faced the purple drapery. It radiated light and shadow from the candles behind. He pushed her inexorably forward, and the strips of silk brushed across her face, enveloping her for an instant in amethyst, closing around her behind and in front. Master Jamie's hands were at her back. As the silk fell away from her face, he gripped her shoulders.

Behind the curtain, the altar was empty, with candles burning all around it. The rising hymn filled the space and drowned out any other sound. Master Jamie moved her up the steps until she stood in the midst of the candelabra, and then gently faced her back toward the purple curtain.

She didn't see the man in the shadows below the pulpit until he stepped forward.

He was a stranger, with elegant clothes and pale eyes and a high wig, white as chalk. He looked up at her from the base of the steps as if she were something holy, something extraordinary and fascinating, and for a confused moment it almost seemed as if it were possible she truly was going to ascend to somewhere beyond this reality.

When he moved, it was with a sudden eagerness. He strode up the steps, took her face between his cold hands, and ground his mouth brutally into hers.

The dreaminess of the moment shattered. While the hymn went on, Harmony fought, writhing and jerking to

free herself, but Master Jamie had her hands; he bound
them behind her. Both men shoved her back. The stranger
held his hand over her mouth. Harmony struggled to bite
him, until Master Jamie slipped a soft rope around her
neck and drew it tight. Pain choked her; she bucked frantically against the hands that held her. The hymn swelled
to a roaring in her ears and blackness closed in.

It seemed only an instant. She came to her senses in
confusion, gasping for breath. The long hymn was drawing to its last ecstatic chorus, bouncing through her ears
in waves of fear and frozen trembling. She was bound with
her hands above her head, her back arched over the altar
and her throat burning. They'd taken her dress; she'd only
her shift to cover her bare skin as the stranger leaned over
her, his mouth against her ear.

"Make a sound, and I'll kill you," he said—and the
cord around her neck tightened slowly.

She heard Master Jamie's voice, raised again to the congregation. He was going on with the service, speaking of
his joy; preaching of God and his goodness. ·

The stranger smiled and put his hand to her throat, caressing the silken rope. He leaned on her heavily. Another
hymn began, the innocent female voices rising in exhila-
ration.

"Please," she whispered. "Don't."

He smiled. He pressed his thumbs into her throat. She
tilted her head back, struggling against it.

His breath came fast, blowing humid heat on her skin.
He filled up all her vision, blocking the candles, his face
a dim silhouette that seemed to waver and flow in her
terror. The sound of everything throbbed unnaturally;
when he ripped her shift open, she couldn't even hear it
for the strange pounding that seemed to be growing and
growing and growing in the song, rising over it, until the
voices faltered and the thundering exploded into screams.

The man above her went still. Harmony sucked in air.
Strange sounds echoed in the church, squeals and shrieks
and the clatter of horseshoes. *The Prince,* she thought, and
knew she must be dreaming, must have gone mad; it was

the church and no horse would be in it, nothing real would make that sound of hooves on stone.

The weight lifted from her body. She could suddenly see beyond the stranger as the purple silk pitched and twisted and fell away. The screams of shock and confusion reverberated in her ears. She saw the white horse emerge from a cascade of violet, the center of a nightmare scene: all of Master Jamie's flock crowding away, out of reach of the whirling sword that cut at the silk and sent it flying; out of reach of the horse's hooves as it reared; out of reach and scrambling back from the wild rider in the painted mask.

The silver flashed on his gauntlets as he turned the horse and drove it up the stairs. Harmony couldn't close her eyes, she couldn't even move as the horse lunged toward her, huge and looming, its mane flying out in luminescent strands of fire against the candles. The other man had disappeared from her vision; it was only the horse and rider and sword she saw, the flash of steel that swung wide, whistling through the air over her head. Her hands and throat jerked painfully for an instant, and then her arms dropped free.

She slipped, sliding to her knees, unable to make her legs obey her. The horse's legs and hooves seemed enormous, appalling, too close. She staggered back, her torn shift gaping, as the animal danced sideways toward her. A black and silver hand opened in her face, offering support, but she shrank against the altar in panic.

"En avant!" he shouted, leaning down.

She looked up into the dazzling mask, trying to find the eyes behind it. There was nothing but glitter and darkness. He grabbed her suddenly by her bound hands and lifted, hauling her in a bruising, tearing pull halfway up onto his thigh. His arm came around her waist and dragged her over the pommel onto her stomach.

She tried to help then, struggling, trying to draw her knee up beneath her. The horse turned. She felt herself sliding. She whimpered frantically, making a desperate heave with her arms and elbows to stay on. Steel clashed;

the horse whirled again. Beyond the saddle and the Prince's
thigh she caught a glimpse of the stranger.

His wig had flown askew, but his face was set in murderous intent. He ducked the Prince's sword and attacked
with his own. Harmony pulled her bound hands over her
head and turned her face into the horse's shoulder as the
blade came at her, heard the ring of steel and harsh breath
of the man above her as he fought. Her chin banged painfully on the saddle; the pommel pressed sickeningly into
her stomach.

The horse moved, rocking her forward as it plunged
down the stairs. She began to slide off, feet first. A solid
hand clamped down on her buttocks and shoved her back
to bumping equilibrium.

She let herself go limp. For an instant, she turned her
head, opened her eyes and saw the pews flicker past upside
down. The rider leaned forward over her. They passed the
inner door, the air growing frigid on her bare legs. She
saw splintered slats of wood on the floor and one great
oak door hanging loose on its hinge, just before the horse
jolted down the outside stairs into the night.

The white horse hit the pavement at a bone-jarring trot.
Shouts followed them, all male, receding into the distance
while Harmony wriggled and panted and tried to hold on
to her position.

"*Merde,*" the Prince muttered, shoving at her rump.
"Leave off squirming, will you?"

The horse broke into a gentle, rocking canter, making
it far easier to obey the command than it had been at the
bouncing trot. The loose reins flapped in her face. She felt
his body twist above her, heard the hiss and rattle of metal
as he sheathed his sword. With both hands, he hauled her
upright against his chest.

She flailed at the change in balance. His arm pressed
into her middle like iron, choking her breath. She managed to kick her legs over the horse's neck and took a deep
gulp of frigid night air as he loosened his hold.

"Th-th-th-thank you," she gasped, her teeth chattering
in fear and cold.

"You're welcome," he said, in an amused voice.

She shuddered, trying to draw her torn shift together.
He brought both arms up around her, enveloping her in
the warm folds of his cloak.

Harmony sat with her bare legs against the saddle and
his thighs, staring dully at the white shadow of the horse
in front of her. "Ohh," she whimpered, swallowing a
sob. Her head drooped forward. "I'm afraid I—I might be
sick!"

The horse danced suddenly sideways and halted. The
cloak opened and he bent her over the stirrup, holding her
by the shoulders as dry heaves racked her body.

When finally the nausea subsided, she closed her eyes
and hung feebly, unable even to straighten up. Just breathing was an effort.

"Better?" he asked, in that low, sweet voice she knew
she would remember all her life.

She nodded. He lifted her upright and let her rest back
against him, drawing the cloak up again as the horse began
to walk forward. Harmony looked around at the shadowy
road. They were just passing beyond the last house.

"We should run," she said in a shaky voice. "They'll
be after us."

"We can outdistance them."

"You saved me," she said. "You saved me."

"Aye." His gloved hand rested solidly over hers.

"I love you!" she blurted, and began to cry, breathing
in deep, throttling sobs.

He chuckled softly. The horse lifted its poll and broke
into another easy canter, without the guidance of the slack
reins.

Harmony managed to suppress her sobs. "Did you kill
him?" she asked.

"What a bloodthirsty lot you damsels are. Kill who?"

"That awful man. He tore my shift. He was going to
. . . to—" She struggled for breath.

"Ah. That man."

She shuddered.

The Prince said quietly, "I didn't manage to kill him,
more's the pity. I couldn't maneuver in there, not with you

aboard. But I don't think there will be another of Chilton's 'ascensions' soon.''

"No," she whispered. "Everything's falling to pieces. Everything's mad. The beast . . . the witch with the sword . . .'' She swallowed. "Perhaps it truly is the devil, come to torment Master Jamie.''

"Then he'll have to queue up and wait his turn.''

She leaned back against him: the only secure warmth in a shifting world. Each swinging stride of the horse pressed her into his chest.

Tears ran down her cheeks. She lifted her hand beneath the cloak and brushed it against her face. "Forgive me," she mumbled. "I shan't cry.''

"Don't regard it," he said comfortably. "I'm perfectly accustomed to female watering pots.'' He picked up the reins and turned the horse off the road, heading up onto the starlit heights of the fell.

It really was too bad, S.T. thought, that Leigh hadn't been there to see him ride into the church and rescue Sweet Harmony.

Too damned bad. He hadn't needed his rapier, after all.

Harmony lay back against him, her face turned into his chin, as Mistral picked the way in the dark. S.T. could feel her light breath on his throat.

She'd believed in him. She'd been sure he'd deliver her. No doubt it was for the best if she never realized just what a near-run thing it had been, arriving in time.

The cave for which S.T. headed was of Nemo's finding, discovered one night while he fed the wolf secretly, slipping out with a brace of pheasant or hares or whatever he could manage to acquire without causing comment. Nemo could hunt everything from fish to ravens to mice for himself; he could survive for days on nothing at all, but if he went hungry enough to begin killing sheep, it would raise the whole countryside. There'd been no wolves in Britain for generations, but memories were long.

S.T. wasn't sure if anyone else had heard that one lonely howl this morning. Likely the wolf had been drawn off after Leigh when she'd ridden out, for which S.T. was grudgingly thankful. She'd still not returned by the time he'd managed to force the girls into leaving with him, but there'd been no time to go out searching for her.

Mistral lifted his head and uttered a soft nicker. S.T. ducked to avoid the low hanging branches as they plunged down a small path through the underbrush.

Properly speaking, it wasn't a cave at all, but an ancient, underground room built of arched stones, the entrance stairs and heavy iron door completely obscured by dirt and bushes. The area around was a mass of Roman ruins, a lonely outpost near the river. When Charity and Dove had adamantly refused to go to Hexham, S.T. had piled them together on black Sirocco with a promise that they could help him, and led them here.

Amid wails of protest, he'd left them.

He didn't really expect them to be waiting in the dark; he'd reckoned they'd head for the nearest farmhouse, but Sirocco was still staked out where S.T. had left him. When S.T. called their names, a pathetic pair of voices floated out of the murky opening.

Harmony stirred in his arms. S.T. swung down, shoving aside a branch, and peered into the dark cavern. "Halloo! What's become of the candles I left you?"

"I dropped 'em where'us can't see," said Charity in a small and trembling voice.

"We're afraid of rats," Dove added wretchedly.

S.T. walked back to Mistral and gave Harmony a lift by the waist. When she was on the ground, he dug a flint and taper out of his saddlebag. In the flickering light, two pale faces stared up at him out of the shadowed hole.

"Harmony?" Charity said on a waver. "Oh, Harmony!" She came scrambling up the stairs through the branches and threw her arms around the other girl. They both began to weep, Charity pulling her own cloak around Sweet Harmony's shivering shoulders. "I didn't never think to look on 'ee again! Yer poor dress—an' yer hands— oh, Harmony, what ha' they done to 'ee?"

"There was a m-man!" Harmony cried, while Charity worked to free the knotted cord around her wrists. " 'Twas horrible; Master Jamie said I was to ascend, but they put a *rope* around my neck, and he . . . and he—'' She broke off into a sob and turned away, chafing her wrists. ''But . . . but now I'm safe. The Prince came—on his horse—in the church, with his sword and everything! Oh—'twas the most tremendous thing. I wish you could have seen it!''

All three of them looked toward S.T. in awe.

''You've got me wishing I'd seen it myself,'' he said, handing the taper to Charity. ''I'll build you a fire before I go.''

''You're going to leave us again?'' Dove cried, her reverence dissolving into dismay.

''There's no time for anything else. I intend to be virtuously sipping punch and toasting my feet beside the Twice Brewed's hearth before Luton returns.''

''Had best hurry, then,'' Charity said. ''I can make a fire,'' she added staunchly. ''Now that there be light.''

''Good girl.'' He caught up Sirocco's lead rope and guided the horse around, dragging the saddle off Mistral and tossing it onto the black. ''Can you find your way to take him down to the river for water?''

''Aye, m'lord!'' Charity said, eager and proud. ''And I'll give'un the nose bag 'ee brung.''

S.T. mounted. Harmony, with Charity's cloak hugged around her, hurried forward and put her hand on his boot.

''Thank you,'' she said in a soft voice. ''Oh—how much I thank you!''

He reached down and slid his gloved finger under her chin. Her upturned face was very sweet, the trace of tears still glistening on her cheeks and lashes. He leaned over, tilted her chin upward, and kissed her mouth. Then he put his heels to Sirocco and sent the horse lunging up the path.

Really, he thought, it was too bad Leigh wasn't there to see it.

Even avoiding the main road and following the wall, he made good time on a rested horse, stopping well off from the dusky lights of the Twice Brewed to remove the mask and change his black and silver gauntlets for plain open-fingered mitts. Sirocco blew restively, swinging his hindquarters in a manner that made S.T. pause and look up, squinting into the dark where the horse was looking.

He heard the sound of the hooves, and leaned over to put his hand on Sirocco's nose, hoping to discourage any equine welcome. But the irregular thud drew nearer; he heard the rattle of stones and then saw the dark shape moving toward him in the night.

He drew his sword. "Declare yourself!"

There was no answer. The shadowy form jogged nearer, until he could make out the dim white blaze and stockings.

"Leigh!" Relief rolled through him for an instant, and then the chestnut dropped to a walk and stuck out its nose to greet Sirocco. S.T. saw the reins dangling into the murk.

He swore. He caught at the chestnut's bit and dragged it forward, trying to see evidence of a fall. In the dark, he could find no sign that the horse had gone down, no mud nor marks on the saddle—small comfort, but a little. It was hard to be tossed from a sidesaddle, with the leaping tree to hold a rider in place, but if a horse reared and toppled backwards that same brace became a trap to entangle her beneath a half ton of flailing horseflesh.

She might be lying somewhere in the dark, crushed and unconscious. Or dead.

"Leigh," he shouted, standing up in his stirrups. *"Leigh!"*

The ghostly frost of his breath disappeared into blackness. He didn't care now if anyone heard him; he didn't care what Luton might suspect—he'd turn out every soul at the Twice Brewed in the search. He listened, damning his bad ear, straining to control his breath and the horses' movements so he could hear any faint response. The light, cold wind brought silence. He turned the horses toward the north.

"Leigh!" he bellowed again, and his voice came echoing back in the night.

He held his breath—and heard an unmistakable whimper. He stiffened, trying to guess the direction, but no hunt proved necessary. The horses both turned and stared, nostrils flaring, as a bobbing gray shape in the obscurity took on the solid outline of a wolf, trotting doggedly forward in spite of an awkward limp.

S.T. sheathed his sword and dismounted. Nemo pressed up against his legs in a subdued vestige of the wolf's usual leaping greeting. S.T. knelt and allowed his face to be washed, searching gently over the thick, cold fur until he felt the matted wound just above Nemo's foreleg.

He didn't probe it, not caring to disturb Nemo's friendly humor. There was little he could see in the dark anyway. The wolf didn't seem too much the worse for his injury, on his feet and able to move, but S.T. had a lump of apprehension in his throat, a nagging sense of dread.

He knelt with the wolf, stroking the deep fur, trying to grasp something that danced at the edge of his memory.

The beast . . . the sword . . . the witch . . .

Nemo. The colichemarde.

The witch—and the way she'd ridden out of that stable as if the furies of hell were at her back.

Like a spark struck into sawdust, he understood. Realization of what she'd done burst full-blown upon him.

"Oh, you little fool," he breathed. "You hare-brained little fool." He stood up and stared around him, feeling blank, feeling the full implication sink into his heart.

Chilton. She'd gone out alone to take him. And she hadn't come back.

"Damn you, Leigh!" he yelled to the night sky. "Damn you, damn you, *damn you!*"

TWENTY-THREE

LEIGH was not afraid of the dark. She loved the night;
had always felt defended by the darkness when she'd
walked out alone beneath the stars. Not specters nor
fients nor fears of the devil's eldritch beasties disturbed
her, if she was outdoors and free.

But to be blindfolded, hurting, lying on the floor with
her hands and feet bound and her ears straining to make
sense of the sounds that drifted to her—that was something
to fear. No creature out of hell could unnerve her more
than the distant screams and shouts of Chilton's followers.

She lay where she'd come to consciousness, racked by
shivering, trying to hang on to awareness amid the swimming pain. Her head throbbed, her cheek rested against a
carpet and her body on bare wood. It smelled of home:
cold and disused, but still a trace lingered of her father's
snuff, of mint and the licorice scent of fennel that the
housemaids had often used to rub the floors.

She was certain she was somewhere at Silvering, in a
large room, from the way the sound echoed each time her
unseen warden moved. She tried to focus her hazy reason.
Not the Marble Hall, for there was no carpet there; not
the Kingston Room, for there the arms of Kingston were
painted on the bare wood, nor either of the resonating
staircase halls with their stone floors and family portraits.
It might be the saloon or the great dining room or the
chamber over the kitchen—or even the gallery of the pri-

vate chapel: all had wooden floors and carpets and echoing space.

When that distant tumult of shouting had erupted, her guardian had stood up and moved away until she couldn't tell where the footsteps had gone. She worked at her bindings, praying that her guard had left the room—it seemed so, for no one chastised her, but she made no headway at all on the cord that restrained her from elbows to wrists, unable even to curl her hands and find the knot.

She was lashed to something solid. Her searching fingers shaped the wood, defining the corkscrew molding. Only one place in the house boasted those elaborate balusters turned in oak: the railing of the chapel gallery, where she'd spent a thousand Saturday evenings sitting between her mother and Anna, listening to her father's mellow voice weave a rehearsal sermon through the peaceful silence.

The footsteps returned, quick and agitated. Leigh tried to go limp, feigning unconsciousness, but the cold made her shiver so hard that she could barely control her movements.

"He's a'coomin' from the kirk," a male voice said, heavy with the familiar dialect of the north. "Thy hour is nigh, witch."

Leigh could hear the shouting, a single voice now, growing louder. It was a voice she'd not heard for many months, but she knew it; would never in her life forget the spellbinding timbre of that preaching. The words said nothing. It was the sound: coaxing and commanding, a caress and then a sudden shout, telling tales of sin and redemption and the glory of God and Jamie Chilton.

It was everything she hated and feared, and it was coming for her.

God. Dear God. Once she would have been glad enough to die, if she could take Chilton with her. Now she wasn't, now she wanted to live, and it made her mind stupid with terror.

Seigneur, she begged silently, and squeezed her eyes shut beneath the blindfold, caught between hysterical laughter and tears. *Seigneur, Seigneur . . . now I need you.*

S.T. saw the lights before he got there: up to the right, the flicker of torches through tree branches, high at the end of the street where Silvering overlooked the town. Almost, he ran—but ingrained years of stealth won out. He'd left Nemo out on the moor, bidding the injured wolf stay where he'd found it. Now he tied Sirocco and kept to the darkest side of the street, his hand on his sword hilt to silence it as he moved.

The lights seemed to coalesce and grow as he neared. By the time he came to the end of the trees, Chilton's bellowing sounded loud and incoherent, and the whole facade of Silvering danced with the pale coral glow from a small bonfire just inside the open gate. The pediment and cornices stood out in lurid relief, the shadows swaying as if the house were alive.

A group of people clustered around the fire and on the stairs, silhouetted by the rising flames. S.T. estimated a score or more, most of them men. The women stood at the outer edge. As he watched, one of the females moved slowly backward to the limits of the firelight, and then turned and slipped away.

Good for you, chérie, he thought.

Something made a noise in the dark close by. S.T. gripped his sword, scanning the area. Just ahead of him, a lone figure stood beneath the trees, well away from the others, watching.

Luton.

S.T. unclipped his cloak and took off his hat, tucking up the cuffs of his shirt to hide the lace. Then he pulled off his cravat and turned down his collar, so as to look as unprincely as possible. He stuffed his neckcloth in his pocket, feeling the cold air on his throat, and walked up to the single figure in the shadows.

" 'Evening," he murmured, attempting cordiality with his blood pounding in his temple. "What's ado?"

Luton jumped a foot, turning to S.T. with a wild look.

"For God's sake—Maitland! What the devil—what are you doing here?"

S.T. shrugged. "Curiosity." He looked sideways at the other man with a faint smile. "Am I too late for the festivities?"

Luton just stared at him, scowling beneath the peaked wig.

"I meant to follow you earlier," S.T. said, "but—ah— one of the girls detained me."

The instant he said it, he regretted the words. Luton might have spoken of the inn to Chilton; the aristocrat might know where Dove and Harmony had come from and how they'd left Heavenly Sanctuary. From there it was but a short step of reason to connecting Mr. Bartlett and S.T. Maitland to the masked Prince of Midnight. 'Twas short enough anyway: S.T. stayed alert and on guard for any attack.

But Luton only said, "We've had some trouble tonight."

"Ah? Pity." S.T. looked up toward the small bonfire. "What the devil's that fellow caterwauling about?"

Luton made a sharp, disgusted move with his hand. "He's gone mad. I tried to reason with him, but he's lost his bloody mind."

"Sounds it, I must say."

"We'd a visit from your highwayman." Luton looked at S.T. again. "Did you know who it was? That cocky French dog, the one they call Seigneur du Minuit. Fair drove Chilton beserk. Fancies it a personal attack. Tried to tell him more likely it was myself—that damned Robin Hood must have got wind of things, but there was no talking sense to him." He turned back toward Chilton as the preacher's voice rose to a screech. "He's positively foaming at the mouth, I tell you. Never seen a man actually do that."

"So the amusement's called off, is it?"

"Oh, 'tis off. All off." Luton curled his lip. "But I've something left to do here."

S.T. was silent a moment. Chilton's crazy voice echoed in the street. As the two of them stood there, another girl stole away, hurrying past them with her cowl pulled around her face. S.T. looked back at Luton, and found the man watching him narrowly.

He brazoned it out. "What's he doing up there?"

"God only knows." Luton grunted. "Keeps roaring on about burning the witch, but there's some of them don't seem to have the stomach for it."

"Witch?" S.T. controlled his voice, keeping it steady, not too loud. "They've caught a witch?"

"So Chilton seems to think."

"Where is she?" S.T. asked casually.

Luton shrugged. "In the house, perhaps." He pulled at his lip. "What are game for, Maitland? Why'd you follow me here?"

S.T. smiled. "Sport."

Luton fingered his sword hilt. "I can give you sport. I mean to silence that raving maggot before he talks too much abroad."

"He does grate somewhat on the sensitive ear."

"I'll not chance his preaching my name wherever he might please. He could ruin me, and others besides." Luton drew his sword. "I wouldn't put anything past him now, him and this lot. They're maniacs. Dangerous. All of 'em. Do you see they've got pikes? 'Tis only the most fanatical left now. The others have all bolted."

S.T. moved his hand toward his sword hilt. Luton glanced down, following the motion.

The basket hilt of the broadsword gleamed in swirling bars of metal: unique and memorable, its uncommon beauty obvious even in the dancing light.

Luton's face froze in recognition.

"Bastard!" He stared up at S.T. "You lying bastard— you're *him!*"

S.T. jerked the sword free, just in time to swing it up into a desperate parry against Luton's instant attack. The metal clashed. Luton disengaged and came back furiously. S.T. could barely see his opponent's rapier in the dim light, but the broadsword was like a ribbon of red and silver. He kept it close to guard his throat, not daring to open his defense by swinging wide to make a cut.

Luton was fast and angry, closing and closing again in spite of the broadsword's advantage of length. "I'll kill you, you lying snake! Interfere, will you?" he panted. "I'll kill you for it—you and that madman both!"

S.T. countered the attack silently, pulling his stiletto from beneath his coat to use in his left hand. He lunged and parried, saw an opening in Luton's overbalanced stance, and made a thrust that pinked his ribs. Luton flinched and sucked in his breath, renewing his onslaught with an angry grunt.

With a rapier and a little more light, S.T. could have disabled the man in three strokes. Luton was an adequate swordsman, no better than average and breathing heavily already, but S.T. could not see the other blade. He had to fight by instinct, by watching the pale bob of Luton's cuff and extrapolating the motion into a thirty-inch sword. It caught him once, a blaze of pain as the point sank into his upper thigh.

He stepped into the burn, the way he'd learned a thousand years ago in a hot and dusty yard in Florence: facing the best with unprotected blades, under a master who had no patience with weakness. A yelp and a disengagement had earned a beating then; now it would earn destruction. S.T. caught Luton's rapier on his hilt and drove it upward with all his strength, attacking when retreat was expected, throwing Luton's arm in the air with the force. As Luton lunged forward to regain his position, S.T. met the whizzing rapier with the cutting edge of the broadsword, both weapons colliding with the full violence of their momentum.

The jar went through his hand to his shoulder. The rapier snapped like bone against the heavier sword.

Luton gave a howl of fury. He flung the broken weapon aside. S.T. heard it clatter on the street, but he wasn't concerned with Luton any longer.

Something had happened at the mansion. People ran out the front door, carrying torches and throwing them on the bonfire. As S.T. stared, a flaming glow rose at two of the windows—*inside*—and Chilton appeared at the open door, holding two flaring torches in his hands. He was bellowing of persecution, backlit by interior flames. Smoke began to creep in dark blurry fingers above him, out of the top of the door, crawling up the luminous facade.

S.T. ran. He mounted the steps three at a time, tripping on his sluggish leg. Someone came running down, as if to push him back, but S.T. brandished the sword and struck the man's pike aside.

"*Is she in there?*" He hurled himself at Chilton, the broadsword still in his hand.

Something cracked in his ear.

Chilton looked at him, a sudden stillness, his mouth open silently and a blossum of red against his white collar. Then he wasn't standing; he was nothing but a sprawled heap in the doorway. As he dropped, a new chorus of screams broke out. S.T. stood above him, staring down in astonishment, and then twisted around to look over his shoulder.

Above the bonfire and the shocked faces of Chilton's crowd stood Luton, balanced on one of the stone pedestals by the gate, his arm around a bar, working frantically to reload his pistol and aim again.

S.T. turned back, springing over Chilton's body and diving into the smoke.

A choking black pall hung at the ceiling, billowing over the cold spread of marble floor. The grand hall danced in firelight. Dark smoke poured from the upholstered seats of a pair of elegant chairs thrown together and set alight at the center, flowing upward into obscurity. His eyes watered; he dragged his arm across them and squinted. Through all the open double doors—before him, left and right—S.T. could see draperies burning in the rooms beyond.

His injured leg wouldn't obey him, trying to buckle under his weight. He staggered and stood straight, tossing down his sword and sheathing the siletto. The sound of the fire came to his good ear like a single bellowing wind, a furnace, a dragon roaring at his left ear, swinging with him wherever he turned.

"*Leigh!*" he shouted. "*Are you here?*"

And then doubled over in a fit of coughing.

He shouted again, plunging forward past the double doors into the saloon, where flaming curtains lit the portraits and the paneling, licking in bright greed up the pale green drapes, dropping small blazing banners of fringe that hissed on the floorboard and smoldered in the carpet. He spread his neckcloth over his nose and tied it, coughing, ducking below the hanging smoke.

He heard her voice, he was certain of it. He was sure he heard her over the sound of the fire—but he could not tell from where.

All the sound came to him from the left. From his good ear. An open door led out from every side of the saloon. He stood in the middle of the burning room and didn't know which way to go.

He snatched up a rug from the hearth, beating it against the flames that rose up the curtains next to the door on the left wall. Smoke and heat engulfed him; he staggered back, his eyes tearing, and pulled the rug over his head to make a dash through. On the other side was another hell: the flaming curtains cast a bloody red glow on the scarlet wallpaper.

More smoke. More doors. He yelled again.

He stood fixed, sweating, turning his head and trying to listen above the crackle and sucking *whoosh* of the flames. Smoke hung everywhere, a lowering murky cloud lit by flickers of orange and yellow, the bitter taste of charcoal in his mouth and throat. He had to bend over to breathe. A smoky billow erupted suddenly into a sheet of flame from the skirting on a window seat. He jerked away, shielding his face from the blistering heat.

He limped to the nearest door and went through, found a hall and a breakfast room untouched by the fire, dimlit in the reflected flames from the other rooms. Her voice sounded: very faint; high-pitched and muffled. He yelled for her and it came back louder.

There was panic in the sound. It sent him blundering down the smoky hall into the darkness.

He ran into something that whacked his injured thigh and doubled him over in agony. For an instant he couldn't move. He pressed his palm over the wound, coughing and groaning. When he put his hand up to his eyes in the murk, he smelled fresh blood and felt the abundant liquid smear on his skin.

"Devil take it," he muttered hoarsely. He pulled down the neckcloth from his mouth. *"Leigh,"* he shouted to the black ceiling. *"For God's sake, where are you?"*

No answer that he could hear. Cursing weakly, he retied the neckcloth over his face, turned, and blundered back toward the glow of the fire.

Smoke grew thicker as he neared the doors. He gulped a breath, wincing back from the inferno in the crimson room, coughing and bending over to find air as heat poured out.

His head pounded from the smoke; he braced his hands on his knees and took a painful breath. His injured leg trembled, threatening collapse.

With a helpless sob, he pushed himself upright, pulled the rug around him, and plunged back into the red drawing room. He moved toward another pair of doors—stood in that opening and shouted her name into the firebox of burning drapes that lined the walls of the room beyond.

No answer.

He shouted again, his voice muffled by the neckcloth. Only the blowing noises and blister of flames came back. His leg kept buckling with each step as he lurched back to the last pair of doors. The green saloon again, lined in flames on the outside wall.

He yelled for her . . . but the flames were too loud now—he could not have heard her even if she answered.

A burning gilt pelmet crashed to the floor halfway down the room. S.T. forced himself to go forward. He moved in a half stagger, half crawl, tears coursing down his face from smoke and frustration. Every room seemed like a nightmare, lit by burning tapestries or drapes that glared through the blinding smoke.

He wasn't sure how much longer his leg would support him. His voice had gone to a croak. But he kept on yelling for her, a raw sound, until he didn't have the voice or breath to do more than weave crazily through the glare and smoke to each door. He was afraid he would pass out;

his lungs already labored just to keep him on the edge of consciousness.

Smoke and tears blinded him, made everything a smear of dark and light. When he opened the last door he couldn't even close it; he hung on the knob, his knees caving under him as he fell through.

"Seigneur! Are you here?"

He heard her voice, clear and close. His eyes refused to open to another smoky hell. She called again, and began to cough. As his brain cleared, he realized the flames were behind him, sucking and blooming on the cool air that poured past his face.

He wrenched his eyes open, saw the cold darkness ahead and staggered up, slamming the door to shut out the fire.

"Leigh." He could barely make a sound. Ahead of him, dim columns rose into blackness far above.

"I'm up—here." She choked on the words.

He stumbled to his feet, his leg trembling with pain. "Where?" he croaked, pulling the neckcloth from his mouth.

"Up." The word echoed, dissolved in a gagging cough. "The—gallery. You're in the family chapel."

He couldn't seem to think. It was hard enough to breathe, to drag air into his burning throat and lungs. "How?" he whispered. "How—I—" he lifted his head feebly "—up there?"

"The stairs—in the chapel—sitting—room." Her husky voice drifted eerily above him. "Left. Door to the left. Next . . . room."

He wet his lips and glanced left. He could see the door she meant by the glow along the floor. Smoke curled under the panels, sliding up the wood.

He groped to it and grabbed the brass handle. Pain flashed across his hand; he jerked back and the door exploded open.

A boom of flame and smoke flung him backwards. The room roared, his back hit the floor and he·pushed up, terrified by the rampart of fire sucking air and life into a howling blaze beyond. His body felt seared, burning where his clothes touched his skin. He scrambled onto his knees, barely aware of the flames that colored the wooden panels in weird translucent light, curling peels of varnish that withered and vanished into charcoal. Kicking out with his boot, he slammed the door shut on the destruction. He stumbled up against a marble column and hugged himself against it, clasping the cool stone to his scorched face.

"Seigneur!" Her voice was a squeak of anxiety. "Are you there?"

"I can't—go that way," he gasped. "Sunshine—"

"The pulpit." The words floated down out of tenebrous shadows. "Can you climb up the pulpit?"

He peered blearily at the dark mass of wood beneath the gallery. The curved steps led up almost a man's height to the pulpit, and then a heavily carved canopy doubled that. The top touched the base of the overhanging gallery floor.

He put his hand on the ornate wooden stair rail and dragged himself up the steps, using his unburned hand to take his weight and ease the strain on his injured leg.

From the black interior of the pulpit, he gripped the edge of the canopy and hiked himself up. His knee wedged against a wooden carving on one side. He put his strength into the push and tried to climb, grimacing against the pain.

A sudden cough racked him, his lungs protesting the effort in the condensing smoke. He lost his hold, grabbed with his burned hand, and fell back, grasping for purchase with fingers that screamed in agony.

"Here," she said. "Can you reach my hands? Just get my hands free."

He squinted upward. He saw movement in the obscurity, heard a frantic thumping as she maneuvered. The pale shape of her hands appeared through the rail.

He let go, dropping to the pulpit floor, and rested his head back against the podium. It took a monumental effort to push upright and drag his stiletto free.

In the smoky darkness he could barely see; he had to feel for the cord, and she yelped when he slipped the blade underneath the knot.

"Sorry," he muttered, sawing as carefully as he could

manage. The cord fell loose. She pulled away before he got it unraveled.

"Give me the knife," she hissed, reaching through the banister. "My legs!"

He flipped the stiletto and laid the handle in her open hand. "Have a care."

"Aye—I'd rather not have my ankle sliced off, too," she muttered with a little gagged cough. "There—that's got it. Come on!" She stuck her hand through the railing again.

"Up there?" he rasped.

"Are you going out the way you came in? There's no other down there."

He glanced toward the closed door of the chapel. Flames glowed beneath the edges, blurred by sliding smoke.

"I'll help you, Seigneur." She stood up and leaned over the rail. "Grab my hands."

"Do you propose to pull me up?" he grated dryly.

"We'll do it together. Do you think I'll leave you?"

"Together."

"Come on!" she urged. "Get up on the parson's seat and give me your hand!"

"Nay—you won't hold me." He searched in the black cavern of the canopy and stepped up onto the seat. He found the carving with his knee. "I can do it myself." He shoved upward, grabbing in the dark for purchase among the carvings on the top of the canopy, but his blistered fingers couldn't take the full weight of his pull. He strained, grunting through his teeth, and fell back.

"Give me your *hand!*" she cried. "What's wrong with you?"

He hoisted himself onto the seat again and grabbed the carvings, kicking off hard with his good leg for leverage. For an instant he swung from his hands as he tried to heave his upper body onto the roof. His tongue tasted of fresh blood and charcoal. He heard himself, whimpering like a puppy while his injured leg blazed with pain and his fingers felt as if he held them to a red-hot forge.

Suddenly he felt her hands around his arms, dragging

hard, stronger than he ever would have thought a female could pull.

The grip gave him the half inch that he needed. He thrust his knee over the top of the canopy, unable to contain a sob as he dragged his other leg up. But then he was on top, breathing hard in his raw throat.

"Hurry!" Leigh's hands groped for him. "This way—there's a window."

He levered himself over the rail, stumbling after her. She was already leaning out the open window. She hiked her legs across the ledge and dropped down. S.T. peered out, and saw with relief that the ground was only two yards below.

He hauled his injured leg over the sill, turned around and braced his foot against the wall, easing himself down into the tangle of weeds below. He stood holding his aching thigh, drinking deep draughts of sweet air and choking in between each one.

Leigh gripped his arm, pulling at him. "Come away—get away from the house!"

He let her drag him, coughing and tripping, into the cold darkness. When he found his breath he straightened up, groped, and caught her shoulders, grabbed her face between both hands and kissed her roughly.

To his amazement, she dug her fingers into his hair, returning the kiss, trading the burnt taste of charcoal and blood, pressing herself to his scorched body until he almost fell off his balance with the force of it. He clutched at her shoulders as she pulled abruptly free.

"God damn, Sunshine," he breathed.

"I knew you'd come," she said, and turned away toward the dark.

S.T. stared after her through the smoke. He felt his burnt face break into a painful grin. He leaned back, turned his face to the sky and sent a raucous howl of elation into space.

It ended up in a coughing fit.

"You put me forcibly in mind of a Bedlamite," she snapped out of the darkness. "Come along to where it's safe, will you?"

TWENTY-FOUR

S.T. made it as far as the line of trees that edged the overgrown garden. He caught at one of the trunks as Leigh passed it, sagging against the bark.

"Si' down," he croaked. "Have to . . . rest."

His injured leg crumbled beneath him. He put his arm around the tree and slid to his knees.

Every breath was punishment for that one elated whoop, burning down his throat and into his chest. Leigh crouched beside him. He could see part of her face, illuminated in yellow by the flames.

She pulled his hand away from his leg and bent over it. Then, without a word, she untied the neckcloth hanging loose around his throat and knotted it over the wound. S.T. gritted his teeth against a groan. The sword cut hurt, but it was his seared skin that took up all of his awareness. Everywhere his clothing rubbed him felt blistered. The cold air on his face and hands was like ice on fire.

"You didn't tell me you were hurt," she hissed. "Impossible idiot!"

"Hurt?" he repeated in a grating voice. "*Sangdieu*, boiled lobsters have felt better."

She shifted out of the light. "Where are you burned?"

He lifted his hand and turned it over. The smell of charred wool rose strongly, mixing with the sweet odor of woodsmoke. "Palm's the worst, I think."

"Where's your knife?" She took his wrist in her hands,

more gently than she'd touched him before. "I'll have to cut your mitt off."

Before he had a chance to protest, she'd felt at his waistcoat and found the stiletto. S.T. panted, gritting his teeth as she slit the wool across the back of his hand and began to peel it from his palm. An involuntary shudder gripped him.

"Lie down," she said, abandoning the project. "Do you feel light-headed?"

He swallowed, leaning against her, suddenly shivering uncontrollably, hot and cold at once. "M'all right," he said, but it felt damned good to allow her to do the work for him, supporting his shoulders until his head rested on the ground. The slight slope sent fresh blood to his head, clearing the mist.

"Bells?" he mumbled, wincing again as she renewed her effort to strip the burned mitt from his hand.

"Aye—they're ringing alarm at the church. Stay here," she said, as if he had any intention of moving. "I'm going for water."

She darted away, and S.T. realized the night was beginning to spark with more than the fire. Distant shouts drew nearer, and torches flared. He straightened up on his elbow and looked around. "Wait—" He couldn't force his voice past a gritty rasp. "Leigh, wait!"

She didn't turn, already too far to hear above the flames and commotion. A bucket brigade was turning out from somewhere, men and women with ruddy faces and working clothes—a few of Chilton's girls, but more of the gathering forces of the neighborhood come to fight the fire, the way they'd banded together for centuries against a common enemy. Leigh ran down the hill and accosted one of the men, pointing and shouting in his ear. She reached out and put her hand on the arm of a girl with a bucket.

They turned together and came back. S.T. sat up against the tree, his instincts crying out that he'd best fade into the darkness before he was trapped here, injured and defenseless. He got to his feet with an effort, but Leigh was there before he could make any coherent decision.

"Put his right hand in the water bucket," she told the girl, and went striding into the darkness.

It was just the sort of autocratic demand that one of Chilton's converts had been trained to obey without question. The girl took S.T.'s wrist and plunged his hand in the water.

"Lord!" He sucked his breath at the frigid bath. The water must have come straight out of the ice-covered river. But she held his hand down, and after a moment the burning in his palm subsided to a dull throb.

Leigh returned, carrying a branch that appeared to have been hacked right off the nearest bush. With his stiletto, she began to strip the bark and toss it into the bucket.

"What's that?" he asked suspiciously.

"Alder bush. I'll make a poultice after it soaks. Do you sit down, Monseigneur—you've been heroic enough for today. Standing up only proves you a blockhead."

He smiled, a painful process. "My sweet Sunshine."

"Don't talk, either, if you please. The smoke will have burned your lungs." She took the water pail from the other girl. "Bring a link for me."

S.T. shook his head as the lass trotted away. "No torch. Don't make such a fuss. Just—"

"I need light," she interrupted. "I want to examine your leg."

"And put me to bed and brew a posset, after which you'll pour invigorating broth down my throat? It won't be necessary. I don't think I'll linger here overlong, Sunshine."

She looked up abruptly.

S.T. pulled his burned hand from the water and shook it. He tilted his head, nodding toward the crowd that gathered downhill. "M'thinks I recognize a justice of the peace, if a decade of dodging the breed gives me any aptitude."

Leigh turned around. Below, a sturdy squire who had arrived on horseback was gesturing and yelling instructions.

"Mr. MacWhorter," she said. She blew a puff of frost, as if the name annoyed her. "You're right; he's one of the magistrates.'' Then suddenly her body stiffened. She looked from the squire to the retreating back of the girl in the pale cap. ''Where's Chilton?'' she asked sharply.

S.T. reached out with his unburned hand. He caught her shoulder and turned her toward a limp body that lay a few yards off from the tumult. No one attended it—there was just a black cloak thrown casually over the head and shoulders.

Leigh stood still at the sight. S.T. kept his hand on her shoulder.

She stared at Chilton's body, and then up at Silvering. The bucket brigade flung their puny offerings at the house, trying to wet down what had not yet caught fire, but smoke poured from the open front door. The windows of every downstairs room glowed angry orange and yellow.

S.T. saw the truth of it hit her. All the horror held in check by their struggle to escape, all the reality of what had happened—it came to her in that silent moment. She stood immobile, ignoring his touch, ignoring the shouts, just gazing at her home as it burned.

So here is it is, S.T. thought. *Revenge.*

''Sunshine,'' he said, his voice low and hoarse. He pressed her shoulder, half expecting her to whirl away from him as she always did, rejecting any human comfort. But she didn't. She closed her eyes and leaned against his hand. When he drew her back, she turned her face into his chest as if he could hide her.

He held her close, in spite of the pain of her body compressed so tightly to his burns. He wanted to hurt; he deserved to smolder in hell for what he'd done.

He couldn't have Leigh. He knew it; he'd known it from the beginning.

His moment was over now.

Au revoir, ma belle . . . the time has come for us to part . . .

Same verse as always. Same song, same ending. He had to leave. He could not stay.

He thought: *she was right.* She'd called him a liar, looked ahead and seen this culmination, faced what he had not brought himself to confront. It came too soon, this farewell; he'd thought there would be more time. It crept in the background and then materialized, like death, denied and denied and still inevitable.

"How did you do it?" she asked dully, and for an instant he didn't understand the question.

Then she lifted her head and looked toward Chilton's body.

"I didn't." S.T. took a deep breath into his burned lungs. "Another killed him."

But 'tis I who'll be accused.

He didn't say it. He just stared grimly past her at this honest country squire, all these upright people who hadn't stood against Chilton for her. They were fatal to him. He'd shown himself here, and now he had to go, as he always did, before the excitement died down and law-abiding people began to talk. Began to piece things together.

It was happening already. The capped girl who'd brought the bucket reached MacWhorter's stirrup. She spoke to him far longer than a mere request for a torch required. As S.T. watched, the squire dismounted. She pointed, and MacWhorter grabbed a lamp to light the way. He began to climb the hill toward S.T. and Leigh.

S.T. shoved himself off the tree, standing straight. He kept his arm around Leigh, but she instantly moved back, looking over her shoulder. A shout rose up, and the firefighters shrank away as two windows imploded and the flames shot out, licking up the stone walls.

His grip on her tightened. He wouldn't leave her yet. Not now, when she needed him. Not this way, like some sneak thief, running from a solemn-faced, beak-nosed, backwater magistrate.

Even from a distance, S.T. could see the man's expression change in the torchlight as he recognized Leigh. The squire stared at her, and then handed the lantern to the girl and put out his hands, striding forward.

"My lady!" he shouted above the sound of the fire. "Lady Leigh, good God—this is extraordinary!" He plowed up the hill. "We'd no notion you'd come home, and that chit says you were *inside*—" He reached them, shook Leigh by the shoulders and pulled her against him. "Child, child, oh my God, what are you doing? What's happening?"

Leigh endured his embrace for a moment and pressed herself free. "Can they save the house?"

He wet his lips and glanced away. "I'm sorry. I'm so sorry. There'll not be much chance."

" 'Tis all gone then. Everything." She looked at S.T. with a sudden intensity.

He didn't understand that look. There was no blame in it. She seemed almost expectant, as if he could say something that would change it all. He met her steady gaze and thought that if the magic words existed that would turn time back and let him do it all differently, he would have sold his soul to buy them.

She was still watching him. Abruptly she put up her hand and touched his blistered face. "Your poor eyebrows," she said. "With the devil's curl all burned away."

MacWhorter looked at her as if she were mad. "Milady, come away from here. You've had a terrible shock. I'll send you home to Mrs. Mac, where you can be made comfortable."

Leigh didn't take here eyes off of S.T.'s face. "He saved me, Mr. MacWhorter," she said. "He searched the house until he found me."

For the first time, S.T. received a direct look from the squire, an uncomfortable glower, as if it were a trifle inconvenient to be introduced to this particular hero. "We owe you our deepest gratitude, then, sir."

S.T. bowed slightly. His leg ached and stung, but he stood stiffly, with his weight on it.

"Mr. Chilton is dead," Leigh said.

MacWhorter cleared his throat. "Yes. I—uh—examined that." He raised his voice above the noise. "Unfortunate man. Shot." He looked at S.T. again, a narrow assessment.

S.T. stared back.

" 'Twill be necessary to ask some questions," the squire said loudly.

"Will it?" Even amid the popping roar, the acid in

Leigh's voice came clear. "You never asked them before."

MacWhorter scowled. "We'll convene a jury."

"Do that," S.T. said in a grating voice. " 'Tis safe enough now, I expect."

MacWhorter answered that with his chin jutting. "I'm afraid I must ask your name, sir—and what your situation may be."

"Samuel Bartlett. I'm putting up with the landlady at the Twice Brewed Ale."

"And your business?"

S.T. smiled crookedly. "Beyond rescuing the odd damsel . . . I'm touring."

"The law does not appreciate levity, Mr. Bartlett." MacWhorter gave him a cold eye. "I've had reports of disturbance in the past several weeks—suspicious characters at the Twice Brewed."

"Did you investigate?" Leigh enquired in a mocking tone. "Find it necessary to ask questions?"

"I was on the point of it, indeed I was."

S.T. put his hand on the tree trunk, surreptitiously supporting himself. "The man you want is George Atwood. Lord Luton. He shot Chilton."

"And how is this?" The squire lifted his eyebrows and tucked his chin. "Do you say you saw it?"

S.T. looked toward the burning building. "Aye, I saw it."

"A lord, you charge! I'm to think some lord just happened by and shot the man? What for?"

"Ask the girls," S.T. said. "I left them at that ruin by the river, where the Roman bridge used to be."

"Witnesses to the murder?"

S.T. moved his hand impatiently. "They didn't see Chilton shot. They can tell you about Lord Luton, not that you'll ever catch him now. He'll be long gone away from this place."

"It seems to me passing strange that this Lord Luton should appear and disappear so conveniently," MacWhorter said. "What is your piece in the affair, Mr. Bartlett? How come you to be here at such an hour?"

"I was taking the air, Mr. MacWhorter," S.T. said huskily. "Why else should I be here?"

The magistrate's Roman nose flared in contempt. "Taking the air. Mounted upon a black horse, perhaps. I'm told there's one such tethered behind the last cottage, with a black-and-white mask in the saddlebag."

Another set of windows shattered, sending shouts and flames into the sky. The fire set MacWhorter in lurid silhouette as he leaned toward S.T.

"D'you think to slip away from justice yourself, Mr. Bartlett? There have been rumors of you and what you are. 'Tis my belief that I could ask a few more questions to the point. 'Tis my belief that you just might be the man who shot him yourself, sir."

"I would have been," S.T. said, his voice grinding, "but Luton got there first."

Leigh touched his arm, as if to silence him.

S.T. raised her hand and kissed it, held it tight in his. "Nay, shall we forgo all this ingenuous posturing? You know what happened here, MacWhorter—you know all about it. One green girl has done what you and your fellows were afraid to do, and contrived to break the spell that held this place." His voice grew hoarser as it rose. "You're safe now, you and your family. *You're* safe—and you stand here while this house burns and have the brass to speak of juries and justice." His lip curled. "Aye, hold me for questions, you cowering bastard, if you think you'll sleep better at night for hanging somebody."

The squire's mouth was tight. He glared at S.T., breathing heavily through his nose. "I can guess what you are, sir. A common outlaw!"

"And I know what you are," S.T. said. "I don't have to guess."

MacWhorter looked away, toward the milling crowd of the bucket brigade. The heat from the fire glistened on his forehead. His jaw twitched.

"Get you gone," he said savagely. "Get out of sight, then; leave my district." With a brusque move, he turned away, and then looked back. "Take your sword and that mask. You're safe 'till the morning, before I mount a posse to hunt you down on charges of murder and thievery.''

The light from his lantern swung wildly as he stalked downhill.

S.T. leaned his head back against the tree, closing his eyes. The sound of the fire whooshed and crackled in his good ear, black smoke dominating taste and smell. He hurt all over; even his eyes felt swollen and gritty.

"I'll bind your hand," Leigh said.

He opened his eyes and saw her reaching into the dancing shadows at their feet, collecting the strips of bark from the bucket. When she straightened up, he caught her wrist. He couldn't really see her face: it was she, now, cast in shadow against the background of the blaze. The bright flame haloed her hair, caught the curve of her cheek. He pulled her toward him with no intention but to put off going, to pretend he could hold her forever, his face pressed into the curve of her shoulder where smoky scent and pain and the reality of her filled up all his senses.

"I don't want to leave you," he said harshly, and then gave a tortured laugh, muffled in her coat. "Oh, God— that's one of them, isn't it? One of the things I've always said. 'I don't want to leave; I love you; I'll be back' . . ." He held her tighter. "Jesus, Leigh—what have I done?''

She turned her head, pressing her cheek against his. Her skin felt cool on his blistered face.

He couldn't say more. *I need you, I'll never forget you.* Every word that came to him, every promise and vow that rose to his lips seemed worthless, turned to dust because he'd said it all before. Had he ever meant them, those pledges to return? Even once, had he ever found leaving harder than staying?

He held her close and reckoned wildly, trying to find some way out, some chance that his arrest wouldn't lead straight to the gallows. He might elude the murder charge—there was evidence enough to cloud that . . . but all of his past ensnared him. Once caught, he was finished. He'd crimes enough awaiting payment.

It was Leigh who ended the embrace, ever-practical, pushing away to search for his burned palm and make her poultice of bark and torn cloth. He stroked her hair with his free hand, watching her work by the light of her blazing home.

"The alder should be boiled," she said. "But this is better than nothing."

She lifted her head, the task completed. S.T. looked down at his bandaged hand. Time seemed to be running past like water, unstoppable.

"Leigh," he said. "Where will you go now?"

She was only blackness against the fire; he couldn't see her face at all. "I don't know," she said.

"You have family?"

"A cousin. In London."

"By what name?"

She turned a little, and the fire showed him the outline of her cheekbone and her lips, smooth as marble, expressionless. "Clara Patton."

"Go there," he said. "I'll find you."

She looked back at him, a mysterious shadow again. "Why?" she asked.

Because I can't live without you. Because I love you. Because it can't end like this.

All those things he could not say. All those lies he'd told in his life.

"I have to," he said fiercely.

"Foolish man," she said, barely audible above the fire.

"I have to find you again. I won't let you go—I can't . . . it's impossible," he said incoherently. "My leaving. Now. This way. I'll think of something."

"Think of what?" There was a strange note in her voice. "A secret signal? Two candles in the window when 'tis safe to meet me in the garden?"

Like an abyss, that future opened before him. He felt drowned, helpless, as shocked as if she'd tossed the bucket of icy water in his scorched face. He saw it; he knew it so well, that garden tryst, but now the excitement of it tasted bitter, the romance twisted into punishment.

"Not that," he said. "Never that way, not for us."

"What way, then?"

He closed his right fist, feeling the burn. "Sunshine—Sunshine—damn it all . . ."

A dense wave of smoke drifted toward them. S.T. squinted against the stinging murk. Coughing doubled him over; when he found his breath and straightened, he saw that a small fire engine had been maneuvered into position. A team of men worked the pump, sending a wobbly arc of water into a window while the bucket brigade toiled to refill the reservoir.

"Too late," Leigh said. She wiped her sleeve across her eyes: tears or smoke, he couldn't tell.

"They might—save the wings." he managed to say, swallowing in his tortured throat.

She shrugged. "It doesn't matter. It's all gone now."

"Leigh—"

She looked back at him. He could see her clearly now in the glare: she had that expectant look again, a little upward tilt of her chin, a slight parting of her lips.

"I love you," he said in his rusty voice. "Will you remember that?"

The expression faded. She smiled a little, sadly. "I'll remember that you said it."

"I mean it." His voice cracked.

She picked up the water pail. She was going to walk away; he saw that, and panic welled up in his chest. He caught her arm.

"You'll go to your cousin?"

Her eyes lifted to his. Not expectant or questioning or unhappy, but a glance like a saber flash. "I'm not sure," she said deliberately.

He held steady under that challenge, refusing to surrender, to admit defeat, to call this the end. "Where else will you go, then?"

"With you."

She said it simply. Quietly.

He stood there, breathing in his aching throat.

Amid the sound of fire and the haze of smoke; the heat and pungent smell, the bitter taste, he found what had eluded him all his life. It came as a gift, unadorned;

unembellished by all the sweet ribbons and charms that disguised lesser tokens.

She didn't say she loved him. She didn't need to say it. With two words she humbled him.

Her eyes were intense as she watched him: proud and severe, a goddess with a soul of flame. That look offered and demanded at once, asked for the truth, commanded honesty.

It burned him all through, seared away the fantasies, left him with the devastating face of reality.

He dropped his hand away from her arm. "I can't take you with me. Not now, with MacWhorter and his bloodhounds upon me. How can I take you now?"

"I'm not afraid."

"Wait for me," he said. "I'll find you. I'll—think of a way for us."

She bent her head. He read contempt in that bending, and it shattered him, broke him at his heart. He felt too ashamed to touch her. All of his past, all of his folly—it came to this. She offered him a fortune and he had nothing to give in return but dreams.

Dreams had always been enough, before. No one had ever asked for more.

"It won't be long," he said, his voice harsh. "This stir will settle soon enough."

She looked up, looked through him. Without words, she mocked his promises.

"I'll think of a way, damn you!" He leaned his head back against the tree, watching sparks fly up into the black sky, winking in and out of the bare branches. "Believe me—just believe in me!"

"That isn't what I have to give you," she said, and suddenly her voice was no longer so controlled. It trembled, the only betrayal of emotion in her. "I can't be a maiden in distress for you always. I can't be your mirror. I can only go with you if you ask me."

Anger seized him. He pushed himself away from the tree, oblivious of the pain in his hand. "I'm asking you to wait!" Frustration and smoke destroyed his shout, fractured it to a broken snarl. "To have some faith."

She stared at him, so beautiful, so distant, no trace of devotion or fondness or acquiescence. He couldn't tell what she felt, what she thought.

"You should go now," she said at last.

"Will you wait?"

She looked at the house, at the conflagration that had been her home. "I've nowhere to go, have I?"

"Your cousin's. Clara Patton, in London."

With a strange shake of her head, as if clearing it of some cobwebby mist, she said, "I've let this happen. I've done this to myself. I knew. I knew. And I let it happen."

His moment of wrath dissolved. He lifted both his hands, pressed his fingers on her cheeks, the bandage a pale shape against the shadow at her throat. He kissed her. "In London. I'll be there."

He felt the tears tumble down her face. They smeared on his burned fingers, cold and stinging.

"Go," she said, pushing him away. "Just go."

He took a step, but she twisted and turned. She dropped the water pail and strode down the hill, leaving him with only the wet trace of her tears on his hands.

He watched her until she reached the fire engine. MacWhorter met her; the magistrate looked at Leigh and then up the hill.

There was no reprieve there, only a cold stare that challenged S.T.'s lingering.

He looked over at Chilton's body. A familiar unsheathed blade lay near it. He limped down the slope and picked up his spadroon, found his silver-edged tricorne cast in the shadows nearby. Then he pulled his cloak off Chilton's body. They'd closed the preacher's eyes, but his white face was underlit by an eerie copper blush from the reflected flames.

"You won't need any extra warmth where you're going," S.T. muttered, taking his cloak as he turned away.

No one paid him any attention. He couldn't see Leigh anymore among the rush of silhouettes and torches.

He turned back and hobbled up the hill into the dark.

TWENTY-FIVE

THREE months was enough. Three months of hunching over an open fire, shivering through a Scottish winter while hidden in a cave at the head of a steep and narrow glen—it was more than enough. Perhaps Bonnie Prince Charlie and his barefooted highlanders had found this sort of thing diverting, but S.T. was sufficiently poor spirited to be altogether wretched.

In former times, he would have made his way directly to London before any alarm could spread quickly enough to ensare him, going to ground in the crowded haunts of Covent Garden or St. Giles, where he knew whom to trust and whom to avoid, and what accommodations his gold would buy. But he couldn't take Nemo so far on a wounded leg—nor himself, not while his hands and face burned and the sword cut flashed agony up his thigh with every step that Mistral took.

He didn't have the willpower anymore. He didn't even have the desire.

So he'd gone north instead of south. In a cleft of rock, mantled with snow and fringed with dark pines, he and Nemo limped and groaned and curled together to keep warm, poaching heathcock and white hares and the occasional sluggish trout from a deep hole in the stream that belonged to some unknown landlord, filling out supper with oatcakes. Forage for Mistral was even harder. Beyond the oats S.T. had brought along, the horse had to nibble lichen and paw for grass and bracken beneath the snow along the banks of the burn.

S.T. was cold. He was hungry. He was lonely. He was too old for this.

He spent his time thinking. And the more he thought, the more he despaired. He couldn't have Leigh and stay in England. There was no hope of it. Aye, he'd his safe houses, his real name, but there was always the hazard of exposure. Especially now, when Luton had seen him, knew his face and name and mask. To live a reckless life alone was one business: to live knowing that every moment he spent with her put her at risk of hanging with him was another ordeal entirely.

There was only exile—only the pointless life where she'd found him amid his half-finished paintings—and when he tried to imagine asking her to give up all her future and join him in oblivion, he knew the humiliation of it would paralyze him.

So he delayed, failing his promise, freezing and moody. When the first thaw came, he mounted Mistral and headed down the glen with Nemo trotting behind. The wolf had healed, but S.T.'s injured thigh still ached. He didn't know where he was going or why, particularly, but he was damned if he'd cower in some freezing cave the same way he'd crawled off for safety to Col du Noir nearly four years ago.

He felt lost; pointless and gloomy. He traveled slowly, avoiding towns, crossing the border through the wild Cheviot Hills, in the country where the cattle reivers made their nighttime raids and then vanished back into the mists.

Moving across country, stopping sometimes at a solitary farmhouse to ascertain his direction or buy some food from some taciturn housewife, he wandered as far south as the lakes of Westmoreland. He'd been traveling for a week when he rode down out of the foggy bleakness of Shap Fells into a clear twilight, saw the town of Kendal nestled in its fertile valley, and had a sudden notion to spend the night in a bed.

No one knew him in Kendal. He'd ridden through once

or twice, but never stopped or used a name, his own or any other.

He whistled up Nemo, who was hunting mice in the heath. There were farms and cultivation nearby; S.T. couldn't allow the wolf to roam free while he stayed in town. He made a collar out his much-used cravat and tied Nemo to the lead rope before he remounted.

In his black cloak and point-edged hat and sword, he'd looked gentlemanly enough, so long as no one took serious exception to the grime on his linen shirt. He pulled his lace cuffs down out of the protection of his coat sleeves, changed his mitts for his silver-studded gauntlets, dusted off his hat as best he could, and prepared to be eccentric.

Nemo displayed some reluctance to join the late straggle of traffic on the road, but with a bit of firm coaxing, the wolf consented to trail alongside Mistral on all four feet instead of being dragged on his haunches. After a half mile, when no females approached to menace him, Nemo began to relax and trot ahead as far as the lead allowed, swinging back and forth across Mistral's path and necessitating numerous transfers of the lead rope over the horse's ears from one side to the other.

No one among the sparse collection of pedestrians and broad-wheeled wagons seemed to take any notice of S.T. and his companion, but when they neared the outskirts of town, a stage coach came lurching along the road toward them. As S.T. drew Mistral off to the side to let it pass, someone on the roof yelled at him. All the passengers on top turned and stared through the twilight as the coach rolled past, leaning out over the Lancaster-Kendal-Carlisle sign on the vehicle's rear wall.

Nemo took exception to the attention, and made a quick snarling dash after the receding wheels of the conveniency. S.T. spoke sharply and yanked him back, but the wolf showed no sign of remorse, only turning around and resuming his position ahead of Mistral with a satisfied air.

The neat town of Kendal was still busy, even as darkness approached. Windows in the limestone and plaster houses shone with lights reflected back by the river. Above it all, the black ruins of a castle brooded on a steep hill beyond the town. S.T. rode beneath the post horn that hung from the sign of the King's Arms and dismounted inside the stable yard, joining the crowd lingering around the office to inquire after parcels that might have arrived on the departed stage.

An officious youngster went striding about through the waiting group, distributing a handbill and bawling, "Proclamation! Proclamation, here, sirra—Proclamation!" He thrust one into S.T.'s hand, skipping back from Nemo's warning growl with a good-humored grin. S.T. glanced down at the paper.

For Acts of Highway Robbery, Mayhem and Murder
Sophocles Trafalgar Maitland
One Thousand Pounds
The aforementioned Highwayman being Possessed of a
Pale Gray Gelded Horse and Large Dog, this Dog
yellow-eyed, marked with cream and black, being in
Truth a Wolf—

S.T. didn't stop to read more. He swallowed the curse that sprang to his lips and crumpled the paper in his hand. For an instant pure panic consumed him; he stood there in the midst of a crowd where every third man was studiously engaged in reading a detailed description of his person, from his hair to his silver-trimmed gauntlets—*one thousand pounds*—Almighty God—*one thousand pounds!*

He took a deep breath, pulled down his hat, and remounted Mistral.

Just at the moment he reined the horse left, Nemo found something to interest him to the right. The wolf crossed under Mistral's nose, dragging the lead across the horse's chest. Mistral arched his neck and danced in protest of the contradictory signals. S.T. forcefully urged him right, and Mistral took the impulsive cue in full seriousness: the horse shifted his weight back onto his haunches as he'd been taught and pirouetted with his forefeet in the air.

On a battlefield it would have been a magnificent move: in a stable yard it made the woman scream and the ostlers lunge, and suddenly everyone seemed to be converging; staring, shouting and pointing and waving their handbills.

They recognized him. One moment he'd been just another traveler in the bustling yard; the next he was the highwayman.

S.T. put his hand on his sword. But he didn't draw it, not in a crowd of townspeople. The rope tightened around his fist as Nemo flew into a fury, sensing the threat and the excitement, snarling and lunging the length of his lead, flinging his full weight against S.T.'s arm. S.T. wrenched the lead forward, dragging the furious wolf back, driving Mistral toward the arched gate amid the commotion.

Bystanders who'd moved into his path to block the quarry suddenly lost their courage as Mistral plunged ahead. But Nemo's repeated leaping attacks sent shocks of contrary force against S.T.'s body, a hundred pounds of flying wolf enough to throw his control into disorder.

Mistral reared in alarm. S.T. felt him flailing, tipping under the unbalanced load. A sea of people seemed to surround them. In a split second between allowing Mistral to fall and holding Nemo, S.T. flung himself forward onto the horse's neck and released the lead.

Mistral came down on his forefeet. S.T. slewed around in the saddle to call Nemo, desperate, his chances evaporating by the moment as ostlers and postilions stretched to seize his bridle. The wolf made a wide swing, snapping and snarling. The shrieking spectators shrank back, and in that instant S.T. collected Mistral, looked forward and saw his path blocked by an empty phaeton as a crowd of boys dragged it across the arched entrance. He didn't think; he put his spurs to the big horse and drove on, mind and body and heart all focused on the dark opening above the vehicle that was freedom.

Mistral made two galloping strides, all he had room for, and launched into the air. Light became shadow; S.T. leaned back with the impulsion, flying, an instant of unnaturally slowed perception in which he saw the seats of the phaeton below Mistral's shoulders and the black loom of the arch like a grasping hand above—and then they were down, with a heavy jar and a splash in the puddle under the arch.

Another bound took them into the street, with S.T. reining back, asking Mistral's best and getting it, going from full gallop to collection and turn in three strides. He saw Nemo come racing out from beneath the phaeton. For an instant he thought they would make it; he shouted to the wolf and leaned back over Mistral's neck—but then Nemo's head jerked backward. The wolf flipped, spun by the dragging lead as it jammed under the phaeton's rear wheel.

Nemo went sprawling on his back in the mud puddle. S.T. reacted in a frenzy, barely aware of the gathering tumult in the street, spurring Mistral back toward the arch as the wolf scrambled up and threw himself forward. One of the postilions jumped up over the phaeton and grabbed the rope. With Nemo straining after S.T., the boy knotted the end of the lead around a wheel spoke.

S.T. rode into the arch, driving the postilion back with a wild swipe of his sword. He leaned down, trying to cut the rope with his broadsword, hindered by Nemo's confused circling, trying vainly to free the wolf even while the crowd sealed his path to liberty; trying and trying as Mistral's hooves echoed with the shouts inside the arch; trying still as the trap closed, as Nemo abandoned his belligerence and attempted to jump up and lick S.T.'s hand; as someone took a hold of Mistral's bridle, as pistols and a fowling piece leveled from the crowd . . . still leaning over, his arm slack, his sword suspended, burying his face in Mistral's mane.

For the first time in his life, S.T. was imprisoned. It could have been worse, he knew that much. Far worse. The Quakers who ruled Kendal kept a gaol as neat as their prosperous town; they brooked no taunting or throwing of dead cats, and neither were they pleased by singing of chants in support of the prisoner. S.T.'s arraignment and detention were uncommonly peaceful.

They allowed him to keep Nemo in his cell, and even authorized two daily walks for air and exercise for both S.T. and the wolf. Nemo was muzzled and S.T. shackled for these expeditions, a mortification that would have been unbearable if not for the townsfolks' friendly attitude. Escorted by two constables and the wolf, S.T. walked the length of the high street, stopped at the King's Arms and visited Mistral, and walked back, returning the frequent civil salutations with a genteel nod. His apparent popularity might have been somewhat more gratifying had S.T. not known that his thousand pound prize was to be awarded to the whole town of Kendal, and the city fathers had agreed to use the plunder to convert a town house into public assembly rooms for the entertainment of the good citizens at cards, plays, and balls.

He didn't doubt they'd attend his execution with the same enthusiasm—but that awaited the county assizes and his trial.

It all seemed fitting, in its way. He was a favorite even in his downfall, a properly dashing fellow who didn't give a fig for his circumstances. S.T. knew how to play the part. He'd played it for years.

For three weeks he waited, until a constable came one morning and said there was a gentleman to see him. The tardiness of the summons was unsurprising. Upon his arrest, S.T. had sent a letter to his father's elderly lawyers soliciting the favor of their counsel. Since they'd already looked upon him askance when he'd only been the disreputable heir to a dwindled estate, he hardly expected to find them enthusiastic about defending a prince of the highroad. But he'd an added intent: he wanted Nemo and Mistral provided for. He had worried over that the most, lying on his cot at night and staring at the ceiling, stroking Nemo's head as the wolf lay on the floor next to him.

The only person he trusted to take care of them was Leigh. That much she owed him. He'd thought on it long and hard, tried to imagine her so cold as to give his full name to the Crown's authorities . . . and wasn't certain. But he had no one else. He'd already committed Sirocco to her care when he'd slipped back to the Roman ruin that night and traded horses, sending Chastity and Sweet Harmony and Dove to Heavenly Sanctuary on the black to entrust themselves, also, to Leigh's practical good sense.

He believed in her. He tried and tried, and could not imagine that she would betray him.

Not Leigh. She did not have dishonor in her.

So now she was going to find herself appointed executor of the last will and testament of Sophocles Trafalgar Maitland, and heir to a wolf, a horse, assorted half-finished paintings, a ruined castle in France and bank accounts in fifteen towns scattered all over England—if the Crown didn't seize the funds as forfeit.

Remember me, he thought. *Just remember me now and then.*

When the constable came, S.T. reached in his pocket for the folded scrap of paper where he'd written down all the banks, allowed himself to be handcuffed, spoke firmly to make Nemo stay, and followed the man outside the cell. He'd expected to meet the solicitor in the constable's office at the gaol, but instead he was taken outside, escorted by both officers, across the street and into an alleyway past stables and garden gates, and finally down the steps into the servants' entrance of a substantial home.

The cook and scullery maids all lined up, wide-eyed, as S.T. and the constables passed through the kitchen. "Mind you don't be catchin' flies on yer tongue, Lacie," one of the constables growled, giving the youngest maid a friendly cuff.

She dropped a curtsy. "No, sir, Mr. Dinton! No' me, sir!"

S.T. glanced at her as he passed. He smiled from the corner of his mouth. She giggled and curtsied again, and Cook hissed an order to get back to work.

The constables clumped up the narrow stairs with S.T. between them. They met a stern-faced housekeeper on the landing. "This way," she said grimly, and opened the door to a comfortable library. The street-side curtains were drawn shut, the red brocade allowing only a sliver of daylight through, but a fire blazed in the hearth and a generous set of candles lit the room.

"Mr. Dinton and Mr. Grant are to wait across the way, in the small parlor." the housekeeper announced.

"What—and leave 'im here alone?" Dinton objected.

"You are instructed to chain him to the table," she said, her nostrils flaring as if merely repeating the order offended her. She waited until the muttering peace officers had seated S.T. and locked his wrists together around the table leg.

"I only want to make a will," he murmured. "I don't see what all the kickup is about."

The housekeeper looked down her nose at him and ushered the constables out, closing the door with a thump. He heard their footsteps cross the hall, and then another door shut. The housekeeper's shoes clicked away.

He waited. This seemed a monstrous amount of trouble for a common prisoner and his disinclined defense counsel.

Another set of footsteps approached the door, ponderous squeaks along the floorboards in the hall. S.T. leaned back against his chair with his shoulders straight, feeling tense and embarrassed and determined not to show it.

The corpulent figure who opened the door and thumped into the library was a complete stranger. S.T. sat looking up at him, waiting for an introduction, figuring his own identity was obvious enough.

For a silent moment, the stout man gazed at S.T., looking him over as if he were some object on the market, walking left and right with the floor complaining at each step. In spite of the fleshy figure, his turquoise silk coat had the cut of a fashionable tailor, and his neckcloth was spotless linen. He stopped and stuck out his lower lip, his hands in his waistcoat pockets.

"Care to examine my teeth?" S.T. asked curtly.

"Don't be impudent."

S.T.'s handcuffs clashed as he tightened his fists against the chair. "Then don't stare at me as if you're some bumpkin at the king's menagerie. I want you to draw me up a testament before we talk of the trial."

The bulbous eyes lowered. "I am Clarbourne," he announced icily.

S.T. lifted his chin, frowning. He gazed at the proud, immense figure, the heavy jowls and powerful shoulders. Then it struck him, with such force that he uttered, "My God!" and threw back his head with a bark of black laughter. "Clarbourne! Egad, I thought you were my lawyer—and lavishly overdressed for the business at that."

The Earl of Clarbourne, maker of ministries, favorite of the king and prime force within the exchequer, appeared to find no humor in the misunderstanding. His wide mouth drew downward contemptuously. " 'Ware the liberties you take, sirrah."

S.T. eyed him with suspicion. "What the devil does the treasury want with me?" He looked up slantwise, breaking into a sly grin. "Perhaps you'd like to appoint a Highwayman-General to supplement the coffers? I'm perfectly willing, but I shouldn't think you in need of any amateur help with the enterprise."

Clarbourne regarded him with distaste. "I have come to inform you of your situation, my dunghill cock." He folded his hands behind his back. "The Crown is in possession of substantial evidence of the activities of this so-called Prince of Midnight. Sufficient to hang him a score of times over if it so pleases His Majesty."

He paused, allowing a portentous silence to fill the room.

"I thank you," S.T. said. "Most kind of you to come all this way to share His Majesty's view of the matter."

Clarbourne drew a snuffbox from his waistcoat and took a pinch, sneezing heavily. "Your name is Maitland," he said. He walked to the windows and drew one of the drapes aside a crack with his forefinger. "Sophocles Trafalgar Maitland, so says the family Bible which your father's solicitors consulted on my behalf. Lord Luton confirmed your identity.'

S.T. waited, keeping his face impassive.

Clarbourne rubbed his nose and sniffed. "This—person— by the name of James Chilton, who was so disobliging as to get himself shot . . . there is some question as to who did the foul deed. I understand that you accuse Luton. He is so amiable as to accuse you. It is all very boring and inconvenient. At a trial"—he squinted out the narrow gap—"witnesses would be called. Questions would be asked. Certain—circumstances—would inevitably come to the public notice."

"Circumstances?" S.T. murmured.

"I have a daughter," Clarbourne said suddenly.

S.T. went still, gazing at the huge silhouette by the darkened window.

Clarbourne dropped the curtain. "The Lady Sophia." His lip curled. "An exceedingly silly girl. She has lately been calling herself Dove of Peace."

A carriage passed in the road outside, the clatter of hooves and grate of the wheels the only sound in the quiet room. Clarbourne chafed his hands behind his back and then turned slowly to look at S.T. with heavy-lidded eyes.

"Ah," S.T. said softly. "Here's a heat."

"A heat indeed. Lady Sophia is betrothed. The family settlements are of some consequence. You may not realize that she has been—abroad—for the past year. Perhaps there would be some confusion at your trial, and girls in whom she has foolishly confided would mistakenly declare that she has been—elsewhere." He shrugged. "Perhaps not. I am not a man who likes uncertainty." The earl took another pinch of snuff. "I do not choose that any trial should take place."

S.T. looked down at his lap. He took one breath, and then another, keeping them even.

"Can you guard your tongue?" Clarbourne asked.

S.T. lifted his head and met the man's eyes. "Only give me sufficient reason."

Clarbourne stroked his forefinger across his upper lip. He stared at S.T. like a huge, sleepy toad staring at a fly. Then he reached inside his coat and drew out a folded parchment embellished with dangling seals. He trod heavily to the door, paused, and dropped the thick vellum on a small ebony table. "His Majesty's full pardon," he said.

"You do not sully my daughter's name by hazarding to speak it."

He opened the door, stalked ponderously out, and closed it behind him.

S.T. stared at the folded parchment. He leaned his head back and rested it on the chair frame, with a slow, incredulous grin spreading across his face.

TWENTY-SIX

A FULL month he'd been in London. A month he'd known where to find her at her cousin's house in Brook Street. He had not gone. Every morning he rose and dressed and called for a chair to take him, and every morning he'd found some distraction, some trivial errand, some chance-met acquaintance, some reason why it would be better to wait.

Perhaps he would see her at the new Pantheon or a garden *musicale*, somewhere more romantic than a drawing room crowded with morning callers. Perhaps he would meet her on the street and take her hand and see her face light with pleasure. Perhaps she would hear of his pardon, recognize his success; perhaps she'd write a letter, send a message, do something—anything—oh God.

For a month, S.T. had been the darling of the London social season, the prize of competing hostesses and an absolute sensation when he'd appeared at a Vauxhall masquerade in his harlequin mask and silver-studded gauntlets. His family name had always given him entree into society, and in the past he'd been welcome as one of those not-entirely-respectable guests who added a bit of spice to the list . . . but now, revealed as the Prince of Midnight, he found himself the rage.

He spent his free time rehearsing the words he'd say when he saw her. At every entertainment he moved restlessly through the crowds, edgy and brooding until he was sure she wasn't present, and then he could be at ease.

After the first fortnight he began to realize that he wouldn't
meet her; she hadn't been into society at all—no one knew
her, no one spoke of her, and the ladies began to tease
him about becoming sadly tame and approachable after
all.

He even accepted an invitation to Northumberland's ball.
The last time S.T. had been Hugh and Elizabeth Percy's
guest at Syon, he'd spent his days gambling and sleeping
late and his midnights making love beneath a scaffold.
Percy had been a mere earl then; now he rejoiced in a
dukedom. Tonight the scaffolding and the illicit lover were
long since gone, and the interiors that Robert Adam had
refitted shone in all their rainbow glory: veined marble of
red and green and gold, patterned floors and gilded statues, carpets specially woven to reflect every complex de-
tail of the painted and plastered ceilings. Within it all
moved the duke's guests, as bright as exotic birds in a
flowering jungle, fluttering fans and gracefully flicking lace
cuffs, smelling of perfume and wine and a social squeeze
on a warm June evening.

"I shall simply *die*, I promise you I shall," Lady Blair
simpered to S.T., "until I make you tell me what became
of my pearl tiara with the darling 'ittle-weensy diamond
drops."

He lifted his finger and flicked playfully at the emerald
that dangled from her ear, allowing his hand to brush her
white throat. "Methinks I gave it to your second housemaid." Smiling, he brought his hand back to his lips and
kissed it where he'd touched her. "After you dismissed
the chit for impertinence. Did your husband buy you nothing better to replace it, *ma pauvre?*"

She gave a delighted shiver, her bared shoulders wriggling and her mouth in a babyish pout. "Oh—p'rhaps I've
been wicked to someone else, an' oo'll steal my earrings,
too."

"Perhaps I shall." He looked into her eyes. "And demand a kiss at sword point on the open heath."

She laid her closed fan on his sleeve and rubbed it up
and down the green velvet. "How very—violent," she
murmured. "I'm certain I should scream."

"But that only makes it all the more interesting." S.T. turned his head. "And what if your husband should come to the rescue? I see him galloping this direction now, armed with champagne and a glass of claret."

She rolled her eyes meaningfully, but S.T. only smiled and inclined his head in a polite bow to the ruddy-faced man who wove toward them through the crowd. "Lord Blair," he said. "Well met."

The man returned a cold nod. "Maitland," he said shortly. He handed his wife her champagne and pulled out a lace handkerchief, dabbing at the perspiration that beaded at the hairline of his powdered wig.

"We were reminiscing," S.T. said. "I was just about to complain to Lady Blair that I carry the scar from your sword to this day."

"Eh?" Lord Blaire's scowl lightened. "Good God, that must have been ten years ago!" He squinted at S.T. "I thought mayhap I'd pinked you, but I wasn't certain of it."

"I was laid in my bed for a month," S.T. lied cheerfully, and then perjured himself beyond redemption by adding, "You've a wicked twist to the left in *quinte*. Caught me entirely by surprise."

"Did it so?" Lord Blair's color heightened. He glanced left and right and then leaned toward S.T. "I've said nothing in public about crossing swords with you," he muttered. "Didn't really think—that is—one doesn't wish to puff off one's bravado, you see."

"Certainly not." S.T. winked. "But you won't take it amiss if I should warn anyone off from a quarrel with you."

Blair cleared his throat, turning very bright red. He grinned and clapped S.T. on the shoulder. "Well, shall we let bygones be bygones, eh? You'll allow you were a bit misguided to be lying out for Lady Blair and myself— but I don't doubt the most of your victims got their just deserts."

"I like to think so," S.T. murmured kindly, and took his chance to move away. The second housemaid, if he remembered aright, had been dismissed for the imperti-

nence of allowing herself to be raped and impregnated by
the heroic Lord Blair. S.T. left the champion expounding
to his wife upon a fight that had never taken place beyond
his hopeful imagination and one halfhearted sally with a
smallsword. No Englishman but Luton could truly claim
to have put a cut on the Seigneur du Minuit. Luton, however, was not here to assert the honor, having apparently
been persuaded that it was in his interests to take an extended tour of the continent.

Perhaps the Duke of Clarbourne had paid for his passage.

"You're perfectly shameless," a female voice said in
his left ear. S.T. turned around and bowed to his hostess,
lifting her hand to kiss.

"But not boring, I hope," he said. "What misdeed do
you intend to tax me with? I'm certain I never robbed a
duchess."

"Oh, too timid for that by half, I don't doubt. I'm not
made of such paltry stuff as Blair." She tilted her chin
and looked down her patrician nose at him.

"Certainly better with a sword, I'd wager."

The duchess tossed her dark curls. "There—I said you
were shameless. Poor Blair is trying to convince anyone
who will listen that he had the wherewithal to wound you!"

S.T. smiled.

"Did he?" She lifted her eyebrows.

"I'm not at liberty to say, madame."

"Which means that he did not," she said in a satisfied
voice. "I thought as much—and so I'll reply to anyone
who asks. I'll give that little smile, just the way that you
do, and whisper: 'He told me he wasn't at liberty to say.'
'Twill drive Blair mad, won't it?"

"What a diverting thought. How does your charming
niece go on?"

The duchess fluttered her fan. "Oh, she dines at eight,
goes to bed at three, and lies there until four in the afternoon; she bathes, she rides, she dances . . . you may see
for yourself—if you can make your way through the flocks
of languishing gentlemen."

S.T. didn't need to look to envision the young lady in

question surrounded by a ring of enthusiastic admirers. "I believe I'll conserve my strength."

"She's saving the first polonaise for you, if you believe you can dodder through it, my poor weakling."

He bowed. "But perhaps you have this set free yourself, duchess? While I still maintain some slight degree of vigor—will you honor me?'

She smiled and held up her hand. S.T. led her past the fluted columns to the white and gold ballroom, where the crowd coalesced into an elegant group at the first stately strains of music.

At the head of the set, he bowed as his partner curtsied. He moved through the familiar steps, making the sort of light conversation that he'd learned at his mother's knee. Not for nothing had Mrs. Robert Maitland been the toast of London and Paris and Rome in her day. S.T. reckoned that he had idle party chat bred in his blood.

It needed only casual attention to make himself pleasant and execute the changes to the strains of flute and hautboys and harpsichord. He cast a glance down the set as he lifted the duchess's hand and circled.

He saw Leigh.

Only pure instinct kept him moving. He finished the circle and went down the set in mechanical response to the duchess's steps, not hearing the music, not seeing the dancers, aware only of the monumental disaster that was about to put him across from her in the set.

He couldn't tell if she'd seen him. Her face was composed, utterly gorgeous, all her hair piled and powdered on her head and that tiny black patch at the corner of her lips. He couldn't seem to draw his breath quite deep enough in his chest; when he reached her end and paused at his place opposite her in the pattern, his body just took its own course, independent of his mind. He didn't even look at her; he only lifted her hand, circled, and passed on up the set.

After he'd done it, he began to breathe too fast. Idiot! Bleeding *blockhead!* Of all the things he'd meant to do when he saw her, of all he'd planned to say, composing the words over and over in his mind until he got them right—oh lord, oh Jesus, oh sweet bloody *hell* . . . he could not believe what he'd just done.

He'd just cut her. He'd given her the cut direct. Perhaps she hadn't realized it—maybe she'd done the same thing to him. Maybe somehow, in some perfect world, she'd managed to overlook six feet and one inch of ex-highwayman, and after this interminable dance he could go to her and make his speech and she would understand.

But he looked at her and his heart froze in his chest, and all the pretty words just vanished.

The music lifted and came to an end. S.T. offered his arm to the duchess. For an awful instant, she seemed inclined to turn toward the foot of the set, but then someone called to her from the ladies' anteroom. S.T. took his chance and squeezed her arm, guiding her in the safe direction.

Leigh pressed her cheek against the carved oak paneling of the passage where she'd come to hide herself after the dance. Impossible to stay amid the music and laughter, unthinkable to see him again and have him look past her as if she weren't there.

She didn't know what she had expected. A declaration? The Seigneur on his knees at her feet? A chance to tell him what she thought of him?

Liar! Hypocrite! Treacherous, preening cockerel, all dressed in his green and gold with his remarkable hair tied casually at his nape, not even powdered for decency, gleaming in the candlelight.

Oh, all the nights she'd lain in her bed, afraid for him, wondering where he was and how safe. All the mornings her heart had pounded in her throat as she tried to speak casually of the papers to her Cousin Clara. Any news of note? Any weddings, births, broken engagements? No highwaymen arrested? Oh, yes, what a sad bore. No, please, she didn't think she felt up to going to the theater tonight.

And then, in one day, the announcement of his imprisonment and pardon and arrival in London.

She'd waited.

Why, why did she let it hurt like this?

She hadn't expected love, oh, no; she hadn't believed in him for one instant. She'd known him for what he was. And yet she'd turned around with Silvering and everything left of her life burning down before her eyes, and laid her heart and being at his feet.

Why hadn't he come?

She truly hated him. Hate seemed to fill up her life; she still hated Jamie Chilton in his grave, and Dove of Peace, and all the silly girls who'd come to Leigh and said Mr. Maitland had sent them to her because she would know what to do.

Of course she knew. It was easy enough to browbeat Dove into admitting her real name, easy enough to predict that the powerful Clarbourne would take back an heiress of Lady Sophia's substance no matter where she'd run away to. Sweet Harmony, too, had a family anxious to have her back, willing to go to any length to cover up the scandal. Leigh had settled Chastity; she'd made certain all of them made homeless by her revenge on Chilton had somewhere to go—but she didn't forgive. She hated every one of them.

Mostly she hated S.T. Maitland. And herself, because she was a great fool to hurt, and hurt, and hurt.

She should not have come out to this affair. Of course he would be here, basking in his legend. She'd heard about Vauxhall—attending in his mask, the puffed-up coxcomb; he'd even had poor Nemo along and terrified all the ladies. Never mind that the wolf must have been more frightened than any squealing courtesan. S.T. knew how Nemo was with females. Leigh should have stayed home at her cousin's the way she had for months—waiting, hoping, hating.

She was afraid, too, frightened of what she found herself becoming. She felt that she was transforming into a malevolent black spider, hunched back in her crack, staring out at the world and despising everything and everyone for having what she did not.

Someone came into the passage; she heard the door open and the sound of distant music grow louder. For a moment she nearly turned and fled, unable to face any sympathetic inquiries into whether she felt quite well, but that course only promised even closer questions. So she stood where she was, stiff and proud, facing the doorway into the hall.

"Leigh?" he said softly, and at the sound of that voice her chin rose higher and her back grew even stiffer, her fingers closing on the edge of a table until they hurt.

The Seigneur came from the shadow into the pale edge of the light. Leigh glared at him, daggers and swords and lances, only wishing looks could kill. But he stayed there, very much alive, a-shimmer in the soft light from the chandelier over her head.

"I wanted to see you," he said quietly.

She kept her chin high. "I beg your pardon?" Her voice was frigid.

"I wanted to see you," he repeated. "I . . . don't know why I didn't come."

She simply stared, willing away the blurring in her eyes. When it threatened to spill over, she turned her face sharply away.

"You've heard that I'm pardoned?" he asked.

"I believe it's common knowledge," Leigh said tautly.

He was silent. She stared at the corner of the table, watching the candles overhead cast a soft reflection of her face in the polished wood.

"Leigh," he said in a queer voice, "would you do me the honor . . ."

His words trailed off. She looked up. He was gazing at her, as if he thought she might speak. When she met his eyes, he looked away, almost as if he were embarrassed, and inclined his head in an awkward gesture.

"I'm not dancing any more tonight, thank you," she answered woodenly. "I've the headache."

He looked down at the tassled handle of his dress sword, fingering the braided silk.

"I see," he said. "I'm sorry."

He made a brief bow, turned, and vanished back into the shadows of the unlit hallway.

Leigh swallowed. Weeping was beyond her now. Tears were not enough.

* * *

S.T. presented himself in Brook Street the next afternoon. He had to do it. He had to. He stood in the hall
while his card was sent up to Leigh, his mouth set, his
eyes focused straight ahead on the fifth stair, rehearsing
his lines over and over.

He found the extent of his courage in that wait, and it
was mortifying.

The butler showed him up. While the servant intoned,
"Mr. Maitland," S.T. stood in the drawing room door,
searching among the callers drawn up in a circle of
chairs, but it was a plump, petite woman he'd never seen
before who rose and met him at the door.

"I am Mrs. Patton," she murmured, as the general conversation resumed after a moment's significant pause. "My
cousin hasn't yet come down."

S.T. bent over her hand, the lace at his cuff falling in a
pale foam. "I'm honored to pay my respects," he said,
maintaining a formally neutral manner, unsure of his re-
ception—whether his notoriety would earn him a rebuff in
this respectable household. "I fear I'm a stranger to you."

But Leigh's cousin, Mrs. Patton, only looked up at him
curiously a moment. "Then do come and make yourself
known," she whispered. Her round face dimpled provocatively. "Not that your interesting reputation doesn't precede you! We're all agog to meet Mr. Maitland. I'm sure
I didn't collect that Lady Leigh had your acquaintance, or
I should have pressed her to present you, sir."

"It has been my loss alone," he said politely.

She smiled in knowing appreciation. "You will have
met her in France, I don't doubt? That unhappy child—
she wrote us almost nothing while she was away." She
leaned toward him. "This has been so difficult for her,
you know," she said in a low voice. "So good of her
mother's friend—Mrs. Lewis-Hearst, was that her name?—
to take her away for a change of scene after the tragedies.
I grieve that I could not have done it myself, but I was
confined with my little Charles. But, oh—'twas too much,
far too much for a mere girl to bear. Poor love, I've wept
for her! And to be gone for so long! Over a year! We had
one letter, from Avignon—I suppose she could not bring

herself to write. And then this fire—it is beyond enduring." Mrs. Patton laid her hand on S.T.'s arm. "The truth to say, I do not think she improves. I finally succeeded in enticing her out last night for the first time since she came to us, and today . . ." She shook her head sadly. "I'm glad you've come calling, sir."

"You're generous," he said, "to welcome me. I did not expect it."

"I believe she needs—a diversion." Mrs. Patton frowned. "She will not see her childhood friends since she returned, and no one else has asked for her." Then she impulsively took his hand. "Mr. Maitland—I declare I would welcome the chimney sweep, if he could make her smile, just once, as she used to do. You cannot know, if you met her—after . . ." She colored and bit her lip. "But listen to me! Chimney sweep—what a dreadful comparison! I'm sure your soul is nowhere near as black as a sweep. The past is past, of course—I should be most spiteful to hold against you what the king himself does not, shouldn't I? Besides—" She peeked at him mischievously. "You are quite a drawing room prize, you know. I shall be telling everyone that the notorious highwayman came to call quite out of the blue!"

"Thank you." He searched for words, and then glanced at her plump, gentle face. "For your warm heart."

The mischief vanished from her expression. She tilted her head and looked at him with a new interest. "What an unusual man you are, to be sure!"

S.T. shifted, not entirely comfortable under the feminine shrewdness of that look. "Do you think the weather will hold fair?" he asked casually.

"I've not the faintest notion," she said, drawing him toward the circle. "Now, come along and have some refreshment. Mrs. Cholmondelay, may I present Mr. Maitland, our so-shocking highwayman? Do keep him amused. I shall just pop upstairs and see what is detaining Lady Leigh."

S.T. stood sipping tea, all that was offered, and exerted himself to make conversation, doing his best to appear as tame as possible to these worthy ladies. Their initial wariness began to thaw, and by the time Mrs. Patton returned, they had extracted from him the interesting information that he was staying with the Child family at Osterley Park, and were deeply engrossed in questioning him on Mrs. Child's new chairs with the backs taken from the pattern of antique lyres.

Mrs. Patton walked over to him. "I must give you my apologies, Mr. Maitland. Lady Leigh is indisposed. I fear she won't be joining us today."

S.T. lowered his eyes before her searching glance. Of course Leigh wouldn't see him. Damn—what could he expect? He felt himself flushing. All the ladies were looking at him. "I'm sorry to hear it," he said, his voice rigidly dispassionate.

Mrs. Patton took his hand as he bowed in parting. "Perhaps another day," she said.

He felt the small folded paper pressed into his palm. His fingers closed around it. "Another day," he repeated mechanically.

The drawing room door closed behind him. He stopped in the dim hall and flipped open the note.

She is walking in the garden, it said succinctly. *Jackson will show you.*

At the foot of the stairs, the butler stood looking up expectantly. S.T. took a deep breath, crushed the paper in his hand, and descended.

Leigh had grown to accept the way her mind played wistful tricks on her. The way a certain sound could cause her to turn, expecting to see her father behind her, or a pretty gauze make her think, "Anna will like that." At first such moments had been frequent, like the dreams, but slowly they'd faded and grown more rare. Still, when footsteps and the scent came to her—the strong, unmistakable burst of newly cut lavender—she lifted her head from her book without thinking, and then realized as she did it that the vivid premonition was only fragrance and memory, and not a person in reality—not a place she'd been, where dust and sunlight mingled in a ruined courtyard.

She would not turn and find the Seigneur standing there
among his wild lavender and weeds.

She closed the little octavo volume of *A Midsummer
Night's Dream* and leaned her head on her hand, awaiting
her cousin's soft insistence. Clara truly wished to help,
Leigh knew, and yet the pressure to return to life, to the
outside world, only made Leigh more unhappy and angry.
She had nothing; no one and nothing. It had all betrayed
her—even her revenge, which had lost her Silvering and
gained her only bitterness.

And worse, worse . . . to still hurt. To long not only
for the family she'd lost but for a man who knew nothing
more of love than flirtation and lust. Who could look
through her as if she didn't exist, and then callously ask
her to dance.

To have tried so hard to barricade her heart against him,
and to have failed so monstrously.

She heard the footsteps come to a stop on the gravel
path before her, but she didn't want to lift her head and
open her eyes. She only wanted to feel nothing. Not to
think, or endure, or even exist.

"Please," she whispered, "Clara, please—just go
away."

There was a soft rustle of silk. Warm hands cupped her
cheeks—not a delicate feminine touch, but strong and gentle fingers that cradled her face, bringing the intense perfume of crushed lavender, the brush of the thin, aromatic
leaves on her skin. She opened her eyes and he was there,
on his knees, concrete and real in front of her.

"Sunshine," he said softly, and drew her close to him,
holding her head against his shoulder.

For a moment it was everything: comfort and union and
love that she desperately wanted, love the way she'd known
it all her life, secure and unshakable. She pressed her face
to his coat, her throat aching. "Oh, you are so dreadfully
good at this, aren't you?" she whispered. "Damned charlatan."

He didn't speak or shake his head. He didn't deny it.
Leigh spread her hands against his shoulders and straightened, pushing upright. Perfumed powder from her hair

dusted the wine-colored silk of his coat, mingling with the scent of lavender from the bruised stems in his hands.

He laid the tiny, broken bouquet carefully on the marble bench beside her. "I saw them by the doorstep," he said, without looking up. He fingered one of the crushed flowers, and then asked quietly, "Are you going to send me to the devil?"

She gazed at his bent head. He lifted his face, regarding her soberly, his green eyes and wicked eyebrows steady, slightly uncertain, like a watchful satyr in the shadows of a deep wood.

"I'm sure my cousin won't mind if you pick her flowers," she said, deliberately misunderstanding.

He released a slow breath and rose. Leigh gazed at the cut-steel buttons on his coat. She kept her hands locked in her lap.

Turning a little aside, he brushed the open bloom of a pink rose with his knuckles. "Leigh, I—" He pulled one of the petals loose. "I know you're vexed. I'm sorry I didn't come sooner. I'm sorry."

"You're very much mistaken," she said. "I never expected you to call."

He plucked another petal. He held it between his fingers and tore it down the middle, folded it, and tore it again. "You didn't?"

She looked up at him. "Why should I?"

The torn pieces of rose petal fluttered to the ground. "No," he said in a low, dull voice. "Why should you?"

Leigh watched him pull two more petals and roll them between his thumb and forefinger. He kept tearing the petals loose, one by one.

"I came because I wanted to see you," he said abruptly, frowning down at the half-destroyed rose. "I want to talk to you." He plucked another petal. "I need you."

She gripped her hands together in her lap. "I find your conversation does not amuse me."

"Leigh," he said ruefully.

Leave me alone, she thought. *Go away. Don't begin this farce again. Please don't.*

He fingered the drooping flower. "You're still angry."

"I am not angry. I have done what I set out to do. I only wish—that my home had not burned."

He closed his eyes. "I shouldn't have left you there alone. I didn't want to." The rose petals fell in a shower, leaving the flower barren. "I was a damned fool."

"You were in jeopardy. Why should you linger?"

He turned his head with a faint, harsh chuckle. "This is like a nightmare. You're saying all the wrong things."

"Indeed?.I must beg your forgiveness."

"Leigh . . . I'm pardoned," he said.

"I am aware. You have my congratulations."

"Leigh—" His voice had a strange emphasis, almost a pleading in it.

She looked up at him. He stared at her, and then lowered his eyes to the rose.

"Will you do me the honor—" He gripped the stem of the denuded flower, breaking it off in his hand. "—of . . . ah . . ." He twisted the green stem into a deformed circle.

The restless movement brought a thorn against his thumb. He pressed the prick into the pad of his finger, clenching his fist, slowly driving in the thorn as if he didn't even feel the pain. "Will you do me the honor—" he began again.

Leigh lifted her head, watching the thorn and the bright spot of blood it drew, a new perception slowly dawning on her.

She met his eyes. His face was set, almost white. He took a step back and said, "May I have the honor of a dance at Mrs. Child's ridotto Tuesday next?"

TWENTY-SEVEN

MR. Horace Walpole stood with Leigh and Mrs. Patton in the eating room at Osterley Park, where their hostess had provided a running supper after the harp concert. "All the Percys and Seymours of Syon must expire of envy, don't you agree?" Mr. Walpole waved his handkerchief fussily and looked up around the walls and ceiling at the white-painted plaster filagree on grounds of pink and green. "Yet another chef d'oeuvre of Adam! Such taste! Such profusion!" He leaned a little toward Clara. "Such expense!" he murmured. "Positively bacchanalian."

"But where are the chairs?" Mrs. Patton said, turning. "I want to see the chairs shaped like Apollo's lyre!"

"Against the wall, Cousin Clara," Leigh said, nodding toward a corner of the crowded room. "There is one."

"How very modish! Come, Mr. Walpole, I want to sit on an example of these wonders."

"And so you shall, m'dear. But the dancing begins; this is a very forward entertainment, you see . . . Mrs. Child doesn't wish anybody to be so antiquated as to sit down to supper together in a proper manner. We must be modern. Can I not persuade you to exercise yourself in the gallery? 'Tis full a hundred and thirty feet long, you know."

"That is a compelling length," she agreed, "but if I wish to exert myself, I will crane my neck to view the Rubens ceiling in the staircase. Take Lady Leigh instead."

"With infinite pleasure." He bowed to Leigh, flourishing a leg in the finicky tiptoe way that he had. "If she is agreeable?"

Leigh accepted his offered arm. She had not planned to attend this affair. She'd told S.T. that she wouldn't. But in the days between, she'd kept thinking of those moments in her cousin's garden, the way he'd held the broken rose until it drew blood. This morning at breakfast she had shocked Clara, and even herself a little, by agreeing with her cousin's daily mechanical suggestion that Leigh attend whatever event was scheduled, and consented to ride out of the city to Windmill Lane for the Childs' private ridotto.

Clara had responded with enthusiasm, insisting that Leigh appear in one of the new gowns her cousin had ordered. Mrs. Patton's seamstress made the tucks and alterations on the watered violet silk within an hour, flicking and tugging at the ruched silver lace to make it spread properly over Leigh's elbows. With her own hands, Clara chose a fan and an amethyst necklace especially to match the flowered embroidery on the stomacher and draw the desirable amount of attention to Leigh's décolleté neckline. The rest of the day passed in bathing and perfuming and having her hair dressed: padded and curled and set with feathers while the coiffeur complained bitterly over the shortness of her locks.

She had not yet seen S.T., not during the concert, when the Childs' green damask drawing room had been full of seated guests all facing the harpist at the head of the room. Nor had he stood with his hosts when they greeted their visitors, nor been amongst the cardplayers in the library. She had begun to think he must have left Osterley, when she saw him come into the gallery at the door halfway down the long room.

Mr. Walpole was leading her into the dance. She only had time to glimpse the Seigneur's golden figure in his bronze velvet and blond lace before she had to turn and step into a animated gavotte. Through the figures she could sometimes see him; he hadn't moved from the doorway, but stood there with his hand on the hilt of his dress sword, leaning casually against the frame.

Something strange welled up in her, something light and giddy. She found herself smiling. She discovered pleasure in the dance, in the party, in prim Mr. Walpole and the color of the wall hangings.

He was here. He hadn't gone away.

When the dance was over, she followed Mr. Walpole off the floor away from the Seigneur. She had no choice; she could not bring herself to approach him even if it had been proper. How strange it was that she had come to this—alienated by etiquette and emotion from a man who had taken her to bed. Who had touched her bare skin, kissed and caressed her and whispered that he loved her. Who had shared life and death, the taste of smoke and blood. She wanted to ask him where Nemo was, how Mistral fared; if the horse had learned new tricks. She wanted to tell him that Sirocco and the chestnut were sound and well cared for in Mr. Patton's own mews, exercised daily by a boy she'd chosen herself. She wanted to speak to him of all these things—matters that had not occurred to her in the garden, questions that seemed to have bubbled up through the ice in her soul as it cracked at the memory of that tortured rose.

Clara was just wandering out of the eating room with a little covey of friends. Mr. Walpole immediately pressed his desire to partner her, and found her willing this time. Amid a flutter of conversation and gallantry, Leigh stood quietly and watched her cousin move out on Mr. Walpole's arm into the gallery. The music began. Fans quivered and jewels flashed around her as the ladies nodded and the gentlemen smiled. Someone touched her elbow from behind.

"M'lady," the Seigneur said. "My dance."

There was no grace in his invitation, none of the elegance she knew he could apply in abundance. He stood indolently, with one hand braced on the back of a pea green damask chair. But his jaw was set hard; he looked at her intensely, without wavering.

Leigh tilted her head and gave a small, assenting curtsy.

The shy smile kept pursing the corner of her lips, impossible to govern. He straightened. When he let go of the chair, he moved oddly, faltering for an instant, and as Leigh took his arm she caught the faint odor of spirits.

They joined the set. As they took their positions, he overbalanced a little, using her arm to steady himself. She looked up at him through her eyelashes. Perhaps he had been dipping too deeply for an ambitious country dance.

But the dancers were already lined up, saluting one another with bows and curtsies. The Seigneur made only the barest of nods. He was staring hard at her face, frowning, his eyebrows giving him an air of fiendish intensity. A trickle of perspiration marked the light powder at his temple. She felt a surge of love and kinship: so familiar, so much a part of her past and present he was, that the months of black hurt and despair seemed to grow dim, fading away into distance.

In time to the music, the couples joined hands and stepped toward each other. He moved with the rest, advancing a stride, his hand tightening suddenly on hers. For an instant, she held the whole weight of his move on her lifted arm, and then he pushed off. He wavered as he stepped back, swaying a little, never taking his eyes off Leigh. The couple at the top of the set came down the line between them, the ranks opened, and he gripped her hands hard as the circling began.

Leigh was holding him steady by main force; they made the circumference of the square, but when the partners left one another and began to go round in opposing circles, alternating hands with the oncoming dancer, he lost control. He pulled the first startled lady off balance, swinging too far and stumbling into her partner, his shoulder striking heavily against the other man's.

The set broke into confusion. The Seigneur stood with his legs spread, his intensity gone to a look of pure despair while the rest of the dance went on beyond him.

Leigh saw the desperation in his face, and suddenly she understood.

She let go of whoever held her hand and stepped quickly

toward him, smiling contritely at the other dancers. "Odiously foxed," she said, shaking her head.

He kept his gaze fixed on her, breathing unevenly. When she clasped his arm, he resisted the turn. She could see the panic in his eyes.

"Mr. Maitland—" she said soothingly, "let us take some fresh air and allow the dance to go on."

His fingers closed on her upper arm as if it were a lifeline. "Slow," he muttered under the music. "Oh, God, don't let me fall. Not here."

"No, I won't. They only think you're drunk as a fiddler."

The set made up behind them, with a few joking shouts and the bustling in of another couple. The crowd on the sidelines parted amiably. The Seigneur's rigid grasp loosened a little; he seemed to find some stability as they moved in a straight line through the doorway into the grand entrance hall.

In the sudden, cool dimness, they were almost alone. Only a few couples strolled through toward the drawing room from supper. Pale stucco pilasters, Roman urns and statues gleamed softly against the ash gray background, a tranquil contrast to the light and color that revolved in the other rooms. Leigh paused, but the Seigneur moved ahead.

"Outside," he said. "I want to be out of here."

A footman opened the front door. Night air enveloped her. The courtyard was unlit, bounded by the dim hall and two wings with darkened windows. At the far end rose the shadowy Greek columns of the outer portico. S.T. kept walking.

They reached the first row of pillars. He went past those, came to the second rank of temple columns, and stopped. She felt him take a convulsive half step, steadying himself. Just ahead was the great flight of stairs that led from the driveway up to the court. Leigh could barely see the pale mass of stone, but she knew it was there. She'd viewed it by daylight. At a London entertainment they would not have arrived until after eleven, but everyone came out into the Middlesex countryside so near to Hounslow Heath well before dark. Later there would be a convoy of carriages returning to London under an armed guard generously provided by their hosts. No one went home early or alone.

Too many highwaymen.

S.T. released her and leaned heavily against a pillar. "Damn," he whispered harshly. "Damn, damn, *damn!*"

"When did it come upon you?" she asked, not needing any explanation of what ailed him.

"This morning." His voice was bleak. "I woke up and moved my head, and the room went spinning." He made an angry sound. "I couldn't believe it. I thought it would go away. I thought—if I came down—I could control it. But I'd forgotten . . . lord, 'tis too easy to forget the way it feels! I thought I could dance." He blew a sneering hiss. "Dance!"

Leigh was silent. She watched him, her eyes on his dark outline against the pale column.

"You don't think anyone guessed?" he asked.

"No," she said.

"Drunk," he muttered. "How charmingly vulgar! The celebrated Prince of Midnight just becomes a drunkard and fades into the woodwork."

"Have you been drinking?" she asked softly. "Perhaps—"

"Don't I wish! Aye, I've taken a drop of brandy. Would I were three sheets to the wind," he added savagely. "Mayhap then I wouldn't care the deuce about it."

She moved away a few feet, down the steps, and sat on the stone rampart that flanked the stairs. The wide slab was cool and hard beneath her hands.

"I won't be able to ride," he said with a kind of frantic wonder.

"We'll find a physician." She kept her voice firm and steady. "We'll cure you."

If he had anything to say to that, he kept it to himself. Music drifted on the light breeze. Somewhere off in the distance, a lamb was bleating for its mother, an anxious counterpoint to the gay melody.

"Where is Nemo?" she asked.

"Locked up in a box stall all day. Child's been a rare

sport about him, but I don't dare let him run in the park alone.''

"Shall we go and take him out?''

"Now?'' He snorted. "Not unless you believe yourself competent to stay up with a wolf's pace in that prodigiously flattering ballgown. Because I assure you that I cannot, my love.''

As her eyes adjusted to the darkness, she could see the silhouettes of trees on the horizon, and the glimmer of starlight on the little lake across the park. "Am I your love?'' she asked.

The faint light from the doorway fell across him, illuminating his face and clothes and the pillar in chiaroscuro: color brushed against ebony, as if he were one of his own intense paintings.

"I beg you not to mock me,'' he said. "Not just at this moment, if you please.''

"I'm not mocking you.'' She paused, and added shyly, "Have you not lately been wishing to ask me for some particular favor? Some 'honor' I might do you, as I thought.''

He turned his face away. "A momentary lunacy,'' he muttered. "Don't regard it.''

Her tentative smile faded. "Don't regard it?'' she asked uncertainly.

He stood silent.

A chill hand stole around the fragile glow of happiness that had been growing in her heart since she'd first seen him standing down the length of the gallery. "Don't regard it?'' she repeated in a dry throat.

He turned his face away from her.

The air seemed hard to draw into her lungs. "You're not . . . staying,'' she said faintly.

He moved with a jerk, beyond her reach, a shadow against shadows. "I can't,'' he snarled suddenly. "I can't stay!''

Leigh took a breath. She stood up. "I have been correct all along, then,'' she said stonily. "Your notion of attachment—of love—is no more than gallantry and passion. You have bound my heart to no purpose. You have dragged me back into the world for nothing but your own indulgence."

"No," he whispered. "That's not true."

Her voice began to tremble. "Then tell me why. Tell me why I must be brought to care, and then deserted. Tell me why I must be made to hurt again. You don't even have your outlaw apology now. It is only heartless indifference."

"You don't want me like this! Look at me!"

"What do you know of what I want? So busy as you are with being the Prince! With this mythical highwayman so famous for his exploits." She snapped her fan open, making an elaborate curtsy on the top step. "When take you to the road again, monsieur? What do you next to earn your renown? Or will you live upon your erstwhile glory forever?"

"Oh, no . . . not forever," he said softly.

"No, indeed. They will forget you soon enough."

"Aye. That they will." His quiet voice held a sardonic note.

Leigh turned away, facing the open park. She put her fingers against her lips. Her body shook. Far away on the horizon, beyond the dark bulk of the trees, the sum of a thousand little crystal globes on the streets of London cast a faint glow into the sky.

"I won't forget," she said.

He touched her, his hand resting against the curve of her throat, fingering the powdered curls at her nape. "Nor I. I'll remember you all my days, Sunshine."

She bit her lip and turned on him. " 'Tis little enough to undertake. Such a miserable small promise."

He dropped his hand. "And what more do you fancy?" he asked bitterly. "Le Seigneur du Minuit! A ten-days' wonder, now that he's caged up and petted and made into naught! Aye, they'll tire of me. Do you think I've not reckoned it? What else can I give you?"

"Yourself."

"*Myself!*" he shouted, and it echoed all over the courtyard. "What am *I?*" He let go of the pillar and turned, then leaned back against the marble column with his fingers spread and his cheek against the stone. "I'm invented! I made a mask, and I invented myself. And everyone believes in it, save you."

Leigh stood silent.

"You've made of me an arrant coward, do you know it?" He laughed, a hollow sound in the empty courtyard. "I never was truly afraid of anything, until I found myself pardoned."

"I don't understand," she said painfully.

"Don't you? I think you understood from the start. You scorned it all, Sunshine, all the illusions. You never suffered anything but honesty, but I'm all fraud and fabrication. And when it came time to offer myself in truth, I found it out. Damn me, but I found it out." He pressed his forehead against the pillar. "Curse you—Leigh, why wouldn't you believe in me? You're the only one. The only one who wouldn't believe. And now it's too late."

She stood with her arms folded, pressed against her sides. She was shivering inside. "Too late for what?"

"Look at me." He pushed away from the column, holding on at arm's length. "Devil out of hell—*look* at me!" he yelled to the sky. "I can't stand up without my head spinning! You can't believe in a farce."

"No, I can't," she cried. "I never could!"

He scowled. "I'll go on a ship. It worked once." He made a frustrated sound. "But then what? So it cures me again. How long does it last? When next do I wake up a buffoon?" With a harsh, angry chuckle, he let his shoulder hit the pillar and stood leaning hard against it.

"It doesn't matter," she said in a tight voice. "None of that matters!"

"It matters to me," he said inflexibly.

Leigh felt a sensation of drowning creep upon her, a powerless sinking beneath forces beyond her ability to vanquish. "And you'd leave me for that? Are you really so proud?"

He stared past her into the darkness, into the empty park, the cool night. "Is it pride?" His voice changed. She could barely hear it, soft as it became. "I wanted to bring you the best of myself." Still he did not look at her. "It seems to me 'tis love."

A minuet floated on the night air, pianoforte notes that followed one another in a thin waterfall of melody.

"Monseigneur," she whispered. "You don't know the best of yourself."

He lifted his hand and rubbed his ear, the blond lace swinging in a pale, graceful tumble from his wrist. "Aye—wonderfully elusive devils, my virtues are," he said ruefully. "Can't seem to keep a grip on 'em at all."

Leigh spread her fingers over her skirt and took a step away from him. "Courage is a virtue, is it not?"

He turned his head toward her. His face was in shadow; the velvet of his coat burned a dull, tarnished gold where the light fell across his arm. "One of the greatest."

She said, " 'Tis strange, then. Why have I so often wished you had less of it?"

"I don't know." He sounded disconcerted. "Perhaps I've not so much as you think."

She gave a little helpless laugh. "Or perhaps you've more—God help anyone who might wait for you and worry."

Behind her, he stirred; his dress sword made a metallic sound against the marble column. The minuet tinkled like a gay pirouette to its conclusion. Amid the sound of a muffled, genteel tribute from the guests, she closed her fist around her folded fan, crushing the feathery trim.

"Do you love me at all?" she asked suddenly.

He moved closer to her, close enough that she could feel his presence shield her from the almost imperceptible breath of evening air.

"Sunshine . . . I love you. I cherish you. But I can't stay. Not like this."

She bent her head, fiddling with the fan. "I wonder, Seigneur—if virtues are so important; if offering the best of oneself is so imperative . . . how did I ever manage to inspire such regard in you?' She gazed out at the park and bit her lip. "You've seen naught of me but my unloveliest scars, that's certain."

"You're beautiful."

She looked back over her shoulder. "Is that why you love me? For my appearance?"

"No!"

"What, then? What virtues can you see in me? What of my best have I offered you?"

"Your own courage," he said. "Your steadfastness. Your proud heart."

She smiled ironically. "As well love one of the king's Horse Guards, Seigneur, if 'tis pride and staunch courage you admire."

"That isn't all." He stepped closer, clasping her shoulder. "Not nearly all."

"No? What more of my best have I given you?" She bit her lip. "Bitterness and vengeance and grief—are they so enchanting? What have I done to match your renowned horsemanship, your mask, your sword, all of your celebrated daring, Monseigneur du Minuit?"

His hand tightened. She felt his breath on her bare skin, quick and deep. His head was bowed, his face turned a little toward her hair, not quite touching. "Pride and courage. Beauty. All of that. All of that, and . . ." He pressed his mouth to her hair. "I can't—explain it well."

Leigh stepped out of his hold and turned, opening her battered fan and staring down through the dimness at the painted design.

He made a move, as if to reach out to her again. Then he dropped his hand. "You're lovely," he said, with careful emphasis. "Lovely and brave and . . ." He came to a precarious pause. "But it is not that. 'Tis none of that."

Beyond the portico, across the unseen lawn, the lake held a faint reflection of starlight and distant lamps.

He stared into the dusky oblivion. He shook his head and gave an uncertain, suffocated laugh. "You're the one who said 'together.' "

She lifted her head and looked at him.

The remote lamplight caught his expression as he met her eyes. He stood frozen, as if he had only just heard his own words. There was discovery in his face, a quiet shock, a comprehension.

"Aye, together," she whispered, standing taut and trembling. "Side by side. A family."

"Leigh." He sounded desperate. "I don't know how. I've never . . . no one ever . . . I don't know how to do it!"

"How to do what?" she asked in amazement.

"How to stay! How to be a frigging family, for God's sake. All I know is what I've been. I've tried—everything I've tried you've scorned; I tell you I love you, and you tell me I know nothing of it. I've shown you my best—I fought, I rode, I was everything I could be and it wasn't enough. And *now*—now it's gone again, now I'm no more than a—" he made a fierce gesture—"a shadow! No more than what I was when you came to me . . . now do you say you want me? If that's 'together,' if that's what love is, that I come to you out of weakness—Leigh . . . I cannot. I can't do it."

She gazed at him. Bright music drifted on the still air.

"Seigneur," she said. "I love an allemande. Dance with me."

"I can't dance!" he said furiously.

She took his hands. "Dance with me."

"I can't—my balance—"

"I'm your balance." She closed her fingers hard around his.

He tried to pull away, and then suddenly his grip tightened on her hands. He lifted them to his mouth. "Ah God, you are . . . you are .. and what can I give you in return?"

"Give me your joy, Seigneur." She pressed her forehead against their clasped hands. "Oh, give me your joy. I can go on alone if I must. I'll endure, oh yes—I'm too strong to break. And I'll grow old and turn into stone if you leave me. I'll never look up and see you play with the wolf; I'll never hear you call me sweet names in French; I'll never learn to beat you at chess." She shook her head violently. "Please . . . dance with me. Take me to Italy. Paint me in the ruins at midnight. Give me all your mad notions and your crazy heroics and your impossible romantical follies. And I'll be your anchor. I'll be your balance. I'll be your family. I won't let you fall."

His hands opened. He slipped his fingers over her cheeks, cupping her face between his palms.

She felt hot tears fill her eyes. "I'm so weary of grief and hate." She bent her head and stepped away, looking up into his face. "I want a chance to give you the best of myself, too."

Far off beyond the lake, a crane made its warbling whoop, exotic and startling against the background of the harpsichord. He lifted his hand, touched her cheek, caught the single tear that tumbled down it.

She bit her lip. The tears came, impossible to stop. "I love you," she said in a cracked voice. "The truth is, Monseigneur . . . I need you more than you need me."

He was silent, his hand against her skin, warm against the night air.

"Don't let that happen to me." Her words shook. "Don't leave me to be what I'll become without you."

"Sunshine," he said huskily.

"That was what my father called me." She kept her body still, holding his look. "If you go away from me, Seigneur—if you go away—" She spread her hands helplessly. "Tell me then . . . when will I ever be Sunshine again?"

He bent toward her, his mouth barely touching the corner of her lips.

"Always," he whispered. "Always. Smile for me." ·

She took a tremulous breath. Her lips quivered, pressed together.

"I'm afraid that's a pretty feeble attempt." He put both his hands on her shoulders and gave her a little shake. "Try again, Sunshine. You've asked me to dance—now you'd best cultivate a sense of humor."

EPILOGUE

OUTSIDE the silent interior of the riding school, the bells of Florence filled the early air: bright quick tones, and beneath them, the deep, slow notes that tolled in time to the pale horse's stride. Leigh looked down from the arcaded balcony into the school, her hands on the wide stone rail. She watched mount and rider canter leisurely around the huge oval of tanbark with a motion as methodical and easy as a rocking horse, moving in and out of the sun shafts where the sheen of dust motes drifted, kindled by the light of the towering windows overhead.

Mistral was bridleless; S.T. rode bareback, dressed only in boots and breeches, with his queue trailing down between his shoulders in careless gold and shadow. The horse halted, retired three steps, and made a perfect *demi-volte* on two tracks, marking one half circle with its forefeet around another made with its hind legs before it started off in the other direction again at a canter, while the man on its back never seemed to move.

She smiled, leaning her chin on one hand. The spectators' balcony was empty except for herself and Nemo, who lay napping in a cool corner. No one came here now: with Italian hospitality S.T. had been invited by one of his Florentine intimates to make all the use he would of this palazzo; the cavernous apartments and riding school were completely at his service. It was nothing, the marchese said; make free of the empty palace; his family and his stable summered at some country villa in the hills.

It was the one place and time of day in Florence that she could be sure to find S.T. alone. He was convinced that it was the riding that kept his equilibrium—that a month on foot in London was what had renewed the affliction. Leigh wasn't so completely certain, but she saw the logic in it. The whole notion had come of an off-hand musing of hers, that if a rough sea could cure him, then perhaps constant lesser motion might have some influence. He'd seized on the idea like a drowning sailor on a floating log. She couldn't have kept him off a horse, concerned for his safety or not. As soon as the notion had struck him, he'd had one of Mrs. Child's steady cobs saddled. After a lengthy argument, at Leigh's insistence he didn't ride free, but spent hours circling at a trot on the longe, with his hand gripping the pommel and an elderly groom holding the longe line.

It had mortified him, of course, to be longed like a boy at his lessons. No miracle took place: he didn't dismount steady on his feet. The progress came in small increments, but by the time two months had passed and they were ready to board a packet for Calais, he claimed he was only dizzy if he closed his eyes and turned sharply.

Leigh fared worse on the smooth crossing than he did. He was disgustingly cheerful when they arrived, and after they'd taken ship for Italy and spent forty days fighting contrary winds, he arrived at Naples and danced with her at the English ambassador's ball the same night.

She supposed that he didn't know she came to watch in these quiet dawns at Florence; he never looked up from his silent concentration on the endless sidepasses and airs and changes of leading leg, the magnificent dance of man and horse to the sound of the morning bells. She carried her sketchbook, but she'd long since given up trying to reproduce the columns of sunlight and the heavy shade, and Mistral's motion and power and beauty. She could not duplicate it on paper, so she engraved it on her heart.

Down the length of the balcony, a servant appeared, hovering discreetly beneath the arch of red and black marble at the entrance. Leigh passed quietly along the gallery and accepted the thick, bundle of letters from the youth.

The servant withdrew with a bow, never once raising his eyes above the hem of Leigh's dressing robe. It occurred to her that the marchese's well-trained staff was unaccountably loath to disturb these morning sessions in the school with any offer of service. She'd left specific instructions that these particular letters were to be brought to her as soon as they arrived—but never before had an attendant shown himself at the balcony entrance.

She'd learned a bit of the native character in the past three months they'd been in Italy. Such diplomacy must have a reason—such rare and curious privacy a rationale.

She walked slowly back down the balcony. S.T. did not glance up from his concentration. Leigh rested the parchment against her lips, looking down at him thoughtfully.

Perhaps he knew she came to watch him after all. Aye—he'd know something like that.

She retired back into the shadows of the balcony and broke the seal on the letters. Within the packet were all the documents she'd been awaiting. She glanced at Nemo, who rose from his corner and came trotting after her to the far end of the balcony and down the stairs that opened to the deserted stable on one side and the school on the other.

Mistral saw them first; his ears pricked forward and then back, and S.T. looked up. He smiled. The horse circled, its tail flowing out like a milky banner, and came to a halt in front of her, its head and shoulders in a brilliant ring of sunlight that caught S.T.'s hair and contoured his bare chest in shadow.

Facing him, Leigh felt a sudden shyness. She'd taken the steps that led to these letters on her own authority. It was possible that he wouldn't care for it. Doubt made her take refuge in gravity. Instead of answering his smile, she only curtsied somberly. "Good morning, Monseigneur."

His good-humored expression faded. He tilted his head. "What's wrong?"

She looked at Mistral's feet. "Nothing's wrong. I wished to speak to you. I've had these . . . letters."

"Ah," he said. "Letters. Very mysterious."

" 'Tis a deed," she blurted. "To your father's estate."

He gazed at her. "To what?"

"To Cold Tor. Your father's house." She saw the change in his face, and added in a rush, "We need a home, Monseigneur. I've had the mortgages cleared—there was a tenant in it, but he'll be removing directly. My cousin Clara's husband says 'tis in remarkable repair, beyond the gutters need new leading; he went into the country to look about it—there are twenty-six bedrooms open, and a good dower house, and stabling for three-score of horses."

"Twenty-six bedrooms?" he echoed in bewilderment.

"Aye." She put her hands behind her back. "All furnished."

"And you bought it?"

"There was no need to buy it. 'Twas entailed on you at your father's death, as surviving male issue." She frowned at him. "Didn't you know it, Seigneur? I discharged your mortgages. We can live there."

He simply stared at her, while Mistral lowered his head and rubbed it against a foreleg. "I don't even know where it is," he said in a low voice.

Leigh gave a nonplussed little laugh. "But 'tis in Northumberland! On the coast, not thirty miles from Silvering. How could you not know that?"

He shrugged. He looked down and curled his fingers through Mistral's white mane. The sunlight streamed down on his hair.

Leigh watched him twist the pale strands around his fist. "Do you wish I had not done it?" she asked quietly.

He shrugged again and shook his head. "I just— wondered why."

"We need a home. Silvering is gone. 'Twould be a king's fortune to rebuild, and I . . . I do not wish it. To purchase another estate the equal of yours, when there were only the mortgages that bound it—I didn't think it practical."

He smiled dryly. "Or think to ask me."

She bit her lip. "Well . . . I know you, you see, Seigneur. You would have us camp under the sky at Col du Noir, living among the ruins and eating wild honeycomb and manna for the rest of our lives."

"Nay—I thought of that, before I was arrested." His mouth tilted wryly. "I knew you wouldn't like it."

"We need a home."

He leaned down and took her chin in his hand. He looked into her eyes. "You aren't happy here?"

Gazing up at him, at his haloed hair and his green eyes, the faint shimmer of exertion that clung to his bare skin in the heat of the summer morning—she could not stop her smile. "Oh, aye, I'm happy, S.T. Maitland," she said softly. "You look an intriguing Italian bandit in that state of dress." She lowered her eyes modestly. "I only mention it because perhaps you may not realize the full effect."

His fingers tightened a little on her chin.

"But then," she added, lifting her lashes, "I suspect that you realize it full well, don't you?"

"I do have hope," he murmured provocatively. "Particularly of the 'intriguing' part."

She put up her hand and gently disengaged his fingers. "But we were speaking of practical matters. Of making a fixed home. I believe that Cold Tor is the most reasonable choice."

"You've been my wife for nigh a year," he said. "Why is this suddenly such a topic of interest?"

"We need a home."

"My home is with you, *bellissima.*"

"Yes, that's very charming, Seigneur; I value it very much, but we need a settled abode."

"Why?"

"We cannot drift over Italy forever."

He leaned back on one arm, his palm braced on Mistral's hip. "Only a fortnight past you wished to see Venice. And the lake at Como."

Leigh evaded his eyes shyly. "I find that I grow weary of traveling."

He was silent, watching her. She felt warmth rise in her throat and face.

She hugged herself, feeling desperately bashful. " 'Tis time to go back to England," she said.

He inclined his head, looking puzzled and wary—perhaps even a little hurt.

"Please," Leigh said, somehow unable to find better words. "Take me home."

He studied her. Mistral moved restlessly, dancing two steps sideways. S.T. controlled the horse and slanted her a bemused look beneath his lashes.

"Sunshine," he said in a strange voice, "are you trying to tell me something?"

She swallowed and nodded.

He sat still. She couldn't detect what he thought. When she could stand it no longer, she went forward and put her cheek against his knee, sliding her fingers around his boot, enveloped in the scent of Mistral and warm leather.

"*Bella donna . . . tesoro mio . . .*" His hands pulled her closer, tangling in her hair, knocking the loose pins free as he bent down and pressed his mouth to the top of her head. "Oh, my God, *caruccia, dolcezza,*—is it true?"

"I think so," she said, muffled against his boot. "'Twill be born in the spring, the *donna* said."

"Little wife!" He laughed into her hair. "Twenty-six bedrooms, *cara?* You go to nest with a vengeance."

She lifted her face. "I'm only being practical," she said defensively.

He sat back and let go of her, shaking his head. "Why is it, sweet *chérie,* that every idea your brain produces instantly becomes practical? Now, if I'd taken a notion to pruchase some fine palace here in Tuscany boasting a mere fifteen chambers, that would forthwith be declared a wildly reckless fancy."

"And so it would be," she pointed out. "We're not buying Cold Tor. 'Tis already yours."

He sighed. "You want to go to staid England, do you? You asked me to make you a romantic, and I've failed utterly. I showed you Rome in the moonlight, and you quoted something from the Stoic philosophers. At Sorrento you thought only of turtles."

"The pot was copper, Seigneur! If the cook had left turtle soup in it overnight, 'twould have poisoned us all. Sorrento was beautiful beyond anything."

"Turtles," he repeated glumly.

"I loved Capri. And Ravello."

"You didn't wish to see the sunset from Monte Stella."

Her mouth fell open. "Now that is a wicked exaggeration, if you please! When I'll never forget how the sea turned golden and the light lay on the rocks and it seemed as if one could drop a stone right down into the water, 'twas so high and steep. I only said we should return before it was utterly dark, because of the brigands in the forest."

"Brigands!" He leaned over. "I can contend with *brigands,* can I not? I am one, my heart."

The corners of her mouth turned upward. She lowered her eyes demurely. "Indeed, I've managed to commit one romantical folly in my life. I ran off with a brigand. My mama would have wept."

He gave an unimpressed snort. "That's nothing. Listen to me, *cara,* this is a disaster. Twenty-six bedrooms! I know what will happen now. You'll become a prodigious excellent parent. You'll organize us. You'll talk all the time of mattress ticks, and cook maids, and mortgages. You'll carry a lot of keys at your waist, and jingle authoritatively. We'll have a governess and a kitchen garden. You'll be terrifying."

She kept her gaze lowered and pressed her lips together to prevent a smile. "No doubt we'll have a garden, I shan't carry keys, if you don't like it."

"*Molto prammatica* Signora Maitland," he said sternly, "before we leave Italy, I want you to have an impractical thought."

Leigh gazed at Mistral's hooves. She slowly drew her eyes upward to the slope of the horse's shoulder, the Seigneur's leather boot, the shape of his leg resting easily against the animal's strength. Her glance lingered on his bared chest in the shaft of sunlight. She smiled a sly, subtle smile and met his eyes.

He cocked his head. Leigh felt herself blushing at his quizzical expression. She almost lowered her eyes and looked away before the comprehension dawned on his face.

Then his devilish eyebrows lifted, and he grinned slowly.
"Oh, Sunshine . . . that *is* impractical."

Leigh ducked her head. "I don't know what you're talking about."

"Impractical," he mused. "But most provocative."

She cleared her throat.

He leaned backwards, resting his elbows on Mistral's croup. "The French have a name for it."

Leigh gave him an arch look. "They would, of course."

"Liaison à cheval," he murmured, swinging his boots slowly back and forth. Mistral's ears pricked backward.

"I believe you made that up."

" 'Tis the more delicate usage." He pushed himself upright with an easy shove. Mistral began to sidle closer to her. Leigh stepped backwards, shaking her head.

"It was only an absurd thought," she said.

"Outrageous," he agreed. "There's the mounting block."

"Really, Seigneur—no."

Mistral moved to cut off her retreat. Snorting softly, his head high, the gray stepped sideways, herding her gently between the wall and the black-veined block of ornate marble steps.

"I didn't mean it," she said. " 'Tis ludicrous."

S.T. reached down and caught her hand. He lifted it and kissed the back of her fingers. "Step up, *amante mia.*"

"My condition . . ."

He made a low growling sound, pressing her hand to his mouth. "Aye—it makes me want you," he said against her fingers. "Right now."

"Someone will come," she said breathlessly.

"Subdue those practical thoughts. No one will come. They're Italians."

"Aye, Italian! The most sociable of national souls."

"Ah, but we're too outlandish to bother about. 'Tis a sad case when a man grows stupid on his beautiful wife." His hand urged her up onto the first step. "A pure scandal. She ought to be abroad with her chosen cicisbeo like a proper lady, but he forces her to spend all her mornings in a horse barn, gazing down upon him until she must go mad with the tedium of it." He lifted her hand again, assisting her up onto the mounting platform. "I'm afraid we're considered indecently odd already, m'dear. Fortunately we're English, so we can get by with anything."

Leigh stood on the top of the mounting block, just below eye level with him. Mistral sidestepped close to the block, and then backed up until S.T. was even with her. She looked at the pale horse dubiously.

S.T. stuck out his boot. "Put your foot on my ankle. No . . . not that one—your right. How can this come about with you in back of me, my foolish love? In front—there, give me your arms, ho—ho . . . whup—*ho!*—Mistral!" He caught at her as the gray shied back from the sweep of her gown across its neck. Leigh gave a little yelp and fell into place against S.T.'s chest, clutching to hang on as the horse ducked and jumped skittishly. Her legs slid up over S.T.'s, around his waist; she fell backwards, but he pulled her tight against him as he grabbed Mistral's mane with one hand and followed the horse's motion, holding them both on board. "Ho . . . ho . . . Mistral, you old villain, be civilized," he muttered, as the horse broke into a canter.

Leigh held on, frightened, her feet dangling in time to the awkward plunge, feeling like a sack of flour bumped between a wall and floor. One of her slippers fell free. The other hung from her toe. Through the skirts of her shift and the dressing robe, she bounced against Mistral's back and withers and S.T's solid weight.

"Relax," he said in her ear. "You make this difficult." He let go of Mistral's mane and pulled her against him. She squeaked in dismay at the greater range in his motion, but his arms gripped her, forcing her to follow his upper body, molding them into one unit moving in time.

"Give yourself to me, *cara*," he murmured. "Don't fight me. Be soft . . . be supple . . . rest here—you don't have to work at all."

He cradled her cheek against his shoulder. Leigh realized she was straining and stiff, opposing all his movement.

"Have faith, Sunshine," he said. "Let go and trust me."

Her other slipper dropped away. Slowly, uncertainly, she eased her desperate hold and relaxed into him.

And suddenly it was easy. Suddenly the stiffness seemed to disappear from Mistral's gait, her backbone ceased to bounce uncomfortably, and she was flying: cradled against his chest and rocking effortlessly with the fluid rhythm of the canter.

They circled once, and she could feel the small variations in his leg and seat that sent Mistral onto a new lead and a turn the other way. They made a figure eight that flowed into a serpentine, curving up and down the whole length of the school. Above the rustle of her skirts, she could hear the beat of Mistral's hooves. The horse's breathing softened to a mellow, even snort in time to each stride as they worked. The walls of the school flew past, dark and light and dark and light in the sun shafts.

Another circle, this one smaller and smaller, caving in on itself, and then spiraling outward again. She caught a glimpse of Nemo, lying sprawled in the tanbark by the stairs, snoozing unconcernedly. S.T.'s queue brushed her hand in time to Mistral's cadence. Her own hair had come free—it swept against her cheek each time Mistral's shoulders swung upward, marking the free fall of her body in that moment of suspension before the next stride.

Aye, like flying it was; like easy swinging above the earth, with the air passing swift and soft as a bird's wing while they circled the school.

S.T. gripped her tighter, shifting his weight back just a fraction, and the horse came to a round halt.

Leigh let out a long breath. She put her forehead against his shoulder and laughed. "This is monstrous fun."

"Hell"—he was breathing deeply—"we haven't even got to the fun part."

"Take me round again," she demanded.

She felt the subtle shift of his body. Mistral gathered himself directly into a canter stride, rising high enough to make her give a little shriek before the horse settled into its easy tempo. Laughter bubbled up again as the wind

swept her hair and the sunny columns flew past like a
carousel. Her arms slid upward; she held S.T. around the
neck and kissed his throat.

He turned his head and tried to kiss her mouth, but she
buried her face in his shoulder. She put her tongue against
his bare skin, tasting salt and heat. She trailed kisses up
the side of his throat in time to the motion that brought
her lips against his skin.

"Sunshine," he said hoarsely. His hands slid down as
she swayed against him; he cupped her buttocks and
pressed himself toward her.

Mistral broke to a trot.

S.T. cursed. Leigh bobbed, her body in uncontrollable
opposition to his at this new and bouncing gait. She clung
to him, giggling wildly. Mistral picked up the canter again.

"This isn't going to work," S.T. muttered.

She wriggled closer into his lap, turning her mouth to
his ear. She felt secure enough now to lift her legs and
curl them around his hips, resting on his thighs and the
support of his hands beneath her. "Try harder," she said
provocatively, and touched the curve of his earlobe with
her tongue, playing and sucking each time she could reach
it.

He reacted to the fondling; his already heavy breathing
grew labored and his hands gripped her. He made a low,
deep sound, trying to pull her closer yet. Beneath the
dressing robe and layered shift, she wore her silken stockings and nothing more. As he moved with the horse, she
pressed against him on each stride, her body meeting his
in the most openly wanton manner.

She lay back the length of her arms, letting him take
her weight on his shoulders. His bare skin felt very hot
beneath her hands. Her hair fell free, flying around her
head as she watched the sunlight in the tall windows tilt
and spin above her.

His face was the one steady thing in her field of vision;
he looked aroused and intent, watching her, his lashes
lowering slightly with every swing. She tossed her head
back, arching against him like a cat.

He blew a harsh breath and braced. Mistral came to an

awkward halt. S.T. dragged her up into his arms, kissing
her fiercely, his fingers pressing her hard, his hold twisting
the linen amplitude of her skirts up around her waist and
shoulders.

Mistral retired restively. As the horse pranced, Leigh
let her body ride S.T.'s, anchored by his embrace and his
mouth deep and aggressive on hers. With an impetuous
move he pushed his arm between them, still holding tight
with one hand, keeping her lips against his, invading and
sucking at her tongue as he searched amid the disorder of
her shift and released his breeches.

"Luscious wife." He cupped her buttocks and brought
her against him. His breath rasped. "My beautiful
wife—" He bent his face to her shoulder, pushing slowly
into her as she straddled him. Leigh dropped her head
back. She pressed her nails into his bare skin. The horse
moved uneasily, but it only drove him deeper, a full and
hot possession. He kissed her chin and throat. "My delicious, erotic little mother," he muttered roughly, "I want
to devour you."

"Take us round again," she said recklessly.

He gave a shaky laugh. "Dangerous, my sweet. This
poor animal doesn't know what to make of it all."

She moved her hips provocatively and touched her
tongue to his lower lip. "Take us," she whispered.

S.T. closed his eyes. She nibbled and licked gently at
the corner of his mouth. He felt heat shower through him,
felt the urge to shove into her in response, felt his muscles
taut, close to shuddering with the conflict between his de-
sires and his brain.

His arms locked around her as he seized Mistral's mane
in both hands. He kissed her with vehemence, his tongue
greedy, exploring her sweetness. "Hold on to me, *caruccia.*"

He moved then as he wanted to: he drove into her tight
warmth—and that same delicious thrust was the signal that
sent Mistral rocking into transition. Bound as she was between his arms, the full power of the horse's motion flowed
up through his body and into hers. Leigh clung to him.
S.T. groaned with the pleasure of it, felt the canter stride

swing downward with an exquisite sensation of withdrawal, and thrust again. The gray responded with a longer stride.

S.T. gritted his teeth on a sob of frustration, unable to push deeper into her with his own force, not without impelling Mistral faster with each stride into a headlong gallop. He had to let the natural motion of the horse control it all, and that was lascivious agony: so deep and yet not deep enough; he wanted to move, harder, ah God, he wanted to push her down and take her with all the strength in his body. Her face was buried in the curve of his shoulder; her hands kneaded the back of his neck.

Mistral swung in a wide turn. S.T. was beyond guiding the horse in disciplined circles. He didn't care what track they took; the lust to drive to a climax penetrated all his concentration. Her loose hair swept in his face, soft and scented. He thought of his child in her, of her body stretched beneath him on a wide bed, while Mistral's canter moved him rhythmically in an act of holy torture.

He could feel her impassioned response growing, the way she pressed him in demand, with her breath coming in short delicate huffs in his ear. But he couldn't move; he couldn't finish; he could only bear the sweet throbbing heat of her, the compelling weight across his thighs, the ravishing slide of his body inside hers. His fingers curled into Mistral's mane until it hurt. She trembled and quivered and flexed against his chest, drew her feet down against his legs and the horse's flanks. The move brought her closer, impaled her heavily each time Mistral's shoulders rose, and S.T. knew he was going to perish of this pleasure.

"Stop," he gasped. "I want to stop—"

He tried to brace back and halt the gray, but his finesse had left him. Mistral danced sideways, confused and irritated at the disordered signals. S.T. slipped backwards, lost the joining with a thwarted moan, and let go of Mistral's mane. He grabbed Leigh around the waist.

"Enough," he said in a gritty voice, holding her tight as he leaned back and hiked his leg over Mistral's neck. They dismounted in a stagger and tumble of dressing robe. Mistral shied and leaped aside, thundering off down the school, but S.T. didn't care what became of the horse as long as it was out of his way. He moved on the edge of ferocity, taking his wife down in the clean, sharp-scented bed of tanbark, pushing into her with all the force of his readiness.

She laughed, throwing her arms around his neck as he strained against her. He rose on his elbows, gripped her wrists, pulled them away and spread her arms beneath him. As her robe fell open, revealing the base of her throat, he saw the tiny silver star nestled against her skin. He kissed it; he kissed her, held her fast as he possessed her. She shivered and arched her belly upward.

He felt the pulsations come deep inside her, the feminine peak of excitement. That ardent response and the knowledge of his child—his—within her . . . it sent him instantly, blindly, hopelessly into explosion.

His body held hard in suspension in the aftermath. He worked to find his breath. He hung his head down, brushing her shoulder.

She smoothed her hands down his bare back, hugging him gently. Her soft, quick breath caressed his ear.

"We'll name her Sunshine," he said into her hair.

"We will not." She tugged at his queue. "That's my name."

"*Solaire.* That's near enough."

She trailed her hand over his shoulder. "And very beautiful."

"I'll teach her to ride. I'll paint her. I'll paint you both together." He curled his hand into a fist. Between a laugh and a sob, he said, "I'm coming unhinged. Twenty-six bedrooms, for God's sake. What am I going to do?"

Her fingers danced on his skin. "Make us a home, Monseigneur," she said. "And make love to me in every one of them."

Acknowledgments

THIS book took a whole team to pull together. Many, many thanks to Gwen Duzenberry, Ann Bair, and Terri Lynn Wilhelm, for all the help and hospitality. And on the West Coast, I owe sincere gratitude to Kathleen Sage and her own real-life fire fighting hero, Larry . . . may he always come home safe! Linda Bartell knows what her contribution was. I also wish to acknowledge the remarkable horse sense of Mr. John Lyons, a cowboy with the talent to work miracles—and the rare gift to show in his training seminars how others can work them, too. I, and a certain strong-minded chestnut gelding named Splash, salute you. It took us two days, but we now load into the trailer with the aplomb of the true world traveler.

The historical use of dressage and equestrian terminology is varied and inconsistent. In addition to modern sources, I've based my usage on *The History and Art of Horsemanship* by Richard Berenger, Esq., Gentleman of the Horse to His Majesty, 1771.

Amid all this generosity and these experts, any mistakes, exaggerations, and—I confess it—romantical follies are mine alone.